DREAMER

Also by Daniel Quinn

Ishmael
Providence: The Story of a Fifty-Year Vision Quest
The Story of B
My Ishmael
Beyond Civilization: Humanity's Next Great Adventure
After Dachau
The Man Who Grew Young
The Holy
If They Give You Lined Paper, Write Sideways
Tales of Adam
Work, Work, Work
At Woomeroo: Stories

DREAMER

DANIEL QUINN

This is a work of fiction. Names, characters, places, and incidents either are the product of the author's imagination or are used fictitiously. Any resemblance to actual persons,, living or dead, events, or locales is entirely coincidental.

Front Cover Art © choikh – fotolia

ISBN-13: 978-1481850063
ISBN-10: 1481850067

For Michael Schillace, who
wouldn't let me get away
with neglecting this book

INTRODUCTION

Dreamer was written in 1985-86, in between the sixth and seventh versions of the book that would ultimately become *Ishmael* (which was version eight). Although it was written in New Mexico (at a time when I and Rennie, my wife, were publishing *The East Mountain News*), it's set in Chicago and drew upon my experiences there as an editor and freelance writer and my close association with several of that city's fine graphic designers, particularly the much-missed David Lawrence.

The manuscript was agented by that "Prince of Agents" Scott Meredith, whose readers were, I'm afraid, not quite sharp enough to recognize some of its fundamental flaws. It traveled from publisher to publisher for a year before landing on the desk of Melissa Ann Singer at TOR Books. I was fortunate in that she enumerated its flaws in detail but was sufficiently impressed with the book to give me a chance to remedy them. I agreed with her assessments entirely, provided an outline, which she ap-proved, and went ahead with the revision.

It came out in softcover in 1988. Although included among the year's best in Ellen Datlow's influential annual review of fantasy, it was not a commercial success and was soon out of print. It nonetheless continued to enjoy an underground notoriety and in 1995 was included in a "Horror at the End of the Century" list published in the *New York Review of Science Fiction.*

TOR reverted the rights to *Dreamer* to me in 1997, and I'm pleased to be able to make it available once again in this new edition.

Daniel Quinn, 2013

PART
ONE

I

GREG DONNER WOKE to the buzz and clatter of an old neon sign hanging just outside the window. He watched it splash red and green by turns on the dingy, cracked ceiling and wondered where the hell he was. Still half asleep, he wasn't particularly worried about it; it would come to him in a moment.

There was something familiar about the bed he was lying in, with its worn chenille bedspread and its hideous white-painted iron scrollwork at head and foot. It was an old, tired bed, and it sagged under his weight. Awake, Greg would have known it immediately as one that had once stood in an attic room in an Iowa farm-house. Now, in his dream, running his fingers through the old chenille, he simply had a vague feeling of nostalgia and comfort.

Glancing at the window, he remembered that the neon sign was hanging over a cut-rate liquor store, and he wondered why they bothered to leave it on all night: without looking at his watch, he knew it was three o'clock in the morning. And, without knowing exactly where he was, he knew he had a long walk to get back to his apartment. Fully clothed, even down to his shoes, he had to struggle to free himself from the clinging grip of sheets and bedspread.

He stood up, twisted his clothes back into place, and looked around. Except for the bed, the room was completely empty. It looked like an office that had been vacant a long time. Thinking this, Greg remembered where he was and what he was doing there. This was his lawyer's office—or at least the space in which his lawyer conferred with clients. The exact nature of his legal problem eluded him for the moment; he'd left something undone, and a heavy penalty was about to be imposed on him. Even a term in prison wasn't out of the question.

And so Greg, who managed his waking life without a lawyer, had come to consult his lawyer. With the sure, false memory of dreams, he knew that the lawyer had been furious with him, had berated him like an angry parent. Greg wouldn't be in this mess had he followed past advice, and the lawyer had no patience for wrongheaded clients. He washed his hands of him. Gathering up his papers, he had stormed out of his own office, slamming the door behind him.

Weary and discouraged, Greg had crept into the ancient, sagging bed, and gone to sleep. It didn't matter now. He'd find another lawyer in the morning, a lawyer of a better class, who didn't have his office over a liquor store.

It took him a while to find the door, because it was hidden behind the tall scrollwork at the head of the bed. This was his own doing: He'd taken the precaution of using the bed as a barricade against the lawyer's return. He shoved it aside and tried the door. Locked, of course; the night watchman would've seen to that. Greg shook his head in mild disgust; should have anticipated this, should have planned more carefully. No matter: the lawyer had to keep a key somewhere. Thinking about it, he winced, because he suddenly knew exactly where the key was. He saw it plainly on a ring in the lawyer's pants pocket. Although the man's face was a blur, his glen plaid suit was unforgettable, and it was hanging in a closet miles away.

He fought down the beginnings of panic and tried to consider the problem calmly. There had to be a key somewhere on the premises; in fact, it seemed to him now that there was actually a law to that effect. But when he looked around, it was without much hope. The barren room offered almost no hiding places. Then, with a sigh of relief, he realized where it had to be: under the mattress. But, folding it back, he found nothing but a rusty, twanging wire grill. Greg closed his eyes for a moment to visualize the action of hiding a key under this mattress: it would obviously fall through the grill to the floor.

And there it was, exactly centered under the bed, nestled in a disgusting flock of dust bunnies. Greg fished it out, wiped it off

2

on his pants, and opened the door. *This really is a seedy building,* he thought as he made his way down the narrow, grimy hallway and even narrower stairway to the ground floor. He began to wonder what he'd do if the front door was locked as well. But it wasn't, and he slipped out into the dead still night. He paused uncertainly. The street was totally unfamiliar, totally deserted, totally silent, except for the rhythmic clacking of the liquor store sign overhead. Instinct told him that he was in Uptown and that he was facing Lake Michigan. This meant that home was to his right. Having no other guide, he followed his instinct.

The city was uncannily quiet, with every window black, every car motionless at the curb as though abandoned during a general evacuation. Even the distant hiss of traffic was missing. The streets had the sinister feeling of a backlot film set deserted since the thirties, when long black Packards prowled by with tommy guns bristling at the windows. His footsteps echoed hollowly off the gray buildings around him, and he could well believe they were just facades propped up from behind by haphazard structures of two-by-fours.

Having nothing else to do as he walked, he began counting streetlights: a useless activity, since he didn't know how many he'd have to pass before he reached his own neighborhood. And, having nothing else to listen to, he listened to the echoes of his footsteps. *Footsteps,* he thought, *are signatures—like voices, like faces, like fingerprints—but no one ever listens to them.* Smiling, he thought he began to recognize himself in them: they were tall, good-natured, humorous; a bit awkward, not entirely regular, sometimes seeming to miss a beat, sometimes seeming to add a beat. He frowned, listening more carefully. There were far too many extra beats; it was as though the echoes had developed an echo of their own—as though his footsteps had twinned. With a pang of apprehension, he realized he was being followed through the dark, deserted streets of Chicago.

It wasn't until midafternoon, while reading a story in the New York Times about a lawyer being sued for malpractice, that the image of a glen plaid suit hanging in a closet popped into Greg Donner's mind. Wondering what a glen plaid suit hanging in a closet meant, he laid the paper down on the library table. "Keys in the pocket," he thought. Then it all came back to him, and he smiled, remembering the grotesquely furnished office and the clacking neon sign, and the key hidden absurdly under the mattress. He sighed and glanced again at the news story, turning it around in his mind, looking for an angle. He decided there wasn't one and turned the page.

At age thirty-two, Greg Donner was a moderately successful freelance writer, his specialty being work-for-hire. His clients were not generally publishers but rather book packagers, canny hucksters with keen eyes for the marketplace, whose "packages" included an idea, an author, consultants when needed, market strategies, product management—and ultimately, of course, a manuscript. When they were in vogue, Greg had written about astrology, martial arts, running, assertiveness, and body building, and had tried to satisfy the reading public's insatiable appetite for competence and success with a dozen or so self-help and how-to books. None of them appeared under his name, none had the slightest pretension to literary merit, none was memorable, none had reached the best-seller lists—but then none of them had failed to produce a healthy return on investment, and that, in the wicked world of the capitalist West, is the general idea behind book publishing. He was in the bread-and-butter end of the business and was content to leave the *haute cuisine* to others.

Three weeks earlier, he'd gotten a call from Ted Owens, a literary agent and book packager in New York City, who asked him if he wanted to do a book on personal computers.

Greg had groaned. "I've done two in a row."

"I can believe it," Ted said, and spent a few moments thinking. "I've got something else on a back burner if you want a change of pace."

"Go on, tell me about it. My tongue's hanging out."

"One of the kids on my staff came up with this, and I'm

pretty sure when nobody's in the office it goes 'Gobble, gobble, gobble.' You get me?"

Greg said he got him.

"Okay. It's an annual called *Bizarre.*"

"*Bazaar,* as in the magazine?"

"*Bee-zarre,* as in weird and strange. It's supposed to be a compilation of the weird happenings of the year, with about one-third of the text in cute illustrations."

"What kinda weird? UFOs? Abominable Snowmen?"

"No, not that kind of stuff. Hold on, let me get the file. . . . Okay. A few weeks ago a fifteen-year-old kid in Grosse Pointe Woods, Michigan, walked into a dentist's office, pulled a gun, and said, 'Take the braces off my teeth or else.'"

"Uh-huh."

"Okay. This one's more recent. A ninety-three-year-old woman in West Palm Beach, Florida, was literally spooked to death by the U.S. government, which kept sending her letters saying she was no longer eligible for social security because she was dead. When she went on bugging them about it, they decided to appeal to her husband. They sent him a letter saying, 'Look, your wife can't receive social security, because she's dead, get it?' That really got to her, because her husband had been dead for nine years. She died of heart failure the next day."

"Uh-huh."

"Okay. This one's pretty good. Prince Philip recently visited a factory town in North Wales where better than twenty percent of the people are unemployed. He told a crowd, 'Everybody talks about unemployment. We would do much better to talk about the number of people who are employed.' You want to know why?"

"Yes, indeed," Greg said.

"'Because,' the prince said, 'there are more of *them.*'"

"A penetrating observation. Sensitive, too."

"Yeah. You get the idea?"

"I get the idea. The illustrations really sell the book. The text is virtually just captions."

5

"Yeah, I'd say so."

"I think it could go, Ted. And if it goes . . ."

"Right. That's the point. If it goes, it's an annual event. Easy money in everybody's pocket."

Greg thought for a moment. "And what are you looking for—a sample to show around?"

"Right. Fifty pages or so, with a lot of variety. Probably a waste of money, but I gotta give the kid a chance. You know me, I got a soft heart."

"Sure, Ted," Greg said, "just like heat-fused sand."

Greg started with two clipping services but, checking what they supplied against his own gleanings, found they were rarely able to spot the bizarre when it occurred in straight news stories. They both sent him the story of Fred Koch, who got tired of hearing his name mispronounced *Kotch* and legally changed it to Coke Is It, thereby enraging the Coca-Cola Company. They both gave him the story of a mail carrier who sprayed a toddler with dog repellent because he wouldn't move away from a mailbox. But evidently neither of them saw anything bizarre in the story of a security guard at Beirut Airport who tried to win a promotion and a raise in pay by hijacking a Boeing 707 and threatening to crash it into the presidential palace.

So he reconciled himself to spending the spring and early summer inside the palatially seedy Chicago Public Library, alongside derelicts nodding over their unread magazines and midschoolers whispering over their term papers. He had once described his line of work as offering long hours, low pay, no fringe benefits, no security, and no future, but it suited Greg perfectly, and he couldn't imagine himself in any other.

"Salesman's Dream Foretells World's End," the headline said. A used car salesman in Seattle had quit his job, sold his house, and started gathering followers to accompany him to the top of Mount Ranier to observe the end of the world "in the not too distant future." In itself, it was nothing, but Greg made a note of it in case something came of it later. Then he allowed himself another look at his watch. Five to six: quitting time. The worst of the rush hour would be over and he might even get a seat on the bus. He closed his notebook, slipped his pens into his shirt pocket, and got up to shelve the newspapers he'd been working on. On his way out he stopped in the men's room to wash his hands; after a day of paging through the *New York Times*, they were as black as a coal miner's.

Stepping out onto Michigan Avenue, he decided to walk, at least to Oak Street. It was one of the handful of days Chicagoans receive from the gods as a break between the fury of winter and the swelter of summer, and Greg didn't feel like wasting it in a bus. Besides, he hadn't made his Michigan Avenue tour in a week, and there was no better time for it than now, when the office workers and shoppers had taken themselves off to their suburbs and left the area to its elegant residents.

Greg had grown up a country boy, in a small town outside Des Moines, and so Chicago, being a collection of villages, suited him. He lived in the village known as New Town, where the snooty, lake-facing piles on Lake Shore Drive turn their backs on bar-cluttered Broadway just a block west. Within a ten-minute walking radius of his apartment, he could buy groceries, hardware, books, and records, hear live folk and rock music, go to the movies, and take his choice of Chinese, Japanese, French, Italian, or American cuisines. It was enough. It was like his work: interesting and varied, but miles from glamorous.

The Near North was another village: life in the fast lane, packed with strip joints and clip joints and nightclubs and high-ticket restaurants where conventioneers could leave behind their bucks. Its natives tended to be young, trendy, single, well-heeled, and determined to be in the right place at the right time. But for Greg, the north Michigan Avenue village was the epitome of City: sleek, cool, dignified, civilized, above fashion. Its modest proportions suited him. Park Avenue or the Champs-Elysées, he was sure, would overwhelm him.

After crossing the bridge over the Chicago River, he spent

7

half an hour browsing in a bookstore and left without buying anything. He considered stopping for a drink at The Inkwell and decided against it. He considered calling Karen to see if she wanted to meet for dinner somewhere—but that was only a fantasy. He wasn't quite used to the fact that Karen and he were finished—had to be finished. He wanted to see her, and he was sure she wanted to see him. But an evening together could only prove what they'd already proved half a dozen times in the past two months: what they had wasn't a relationship, it was a crisis. He enjoyed her company and was genuinely fond of her, but she was painfully in love with him, wanted to be his wife. For different reasons, each of them wanted to be with the other, but both knew it had to be left alone to die.

Doing what people at loose ends do, Greg made a plan for filling up his evening. Then he carried it out.

The moment he opened his eyes in the garishly lit room above the liquor store, he knew where he was, and was annoyed with himself. To have stranded himself once again in his lawyer's office was sheer stupidity and carelessness. It seemed so unnecessary, when he obviously wanted to be home in his own bed. With a sigh, he disentangled himself from the sheets, stood up, and straightened his clothes. Then, without having to think about it, he knelt beside the bed and groped among the dust bunnies for the key. He thought, *If I'm going to keep on falling asleep here, I've got to clean up this mess.*

He shoved the bed away from the door and let himself out.

Outside on the deserted street, he unhesitatingly turned right—and was immediately assailed by a doubt. It came to him in a spurious memory that, according to wilderness rescue teams, lost travelers invariably turn to the right, whatever their situation, often directly away from inhabited areas, shelter, and safety. Although his steps slowed for a few moments, he went on, deciding that the fact that lost travelers invariably turn right doesn't mean they're invariably wrong. Nevertheless, from that point on, Greg thought of each block he crossed as one he might have to cross again going the other way. The prospect filled him with gloom.

Looking around, he had the feeling he was moving through a deserted city. There was no resonance of life in the buildings that stared down at him with black, empty eyes; no one moved or breathed in those thousands of dark rooms. The cars at the curb were layered in dust, as if they'd all been abandoned the same day, nosed in carelessly and left to decay. It was inconceivable that life and movement could return to these streets in just a few hours.

There was a rhythm to Greg's journey, a strange parody of the human life cycle, enacted again and again in shadow play. Each time he passed under a street lamp, a compact blob of black was born at his feet, grew long before him, developed a head, arms, and legs, and then gradually wasted away into the darkness ahead. He came to think of it as an unfaithful companion who greeted him cheerfully enough at well-lit street corners but who cravenly slunk off in the tenebrous midblocks, where he needed its company most.

At one corner he smiled, because it seemed to be there waiting for him: an oil stain under the street lamp. He stepped into it and imagined it locking onto his feet. Predictably, it began hustling before him, growing more recognizable as a human form with each step. As it stretched out, its head already melting into the gloom, Greg decided he would keep an eye on it and catch it in the act of slipping away, perhaps darting upstairs to the doorway just ahead. His steps faltered and his mouth went suddenly dry. In the shadow of that doorway he saw a deeper shadow, the profile of a human figure, unmoving. His gait wobbled as he tried to think of what to do. Stop? Turn back? Cross the street? Any of these would make it obvious that he'd seen the figure in the doorway and wanted to avoid him. His legs were carrying him toward a crisis that every city dweller knows in imagination if not from experience: the encounter with violence, perhaps with insane malice.

Greg's brain seemed frozen, but his feet were still moving.

9

See nothing, keep going, he told himself. *Look confident, purposeful.*

He was abreast of the doorway now, and, in spite of his commands, his legs were rubbery and his head felt as if it were going to topple off his neck. But he kept going, fighting with every step the urge to break into a run. *Don't run,* he told himself. *To run is to proclaim your fear, is to provoke the attack.* The safety of the next street lamp lay a hundred yards ahead. Two hundred paces at most. After twenty, the muscles in his back ceased twitching. After fifty, he permitted himself a sigh of relief. *At one hundred,* he thought, *it will be safe to assume that—*

Greg heard another set of footsteps spring to life on the sidewalk, and he thought, *Oh God.*

His body carried on as he began to live through his ears alone, listening compulsively to the quality of the footsteps behind him. Were they hostile? Surely not. Weren't they just stroller's footsteps, very like his own? Perhaps they belonged to someone who was simply walking in the same direction. Were they hurrying? No, they seemed measured exactly against his own. *Wait:* just then they seemed to hurry for a bit, for just a few paces. Like someone trying to catch up unobtrusively.

As Greg walked into the protective cone of light of the street lamp at the corner, he felt it gladly on his face, like sunshine. For a few moments his body, operating on its own instincts, slowed its pace as if reluctant to rush through this zone of safety. But the footsteps behind him came on as before, and he wondered what he was going to do. Stop here and confront his follower? Unthinkable. He pushed himself forward across the street and saw with a sinking heart how soon he'd be walking out of this oasis of light and how far away the next one was.

As he was engulfed in darkness, Greg felt a surge of hope. The footsteps behind him fell silent, and he thought, *He's turned the corner. He wasn't following me after all.* But a moment later they resumed as before; they'd only been lost briefly in the sound-absorbing asphalt of the street.

He stifled a groan and went on, desperately considering his alternatives. There were several that seemed better than passively waiting for the other to do whatever he planned to do, but they all meant acknowledging the follower's menace. And that, Greg knew, you mustn't do: the bogeyman will stay in the closet forever—but only if you pretend he isn't there.

In the midblock darkness the follower was closing the gap between them, was only some ten yards behind now. Greg fractionally increased his pace and looked ahead to the next streetlight. Under it, at the bus stop, was a bench. He blinked, hardly daring to believe his eyes. Someone was sitting on the bench: a woman. Her head bent, her shoulders slumped, she looked lost, discouraged.

In two, he thought, *there is safety.* Now he felt he could hurry more openly. He thought of calling out to her, of throwing out a lifeline of sound to her. *Hello there! My name is Greg! What's yours?* But he didn't. He concentrated on achieving the greatest possible speed without appearing to hurry.

The woman on the bench had heard his footsteps and her head was up now. She was staring straight ahead, following the rule: *See nothing, hear nothing, pretend you're not afraid.*

Finally Greg entered the safety zone of light and felt his back muscles relax. Nothing could happen now. The woman—she looked very young to him—was still staring straight ahead, and he approached her diffidently.

"Excuse me," he said, "I know it's none of my business, but there are no buses running this time of night." She looked up at him nervously and he realized she was a startling beauty: flaming red hair and intelligent, emerald-green eyes. He went on, "This really isn't a good neighborhood, you know."

She said, "I don't know what I'm doing here."

"To tell you the truth, I don't know what I'm doing here either. But I'd be glad of your company if you're headed my way."

She looked around uncertainly. "Yes. All right."

As she got up and joined him, he wondered if he was taking her along for her protection or for his. Perhaps a little of both.

11

Safety in numbers, he thought idiotically.

He held his breath as they began to walk, listening for footsteps other than their own, but there was nothing.

No, not nothing. A presence. He felt that they were being followed silently.

"Why is it so dark?" the woman asked.

He glanced up at the sky. "No stars."

"So they've turned out the stars too," she said mournfully.

"I don't know. It'll be all right." He leaned closer to her and whispered, "I think we're being followed."

"Oh God," she moaned.

II

A SINGLE TABLE IN THE LIVING ROOM served Greg both for dining and working. It was dark and hideous, with curved legs and claw feet, and he treasured it. He'd picked it up for twelve dollars at a Sheridan Road junk shop. Littered with pads of paper, notebooks, pens, pencils, and file folders, it faced a broad window that framed Greg's favorite view in the world: Lake Shore Drive, the Outer Drive, Lincoln Park, and Lake Michigan.

He was sitting at the table eating breakfast when he remembered the dream. As he thought about it, he took a bite of scrambled eggs and watched the lake, which was in one of its leaden, surly moods.

Two dreams in sequence, the second extending the first? He'd never heard of such a thing. Or had he just imagined the connection between the two? No, he distinctly remembered recalling the first dream at the library, and the second was definitely a repetition of it. He pulled a pad around and between bites wrote down the dreams, filling several sheets. When he was finished, he smiled and thought, *By God, next time I'll bring a broom and sweep out under the bed.*

He stood up, stretched leisurely, and looked around his apartment with a delight that familiarity never seemed to diminish. It was virtually one enormous, high-ceilinged room. During the twenties, when it had been new, it had undoubtedly been the living room of a ten or twelve room apartment. To attract renters during the thirties depression the management had been forced to cut all the apartments into smaller parcels, adding closet-sized bathrooms and kitchens as needed. Thus mutilated, the building survived but never prospered again, and it was thanks to its general seediness that Greg enjoyed the luxury of a twelfth floor

13

Lake Shore Drive apartment at a rent he could almost afford. it was his one great extravagance.

Today, Greg decided, he'd spare himself the trip to the library and spend the day writing up the best of the stories he'd collected in the last week. He cleared away the breakfast dishes and settled down at his table to work. From time to time he looked up to gaze thoughtfully at the heaving gray water outside. The lake looked like it was about to give birth to a monster.

At four o'clock he got a call from a client asking if he was free for an assignment. With a pang of regret, he had to say he wasn't. Twenty minutes later yet another client called to ask the same question. Greg was astounded and immensely tickled. To turn down two assignments in one afternoon was unprecedented—incredible! He thought, *Wait'll Karen hears about this!* Then he remembered that Karen would not be hearing about it, and his excitement evaporated.

With a sigh, he sat down and went back to work. He shuffled through his clippings for a while, then pushed them aside in disgust. A few minutes earlier they had all seemed delightfully absurd. Now they seemed uniformly stupid and pointless. His sense of humor gone, he was obviously finished for the day. He pushed back his chair, crossed his legs, and stared out the window. The sullen heaving of the lake matched his mood exactly.

Maybe, he thought, he should take Mitzi to dinner. She'd get a kick out of that. Mitzi lived on the eighteenth floor in an apartment twice the size of his—alone, because she was Going Through A Divorce, an occupation that seemed to require all her attention and energy. She popped in once or twice a week to see if Greg didn't agree that all the saints and angels of heaven would endorse whatever stand she was then taking against her brute of a stock-analyst husband and his battery of bloodsucking attorneys.

She was his age, cute, and badly in need of reassurance. And altering their relationship by asking her out to dinner would be an idiotic mistake. He liked her, he was attracted to her physically, but . . . another Karen he didn't need. Finally he decided to take himself to dinner. He would go to the Tango, one of the neighborhood's more elegant restaurants. But it was far too early for that. He would walk over to the bookstore and see if he could find a thriller worth reading.

And another evening would be gone.

The girl with the flaming hair moaned, "Oh God," and clutched his arm. Greg felt the strength drain out of her, and he said, "Keep walking. It'll be all right." But he didn't believe it. The next streetlight, a long block away, flickered like a guttering candle, and their steps brought them no closer to it.

The presence of the follower gliding silently behind pressed on his neck like an icy hand.

"Look," the girl whispered, nodding to a dimly lit storefront just ahead. An old, balding man in shirt sleeves stood in the window watching them with grave interest. Greg paused in front of him and silently mouthed the words, "Help us."

The old man cocked his head to one side and looked at him curiously.

"Let us in," Greg hissed.

With a theatrical gesture, the old man held up a hand to silence him. Then he painstakingly rolled up his sleeves, waggled his hands to show that they were empty, reached into his pocket, and pulled out what looked like a silver dollar. He held it briefly up for their inspection, then pressed it against the glass. When he removed his hand, the coin remained in place.

"Please," the girl whispered. "We need help!"

Ignoring her, the old man rolled his sleeves down and carefully buttoned them. Then he drew down a black shade that covered the entire window.

Greg saw that the silver dollar had passed through the glass. He pulled it away and examined it. On the front was an exquisitely detailed scene in low relief: A shrouded figure was poling a boat across a murky river, oblivious of the men and women who sprawled and writhed at his feet. Just below the surface of the water Greg could see an octopus grappling with a serpent. Ahead, in rolling clouds of fog, a merman and mermaid embraced and the mermaid seemed to be weeping. A setting moon, barely visible through the mist, gazed blindly and mournfully up into the heavens.

Greg turned the coin over and studied the legend printed there. It read:

GOOD
FOR ONE
CROSSING

III

A NOTICE ON THE BULLETIN BOARD caught Greg's eye as he was leaving the library the following afternoon.

YOUR DREAMS
What Are They Trying To Tell You?

A lecture, with analysis of dreams
submitted by the audience,
by
Agnes Tillford
Author of "Your Dreaming Advisor"
and "Listening to Yourself"

The lecture was scheduled to start in half an hour in the basement hall. Greg hesitated, looked at his watch, and thought, *What the hell, you've got nothing better to do.*

A dozen people had assembled in the lecture hall by the time Greg arrived twenty minutes later—probably, he thought uncharitably, the same dozen who assembled for slide lectures on the ruins at Chichén Itzá and readings by little-known poets—people with nothing much to do. *Like me,* Greg thought.

He found a place neither conspicuously close nor conspicuously far from the front and sat down. A group of four were clustered around the lectern, and one of them leaned against it with a proprietary air: presumably Agnes Tillford, holding a pre-lecture séance. She was a short, blockish woman with cropped iron-gray hair and a cheerful, round face, and her unornamented gray suit had been cut by an expert. Unmarried, Greg judged; not a mother, possibly gay.

A middle-aged couple entered from the back and found seats in front of Greg, and Agnes Tillford cleared her throat authoritatively.

"Before we begin," she said to the room at large, "I'd like to suggest that if any of you have a dream you'd like analyzed, you spend a few minutes now jotting it down." She patted the top of the lectern. "I have paper and pencils up here if anyone needs them." With a smile, she resumed her interrupted conversation.

The couple in front of Greg put their heads together and after a minute of whispered conversation, the man shook his head. "Oh, go ahead," the woman said. "I want to see what she does."

"Give her one of your own," the man said without looking at her.

"I never dream."

"Everyone dreams."

"All right, I never *remember* my dreams."

The man sighed and asked her if she had anything to write on. She said she'd get something. She went to the front of the room, burrowed through to the lectern, and returned with paper and pencil.

Greg looked around. Three or four people were working away, brows creased in concentration.

A few minutes later the circle of admirers around the speaker broke up and scattered into the audience, which Greg estimated to number about twenty. Ms. Tillford took her place behind the lectern and studied her notes for a few minutes, waiting for the audience to settle down. Finally, she looked up and gathered them in with her eyes.

"Along with eating, sleeping, and procreating," she began, "dreaming is a universal human activity. From childhood on—perhaps even from infancy on—every one of us spends part of every night dreaming, whether we know it or not, whether we remember it or not. In fact," she added with a smile, "it has been estimated that we spend twice as much time dreaming as in sexual activity."

A small nervous laugh from the audience.

"Nevertheless—in spite of its ordinariness—dreaming remains a mysterious process to most of us. There are two reasons for this, I think. The first is that there have always been those whose interest has been served by *making* and *keeping* dreams mysterious. In ancient times, the interpretation of dreams was the special preserve of wizards, soothsayers, witches, oracles, mystics, saints, and prophets. Nowadays the interpretation of dreams is the special preserve of psychologists and psychiatrists, who would have you believe that only years of arcane study can enable one to understand this very ordinary process.

"I'm here tonight to show you how to poach on their special preserve."

We smiled politely.

"The second reason dreams seem mysterious is a little more rational. Our dreams speak to us in a strange and unfamiliar language. You might say that we can recognize all the words of this language but can't always follow the syntax. We can recognize the family car when we see it in a dream, but what puzzles us is why it should be lying on its back in the middle of the living room floor."

A little more relaxed now, the audience laughed.

"Writers of popular books on dream interpretation haven't been very helpful in clearing up the mystery. This is because they concentrate on doing what's easy to do—they compile lists of dream symbols. Dream of a purse? That's a womb. Dream of a lance? That's a phallus. Dream of a wall? That's a problem to be overcome. Dream of a rainbow? That's a promise. Dream of a goat? That's a sacrifice you've made. And so on. This isn't to say that these identifications are in error. It's to say that symbols are invariably *static*, whereas dreams are invariably *dynamic*. They tell a *story*, and it's in the unraveling of this story that meaning emerges—not in the identification of symbols."

She paused to let that sink in.

"Why *stories*?" She shrugged. "I don't know. Nobody

knows. For some reason, our unconscious, dreaming self—which I've called our dreaming advisor—prefers to communicate with our conscious, waking self through the medium of stories. And there is no doubt that, at first glance, these stories generally seem absurd, incoherent, and meaningless. And in order to understand them, we have to begin with something like an act of faith. We have to say, 'This story, which seems completely absurd, incoherent, and meaningless, *means* something. In some fashion or other, yet to be discovered, it *makes sense*. Unlikely as it seems, my dreaming self is trying to tell me something. Let's see if I can figure out what it is.' Does anyone have a dream I can use to illustrate what I mean?"

The audience answered with some uneasy shuffling. The woman in front of Greg elbowed her husband in the ribs; he grunted and shook his head. A young woman near the front darted up to the podium and handed over a sheet of paper, which the speaker glanced at, then read aloud.

"'I dreamed that for some unknown reason my mother came to my home to live. When I went to my drawer to get my favorite sweater, I found it had been stabbed in the right armhole seam with one of my wooden spoons (which has a pointed handle). The yarn was all stretched and broken, and I was furious. I knew my mother had done it but she wouldn't admit it. Later I went back to get the sweater, and again there was a wooden spoon sticking out of the armhole seam. I was furious but I still couldn't get my mother to admit doing this.'"

She held up the dream to the woman who submitted it. "This makes no sense to you?"

"No."

She held it up to the audience as a whole. "Does it make sense to anyone?"

Smiles, then shaking of heads.

"I've barely looked at it, but I'll say with complete confidence that this story makes sense. That's where I have to begin or else I'll just throw up my hands in despair."

She studied the page briefly. "What is this story about, in a general way? That's easy. It's about unfinished business between a mother and daughter." She looked at the writer. "The dream makes it clear that your mother has grievously injured you—has injured you to the very heart. That wooden spoon passes through the side of your sweater right to the place where your heart would be. But what really irks you is that she refuses to admit it. She pretends that all is well between you."

The woman laughed. "That's right. The last time I saw her I tried to face her with it, tried to tell her . . . She refused to listen, ended up by saying I needed a psychiatrist."

"You had this dream after that?"

"That's right."

"Okay. This is a commentary on that episode." She glanced at the dream again. "Here is what your dreaming self is telling you. 'Don't expect your mother to change. She's never going to acknowledge what she did to you. On the contrary, if you let her, she's going to keep on injuring you in the same way over and over again.'"

She looked up and smiled. "But that's not all it's saying. What's important to note is that your mother has failed to reach your heart. Your heart is elsewhere—not in that sweater. Does that sweater have any particular significance?"

The woman thought for a moment. "I guess you could say so. It was part of a sweater-skirt outfit she bought for me when I went to college."

Agnes Tillford nodded. "Okay. You're not inside that sweater any more—you're not a schoolgirl any more. In other words, your heart—your attachment—is somewhere else now, belongs to someone else."

"That's right!" the woman grinned.

"So your dreaming advisor is pointing out that the injury your mother did to you belongs to the past. She ruined the part of your life that sweater represents, but she can't touch you *now*. It's also saying you should leave that drawer closed, because every time you open it all you're going to see is that damned spoon sticking out of your sweater. In other words, let it lie."

21

She smiled. "One other sneaky little point. Whom do you stab with a wooden spoon?" She looked out expectantly to the audience. "Come on. A wooden spoon sharpened to a point at one end."

Someone called out, "A vampire."

"Exactly. A vampire. The source of the word *vamp*. Does your mother think of you as a vamp?"

The woman smiled. "I wouldn't be surprised if she did."

Agnes Tillford thought for a moment. I'm going to hazard a guess. Not entirely a guess. You were daddy's darling. Daddy's favorite."

The woman smiled again. "That's right. He was a photographer and he took me everywhere with him. He must have taken a thousand pictures of me in my cute blonde curls."

"Did he take a thousand pictures of your mother?"

"No."

She nodded. "In this dream your dreaming self proposes a motive for your mother's hostility. You vamped her husband and she was just plain jealous. She was afraid of you, and the only thing she could think of doing was to put a stake through your heart, as you would a vampire."

Someone at the back began to applaud, and most of the audience, including Greg, joined in.

"Okay," she said in acknowledgment, "but what I want you to see is not how clever I am but how easy it is. You simply have to let go of your preconception that dreams are incomprehensible. Can I have another one?"

The woman in front of Greg snatched her companion's dream and marched it up to the podium. Tillford scanned it and asked the woman if it was her dream.

"My husband's," she answered.

"Okay." Tillford studied it for a moment. "I see it's actually two separate dreams. Did you have them the same night?"

"The same week," the man said. "Couple days apart."

She nodded. "Two real nifties. Here's the first one: 'A large, innocent white goose was forcing its head down onto an egg.

One after the other, its eyes filled with blood and then it waddle-ed off to die.' And the second: 'A little boy in white started off walking somewhere. An elderly Edward G. Robinson rushed right after him, knowing he was heading somewhere important. I came along behind. The boy climbed up the side of a cliff and onto an incredibly narrow ledge, and Robinson followed him with terrific enthusiasm. I wasn't sure I could make it.'"

She looked up at the writer. "What made you connect the two?"

He shifted uncomfortably in his chair. "I don't know. I don't usually remember my dreams. I mean, I remember them, but don't pay any attention to them. These two, I don't know . . . They seemed special."

"I'd say they are." She looked around the room. "Any ideas? Anything strike anyone?" Nobody moved. "Before the evening's over I hope I'll see some hands."

She looked down at the sheet of paper. "A large, innocent white goose, an egg that's painful to hatch, and a little boy setting off on a dangerous journey to an important but unknown destination. What's this all about?" She looked at the writer. "May I have your name, sir?"

"Lewis. Everett Lewis."

"Thank you. Now. What's this large, innocent white goose? In general—at least as a first hypothesis—you have to assume that an obviously symbolic figure of this sort represents the dreamer himself. So, this is Mr. Lewis, who is depicted in the dream as large and innocent. And, of course, it's the sleeping Mr. Lewis who's doing the depicting here. In other words, this goose is Mr. Lewis's image of himself. He sees himself as large—which is to say, mature—but still innocent. He sees that he's all grown up, but he also feels he hasn't actually begun to live. How am I doing so far, Mr. Lewis?"

Mr. Lewis smiled ironically. "You're doing okay."

"So what's in the egg this goose is trying to break open? He says the goose was forcing its head down onto an egg. Any idea what's in it?" She looked around. "Come on. Somebody think."

A young man near the front raised a hand. "A new Mr. Lewis?"

"Of course! It's desperately important for a new Mr. Lewis to be broken out of that shell to begin a new life. If he can't do it—and it's obviously going to be very painful—then, as he sees it, he's just going to waddle off to die. That's it for dream one."

A hand shot up. "What about the goose's eyes filling with blood?"

She thought for a moment. "This is basically just reinforcement of the point. Bleeding from the eyes suggests tremendous internal pressure. He wants so desperately to liberate that new Mr. Lewis that he's about to explode. Okay?"

"Okay."

"Now, dream two—the little boy in white. Who's that?"

Half a dozen people raised their hands, and she nodded to one of them.

"That's the new Mr. Lewis."

"Of course. The new Mr. Lewis, freshly hatched and rarin' to go. Full of zest and fearless. Exactly where he's headed isn't specified, but he's clearly prepared for excitement and adventure. But the old Mr. Lewis is hanging back. He's afraid to follow this child, afraid to trust his future to this child who has thrown caution to the winds. So what's Edward G. Robinson doing in this dream?"

No one volunteered an answer to this question.

"Edward G. Robinson is one persona of a familiar figure in dreams—the Wise Old Man. Mr. Lewis's dreaming advisor is giving him some encouragement. It's saying, in effect, 'Look at this Wise Old Man. Edward G. Robinson is no fool; he's a sophisticated and experienced man of the world. He knows this child can be trusted. He's not hanging back and fretting about the hazards the child may be leading him into. Follow the example of this Wise Old Man and let the new you be your guide.'"

Mrs. Lewis raised her hand. "Can I add something?"

"Certainly."

"My husband is an accountant with a pharmaceutical

company here in Chicago. Has been for twenty-odd years. But he's also a collector of antiques—and that's where his heart is. What he really wants to do is take an early retirement and go into the antique business full time. But he's so damned worried about providing for the future that he won't do it. That's all."

Agnes Tillford nodded. "Mr. Lewis, your dreaming self advises you to take the plunge. It advises you to break out of your shell of comfort and security and to take the risks of an exciting new adventure."

The applause this time was enthusiastic.

It took Greg half an hour to outwait the half dozen who stayed behind after the lecture. Finally the last one departed, and Ms. Tillford began gathering up her papers. When Greg joined her at the lectern, she looked up, nodded an acknowledgment of his presence, and went on packing her briefcase.

"Can I buy you a cup of coffee?" he asked. "Or a drink?"

She looked at him gravely. "You must have a good one."

"A good dream?" He smiled. "Yeah. Maybe."

She continued to study him. "A drink would be nice. If you mean someplace nearby."

Greg thought briefly. "How about the Blackhawk?"

She nodded and closed her briefcase. "So what did you think?" she asked as they made their way out to the street.

"About the lecture? I guess I have to say I don't believe it."

"You don't believe what?"

"That what you do with dreams is teachable. I think you have a genuine knack. Nontransferable."

She shrugged. "I agree I have a knack, but I've managed to teach it to a few people. Not in an hour, of course."

"My name is Greg Donner, by the way. I forgot to introduce myself."

"I noticed," she said without emphasis.

"And what do I call you over drinks? Ms. Tillford?"

"Mrs. Tillford. Widow Tillford. Actually, people who take me out for drinks call me Agnes."

Greg smiled. "I picked you for unmarried."

"Thanks. I was married for twenty years."

"Any kids?"

"Three. One grandchild so far."

"I picked you for childless, of course." He held the door of the Blackhawk for her.

"Some judge of character you are," she remarked dryly.

Seated and with drinks in front of them, Agnes asked him what he did for a living and he told her. She asked him what kind of writing he did.

"Any kind anyone wants to pay me for. I'm strictly a hack."

She grunted. "I've done enough to know that any kind of writing is creative writing."

"I won't argue with that."

She looked around the room, which was handsome, dim, and spacious. "Do you have any fans?"

"Me? No."

"I do," she said glumly. "Fans are so boring." Greg felt she was trying to tell him something, but he wasn't sure what it was. He asked her if she made a living out of her books and lectures.

"God, no," she replied. "If I had to make a living out of it, it wouldn't be any fun." She looked up at him. "So what is this dream of yours?"

He shrugged. "There's no hurry about that. Believe it or not, I didn't ask you out just to listen to a dream."

She raised her brows. "You're after my body?"

Greg gave her a crooked grin. "You women. All you think about is sex."

They chatted through a couple more rounds of drinks, and he learned that, in her day, Agnes had been a hardhead, a hell-raiser, and a women's liberationist long before it became a movement; when it became fashionable she lost interest.

"Well," she said at last. "We've established that we enjoy each other's company. Now I really would like to hear this dream of yours."

So Greg told her. The whole thing.

"Very interesting, if you'll pardon the expression," she said when he was finished. "And you're sure you actually dreamed these things on successive nights?"

"Absolutely. I wrote them down."

She shrugged. "I've never heard anything quite like it. Not that it matters in particular. The repetition is just a way of fixing the dream in your mind, of drawing attention to it. The dream itself isn't particularly mysterious."

"It isn't?"

"Didn't you just hear my lecture, for God's sake?"

Greg laughed and told her to go on.

"Okay. The dream begins with an awakening. An awakening to what? To the fact that you're locked up in a lawyer's office. What does that suggest?"

"Nothing, to me."

"Chah. You're not thinking. You hire a lawyer to oversee your actions, to restrain you from doing wrong—in short, to act as a sort of conscience."

"True."

"So, in your dream, you awaken to find yourself locked into a life ruled by caution. You're a good boy. You do what your lawyer—the lawyer inside you—tells you to do. You're always careful to do what's proper and right."

"True enough."

"Okay. You'd like to get yourself out of that situation, but finding the key means getting your hands dirty." Greg laughed. "So you wake up to a choice. Stay or go. Stay or go. Green and red lights flash your choices on the ceiling."

"Right. Very good."

"So, in your dream, you release yourself from this barren prison. And as soon as you get down to the street, you're faced with another choice—right or left. In the language of dreams, turning left can mean a turn toward the passive, spiritual side— or toward the dark side, the wicked side. This doesn't feel like the direction you should take. Home is toward the right— toward a more active and positive involvement with life."

He smiled and nodded.

"Okay. Ultimately, what're you looking for in this empty, lonely city? A woman, of course. A woman alone as you're alone. You can protect each other from your loneliness. However . . . a menacing figure is following you and threatens to overwhelm you. And who or what do you suppose that is?"

"I don't know."

"That, dear boy, is your terribly guilty conscience."

"Oh."

"Do you have some reason to feel guilty about looking for a woman to love in this city?"

Greg made a face. " I guess I do." He told her about Karen.

"Well, there you have it then. The lawyer in you—what the psychoanalysts would call your superego—says that, because Karen is in love with you, you should lock yourself in your room and be faithful to her. But you want to be involved with a woman *you're* in love with. Your dreaming advisor is warning you that a lot of guilt is going to follow such an involvement."

"I see that. But what about the old man in the storefront?"

"Ah. You met him in another guise earlier this evening. This is the Wise Old Man."

"He didn't *seem* wise. Why wouldn't he let us in?"

"'Cause he *was* wise. He knew you were in no real danger."

"What about that coin he gave me?"

Agnes smiled. "That's a nice touch. I assume you recognize the boatman on the coin."

"Yes. That's Charon, who ferries the dead across the river Styx to Hades."

"And what do you read in this?"

"I took it to be a warning. The old man was trying to warn me about something."

Agnes shook her head and stared into her drink for a few moments. "Suppose someone handed you a card with a picture on the front showing God seated on his throne, surrounded by choirs of angels and ecstatic throngs of saints. And suppose on the back was printed, 'Admit One.' What would you call that?"

"What do you mean?"

"'Admit One.' Think about it. Suppose someone in real life handed you a ticket to heaven that said 'Admit One.' What would you call that?"

"I'd call it a joke. Something you'd pick up in a trick shop."

"Exactly. The old man in your dream made it obvious he was performing a trick. And a coin showing Charon ferrying the dead across the Styx, marked 'Good for One Crossing' is clearly a joke. You don't need a token to get a ride across that river—and you know that perfectly well."

"True."

"And what's the point of the joke?"

"I'd rather you told me."

"Lazy fellow. All right, here is what your Wise Old Man says, speaking with the voice of experience. 'Okay, sure, if you break out of your self-imposed prison routine and look for a woman you can love, you're going to be plagued with a terrible feeling of guilt. But look here, *it's not going to kill you.*'"

Greg nodded, smiling. "I guess that makes sense."

They had another round of drinks and talked about themselves and about Chicago. Greg offered to see her home to her apartment in Rogers Park.

"Very gallant of you, young man," she said. "But I've been making my way alone in this city for twenty-five years, and I'm quite capable of doing so tonight."

Nevertheless he walked her to the subway on State Street and saw her aboard a train. He could have taken it himself, but he hated that earsplitting subterranean ride. He walked back to Michigan Avenue and took a bus. In his apartment, after still another drink, he fell into bed pretty well drunk. He thought, *At least I won't dream tonight.*

But he was wrong.

Greg stared blankly at the inscription on the coin for a moment, then put it in his pocket. He looked up at the distant streetlight and felt like groaning. While he and the girl had been pleading with the old man, the follower had slipped past and was now lying in wait for them in some shadowed doorway ahead.

"We have to go back," he told her.

"Back?" she whispered, her eyes wide with horror. Without explaining, he grabbed her arm and hurried her along, his mind working furiously. Everything was changed now, and there was nothing left but flight. Now that they'd acknowledged his presence, the follower could abandon his subtle game and pursue them openly. Where in this warren of locked doors could they take refuge?

Suddenly he remembered the observatory. Why hadn't he thought of it before? He could picture it with absolute clarity. Although no such structure exists in Chicago, in his dream Greg was sure he'd seen it a thousand times: a pristine silver dome perched atop a dignified old Georgian house with a dormerless hip roof and a flat roof-deck. Its quaint history came back to him in detail, and he had to struggle to thrust it out of his mind.

"Where are we going?" the girl asked breathlessly.

"Look for a dome," he told her.

"A dome?"

"Look for a dome," he repeated grimly.

Would the observatory be open at this time of night? he wondered, then shook his head at the stupidity of the question. Of course it would be open; the observatory was in constant demand among amateur astronomers throughout the city, and the middle of the night was when they worked.

"Over there!" the girl said, pointing half a block ahead and across the street.

And there it was, gleaming softly against the black sky.

Greg began looking for a place to cross the street, but the cars were all parked bumper-to-bumper. Looking at them now, his heart suddenly thudded: The cars were all *occupied*. Open-eyed corpses sprawled across the seats, leaned brokenly against doors, pressed slack faces against windows: all victims of the creature who was following them, all somehow killed by a single, shattering blow.

They found a narrow break between cars, sidled through it, and hurried across the street. As soon as they stepped up onto the sidewalk, he saw his mistake. On this side of the street, the dome was out of sight. He'd have to hope there was a sign of some sort on the house. Soon they came to a long spiked iron fence, and Greg thought this must be it. A tall, elaborately worked gate appeared ahead. Pausing in front of it, he saw that the elaborate arabesques of the grillwork formed a name: The Celestial Mirror.

They passed through the gate and found themselves in a tangled, overgrown garden. Its neglected condition worried him: had the observatory been closed down? Ahead, he saw that the shattered cement walk led to a pedimented pavilion framed by two-story Ionic pilasters—the entrance to a country mansion.

"Christ Jesus!" the girl hissed and stopped. "We can't go in there. This is *his* house."

"It's all right," Greg said. "This is the observatory. We'll be safe here." And he dragged her up to the front door, which was standing half open.

A circular staircase just wide enough for the two of them to walk side by side spiraled to the roof. Greg couldn't make out the construction of the place, but as they mounted the stairs they seemed to pass many landings, and on each one a painting hung in shadow a few feet from the staircase railing: Adam, Proteus, Quetzalcoatl, St. Michael, Jupiter, Thor, Ahura-Mazda . . . He didn't recognize them all.

Finally, their legs throbbing, they came to the top and found a door that opened out onto the roof. Just a few feet before them, the observatory arose serenely majestic, like a spaceship poised for takeoff. They hurried inside, and Greg shut the door behind them. It closed and automatically locked with a comforting metallic *chunk*, and he shot home two massive bolts at the top and bottom.

As the echoes died away, he became aware of an awesome stillness. This wasn't the chilling, oppressive silence of the street below; it seemed to draw friendly life from the stars that blazed through the slotted opening in the roof. An almost palpable column of moonlight stood in the center of the cavernous room. Beyond it, locked in an intricate gleaming superstructure, loomed the black mass of the telescope. The girl was standing beneath it, staring up in awe. Watching her, Greg noted again how astoundingly lovely she was. In the moonlight, her flaming hair was softened to gold, perfectly offset by her lime-green dress. He walked over to join her.

And the building shuddered as if struck by a giant fist.

He put an arm around her shoulders. "We're safe here," he said, and she nodded. Nevertheless they turned to stare at the bolted metal door.

After a few moments it swung open silently, as if carried on a gentle puff of wind.

IV

SINCE HE WORKED WHEN IT SUITED HIM and not according to the calendar, Greg paid little attention to the days of the week. And so, when Aaron Spaulding called at noon to remind him it was the Friday of the annual design awards show, he had to admit he'd forgotten all about it.

"But you *are* coming to the show, aren't you?" Aaron demanded.

For a long moment Greg struggled to think of some engagement, some pressing piece of work, some indisposition that might excuse him, but he hadn't the heart for it. Aaron was a young and talented graphic designer who did not as yet belong to the elite class of the profession. Half a dozen examples of his work would be on display at the show, and Greg had worked with him on three of them. In fact, Greg himself would collect a few honorable mentions as copywriter on winning projects, but these were perfunctory awards and, coming from a design-oriented show, professionally worthless to him. Nevertheless he knew Aaron would be hurt if he didn't come.

"Sure," Greg said. "What time do you plan to be there?"

Aaron suggested they meet for dinner beforehand, but Greg was in no mood for that. He told him he'd be lucky to get his desk clear by seven or eight.

"Oh," Aaron said, obviously disappointed. "Well, I'll be there all night, till ten or eleven at least."

Greg told him he'd see him long before then.

As a matter of fact, nothing was moving across Greg's desk. He'd spent the morning fiddling with two or three stories, and the results had as much sparkle and wit as assembly instructions for a hand truck. Gloom had settled on him like a bag of sand across his shoulders.

The trouble was he knew exactly what he felt like doing. He felt like calling Karen and taking her to lunch. She would be home; Friday and Saturday were her days off. She'd be home and doing something crazy like washing walls or making new curtains for the windows. She was an intense homemaker.

He knew exactly how it would go if they met.

They'd exchange a kiss as though the hiatus of the past three weeks didn't exist. She'd ask him what crap he'd been eating and tell him he looked lousy and his clothes were a mess. He'd tell her about the book he was working on for Ted Owens and she'd glare at him and ask him if his name was going to be on it. Of course he'd admit that it hadn't even occurred to him to ask.

"Goddamn it," she'd say, "you *make* him put your name on it. I want a copy of that book on my coffee table with your goddamn name on it, inscribed, 'To Karen, with all my undying goddamned love.' Hear me? I'm serious!"

He'd make fun of her motherly concern, and she'd pretend her dignity was affronted. To mollify her, he'd tell her about getting two job offers in a single afternoon, and her eyes would get wide and she'd say, "See, baby? You're gonna be big time!"

And he'd find that his depression had dissipated like fog in the sun. By midafternoon, they'd be a little drunk and a little silly and they'd go back to her place, because, according to her, his building smelled of cockroaches. They'd make playful love on her flowered sheets, order in some fried chicken, and spend the evening in bed watching television.

It was exactly what Greg wanted. And he knew he couldn't have it, because at some point, sure as hell, she would say something like, "You know, for what the two of us pay in rent, we could have a penthouse on the goddamned Gold Coast."

And the disaster would begin all over again.

His spirits still lower, Greg poured himself a drink and spent the rest of the afternoon staring out at the lake.

* * *

By the time Greg arrived at the show, elegantly arranged over most of the first floor of Water Tower Place, everyone was pretty well lit with excitement and booze. It was one of the gala events of the year for the Chicago publishing world, and designers, publishers, editors, ad people, and public relations people mixed with printers, typographers, artists, artists' reps, writers, paper salesmen, and clients of all of them. Except for a couple of editors and a couple of designers, Greg would know and be known to very few of them.

Almost no one was looking at the exhibits. Those who had come to see them had already done so and were now clustered in small groups around the cash bars. Greg fought his way through to one for a bourbon on the rocks, then, plastic glass in hand, began to tour the exhibits.

Virtually anything printed was eligible for entry: packages, brochures, books, advertising posters, record jackets, magazines, stationery, logos, business cards, sign systems, annual reports, and a good many items difficult to classify in any way. In spite of their differences, all were glossily handsome, proclaiming the fact that Money Had Been Spent on them. Most were beautifully printed, and some were visually startling. And, since there were innumerable entry categories, a great many sported ribbons that were not nearly as tasteful as the objects they adorned.

Greg felt a hand on his arm and turned to look down at Aaron Spaulding, darkly handsome and elegantly turned out in a midnight-blue velvet suit and an open-necked ivory silk shirt.

"So you came," Aaron said, sounding disgruntled.

"Of course. I said I would."

"I've got some people I want you to meet. Could be some business for you."

Stifling a sigh, Greg let Aaron lead him toward one of the bars. From experience, he knew Aaron's clients were the sort who insist on putting a writer through four drafts of anything just to make sure they're not being cheated.

He spent the next half hour making polite noises to a large,

35

aggressive toy manufacturer who wanted—or imagined he wanted—a series of teacher's manuals showing how educationally valuable his merchandise could be in the classroom. His diminutive, pop-eyed assistant tried to impress Greg with the size of their sales force and their projections for the educational market, as if he were offering him a vice presidency in the company. What they knew about education and the educational market wouldn't be noticed if it flew into your eye, but, since designing their annual catalog was a big chunk of Aaron's income, Greg nodded in all the right places and told them he'd look forward to working on the project.

Finally, he broke away, explaining that he'd just arrived and hadn't had a chance to see the show. Aaron excused himself for a minute and followed Greg back to the exhibits. "Could be a lot of work there," he said.

"Forget it. It'll never happen."

"You don't think so?"

"He'll talk about it until somebody asks him to spend the first nickel. Then you'll never hear of it again."

"Yeah, I suppose you're right," he said glumly.

"Where's the hospital book, Aaron?"

"Oh, it's over there," he said, gesturing vaguely to his left. "I've got to get back. See you later?"

Greg didn't answer, hadn't even heard the question. He was staring openmouthed at the spot Aaron had indicated: at a girl with flaming red hair in a lime-green dress, facing away from him, toward an exhibit in a glass case.

Leaving Aaron blinking, Greg crossed the room. His heart was pounding, and he told himself not to be stupid; there are ten thousand girls in Chicago with flaming red hair. Drawing up beside her, he didn't dare glance at her face. Instead, he looked at the exhibit, which, he was astonished to see, was the hospital book he'd just asked Aaron about: a full-color, elaborately die-cut production with intricate three-dimensional pop-up illustrations. The card beside it read:

CHILDREN'S BOOK: *"A Visit to the hospital"*
DESIGNED BY: *Aaron Spaulding*
TEXT BY: *Gregory Donner*
CLIENT: *St. Anselm Hospital*
TYPOGRAPHY: *Texthouse, Inc.*
PRINTING AND BINDING: *Greenleaf Press*

"God," Greg said. "Can you imagine grown-ups working on such crap?" He felt a look of indignation slam into the side of his head like a brick. He turned to face her and blinked.

It was she.

Unmistakably. The same wide green eyes. The same fine nose. The same beautifully shaped lips, which were moving. She was saying something to him.

"I beg your pardon. What did you say?"

"I said, who are you to call this crap?"

"Oh." He pointed to the card. "See where it says 'text by'? That's me. Greg Donner."

She peered in at the card and then looked back at him with open puzzlement.

"And I know who you are," Greg said solemnly. "You're the girl of my dreams." Her wide eyes grew wider as her brows rose into a skeptical arch. "I know that sounds like a line, but I'm not kidding. You've literally been in my dreams the last three nights."

She gave him an ironical smile. "Well, it's an original opening anyway."

"However, in all the time we've spent together, you've never told me your name."

"We must have been busy."

"We were. We were being chased."

"Oh. Well, I'm glad to hear that."

Greg blinked, frowned, then realized that what she'd heard was: We were being *chaste.* "Yeah," he said. "Well, here I am wide-awake, and I still don't know your name."

"You didn't read it in your horoscope?"

"No," Greg said slowly. "All it said in my horoscope was that I'd meet a fat woman with a mustache and take her to dinner tonight."

"I'm not fat and I don't have a mustache."

"I know. That's why I don't believe in horoscopes."

She laughed and held out a hand. "My name is Ginny Winters."

He took her hand. "But it was right about my taking you out to dinner."

"It was?" She took her hand back.

"I'm sure it must have been. Horoscopes are always half right. That's why I believe in them."

She laughed and shook her head. "I can see I'm going to have trouble with you. Are you really Gregory Donner?"

"Absolutely. Relentlessly."

Greg felt a tap on his shoulder. A tall, distinguished gentleman eyed him with a bleary smile. "Excuse me, my dears, but this is not a nesting ground. I would like to glom this exhibit."

Ginny and Greg moved away toward the next exhibit. "You're not tall enough to be a model," he told her, "and you're too glamorous to be an editor. You didn't ask me if I buy art, so you're not an artists' rep. Therefore I conclude you are a photographic stylist."

"Pooh," she said. "Wrong again. I'm a graphic designer."

"Ah. And you have some stuff here?"

"A couple things."

Greg said he'd like to see them, and she led him back to a set of portable wall panels that zigzagged across the floor. There she pointed out a collection of stationery that included a letterhead, two sizes of envelopes, business cards, and a mailing label, all with a logo in vibrant circus colors.

"Very nice. What do these people do?"

"They design educational games."

"Ah. I especially like the little guy with the hoop." Central to the logo was a boy in 1930s costume who looked out into the viewer's eye with a knowing leer.

"Yes. I had to go to St. Louis to get him. I couldn't find anyone in Chicago who understood what I wanted."

He turned to her gravely. "As soon as I scrape together twenty-five dollars I'd like you to do some stationery."

She grinned. "This little lot here—all of it four-color—set the client back over three grand in printing alone."

"Gawd," he said.

She led him past a few panels and pointed out a tabloid newspaper. It was called *Pix,* and the flag was done in raw, aggressive calligraphy. Its pages were devoted to avant-garde photography and shrieking verse, and it had an air of harshness and sneering cynicism. "It's a bit daunting," Greg said.

Ginny nodded. "This was the look they were after. It was a whips and chains crowd."

"I've never seen it on the stands."

"You're not likely to. It folded after the second issue. None of them wanted to sell advertising."

"Ah, business," he said. "Anything else?"

Ginny shrugged. "A couple of annual reports. Very Swiss, very elegant. And a line of running shoes."

"Good heavens. I saw those when I came in. It didn't occur to me they were even part of the show."

"Swine. They won second place in some category or other."

"Running shoes, probably."

She shook her head admiringly. "You really know how to make a girl feel good."

Greg thought for a moment. "Do you know Sasha's?"

"Sasha's? What is it?"

"A Russian restaurant. The most romantic restaurant in Chicago. Closed a few years ago."

Ginny laughed. "So?"

"That's where I would've taken you if it was still there."

"Wow. Sounds like it would have been terrific."

He nodded solemnly. "It would have been, believe me. Caviar. Honest-to-God beef Stroganoff. Plush banquettes, nice low-key atmosphere. Still, there's Chez Paul."

39

"Yes," she agreed. "There's still Chez Paul." She looked up at him innocently. "Are you proposing to break the heart of that nice fat girl with the mustache?"

"Oh, her." He waved her away. "There's nothing between us but sex."

"Good. I'm glad. But, honestly, I'm not dressed for Chez Paul." Greg almost told her she was dressed for Chez Paul, Maxim's, the Forum of the Twelve Caesars, or any other restaurant in the world, but caught himself in time. He proposed Armando's as an alternative, and it was accepted.

Over a pair of drinks each they discovered they'd done work for the same companies at various times and shared several acquaintances. During dinner they exchanged sketchy life histories, and over coffee, Greg asked her if she knew Mandarine Napoléon. "No. Is it like Sasha's?"

Greg shook his head. "It's a prince in the world of liqueurs." He signaled the waiter and ordered one for each of them. When they arrived in snifters, she held hers up to the light. "Lovely. Tangerine." She took a sip and said, "Woof. Elegant."

"It goes well with your dress," Greg said. "For that matter, it goes well with your eyes. And your hair. And your complexion."

"I'll keep a glass of it with me always."

"And do you know," he said thoughtfully, "I think I'm already three-quarters in love with you."

Her eyes widened. "What? Only three-quarters?"

He shrugged. "If I said 'totally,' you might think I was exaggerating."

She looked down at her glass, suddenly serious. "Don't be," she said.

"Don't be what?"

"In love with me."

Greg felt her words as a blow to the solar plexus, but he managed to hold onto a smile. "Why not?"

"Just don't."

And Greg, who knew that he was already totally and irrevocably in love, could think of nothing to say. Ginny saved the moment by holding up her glass. "This is marvelous stuff. I thank you for introducing it to me."

"Listen," he said, shaking off his desolation, "that's nothing. I do card tricks."

"I can hardly wait."

Greg was stunned when the maitre d', bowing them out, said, "Good night, Miss Winters."

"What's this," he asked when they were outside, "your neighborhood restaurant?"

"Almost. I only live a couple blocks away. I take a lot of clients there for lunch."

Suddenly Greg pictured them: ruggedly handsome men with manicured nails, fifty-dollar haircuts. and eight-hundred-dollar suits. He was ready to kill them all.

As though reading his thoughts, Ginny looped her arm around his. "But you introduced me to Armando's stuffed mushrooms — and to Mandarine Napoléon."

Greg grinned foolishly, thinking, *boy, you've got it bad.*

In less than five minutes they were standing in front of a tall-windowed graystone apartment building, and Ginny asked if he wanted to come in for some coffee. Greg had spent the last two minutes considering his response to this predictable offer. On a number of grounds — chief among them that he didn't want the evening to fizzle out anticlimatically — he had decided to make an unpredictable response.

"Thank you, lady of my dreams," he said, "but I think not tonight." He smiled at her disconcerted look. "However, I will see you to your door, in hopes of being called upon to trample a dragon or two on the way."

At her door on the second floor, he said, "And when next I come, you can be sure I'll bring a deck of cards."

She laughed. Taking her shoulders he bent down to kiss her, and she offered her lips without hesitation. It was brief, casual, and—for Greg at least—ecstatic. He released her after a moment but couldn't resist the temptation to lift a hand to her cheek. Smiling, she leaned into it lightly.

"It was nice," she said.

"Damned right it was," Greg whispered, and kissed her again, even more briefly. Then he turned and left.

Outside it was all he could do to restrain himself from jumping up and down like a madman or tearing down the street yelling at the top of his lungs. Instead he turned east and with long strides headed toward Michigan Avenue.

God, he thought, *I feel just like that simp in* West Side Story *who swans around singing "Maria! I just met a girl named Maria!" I want to go back and spend the night casting lovesick glances up at her window. Wow. Terrible.*

But he wasn't feeling terrible. He was bursting with happiness, and he thought of dragging Aaron out of bed to release some of the pressure by sharing it with him. Grinning ruefully, Greg shook his head and reminded himself that there is no one in the world more boring than someone who has just fallen in love. What is there to say after you've said "I'm in love"? Greg looked up and smiled at the stars glittering overhead.

After you say "I'm in love," you say, *"I'm in love!"* Wide-awake and stone sober, he considered walking the thirty blocks home. Better sense prevailed, and he flagged down a taxi.

V

GREG WOKE UP THE NEXT MORNING feeling wondrously whole and content. Smiling, he wondered what Agnes Tillford would make of the dream he'd had just before waking. Probably nothing, he decided. Even she'd have to concede that a lot of dreams are just meaningless pranks of the unconscious.

Suddenly bristling with energy and hungry for activity, he rolled out of bed and headed for the bathroom. After a quick shower and a cup of coffee, he lightheartedly tackled the kitchen, which in the past few days had become a bachelor sty of open cans, unscraped dishes, and overflowing bags of trash. When it had achieved a state that would win even Karen's approval, he made breakfast—and afterward tidied up again.

He went through the bedroom and living room just as methodically, picking up odd bits of clothes, shelving books, squaring up stacks of manuscript, dusting window sills, gathering cobwebs from corners. Finished at last by midmorning, he carried a cup of coffee to the sofa to contemplate smugly the transformation he'd wrought on his environment. It had been carried out in a sort of giddy unthinking trance, and it was only now that he understood what he'd been doing.

He'd been getting ready for company. Not for company still to arrive, company that had *already* arrived: *Ginny*.

It seemed to him that Ginny already lived inside of him, that she totally inhabited the interior space that had formerly housed only Greg Donner. It was Ginny who had brought order to his apartment. It was Ginny who wiggled his fingers and toes. And it was certainly Ginny who filled his body with an intensely pleasurable ache of yearning.

For the first time in days, Greg settled down to work without the distraction of wishing he was somewhere else, doing something else. From time to time he would pause over a word, look out at the lake—blue today and scintillating with sunlight— smile, and think: *Ginny*. Then, without a pang, he would go back to work. Effortlessly, he shaped story after story into a tidy package of wit and irony. He found, somewhat to his surprise, that he had a knack for what he was doing, that he was deriving from it a kind of pleasure he rarely experienced in his work.

At a growl from his stomach, he checked the time and was astonished to see that it was nearly four. He'd been working for six hours straight, and it seemed like no more than two or three, he stood up, stretched, and allowed himself to wonder what he was going to do about Ginny. He wanted to call her that instant, to try to see her that evening. Instinct and experience told him it would be a mistake to do either one.

"Don't be in love with me," she had told him. But at the door of her apartment she had responded to his kiss, to his touch. Had responded like a woman who wanted to be loved.

Nevertheless, she had said: Don't be in love with me.

Be casual, be playful, be witty, be fun, be crazy, be tender.

But don't be in love.

All right. Granting that he didn't know what it meant, he could understand it, sort of. Perhaps she'd been hurt in an earlier affair. Perhaps—and Greg winced at this—maybe she meant, "Don't be in love with me . . . because I'm in love with someone else."

He shook his head, rejecting this. Forget what she *said*. Consider what she said more plainly when he kissed her, when he touched her cheek: *Your kiss is welcome; your touch is welcome.*

But don't be in love.

It meant—it *had* to mean—don't overwhelm me. Take it slow. Greg nodded. Yes. He would take it slow. He ached to hear her voice. He yearned to have her in his arms again. But he would take it slow. He would be casual and playful and witty and fun and crazy—and tender.

44

But he would also be in love; his feelings were his own and Ginny didn't need to know about them until she was ready to.

He would wait till next week to call her. Groaning, he thought of the empty days that stretched ahead. Then he thought again: Sunday brunch? Acceptably casual—and leaving less than one day to be lived through without her. Brunch. Then what? An equally casual good-bye? A stroll through Lincoln Park Zoo, for God's sake? He shook his head: brunch was all wrong.

He would call her Wednesday afternoon. Well, Tuesday afternoon. Three days.

On an impulse, he called Agnes and asked if she'd like to join him in a Saturday night pub crawl. "My dear boy," she said. "You're sure you're not after my body?"

"Your mind, Agnes. I love your mind. And the way you hold a martini glass."

"I don't drink martinis, as you well know."

"Oh. Then it must have been someone else."

Agnes giggled and asked him what pubs he was thinking of, his or hers?

"Let's placate my sense of gallantry and say yours."

"That's fine. Except there's only one I regularly crawl in. Freddie's, just south of Evanston on Sheridan." They arranged to meet at eight.

Greg checked his watch and decided he might as well get in another couple hours of work.

Freddie's turned out to be not a pub but a steak house with a separate, cavernously dark cocktail lounge. When Greg's eyes adjusted to the meager light, he saw Agnes waving at him from a booth near the back.

As he slid into the seat across from her, he asked, "Are they expecting an air raid?"

"In the dark night of the soul," Agnes intoned somberly, "it's always three o'clock in the morning."

"Good lord. Are we doing quotations tonight?"

"Let's."

In the course of the evening, Greg told her he'd met the girl of his dreams. She raised an eyebrow and asked if he meant the exact girl he'd dreamed about. When he said he did, she told him to tell her about it.

When he was finished, she smiled benignly and said, "I like that part where she thought you said, 'We were being chaste.' Puns like that are very common in dreams."

"Except this wasn't a dream."

"I realize that." She gave him a speculative look. "You're not thinking this is some sort of preternatural event—meeting someone in real life that you've only known in your dreams."

"Well, not preternatural. But it's certainly a hell of a co-incidence."

"Not really. You're in related fields, you share some of the same clients and acquaintances. It would almost be a miracle if you hadn't seen her around—probably more than once. It may only have been a glimpse, but that would be enough."

"True." He asked if she'd like to hear a couple of dreams.

"Sure. Next to gossip, I love to hear dreams."

"This one I had this morning just before I woke up," Greg said, and went on to describe it. He and Ginny had been back at Armando's. They'd had cocktails and dinner, but he remembered little of that. Then he'd signaled for the check. They dawdled over the last of their coffee and drinks. Soon he realized they'd been waiting an uncommonly long time for their check. Looking around, he spotted their waiter across the room in excited conversation with the maitre d' and some other waiters. When Greg finally managed to catch his eye, he hurried over nervously, and Greg asked what the problem was.

"Oh, no problem, sir," the waiter said, obviously lying. "Your check will be here in a moment. Someone will bring it."

"Why don't *you* bring it?" Greg asked stiffly, but the waiter had already turned away in embarrassment.

Greg shrugged and told Ginny, "It'll be here in a minute." She said nothing. After a few moments she nodded to his left to indicate that someone was coming.

46

It was the old magician from the storefront, still in his shirt sleeves, but lacking the confident air he'd displayed while performing his coin trick. He slid the check across the table and, looking away, said, "I'm sorry, sir."

Greg glanced at the check and blurted, "This is ridiculous."

It was for $643.17.

"I know, sir. Would you like me to go through it for you?"

"I sure as hell would."

The old man took out a pencil and touched the items on the bill one by one, identifying each, and Greg saw that, somehow or other, it did indeed total $643.17. "This is ridiculous," he repeated. "Six hundred dollars for dinner for two?"

"Dinner *and* drinks, sir. The menu does list all the prices, you know."

"I know that, goddamn it, but—"

Ginny put a hand on his arm. "I tried to warn you, Greg," she said in a strangely flat tone. "Don't make a scene."

"Don't make a scene! My God—" Biting his lip, he tried to bring himself under control. "Okay," he said at last and slipped a credit card out of his billfold.

The old man cringed with embarrassment. "I'm sorry, sir, but a bill of this size . . . I'm afraid we must have cash. You understand."

"I certainly do *not* understand," Greg snapped. "Do you mean a check?"

Pained, the old man turned his eyes up to the ceiling. "Ah, no sir. I'm afraid I mean *cash*. A policy of the management."

Greg exploded into wrath. Patrons at other tables turned to stare at him yelling and pounding on the table. "One moment," the old man said. "I'll bring the manager."

Glancing across the table, Greg saw that Ginny was gone. He looked around frantically and saw her standing by the exit, rigidly disassociating herself from him. As he watched, she looked longingly down the stairs to the front door, as if she wished she could leave.

The old man returned with the manager, and a hysterical

argument began. The dream dragged to a close in a numbing chaos of accusations and threats.

"It must've been an unusually vivid dream," Agnes observed.

"It was. So what does it mean?"

She smiled. "That's obvious enough, I think." She regarded him benevolently. "So you've met the girl of your dreams. What was your reaction to her?"

"What do you mean?" When she raised her eyebrows at him, he shifted his gaze to the drink in front of him. "I guess my reaction was a pretty powerful one."

"Don't kid me, sonny. It was the thunderbolt. You fell in love."

Greg shrugged and nodded ruefully.

"Head over heels? The complete madness?" Smiling, he nodded again. "Okay. This is something new for you? Never happened before?"

"No, not like this."

"Then the dream is obvious. Under the delirium, you're a bit apprehensive. You're afraid it's going to cost you plenty. You've never been in love before—maybe the price always seemed too high. But here you are, head over heels, and you're going to have to pay for it at last. And you're worried that it may turn out to be more than you can afford—emotionally speaking, of course. But, once again, the magician—that Wise Old Man of your dreams—makes it plain that your fears are absurd. You know damn well there's no restaurant in Chicago where you can spend six hundred bucks on dinner for two."

Greg nodded. "Very neat. But I don't *feel* worried."

She peered at him skeptically. "Goodness, you must have nerves of steel. No butterflies in the stomach? No fear of rejection? You're confident it's all a sure thing?"

Don't fall in love with me.

He made a face. "Yeah, I see what you mean."

"Anyone in love is in a position of extreme emotional risk. That's part of the excitement, after all."

"True." He looked up at her and blinked. "Would you like to hear another one?"

"Another dream? Sure. As I say, right next to gossip."

He told her about the dream in which he and Ginny had sought refuge in the observatory atop a country house planted in the middle of the city. When he was done, she smiled and shook her head. "You have such straightforward dreams. There's no challenge to them at all. You don't see what this is about?"

"Nope. Next to gossip, I love hearing dreams explained."

"Okay. Your original direction—the direction you took at the beginning of this series of dreams—was toward the right, toward an active, physical involvement. That direction now seems to you mortally hazardous. The menacing follower—your looming guilt—lurks there. So turning back, you go to your left—toward the spiritual and intellectual. You seek an upper room, a lofty place that looks upward into the heavens. This"— she tapped his forehead—is the dome, of course. In other words, you think you can escape your dread of involvement if you keep things on a high intellectual and spiritual plane."

Greg shook his head, unconvinced. "I don't think so. What you're saying makes beautiful sense, but I don't feel any 'dread of involvement.' I really don't."

"Don't you? I thought that's what your problem with Karen is. You want to be pals and she want to be married."

"True. But that's Karen."

She cocked a skeptical eyebrow at him. "Maybe I'm wrong, but I get the distinct impression that all your relationships with women have been on a pretty light-hearted level. Till now."

"Yes, I suppose you could say that."

"But you're absolutely sure you feel no dread of involvement."

He laughed and shook his head in defeat. "Okay, point made. You must have read a book or something. Have you ever considered the proposition that a woman's place is in the cellar?"

And that took them off on another track.

VI

SUNDAY WAS THE ONE DAY of the week Greg never failed to take note of. It was unmistakable, because the Outer Drive, normally surging with energy and life, was as hushed and deserted as a country churchyard—for him a depressing sight. It was a day on which he was particularly vulnerable to depression, thanks to his parents, who had consecrated it a perpetual day of mourning for Greg's older brother, who had gone off to boot camp when Greg was ten and had committed suicide a month later for reasons unknown or undisclosed. From that moment, he had been enshrined as a household god beside whom Greg could never be more than a disappointment. He had been all the things Greg wasn't: a golden boy, cheerful, helpful, eager to please, extroverted, athletic. Greg remembered him only dimly (and guiltily) as an energetic youngster who was good-natured but not terribly bright.

Any other day of the week Greg might take off and do nothing; Sundays he invariably filled with work in order to stifle the nagging voices of the past.

Around noon Mitzi, the *divorcée manqué* from upstairs, called to see if she could drop in that evening. He told her he'd welcome the company, and he was sincere; an evening with Mitzi would mean only one more to get through before he called Ginny. She said one odd thing before hanging up. After a hesitant pause: "I had a dream about you."

"It's the in thing, Mitzi. Everybody's doing it."

"Would you believe what that bastard husband of mine is trying to do to me?" Mitzi asked when she was barely inside the door. "He's trying to get back all the *tapes* he bought for me, for

50

Christ's sake. Have you ever heard of anything so fucking petty?"

Greg agreed he'd never heard anything so fucking petty, and she went on from there through a family-sized bag of potato chips that she'd supplied and four hefty bourbons that he supplied. It took until midnight to review the current status of her grievances and counterstrategies, and when it seemed to Greg that she'd worn herself out on the wickedness of lawyers, he asked her about the dream she'd had.

"Oh, that," she said darting a guilty look at him. "I don't know whether you want to hear about it or not."

"Why not?"

"It was . . . creepy."

"The best dreams are all creepy," he said.

"Well . . . okay." Mitzi closed her eyes dramatically. "We were holding a funeral—all the people in the building, the janitor, even the postman." She made a face. "And it was *your* funeral. We were burying you in back, where the moving vans unload. And we were all saying what a pity it was and what a shame and you just a young man and so on and so forth." She opened her eyes and looked at Greg. "And the weird thing was that you weren't dead. I mean, we *knew* you weren't dead."

"What was I doing if I wasn't dead?"

"You were asleep. You were asleep and you couldn't wake up, and that's why we were burying you."

"Go on."

"I think that's all there was," she said, but went on staring into space. "There was something about letters."

"Letters?"

"That's right. Oh, I remember now. There was a big pile of unopened letters on your coffin. That's why the postman was there. It was a regulation that . . . The reason we were burying you . . ." Mitzi nodded. "I'd forgotten this part of the dream. This is how it began. The postman came in and said, 'What's all this? Why isn't this person collecting his mail? I can't keep delivering mail if he isn't going to collect it.' So we went up to

51

your apartment and found you asleep your bed, and we waited around and tried to wake you up. And the postman said, 'Well, that's it, this man has to be buried, because it's against the regulations for me to deliver mail that isn't being collected, and if we bury him then I can go back and tell them it's okay now, because this man is dead.' And that's why the postman was there: to make sure we really buried you, along with all your unopened mail."

Greg chuckled. "Quite a dream."

"It seemed very creepy at the time. Now it just seems ridiculous. What do you think it means?"

"A dream should not mean but *be*," he said. "I don't think it means much of anything, to tell the truth."

"You don't think it's . . . an omen?"

"Good God, Mitzi. You read too many horror comic books. Applying the Agnes Tillford method to it . . . ." He closed his eyes for a few moments. "I would say it means you're afraid that I'm not always going to be around to give you a shoulder to cry on. It means you're afraid that someday you're going to come in here and find me asleep—which is to say insensible to your troubles."

"Yeah. But what about all those letters?"

He thought for a moment, then smiled. "Those are from my creditors. Knowing how little money a freelance writer makes, you're worried that my creditors are going to do me in and you're thinking of cutting me in on your divorce settlement."

"Shit! Divorce settlement? When those lawyers get through with me, I'll have to borrow bus fare to get to the poorhouse."

And she went on from there until Greg shooed her off to her own apartment half an hour later.

VII

HAVE YOU EVER SEEN *Les Enfants du Paradis*?" Greg asked when he called Ginny on Tuesday.

"No. Is it like Sasha's?"

He thought about this for a moment. "Yes, it's a lot like Sasha's. It's very romantic and comes to a tragic end. But it's not a restaurant, it's a film. A classic film, which everyone should see at least once in his or her lifetime."

A pause. "Then it's too bad it's not playing somewhere."

"Ah," he said, "but it *is* playing somewhere."

"I see. Then it's too bad I have no one to see it with. I hate going to movies alone."

"This," he pointed out gravely, "isn't a movie. This is most definitely a *film*. And I'm perfectly prepared to cross off several items on my social calendar to escort you."

"Then it would seem I'm in luck."

"Absolutely. It's also highly educational. You will learn to say *absolutely not* in an aristocratic Parisian accent."

"Wonderful. I can astonish all my friends."

"Exactly. And afterwards we can astonish all the waiters at L'Auberge by saying *absolument pas* to all of their suggestions."

"What fun. And when were you thinking of all this happening?"

"Well, I've never been much for postponing gratification. Are you free this evening?"

She was, and Greg said he'd pick her up at 6:30.

"Don't be so old-fashioned," Ginny replied. "Where's it playing? I'll meet you there."

He named a small art cinema on the near north side and told her not to be late.

"If I'm not there by seven, I won't be there at all," Ginny

snapped, and Greg's mood of exhilaration sagged like a punctured balloon.

Nevertheless, she stepped out of a cab in front of the theater almost ten minutes before the hour, and his apprehensions vanished. He was delighted to learn they shared a common disdain for munching during movies and both liked to sit up front, to be engulfed by the image on the screen.

But, as they sat waiting for the film to begin, his speech centers became clogged, and he had to fight down the temptation to vocalize inanities like "Have you been here before?" and "I just love old movies." Ginny was equally speechless, and Greg suddenly recognized the old symptoms from high school days.

They were On A Date. Staring straight ahead, he said, "Do you come here often?"

Ginny burst into laughter, and the spell was broken. They traded singles bar clichés until the lights went down and the film began.

Greg noted with relief that it was a fairly good print and for the first few minutes was more alert to Ginny's reactions than to the film itself. When he was assured that she was enjoying it, he relaxed and allowed himself to become absorbed in what was happening on the screen: Jean-Louis Barrault, on a street-side stage in Paris, was miming the activity of a pickpocket that was working the crowd. Greg knew the film by heart and in a few minutes was looking forward to a tavern scene in which the fragile-looking mime fells one of the vile Lacenair's bullies with a dancer's blow. As the scene opened, however, the screen abruptly went dark and the sound failed. After waiting for it to resume for half a minute, Ginny leaned toward him and said, "Is this the good part?"

"This is the dark part."

"Ah. A *film noire*."

Greg grunted.

After ten minutes of sitting quietly in the dark, he said he'd reconnoiter to see what the prospects looked like. He found a small crowd in the lobby exchanging speculations. Apparently a fuse had blown—or something had blown. It was rumored that help was on the way from some unknown corner of the city, but the theater personnel were already handing out free passes to anyone who could produce ticket stubs. Greg produced his, collected a pass for two, and went back for Ginny. "The wires sprang a leak," he told her, "and the electricity all ran out. No more movies tonight."

"Or films?"

"Or films."

She gathered up her things and they left. To Greg it seemed like a bad omen. "All the same," he pointed out, "there's still L'Auberge."

"I've got a better idea," Ginny said. "You took us out to dinner last week. Let's pick up a couple of steaks and take them to my place."

"That sounds fine," he said and began looking around for a cab. Ginny's taking the initiative for the evening was a good omen that offset the bad.

* * *

Ginny's apartment was a revelation to him, and he couldn't quite say why. The large front room was manifestly a work space, with expensive-looking drafting tables, a personal computer and printer, a light table, a waxer, tabourets overflowing with brushes, markers, and templates, racks of press type and a xerographic duplicator. While Ginny was off changing into jeans, he tried to figure out how it also managed to be an elegant living space as well. The graphics on the walls were the sort you find in Michigan Avenue galleries, and the two sofas facing each other across the ankle deep wool rug were in the Ferrari class of furniture, but it wasn't money that had turned the trick. He consigned it to the realm of mystery by deciding it was a designer's room, had been assembled according to principles beyond his comprehension. Beside this room, his own would seem frumpy and boring, and his prized claw-foot table would be a definite embarrassment.

Oh well, he thought, *I just want to be loved for myself.*

55

"There's an ice bucket in the kitchen," Ginny called to him from an adjacent room.

Greg looked around. "Where's the kitchen?"

"In front, to the right."

He'd taken in the extension of the room to the right, but simply as another living area, not as a kitchen. Now that his attention was focused on it, he saw all the required appliances there in plain sight. More of the designer's magic. He found the ice bucket and was cracking ice trays into it when Ginny joined him. Leaning back against a counter and watching her as she reached down bottles and glasses, he decided she was very alluring in jeans.

"Do you have a gorilla suit?" he asked on an impulse.

She put down a bottle and turned to stare at him. "It's at the cleaners, I think. Why?"

"Oh, I was just wondering if I'd have the same reaction to you in a gorilla suit."

She frowned. "If *you* were in a gorilla suit or *I* was in a gorilla suit?"

"Well . . . if you've only got the one, we could share it."

She shook her head, smiling. "You *are* crazy."

"There are two colors," he was saying an hour later, "red and black. Choose one."

Ginny studied the deck of cards face down on the table in front of her.

The steaks had been good, the conversation had been lighthearted, and when Ginny returned with the coffee, Greg had drawn a deck of cards from his shirt pocket.

"What's that?" Ginny asked.

"Card trick. As promised." He shuffled and set the deck in front of her. "Tell me what the top card is." Ginny reached for the deck but he stopped her. "Don't you know this trick?"

"No," Ginny said doubtfully. "How could I know it?"

He frowned. "I thought everyone knew this trick. You honestly don't know what the top card is?"

She laughed and said she honestly didn't.

Greg paused as if considering how to proceed. Finally he shrugged and said, "Well, we'll go on anyway. There are two colors, red and black. Choose one."

"Black," she said after a moment.

"Uh huh. And there are two black suits: spades and clubs. Choose one."

"Clubs."

He looked at her suspiciously. "You *do* know this trick."

"I don't!" Ginny protested. "I swear to God!"

He shrugged, unconvinced. "Okay. There are three kinds of clubs: high, middle, and low. Choose one."

"Low," Ginny said.

"And the low clubs are ace, two, and three. Choose one."

"Three."

Greg nodded. "Turn over the top card."

She picked it up, looked at it openmouthed, and said, "Good lord."

"May I see it?" She showed it to him. It was the three of clubs. "Aha," he said. "You lied. You *do* know this trick!"

"But I don't!" Ginny said. Then she laughed. "How the hell did you do that?"

"I didn't. You knew all the time it was the three of clubs."

"You swine. Tell me how you did it."

He gazed at her with lidded eyes. *"Absolument pas. Jamais."*

"Bastard. Tell me."

He raised his brows innocently. "But I want you to think of me as a man of mystery. How can I be strangely fascinating if I reveal all?"

She cocked her head at him. "And you seriously expect me to share my gorilla suit with you?"

"I'll bet it's all moth-eaten."

"It's not!"

Finally he relented. "It's not really a card trick at all," he said. "It's a psychological trick. Obviously I already knew that the top card was the three of clubs. I just had to lead you to it through a series of apparently arbitrary choices. That's the psychological trick: if you give someone an arbitrary choice to make between two or three things, he'll almost invariably pick the last one you name. I said 'red or black?' and you picked black. I said 'spades or clubs?' and you picked clubs. I said 'high, middle, or low?' and you picked low. You weren't thinking about your choices—you were wondering why I kept insisting you already knew the trick."

"True. If I'd been thinking, I would have said that 'low' should be ace, two, three, or four." She cradled her chin in her hand and stared at him thoughtfully for a moment. "It's true. Now that I know, you no longer seem strangely fascinating."

Greg snorted. "Wait'll you see me in a gorilla suit."

Later, saying good night at the door, Greg felt his heart plunge into his stomach when Ginny frowned and said, "It seems a shame to send you home."

Seeing his face drained of blood, her eyes widened in alarm. "What's wrong?" When he didn't answer, she covered her face with her hands and moaned, "Oh, Greg, I am so fucking stupid!" Then she took him by the hand, led him back to a sofa in the living room, and sat him down. She sat down beside him and looked at him searchingly. "Greg, you are a lovely man. I doubt if you know how lovely you are. I just got used to saying anything at all to you. Do you understand?"

Greg shook his head, not trusting his voice.

"Oh dear." She stood up nervously. "When I said what I said . . ." She paused, searching for words. "There isn't another man in the world I would have said that to, and you're obviously the one man in the world I *shouldn't* have said it to." She closed her eyes. "Oh God, it just gets worse and worse."

She knelt down beside him and took his hand in her own. "Greg, what I'm trying to say is this. When I stood there at the door, I thought 'Wow, it really seems a shame to send this man home.' There's nothing wrong with that, is there?"

He shook his head.

"And if I'd kept it in my head, where it belonged, we would have kissed good night, and you would have gone home, and everything would've been fine. Wouldn't it?"

Greg nodded.

"You wouldn't have felt bad if I *hadn't* said that, would you?"

He shook his head.

She squeezed his hand but felt no answering pressure. "Please, can't we do it all over again without that part? Can't we just pretend I'm not so stupid as to have said that?"

He said, "No," but it came out hoarse.

"Oh, Greg," she groaned, "don't fall in love with me. *Please.*"

"Why?"

When she didn't answer, he took his hand back, went into the kitchen, and made himself a drink. After taking a swallow and clearing his throat, he went back into the living room and stood over her. "Why?"

Ginny, still kneeling on the sofa, shook her head.

"Why? Are you in love with someone else?"

She shook her head. "Don't, Greg. Please."

"Are you a man killer? A Soviet agent?"

She shook her head.

"Do you have some dread disease? For Christ's sake, what is it?"

"Please don't quiz me, Greg."

Suddenly he felt his face flush with anger. He reached down and pulled her off the sofa to her feet. Gripping her shoulders fiercely, he said, "All right. You can tell me not to quiz you. I have no right whatever to quiz you. But you have no right to tell me who to love and who not to love." He shook her like a doll. "Do you get that? You can no more tell me not to love you than you can tell the sun not to shine." He shook her again till her head was bobbing. "It's a thing that's already *happened*, goddamn it!"

Her eyes wide with alarm, she nodded helplessly. Still

holding her in a numbing grip, he snarled, "Now tell me again what a shame it would be to send me home."

"Sh-sh-shame . . ." she whispered, her chin trembling.

"Goddamn right."

A couple hours before dawn, Greg woke from a light sleep and was immediately glad. This wasn't a night to sleep through. Ginny lay asleep on her stomach beside him, and he propped himself on an elbow to study her. This is enough, he thought. He'd be content to spend a week just watching the slow rise and fall of her shoulder blades below the cascades of her hair.

Their lovemaking, at least for him, had been like nothing he'd ever experienced—precisely because it *had* been love-making, not just the quenching of desire, not just delightful play. Holding her, touching her, he'd felt suffocated, overwhelmed, delirious with love. He'd felt no urgency to bring it to a climax. He'd wanted it to last forever, and it seemed to him it had. They had occupied a timeless zone in which tomorrow would never come, the sun would never rise, phones would never begin ringing to signal the beginning of just another workday.

When he'd come at last, it was something other than just a physical release, it was an electrical one. His body had sizzled and his brain had dissolved in a champagne foam. Ginny had fallen asleep with her head pillowed on his chest, and, his arm around her shoulders, he'd dozed off a few minutes later, drunk and exhausted with happiness.

With a sigh, he pulled the sheet up over her, carefully rolled out of bed, and began gathering up his clothes. He didn't want this magical evening to end in a humdrum morning of bathroom visits and breakfast and good-byes. And, having made that decision, he wanted to be gone before she woke up.

Passing through the living room, he considered leaving her a note. But saying what? Nothing could be added to what he'd already said, without words, a few hours before. He let himself out silently, eventually found a cab, and, sitting in front of his window with a cup of coffee, watched the red ball of the sun emerge from the far side of the lake. This satisfying ritual completed, he decided that two hours of sleep wouldn't see him through the day and took himself off to bed.

Silently, as if borne on a puff of wind, the steel door of the observatory swung open. With a thrill of panic, Greg took Ginny's arm and hurried her to the opposite side of the dome, where he began frantically to search for an exit. In his haste, he nearly missed it. It was an elevator door, fitted almost invisibly into the sleek metal wall. A plate beside it framed a single red button, and he slammed his palm onto it.

Nothing happened. The door at the other end of the building closed and locked with an echoing clunk.

Greg hammered on the button with the side of his fist until he felt Ginny's restraining hand on his arm.

"Not that way," she said. "Lightly."

Holding his breath, he touched the button with his index finger, and the door slid open with a gentle mechanical sigh. They scrambled inside, and when the door closed behind them they began to descend, smoothly and silently. Looking around, he thought he'd never seen such an elegantly appointed elevator. The walls, lit from some invisible source, glowed an indescribably delicate red. Handsomely machined brass panels on all sides offered knobs and buttons controlling unguessable functions.

The elevator sighed to a gentle stop, and he waited for the door to open. After a few moments a neutral voice issued from a brass grill over the door: "Yes or no?"

Yes or no? He looked at Ginny, and she shrugged. Greg answered with a shrug of his own and said, "Yes."

The elevator resumed its descent.

Twice more it paused to ask its question and twice more he answered yes. Finally it settled to a halt and the door opened. They stepped out onto a brightly lit street, and Greg realized that, by passing through the house and observatory, they'd reached a parallel street a block away.

Behind them the door sighed to a close, and the elevator began to ascend.

He looked around and saw a subway entrance just ahead. "Come on," he said, taking Ginny's hand. "The trains run all night." They raced down the stairs, through a turnstile, and out onto the deserted platform. He turned to the left, straining to hear the distant roar that signaled an approaching train, but there was nothing.

"Look," Ginny whispered and pointed into the track well. A long table set for an elaborate meal sat astride the tracks, and he groaned. They had stumbled into a subway station that had been abandoned by the city and turned over to private use. No trains ran here.

He looked around desperately for some way out, but they were surrounded by an unbroken, white tile wall. Again and again he swept it with his eyes, looking for some exit other than the one leading back up to the street. Then he realized he'd seen it and missed it. Once more he sent his eyes across the wall, this time fully alert. Then he had it: at a certain point, the wall angled in to form a V. Set into one arm of the V was a door. The other arm was a mirror cunningly angled so as to give the illusion of an unbroken wall. He remembered now that this was how the subway dwellers kept intruders out. It was an effective illusion; even knowing it was there, he had to concentrate to see it at all.

Keeping it fixed in his vision, he held out his hand to Ginny and whispered, "There's a door over here." When she didn't answer, he said, "Ginny, come on!"

Nothing.

Tearing his eyes away from the illusion, he looked around. He was alone on the platform. Ginny was gone. He turned back to the illusion and in the mirror caught sight of her disappearing into the darkness beyond the hidden door.

Behind him a thunderstorm of footsteps broke out on the stairway leading down from the street. Now completely maddened with fury, the follower had found them.

Fear clutched at Greg's heart.

VIII

LOOKING THROUGH THE CLIPPINGS that remained on his desk, Greg realized he was doomed to return to the library. He'd worked through the best of the lot, and the stories that were left weren't worth fooling with. Checking his watch, he saw it was nearly one o'clock: hardly time enough to make the trip worthwhile. He sighed, knowing he was just groping for an excuse to stay home with his bright daydreams. He was in no mood for the gray, hushed confinement of the library.

He wanted to call Ginny. No, that wasn't quite it. He wanted to be where Ginny was. He wanted to look up from his desk and see her working away at her drafting table. He wanted to stroll over and plant a kiss at the nape of her neck. He wanted to see her look up and give him a distracted smile and accept another kiss, this time on the lips. He wanted . . .

God, he thought, it *is* a form of madness.

Mentally gritting his teeth, he gathered up his notebook, shoved a couple of pens in his pocket, and headed for the door.

When he returned five hours later, he was in a foul mood. He'd struck a two-week period that was a dry hole. After nearly three hours of wading through the *New York Times*, he'd come up with two mediocre stories. In desperation, he'd floundered through *Variety*, the *Washington Post*, the *Los Angeles Times*, and even the *Wall Street Journal* for the same period, garnering exactly nothing. He was tempted to call Ted Owens in the morning and tell him the idea was a washout. In a world of terrorist bombings, Star Wars game playing, and famine, no one gives a damn if a man bites a dog. He tossed his notebook on the desk and headed for the bathroom to make a second pass at stripping away the black sheen his hands had picked up from a thousand sheets of newsprint.

A few minutes later he was stretched out on the sofa with his eyes closed and a drink resting on his chest, trying to wash away the blackness of his mood, when the phone rang. His heart stopped and he thought: *Ginny*. Rolling his eyes at his own foolishness, he set his glass down on the coffee table and answered the phone.

"Is this Mr. Donner?"

"Yes."

"I'm calling from Armando's restaurant," the voice announced primly. "We have a small bookkeeping problem here."

"Oh?" Greg wondered if he'd accidentally written them a bad check, then remembered he'd paid with a credit card.

"I was rather expecting you to have called *us* by now."

"Why? What's the problem?"

"I see. You don't know what the problem is."

Greg laughed. "I'm afraid I really don't."

"Well, the problem is the bill I have here. I was wondering what you plan to do about it."

"*Bill*," he said, frowning, completely baffled. "What bill is that?"

"It's a bill from last Friday night, Mr. Donner. I'm sure you must remember it. For six hundred forty-three dollars and seventeen cents?"

Greg felt the blood drain from his face. "You're crazy."

"Oh . . . Well, I must say I don't think that's quite the approach to take to this thing, Mr. Donner. I know you've been a regular customer here, and I'm sure you want to go on being a regular customer here, and —"

"*You're crazy!*" Greg screamed and smashed the receiver down into its cradle.

His legs shaking uncontrollably, he sank into the cushions of the sofa and held his face in his hands. He struggled to think, but his brain seemed clogged with sound: with the rushing of blood in his ears. Finally he dropped his hands and stared at the phone. He tried to imagine it ringing, to remember the sound of its bell. Had it rung at all?

He got up shakily, idiotically put the receiver to his ear, and listened to the hum of the dial tone. Then he cradled it and said aloud, "That didn't happen."

Obviously it *couldn't* have happened.

He turned and stared at the sofa, where he'd been lying just a few moments before, and it came to him: he'd fallen asleep. Lying there with a drink on his chest, he'd dozed off and had a dream. But if that was the case . . . when had he woken up? When you wake up from a dream, no matter how vivid it is, you *know* you're awake and you *know* that what you've just experienced was a dream.

He hadn't woken up.

Christ, he thought, is it possible that I'm still asleep, still dreaming? How do you tell with absolute certainty that you're *not* dreaming? Pinch yourself? Can't you pinch yourself in a dream? He shook his head violently. He *knew* he was awake. But if he was awake, then he'd never been asleep—and the phone call hadn't been a dream.

He stood staring into space for a few seconds, then looked up Agnes's number and dialed it. When she answered, he said, "Agnes, this is Greg. Have you just played a little trick on me?"

"What? What on earth are you talking about?"

He didn't answer. He knew it was all wrong. For her to have impersonated that caller would have been inconceivably out of character. "Do you remember the dream about that ridiculous bill at Armando's?"

"Of course." She sounded puzzled.

"Did you repeat it to anyone?"

"Why ever would I do that?"

"Just answer me. Did you?"

"No."

"Not to anyone?"

"No, dear, not to anyone. Why?"

"Because I just got a call from someone dunning me for the six hundred forty-three dollars I owe Armando's."

He listened to her breathe through a full minute.

"I'm trying to think what the point of this is."

"What do you mean?"

"You have a wonderful sense of humor, Greg, but this is completely over my head."

"I'm not joking."

"You're saying this really happened?"

"Yes."

"Tell me about it."

He told her, and she said, "You were lying on the couch with your eyes closed when the call came?"

Greg sighed. "I've already thought it out, Agnes. I definitely didn't dream that call."

"Of course you didn't. If you had, you'd know it. That isn't what I was getting at."

"Oh. Well, go on."

"In a semiconscious state, as when we're just waking up or just falling asleep, it's not at all unusual to superimpose a dream context on things happening around us. For example, the alarm clock goes off, and in our dreams this becomes a fire alarm or someone screaming. This is a common experience. You must've had it."

"Yes. Go on."

"Okay. Lying on the couch, you were in such a state: semiconscious, on the verge of dreaming. You had a phone call, and you superimposed a dream context on it. The caller may in fact have been trying to sell you a newspaper subscription, but what you *heard* was related to your dream about Armando's. Maybe he said something that *sounded* like Armando's or six hundred, and your unconscious latched onto that and supplied the rest. And by the time you were fully awake, you'd hung up."

Greg nodded reluctantly. . . It fit, barely. It was plausible, or at least credible. He *wanted* it to be credible, because it was infinitely preferable to thinking he'd had an outright hallucination. "Bless you, Agnes. You have saved a man's sanity."

"Good heavens," she said. "Did you think you were ready for the straitjacket?"

"Just about."

"You couldn't pay for our drinks in a straitjacket, honey."

"I know. I owe you a brace of them, love."

Greg's weariness had been washed away with relief, and, without thinking about it, he dialed Ginny's number.

"I'd like to see you tonight," he told her.

A pause. "All right. Can we meet somewhere?"

"What do you mean?"

"I mean, let's have a drink together. Maybe somewhere up in your neighborhood for a change."

He asked her if she knew the Tango, and she said she didn't. "It's in the Hotel Belmont. You'll like it. Very designy. Then you can come up and see my place—it's only a couple blocks away."

"Okay," Ginny said levelly. "Eight o'clock?"

He said that would be fine. But, after hanging up, he didn't feel fine. Ginny had seemed cool and remote. He shook his head, recognizing this as just another symptom; to one struck down by the love madness, every word, every tone, every gesture is a portent of acceptance or rejection.

Thrusting his apprehensions aside, he began to organize something to eat.

"Very nice," Ginny said, surveying the Tango cocktail lounge with a wan smile. "Nice colors. Nice lighting. Though I'll bet people fall over the tables a lot."

The tables, were in fact low cubes, and they *were* a bit awkward.

Greg looked around nervously for the waitress. He'd arrived early to be sure of snagging a corner booth, and there was a half-finished drink in front of him. Finally he caught her eye and ordered one for Ginny.

Ginny looked down at her hands and folded them. He reached over to claim one, and she gave him a reserved smile but didn't quite meet his eyes.

He felt sick with dread.

When her drink arrived he said, "What's wrong, Ginny?"

She shook her head. "I had it all rehearsed, now it's gone."

"Go on."

"I'm sorry, Greg. I'm desperately sorry."

"What is it? Is it something about last night?"

She took her hand back after giving his a brief squeeze. "No. Last night was . . . lovely."

"Then what's wrong?"

"What's wrong," she repeated blankly. Then she looked up at him appealingly. "I wish you'd listen to me."

"I *will* listen to you, Ginny."

She shook her head hopelessly. "I told you not to fall in love with me, and you didn't listen. I suppose you thought I was being . . . coy."

"I didn't know what you were being. I still don't."

She turned her hands up and studied them as if she might find something written in her palms. "It's true I have no right to tell you who to love. But . . . " She broke off with a sigh. "But I have a right to resist being torn to pieces."

"Is that what I'm doing to you, Ginny?"

She shook her head.

"Ginny, you said you wished I'd listen to you. I'm listening. I'm listening as hard as I can."

Suddenly she lifted her head and turned away from him, and he could see tears standing in her eyes. "What you want from me I can't give. And what you want to give me I can't accept. That's what you have to listen to."

"God, Ginny, all I want is what I've had. And I don't even mean last night. I didn't demand that."

"I know." She groped in her purse for a tissue and wiped her eyes. "That was my fault."

"Your *fault*? Jesus, what are you saying? Didn't you want it to happen?"

Ginny nodded bleakly. "I wanted it to happen, and that was my fault."

"I don't understand, Ginny. You say you can't accept what I want to give you. What does that mean? Do you mean you don't want to be loved?"

She leaned over the table and touched the rim of her glass with her fingers but didn't pick it up. "No," she whispered.

"Then you mean . . . you don't want to be loved by *me*."

She answered with a slight shake of her head. A tear dropped onto the back of her hand, and she wiped it away. "I don't mean that either," she said.

"For God's sake, Ginny, I don't understand. I'm trying, but I don't understand."

She nodded and wiped her eyes. "I know. You can't understand, and I can't explain." She stuffed the tissue into her purse and stood up. "And neither one of us can do anything about it."

"God, Ginny, don't leave now," he pleaded, but she was already walking away. He followed her with his eyes till she was out of sight, then glanced dismally down at her untouched drink, thinking: not even that much of me can she accept. It seemed a perfect token of her rejection of him. Empty of feeling he looked around the deserted room.

The bartender pointedly turned his back.

IX

FOR THE NEXT FOUR DAYS Greg haunted his apartment like a ghost. Drained of all substance but grief, he found himself pausing in front of mirrors to confirm his reality. His reflection stared back at him like that of a corpse.

A phone call from Ted Owens on Monday morning forced him back to work. An editor had expressed an interest in seeing a sample of *Bizarre*, and when did Greg think he could get it together?

"It's coming along well," Greg lied. "Another three weeks should do it."

"Editors have short memories, Greg. Could you make it in two?"

"I'll do my best," Greg said vaguely, to get rid of him.

He spent the day at the library and that night took Agnes to dinner at Freddie's to tell her his troubles. She listened gravely and when he was done reached across the table to pat his hand.

"Greg, dear, you are a gorgeous man," she said, "but you have a hell of a lot to learn about women."

"I believe it," he replied. "What did I do wrong?"

"Basically, you overwhelmed her. It's all very well for you to let yourself go the way you did. To lose your mind over a woman after knowing her for a few hours. In fact, it's sort of charming. But a woman learns early on that she can't afford to respond to a man the way a man responds to a woman."

"What do you mean?"

Agnes raised her brows. "Maybe you don't understand men too well either." She thought for a moment. "Let's suppose you're a woman instead of a man. You run into a man who turns you on, and after an hour you tell him, 'Wow, I'm already three-quarters in love with you.'"

Greg blushed.

"Now maybe you don't know it, honey, but nine-tenths of all men in this situation are going to say to themselves, 'Oh ho! What have we here? An easy lay!' Nothing whatever to do with love. A gorgeous woman throws herself at a man and nine men out of ten will gladly take her. They may think she's dumb as a horse or as boring as *Pilgrim's Progress*, but a free ride with a beautiful girl is not to be passed up. You can't be so innocent that you don't know this."

Greg nodded. "True."

"And surely you can see the potential for disaster for the woman who behaves this way."

"Yes."

"Okay. But you didn't hesitate to proclaim your love for Ginny. You knew you didn't have to Hesitate, because women aren't like men in this regard. Unless they're nymphomaniacs or damned hard up, very few women will take a man just because he's available. They generally want something more than an easy lay."

"Also true."

She shrugged. "So what you were asking Ginny to do was to throw caution to the winds and make herself completely vulnerable to a man she's barely met, a man who, for all she knows, might leave her emotionally ravaged in a week."

"I didn't ask that of her."

"Don't be a klutz. Your *behavior* asked it of her. *Demanded* it of her."

He nodded glumly. "So what do I do, Agnes?"

"I don't know. Snag us some more coffee and another drink, and I'll think about it."

When he'd done that, she said, "I really don't know what you should do, Greg. If it were me instead of Ginny, I'd be able to advise you. But I don't know this woman."

"What would you advise me to do if it were you?" Agnes tugged on an earlobe and stared into space for a while. "I'd advise you to think of something."

Greg laughed. "That's a big help."

"I mean it. If I were Ginny, I'd put you right out of my mind. Not because I don't like you, but because you're just too damn dangerous to fool around with."

"So what are you saying? That I should somehow make myself seem less dangerous?"

She shook her head. "No, you could never manage that. Let me see if I can explain. What I sensed in you almost instantly, and I'm sure Ginny did too, is that you have . . . wonderful instincts. The instincts of a wonderful fool."

"Terrific."

"Let me finish. These instincts make you attractive—very attractive—but they also make you dangerous. Okay. Following your instincts got you into trouble. But you've got nothing else to follow to get you *out* of trouble. Don't give up on being Greg. Keep on following those instincts. That's what I meant when I told you to think of something. Keep on being Greg, and do what Greg would do. I don't have any idea what that might be. Only you can figure that out, following your instincts."

Greg looked at her thoughtfully. "So you're saying I shouldn't give up. I shouldn't accept that good-bye as final."

"I'd be a fool to tell you that, Greg—or to tell you the opposite. I don't know Ginny. I only know you, and I trust you. All I can tell you is to trust yourself."

And Greg had to settle for that.

In sleep that night, he wandered endlessly through the corridors of the dwelling that had been made of the abandoned subway station. Sometimes overhead, sometimes in a parallel corridor, he heard Ginny's footsteps. Sometimes he heard whispered conversations nearby and paused to listen; but these were only impossibly muddled echoes, and he could neither understand them nor trace them to their source.

The corridors formed a tortuous and endless maze, and he often suspected he was traveling the same route over and over, but the walls and the countless empty rooms he passed were so featureless that he couldn't be sure. He sometimes heard his follower's footsteps as well, but they inspired no terror in him now. They seemed almost jaunty, carefree. Having herded Greg into the labyrinth, the follower no longer needed to pursue him and was free to go about his own business.

In the end, the walls, doorways, and corners began to stream past him monotonously, at an unvarying speed, and Greg lost all sensation of walking.

The next morning he woke up exhausted and vastly depressed.

X

GREG SCANNED A PAGE of the *New York Times* and thought, *Follow your instincts*.

A newspaper in Tennessee had won a libel suit, ending a decades-old feud between the publisher and a city official. Nothing there. More on the eight thousand dollars the Defense Department had spent on a pair of pliers. Everybody had worked that one over.

He turned the page and thought, *Follow your instincts*. He had several, the first being to continue to sink into depression and self-pity till he drowned in it, till one day someone would discover him sitting in his apartment, a mindless vegetable.

That would show her. Childish.

A gunman had held up a bank and eluded the whole Akron police force by escaping on a bicycle. It needed something else, some capper that wasn't there.

What would happen, he wondered, if he pretended their last conversation had never taken place, if he just called Ginny up and asked her out? He decided that was just an impulse, not an intuition, and his intuition told him it was a rotten impulse.

He paged through the business section without much hope. There was another story in the continuing financial misfortunes of the Hunt heirs. The head of a bank observed, "It's been a tough year for Texas billionaires." Bizarre. Something could be done with it, but Greg didn't feel like lugging it over to the duplicating machine.

Bombard her with flowers, books, boxes of candy, funny little gifts? Incredibly stupid. Completely brainless.

He discarded the sports section unread. He didn't know the names and backgrounds well enough to recognize a bizarre event when he saw one, and if it ever came to the real thing, he'd subcontract the sports side of it. Reassembling the paper, he concluded he knew only one thing for sure: he was wasting his time and Ted Owens's money.

Guiltily, he dug out the story about the Hunt heirs and took it to the duplicator. Then he packed up and headed for home.

It was on the bus, in a window seat facing the lake, that he realized what his intuition was, and it brought a crooked smile to his face. Agnes had been right. He had to go on being Greg. That was all he could do and the best he could do. He couldn't become a figure from a romantic novel, brooding away into a heartrending decline. He couldn't become a whacky buffoon from a Frank Capra comedy. He had to go on being Greg.

And he had to go on hoping. Something would happen. There'd be a day when it suddenly made sense to call Ginny. Or there'd be a day when it suddenly made sense for Ginny to call him. It couldn't possibly be over. On that, his intuition was un-wavering. The happy ending would be there, but he couldn't bash his way through to it. He simply had to let it come. And with that conclusion, he heaved a deep sigh of relief.

Free to think of something besides his grief, Greg consid-ered Mitzi. She had called twice in the past week to see if his shoulder was available for crying on, and, pleading a lot of work, he had turned her down.

Interesting, he thought. In a way, her dream had been prophetic. If she had come to his apartment, she would have found him deeply asleep, completely absorbed in self-pity, lifeless. He would call her when he got home and tell her his shoulder was back in working order.

And he thought: *Greg is also back in working order.*

By Thursday afternoon, fed up with the library, Greg decided he had enough stories to finish the promised sample, and he was back in his apartment by four o'clock —in time for a frantic call from Ted Owens.

"For Christ's sake, Greg, where have you been? I've been trying to reach you all week."

"I've been at the library," Greg replied coolly, "working on a goofy book for Ted Owens."

"Oh. Well, great. Look, the editor I talked to has talked to his people, and I think they're all looniest. They think the *Bizarre* book could be another *Book of Lists*, which is absurd, and they're wetting their pants to have a look at it. Do you think you could get me that sample by next Friday?"

Greg spent a few moments calculating. "I could get it in the *mail* by next Friday. What the hell, you wouldn't do anything with it if you got it Friday anyway."

"I'd give it to the editor if I got it Friday."

"Don't kid me, Ted. All you can do with an editor on Friday is haul him away in a basket."

Ted chewed it over for half a minute. "You'll put it in the mail Friday without fail?"

Greg paused, smiling. "Have you ever thought carefully about that locution, Ted? Without fail? *Fail* is strictly a verb. To do something without fail is like doing something without spend or without destroy."

"Come on, Greg. You'll put it in the mail Friday?"

"Without fail."

After he hung up, Greg did some real figuring and concluded that, at his current production rate, the work he'd promised in a week would take a month. He was going to have to put his back into it: no more leisurely dinners with Agnes, no more evenings frittered away with Mitzi. In the week ahead, Gregory would have to become a very dull boy.

Looking at his desk, he winced. For a year or more he'd been pushing back the jungle of manuscripts, files, half-read books, notes, unfinished letters, and magazines turned open to unread articles. Now he was in for it. Before undertaking this miracle of productivity, he was going to have to waste an hour clearing it off down to the bare wood, a task he considered the most gruesome of his professional life.

After an hour he'd worked his way down, like an archaeologist, to the neat stack of file folders that had remained after his last bout with the jungle. Wondering why he'd thought they deserved a permanent place on the table, he began to go through them. In a file of biographies he'd done for an encyclopedia two years ago, he found an item that gave him an idea. Deciding the idea deserved consideration and that he'd earned a break, he went into the kitchen for a drink and then returned to study what he'd found.

It was an eight-by-ten glossy publicity still of Benny Goodman tilted back in a plain wooden chair while tootling away on his clarinet. Greg didn't have even the faintest recollection of how it had come to be in this file. Probably he'd seen it in the editor's office and asked if he could have it. Possibly he'd swiped it—for what reason he couldn't imagine.

None of this had anything to do with his idea, which he had to admit was an impulse. He spent several minutes studying the photo. It was meant to look like a casual, unposed shot: just Benny Goodman savoring his own music all by himself in an off moment. What the hell, he thought as he reached for a pen and scrawled across the bottom:

To Ginny—
Still tootling away and thinking of you.
Your pal, Benny

And what, he asked, does my intuition have to say about that? Finally he decided. This is the truth I want Ginny to know about me right now, and there's no other way to give it to her. I *am* still tootling away. I've recovered from her inexplicable rejection and am still here, thinking about her. She's the tune I'm playing, and if she looks at this picture a month from now or a year from now, I'll still be playing it. No reply is asked for or needed; I'm not asking her to change her mind. I'm just telling her about *me*.

His intuition told him to send it, and, so as to give himself no time for second thoughts, he slipped it into an envelope with a backing of cardboard, sealed it, addressed it, and carried it out to the mailbox in time for the last pickup. Then, in a giddy mood, he went back to work.

XI

BY TEN O'CLOCK SUNDAY NIGHT, Greg was beginning to believe he might actually meet the deadline. Ted had asked for fifty pages, not because it would take that much to give someone the idea but to demonstrate that there was plenty of good material available. Greg judged that what he'd produced so far, when typed up, would come to about twenty pages. By Wednesday he'd be ready to have a typist in from one of the temporary services to produce a rough draft while he went on writing. Though he hated the damn things, he made a mental note that this was the last project he was going to start without a word processor.

He had the project on track at last, and, pouring his first drink of the day, he wondered why he didn't feel better about it. Up until ten he'd felt fine. The changing of the hour had been like crossing a border into sudden, bleak depression. Then, with a twinge of self-disgust, he realized what it was.

For the past three days, without thinking about it at all, he had begun to build a fantasy: Ginny would get the photo by Saturday. Although he'd told himself that no reply was asked for or needed, she would call. Maybe not immediately, not on Saturday.

On Sunday.

And when ten o'clock—the last of the "civilized hours" for calling—had come and gone, Greg knew he had betrayed himself. It was true that no reply to his message was asked for, but he'd sent it hoping to get one. Now, instead of that, he had an image of Benny Goodman's photo lying in Ginny's wastebasket, buried beneath superfluous dupes, stats, and proofs. By sending it, he'd given her another chance to reject him, and she'd taken it.

For nearly a week, Greg had dammed up his anguish with hope. Now it engulfed him in a flood, and he let himself drown. He went into the kitchen and filled a glass with bourbon. Normally he drank for relaxation; tonight he would drink for stupefaction. It took him less than an hour to achieve it. He staggered out of his clothes and fell into bed like a corpse.

Greg's journey through the subterranean maze was endless, and his body ached to be free of it. He was certain now that he was following the same route, passing the same blind walls, the same corners, the same empty rooms over and over again. But there didn't seem to be any help for it; every turning was forced.

Then he paused to listen. The labyrinth, which before had been alive with echoed footsteps and whispered conversations, was now utterly silent. This meant Ginny and the pursuer had known or found a way out. He closed his eyes and thought, *Of course. I've been following the corridor and it leads nowhere. The way out must be through one of the rooms.* He turned into the nearest—a windowless box with a closet at the left near the back. The closet was empty and led nowhere. The next two rooms were identical. But the closet in the fourth seemed deeper than the others—deep enough so that its back wall, if it had one, was lost in shadow.

He walked in and after a few steps stumbled over a box. Squatting beside it, he saw it was filled with old toys: a Raggedy Ann doll, a teddy bear, some boxed games, a jump rope, a few coloring books, and a flashlight. Rummaging through them, he felt a sudden certainty that he was touching relics of Ginny's childhood. He picked up the flashlight and switched it on. Directing its feeble yellow glow to the back of the closet, he discovered a narrow staircase leading up.

And overhead he heard the low tones of a muffled conversation. Looking at the stairs, he wondered if he'd be able to climb them at all. Only a foot wide, they seemed to belong to a child's playhouse. He'd have to attack them sideways. Sending the dim glow of the flashlight upward, he saw that the stairs turned crazily every few feet: It was a tower of some sort.

After a few exhausting minutes, he arrived at the top and stepped out into a room he recognized as the vestibule of the country mansion with the dome on the roof. To his left was the front door, through which morning sunlight was streaming. Straight ahead was a broad, handsome staircase leading to the upper floors of the house. He heard someone giggle: plainer now, on the floor just above.

He turned off the flashlight and headed for the stairs. At the top he found himself facing a wide hallway. Glass-handled doors to the right and left were closed, but at the far end an open doorway glowed mysteriously, as if the room beyond were the home of a radiant treasure. Approaching hesitantly, he heard a brief whispered exchange from within, then another soft giggle. He stepped into the doorway and saw an elegant pedestal bed that seemed to be framed in sunlight, floating in sunlight. Dazzled, he was at first unable to make out the features of the two figures lying in the bed. They seemed to exchange a glance, then sat up to stare at him with amused curiosity. Both were naked. One was an old man: old but strikingly handsome, with a matinee idol's profile and an abundance of white hair.

The other was Ginny.

As if suddenly self-conscious, she rolled over onto the man's chest, and he put a protective arm around her shoulders. Without looking up, Ginny said, "I told you, Greg. Everyone told you. We told you and told you and told you. We sent you letters and you wouldn't read them. We sent you messages and you ignored them. You just wouldn't listen."

Heartsick, Greg stared at her.

Finally she looked up and said, "There's only one way out for you, Greg. You'll have to use your flashlight."

Dumbly, Greg looked down at it, but it was no longer a flashlight: it was a long-barreled pistol. He lifted it up for a closer examination. It was a handsome object, though it lacked the wicked sleekness of a Luger: blued steel, with hard-rubber stocks. Bringing it closer he saw a design pressed into the stock: the head of a snarling bear in profile.

Without hesitation, he put the gun to his temple and pulled the trigger.

And woke up trembling, with the worst hangover of his life.

Groaning, he stumbled into the bathroom for a handful of vitamin B and aspirin, neither of which helped much, even after another three hours of sleep.

He forced himself to his desk and worked till mid-afternoon. Then he took the phone off the hook and went back to bed.

When he awoke at six, his hangover was gone.

XII

TUESDAY MORNING brought a cold front to Chicago, with leaden skies, a steady drizzle, and high winds that whipped the lake into a fury. It was an ugly day that matched Greg's mood.

He was beginning to resent Ted Owen's project. Ordinarily he didn't mind working hard to meet a deadline, but then ordinarily his life wasn't falling to pieces around him. He urgently needed—or at least wanted— a few days to sort things out, lick wounds, and try to find his emotional feet again, and Ted's project made that impossible. For the next four days, he had to chain himself to his desk and produce bright and witty copy.

By two o'clock Greg had made up the time he'd lost struggling with his hangover and was back on schedule, with a little more than half the writing done. He decided he'd earned half an hour's brooding time and was on his way into the kitchen for a drink when the phone rang. He answered it, hoping it wasn't Ted Owens.

"Mr. Donner?"

"Yes?"

"Hi. This is Phil Dobson. I think I've got a line on that piece you're looking for. There wasn't a whole lot to go on, but—"

"Hold on," Greg said. "You've got the wrong party,"

"Oh. Isn't this Mr. Donner? 984-2754?"

"Yes."

"Well. . . I don't see how I could have the wrong party. Have I caught you at a bad time to talk or something?"

"No." Greg said with a sigh. "Go ahead."

"Well, as I say, I think I've located that piece you're interested in. Actually, it's quite a rarity, a Reising Target Automatic, made in the early twenties. I wouldn't have been able to spot it at all, but—"

"You know," Greg interrupted, "I don't have the slightest idea what you're talking about."

A pause. "Jesus. You called me yesterday afternoon and described a pistol you're interested in: blued steel, long barrel, hard-rubber stocks, with a bear's head in profile ."

Greg's face went cold. "You're crazy."

A longer pause. "Oh," he said finally. "I get it. You found someone who already had it in stock. Shit, man, that's not nice. I spent an hour with the books and an hour on the phone tracking down that piece for yon. If you'd told me you were—"

"What did you say your name is?"

"Christ. Phil Dobson. Dobson Firearms."

"I'll call you back," Greg said, and hung up. He stood blinking for a moment, then reached for the phone directory. Phil Dobson didn't have a display ad, but under his name in the regular listing was printed: *Specializing in Unusual & Collectible Weapons.* Greg dialed the number and the same voice answered, "Dobson Firearms."

Greg's lips and tongue felt anesthetized. He mumbled, "This is Greg Donner again. I'm sorry. I, uh, forgot all about our conversation yesterday."

"You *kidding*?"

"What exactly did I ask you for?"

"Aw, c'mon, man. Gimme a break."

Greg paused, thinking. "Do you have the gun there?"

"No, but I can have it here in an hour. If you're serious."

"This is a pistol?"

"Christ, man, what do you think it is, a musket?"

Greg considered asking him to describe it but decided no description would be good enough anyway. "How much would it cost me to have a look at it?"

"What do you mean, *look* at it?"

"I mean I want to look at it and I'm willing to pay you to show it to me."

Dobson paused long enough for Greg to imagine him scratching his head in frustration. "Look," he said in a strangled voice, "if you're a serious buyer, looking costs nothing. If you're wondering what condition it's in, the guy I'm getting it from says—"

"I'm not interested in its condition," Greg snapped. "I just want to see it."

"Jesus . . . You mean you want me to close up shop and go get this piece just so you can look at it?"

"Yes. How much would that cost?"

"Christ. Twenty dollars. Cash money."

"It'll be there in an hour?"

Dobson said it would.

Dobson's Firearms was a dismal little hole off south Wabash, its windows stained as though permanently blackened by the shadow of the el overhead. When Greg went in, the slender man behind the glass-topped counter squinted at him tensely, like a creature disturbed in its burrow. He said nothing.

"I'm Greg Donner." Dobson didn't move. Facing him across the counter, Greg saw that he was an ancient-looking kid in his mid-twenties, his face crisscrossed with black lines of suspicion and cunning.

"Do you have the gun?"

"I have it." Dobson's eyes held a surly challenge, as if they were discussing the Maltese Falcon.

Greg handed over the twenty dollars, and the little man reached into the case for an object shrouded in black. He set it gently on the counter between them, flipped the corners of the wrapping aside, and there, in a nest of black velvet, lay the gun of Greg's dream. He didn't have to pick it up to recognize it, but he did anyway. Resting in his hand exactly as it had in the dream, it fascinated him, and he lifted it up for a closer inspection, just as he'd done then. After a few moments he realized Dobson was saying something.

". . . not an antique in the strict sense, but highly collectible. If it was in perfect condition—that means the way you would've found it in a dealer's case in 1922—"

"What time did I call you about this?"

"Huh?" His concentration broken, Dobson blinked at him without comprehension. Greg repeated the question.

"What *time*?" He looked astounded, as if time had ceased to exist. "Jesus, I don't know. Two, three o'clock."

"What did I sound like?" Dobson gawked at him, and Greg went on with a sigh. "Look, I know I called you, but I have no memory of it at all. Do you understand? That's why I paid you twenty dollars. I want to hear about it."

"Jesus." Bafflement had smoothed his face and he suddenly looked very young indeed. "I don't know. You sounded . . . *ordinary*. You said you were looking for an unusual gun, and I said I had plenty of 'em. And you said you had a particular gun in mind, and you described it. In detail. I said I didn't recognize it offhand but would look it up and see what I could do."

"Anything else?"

He gazed into space for a moment. "Well, you said you were in a hurry. You said you needed it in a hurry."

"I said I *needed* it?"

"Well, yeah. I think so."

"Did I sound . . . excited?"

Dobson shrugged. "You sounded *ordinary*. Matter of fact. Just like now. You wanted a gun and could I get it for you. Nothing special, except you needed it in a hurry."

Greg turned the gun over in his hands. "What are you asking for it?"

"Ah." Dobson's face creased in a meager smile. "Well, I was just saying, if it was in perfect condition, the right collector would pay three-fifty, four hundred for it. As it is—and I'd say it was in excellent to very good condition—two fifty'll take it."

Greg looked down at the gun again as if imprinting it on his memory, then set it down carefully in the center of its velvet nest. "Thanks," he said blankly and turned toward the door.

"Hey, man, make me an offer, for Christ's sake!" Dobson called after him, but Greg didn't hear it. After walking blindly for two blocks, he stopped at a pay phone and dialed Agnes's number. He told her, "I've gotta talk to you."

"Sure, honey. What's wrong?"

"I've gotta talk to you right now."

"Okay. You want to come up to my place?"

"Yes."

"If you need a drink, I don't keep anything here."

"I need a drink," Greg said.

They agreed to meet at Freddie's in forty minutes.

"Greg, honey," she said after hearing the story, "you've got to realize this is out of my depth."

"You can explain it, Agnes. The way you did the other thing. I need to have someone explain it to me."

She patted his hand, looking a little scared. "Look, you were exhausted and hung over and depressed."

"Yes. Go on."

"And you made a phone call. Then you fell into bed and forgot about it."

"I made a phone call about a gun I'd used the night before to blow out my brains."

"I know, honey," Agnes bleated.

"How could I dream a gun I've never seen, never heard of—an actual gun that exists in the real world?"

"You saw it somewhere, Greg. You had to."

"I didn't. I've never been interested in guns—and this is a rarity. Even the gun dealer didn't recognize it."

Agnes shook her head helplessly.

"For Christ's sake, what does it *mean*?"

"I don't know, Greg. I *think* it means you were exhausted and hung over and depressed."

"And suicidal maybe. Right?"

"Greg, I don't know."

He stared at her bleakly. "For God's sake, say something *useful*, Agnes."

She looked down at her glass. "I can give you the name of a friend, a psychologist. She's old as the hills, but she's the very best. She's—"

86

"I don't want the name of a friend," Greg snapped. He closed his eyes for a moment. "Look, I'm panicked. I can't think about this thing. I need you to think about it for me, but you're panicked too. Stop being panicked and think. Please, Agnes."

She looked again at her empty glass and said, "I need another drink." She got up, and when she returned ten minutes later she set a fresh drink in front of each of them, and Greg realized she'd had another at the bar.

"You're right," she said. "I was panicked."

"Okay. Go on."

"First, call up this guy you're doing the book for and tell him you're going to be a week late. Take off a week and go fishing or whatever you do to relax. Don't stay in your apartment. Go somewhere. Get out of Chicago."

He was shaking his head. "I can't do that."

"For God's sake, tell him you're sick!"

"This man doesn't know sick, Agnes. He doesn't know sympathy. If I had a heart attack, he'd shrug and write me off as unreliable. I'm not kidding."

She sat chewing her lower lip for a few minutes. "All right. If you won't talk to my friend and you won't take a week off, then this is the best advice I've got left, and it may be the wrong advice entirely. You understand?"

He nodded.

"You're under a lot of stress in your work and you're in the midst of an emotional crisis as well. Plus, to repeat, you were exhausted, hung over, and depressed. So you did something weird and then blocked it out of your memory. Okay?"

"Okay."

"Don't blow it up into a nervous breakdown. It was a five or ten minute glitch. Don't brood about it. Let it go and get on with your life."

Greg sighed and sagged back into his seat. "Yeah. I guess that's what I wanted to hear. I guess the advice I was ready to give to myself was to go back, buy the gun, and get it over with."

"Oh, gee, baby." Agnes leaned across the table and grabbed

one of his hands. "Don't even *think* of that. You've got a wonderful life ahead of you. Everything's going to work out, you'll see."

"Yeah. Someday I'll look back at all this and laugh. Ha, ha, ha." And he almost managed a smile.

On the bus back to his apartment, Greg reflected that Agnes had helped him more than he'd hoped for and more than she'd known. He found that, after all, a glitch was acceptable. It wasn't a nervous breakdown or even a psychotic episode. It was just five minutes a bit off the rails. He wondered what he'd been thinking about while he looked through the gun dealers' ads in the yellow pages. Was he seriously considering finding and buying that pistol? That seemed impossible. Even at his lowest, he'd never contemplated suicide. More probably, he'd been motivated by curiosity. Did the gun he'd seen in his dream actually exist? It seemed a point well worth settling—and he had in fact settled it.

But why, exhausted, hung over, and depressed, had he chosen that moment to settle it? And why had he obliterated the call to Dobson from his memory? He shook his head and told himself to knock it off. He'd already lost four hours out of the middle of the day and couldn't afford to lose any more.

He worked until midnight, then took himself, a large drink, and a paperback to bed. Later, as he was drifting off to sleep, he thought, *Please, God, no dreams tonight*. Then he smiled. *I'm safe tonight. In my dreams, I'm already dead.*

XIII

WEDNESDAY WENT LIKE CLOCKWORK. Working from Greg's handwritten manuscript, the typist produced thirty-three pages, while he wrote enough for another five or six. That night he revised what she'd typed up, and on Thursday she retyped it in final form and then went on to the new material. By day's end he had thirty-three pages ready to go and another five ready to be finally typed. With luck—or rather without any bad luck—he was going to make it.

At eight in the evening, Mitzi called and asked if she could come down for a drink.

"Not tonight, sweetie," he told her. "I've got four hours of work to do yet. Come tomorrow and you can help me celebrate meeting a deadline."

"Okay. What time?"

Greg thought for a moment. The last mail pickup at the corner was at 5:40. "Make it six o'clock," he said.

"All right." She Hesitated. "I had another dream about you last night."

"Tomorrow, Mitzi. If at all."

"Okay," she said meekly.

Friday morning the typist finished off the seven pages he'd revised and rough typed another three pages he'd written before going to bed. At two o'clock he hit a bad patch where nothing seemed to work. He swallowed his panic and went through his story file again, while the typist sat yawning, waiting for something to do. At four o'clock he realized he wasn't going to make the 5:40 pickup. This meant a trip to the Clark Street post office. No big deal.

At five o'clock the typist put her cigarettes in her purse and stood up to go. Greg said, "It's worth another twenty dollars an hour to me if you stick around till we're finished. We should be done by seven."

Without much interest she said she was sorry, but she had a train to catch and a date to go to the movies. He offered her thirty dollars an hour and she didn't even hear him. Her interest in money apparently vanished at the stroke of five on Friday. At the door she said brightly, "I'd be glad to come in tomorrow morning at thirty dollars an hour." Greg said he'd think about it and shut the door in her face while she was giving him her phone number.

He considered the situation. Forty-three pages were ready to send. Fifty by tonight was out of the question. He decided forty-seven would do. Or as much as he could get done by nine o'clock. Either way, that was it.

He headed back to his desk, then remembered Mitzi. He dialed her number and told her their six o'clock date was off. "If you still feel like it at nine-thirty, I'll be glad of the company."

"Shit," Mitzi said. "By nine-thirty I'll be half asleep. Let me come down at six or seven. I won't be in the way, I promise."

"What would be the point, Mitzi? I'm just working and nothing but."

She whimpered a little. "I just get so goddamned *blue* on Friday nights, Greg. You know, being all by myself?"

"I know, Mitzi. We'll chase the blues at nine-thirty, I promise. See you then," he added and hung up before she could make any more suggestions.

At seven o'clock he was pulling page forty-five out of the typewriter when he heard a tentative knock on the door. He strode over and flung it open, saying, "Goddamn it, Mitzi." But it wasn't Mitzi.

It was Ginny, looking pale and shaky. "May I come in?" she asked.

Without thinking, he reached out for her and she came into his arms trembling.

"What's wrong?" he asked.

She whispered, "This is my second mistake. Just hold me for a while, okay?"

He held her for a while, then walked her over to the sofa and sat her down. "Tell me what's wrong."

She looked at him bleakly. "There's nothing wrong. I'm *here*, Greg. Do you want me to be here?"

"Forever, Ginny. Forever. But you seem frightened."

"Hold me, Greg. Now that I'm here, don't stop." When his arms were around her and her face was buried in his chest, she said, "Yes, I'm frightened, but I'm here. I always wanted to be here. Do you understand?"

"I understand," he said, though he didn't. "But what are you afraid of?"

She shook her head and brought a hand up to lie against his chest, next to her face. "That part can't change, Greg. Don't quiz me. Just accept me."

"I accept you, Ginny. I love you."

"I love you, Greg."

His chest contracted in exquisite pain and he said, "I was afraid I was never going to hear those words."

"I was afraid I was never going to say them, Greg. It was hard not to, that night."

Greg started to ask her why she hadn't, then told himself not to be a dunce. He reached down and lifted her feet off the floor and lay back on the sofa with her on top of him. For half an hour, except for his hand stroking her hair and her slow breathing, neither moved. Then she used her elbows to prop herself up on his chest. She looked down at him, smiled, and asked if she could have a drink.

"You can, provided I don't have to carry you."

She laughed and rolled off to the back of the couch. On his way to the kitchen, he looked at the desk and winced. When he returned with the drinks for both of them, she was sitting with her shoes off, looking around. "It's an elegant room," she said.

"An elegant room waiting for an elegant tenant."

"You're elegant enough. Show me the rest."

He shrugged. "I won't apologize for the bedroom. I've been working fourteen hours a day and wasn't expecting company."

When she'd had the tour, which she accepted without comment, she paused at his desk. "Is this what you're working on? Obviously it is." She picked up a sheet of typescript, read for a bit, and giggled. "What *is* this thing?"

He explained, and she asked if she could read all of it. "Go ahead," he said. "I've got a few things to do anyhow."

She took the manuscript and curled up on the sofa.

Greg dug up a manila envelope and. scrawled Ted Owens's address on it. Forty-five pages will have to do, he thought ruefully. He went into the bedroom and changed the sheets and pillowcases. Then, seeing that Ginny was still reading, he went into the kitchen and started washing the dishes. She joined him there a few minutes later. "It's good," she said. "I like it."

"You do?" he said, genuinely surprised.

"Yes, don't you?"

"I honestly don't know yet. I'm too close to it. Find any typos?"

"No. But I wasn't looking for them."

"Good. Don't. I've got to get it in the mail."

"'What? Tonight?"

He turned off the water and dried his hands. "Without fail, the man said." He steered her into the living room. "Do you want to go with me to the post office? We could stop somewhere afterwards and have dinner."

She considered this solemnly. "I think I'd rather wait for you here. If that's okay."

He touched her cheek and she looked up. "Anything at all is okay," he said with a smile. Then he made a face. "I'd better cancel my wailing session before I leave."

"Your what?"

He explained about Mitzi, then made the call. When he hung up after being yelled at for a minute and a half, he shrugged and said, "It'll do her good to feel betrayed by someone new."

"I'm sorry," Ginny said.

"Don't be ridiculous."

He paused at the door. "I should be back in half an hour."

She studied his doubtful look for a moment and then laughed. "Don't worry. I'll still be here." She gave him a kiss. "I just want to spend a while getting to know your place."

She was curled up on the sofa with a book when Greg returned, and finding her there gave him an unexpected rush of delight. Making herself at home in his home seemed to set a seal on her capitulation. He asked her what she was reading.

She glanced at the cover and tossed the book aside. "Damned if I know," she said and got up to take him in her arms. "Is it all right if I change my mind about going out? I'm in a mood for celebration."

"That's fine. What mood is your mood in? You want someplace loud and crowded or someplace quiet and intimate?"

After a moment's thought, she said, "First loud and crowded, then quiet and intimate. And then . . .

"And then?"

She laughed. "Then loud and crowded again. I don't want this night to end."

"Then we'll see that it doesn't," he said.

On a Friday night, Blinkers, just a few blocks away, was as jammed as the locker room of a World Series winner, and the addition of the weirder extremes of rock and roll at earsplitting levels made conversation below a shriek impossible. When they'd battled their way to a small table, Ginny looked around wide-eyed and then pulled him closer to whisper a question in his ear.

"Christ, Ginny, you don't have to whisper in *here*," he shouted. "Nobody'd hear you if you put it over the public address system."

"I said, is this a gay bar?"

"Sure. This is a *classy* gay bar, where the professionals hang out—doctors, lawyers, stockbrokers, architects."

Ginny seemed fascinated by the giddy, babbling surge of men endlessly circulating around them, delighted to see each other, all bursting with gossip, all sleekly trim and expensively dressed. "They certainly seem to be having a wonderful time."

He smiled. "It's hard to be glum in a gay crowd."

"I would have expected to feel intimidated, but I feel sort of smug, being the only woman around."

"*Almost* the only woman. The muscular gent in the Pierre Cardin suit at the end of the bar is a bull dike."

"How can you tell?"

"I once spent an evening with her proving she could drink me under the table."

"I don't believe it."

Greg raised his eyebrows at her. "You don't? I lead a very adventurous life."

Half an hour later a slender man in his fifties appeared at their table during a pause in the music and asked if he might join them. After exchanging a glance, they invited him to sit down.

"If I'm intruding," he said, hesitating, "I do hope you'll send me away. I wouldn't want to feel I was simply exploiting your good manners."

Ginny smiled and reached up to take his hand. "Please join us," she said. "You can help us celebrate."

He nodded solemnly and pulled up a chair. "Yes, I had the feeling you were celebrating." Glancing from one to the other, he went on, "The two of you are positively glowing with delight."

Ginny laughed. "In the midst of all this delight how could you possibly pick us out?"

"Ah, this," he said, looking around sadly. "This is largely just giddiness. And lust, of course. My name is Bruce, by the way. Bruce Eddison, two *D*'s, no relation to the inventor." Ginny and Greg introduced themselves., and Bruce looked around again. "Unattached straight people—or semiattached straight people—can never have this kind of fun together because men and women are playing different games. Here they're all playing the same game, so they can just relax and enjoy themselves."

"But not you?" Ginny asked.

Bruce smiled wistfully. "I'm a little old for the game. Or, perhaps I should say that I'm old enough to want something more than the game." He made a face. "I shouldn't bore you. I've just broken up with my lover."

Ginny put her hand over his. "You're not boring us. And you came here looking for . . . company?"

"Yes." His pleasant, horsey face wrinkled into a smile. "And I end up sitting here with you two. Isn't that strange?"

"Why is that strange?" Greg asked.

He glanced at the two of them. "Well, it isn't really. Many people would think it was."

"You mean because we're straight?"

"Yes."

Greg shrugged. "People are people, whether they're straight or gay. Or am I being naive?"

Bruce looked at Ginny, started to say something, and was interrupted by an electronic howl that marked the beginning of a new tape.

Over the blare, Ginny shouted, "Why don't we continue this somewhere else, where we can . . ." She finished with a helpless shrug at the pandemonium. After a moment's thought, Greg suggested the Casbah, a Mideastern restaurant nearby, with a quiet, dimly lit bar and soft, spacious booths. Neither Ginny nor Bruce had ever been there.

"I'm a physician," Bruce said in answer to a question half an hour later, "a profession for which I have little affection and no real talent. However," he added with a smile, "it pleased my parents enormously and has provided me a comfortable income."

"What would you have been by choice?" Ginny asked.

He shrugged. "I'm not sure how to answer your question, my dear. I have a passion, but not every passion can be bent into an occupation."

"Well, what's your passion then?"

Bruce smiled apologetically. "It'll probably sound absurd to you. My passion is family portraits. Snapshots."

"I don't understand."

"It's a little hard to explain. Because snapshot family portraits are so very commonplace and so superficially alike, no one troubles to look at them carefully. No one takes note of what the people in them are actually doing. Oddly enough, these portraits are often shockingly naked statements of family dynamics." He looked at them diffidently. "May I show you an example?" Getting their nods, he reached inside his jacket for a sheet of paper. "This isn't from my collection—I wish it was. It's from an issue of *Parade* about a year back, and I clipped it because it's so very astounding." He unfolded it and passed it across the table.

Greg moved a candle nearer so that they could study it together. He saw four figures: an old woman in front, two younger women just behind her at either side, and a rather sinister-looking bearded man behind them. After a few moments Ginny nodded and Greg asked what made it so astounding.

"The father, a Russian émigré named Pyotr Melandovich, is leaning toward his daughter, is staring at her openmouthed, practically drooling. His wife, standing a little apart from him—actually leaning away from him a bit—is facing the camera, but her sideways glance is fixed on her daughter in a look of intense suspicion and jealousy. At first glance, the daughter seems to be giving the camera a lascivious leer, but if you look at it for a while the lasciviousness disappears and you're left with a very doubtful smile. She's the only person in the picture touching anyone—she has her hand on her grandmother's shoulder. But if you look closely you'll see what an odd gesture it is. Her hand is stiff, she's carefully keeping her wrist from resting on the shoulder, as it would if she were relaxed. And the grandmother is hardly there at all. She's looking off into space, disassociating herself from all of them.

"Three years after this photo was taken, the daughter took an axe to her father in his sleep, after having endured his sexual assaults for more than a year."

"Oh," Greg said. He looked at the picture more closely. "I see what you mean about naked: naked lust, naked jealousy, naked doubt."

"And all while they were posing for a casual snapshot. It really *is* a family portrait."

Greg nodded. "You have others like this?"

"Thousands. Not all as dramatic as this one, but many are. The poses people unconsciously adopt for such pictures are truly amazing. They'll cringe under a touch, they'll use elbows to keep two people apart or to keep someone away. Even the deliberate, playful gestures can be very telling."

Greg said, "I've a friend who does dreams the way you do snapshots. You should get together." Bruce gave him a doubtful look. "I'm not making fun of you. You'd make quite a team."

"Tell me," Bruce said after a few moments, "as a writer, do you think there's a book in it?"

"You mean a collection of portraits and analyses? I don't know. It's an intriguing idea . . . Could you get releases from the people in the pictures?"

Bruce shook his head. "Most I pick up at garage sales and rummage sales and flea markets. There are a few junk dealers who save them for me. But most of the subjects are unknown."

"Then no publisher would touch it. Unless you blocked out the faces, and that would defeat the purpose."

Bruce sent Ginny a bleak smile. "So you see that my passion is one that can be turned to no practical account."

Ginny, who had been slumped back into the booth, leaned forward and smiled. "You could set up a special practice—family portraits analyzed, twenty-five dollars."

Bruce winced humorously. "What a dreadful idea."

A few minutes later he pushed himself up out of the booth and said, "Now I'll take my leave of you dear children. I mustn't monopolize your evening." As they began to protest, he held up a hand. "No, my dears, I'd much rather leave while you're wishing you could have more of me than wait until you begin to wish you could have less of me. Do you understand?"

They said they did and let him go.

Ginny sank back into her seat and sighed contentedly.

"What now?" Greg asked. "Another drink? Or another bout of loud and crowded?"

"Another drink, I think." She smiled. "But one bout of loud and crowded is enough."

They had another drink and, when Greg asked for the check, learned that Bruce had taken care of it on his way out, including the round they'd just finished.

Outside, after looking up at the star-filled sky, Ginny decided against taking a taxi back to Greg's apartment. "Let's walk," she said, "I still don't want this night to end."

Half a block beyond the Hotel Belmont, she stopped and asked if they could get a cup of coffee at the Tango. Greg looked at her with raised brows. "Sure. Why not?" They turned back and he thought, *She really doesn't want this night to end.*

Sitting at the bar, they each ordered coffee and an almond liqueur. When their drinks came, Ginny asked nervously, "It's still early, isn't it?" Greg checked his watch. "Eleven-thirty."

"Then let's move to a table, okay? This feels so . . . temporary."

He laughed, picked up his drink, and led the way to a booth. She slid in, sat back, and sighed. "Much better."

Taking a sip of her liqueur, she sent her eyes around the room. "What did you call it? Designy? I'm not sure I agree. Design that calls attention to itself is bad design, and I don't think this does. Only the message counts, and the message of this room . . ." She broke off and frowned down at her drink. "Sorry," she said.

"For what?"

"I'm babbling."

He squeezed her hand. "Babble on."

She stared into the corner they'd occupied two weeks before, and her eyes filled with tears. "I'm sorry," she whispered. Greg felt the breath go out of him as if he'd been kicked in the stomach.

She blinked away her tears. "I want you to hold me, Greg," she said. "Hold me and don't stop."

He refilled his lungs in a long sigh and kicked the cubical table between them. "I'd be delighted to oblige, but this thing is sort of in the way."

Ginny drained her glass, set it down, and said, "Let's get out of here."

That night in bed, Greg was nearly overwhelmed as they made love. Ginny shrieked like a madwoman, pummeled him with her fists, sprinkled his shoulders with tears, groaned like a soul in despair. And he cursed himself for worrying about what the neighbors must be thinking—and for letting this mundane worry make him impotent.

Finally, after several frenzied climaxes, she climaxed a last time together with him, and collapsed onto his chest, panting. "Don't fall asleep," she whispered. "Hold me." And he held her until her breathing subsided into the regular measure of sleep. He moved his head against the hand cushioning his neck and thought drowsily, *That hand is Ginny's hand.* Then he drifted off to sleep.

And woke up in the morning alone, in a strange bed, in a strange room hundreds of miles from Chicago.

PART
TWO

XIV

COMING FROM A WORLD OF BIRD SONG and wind rustling in the trees, bright sunlight filtered through the blinds on the window. It illuminated a room twenty feet square, decorated in cheerfully warm but muted tones. A large television set faced him across the room. Along the wall at his right stood a well-designed but purely utilitarian desk-bureau combination. *A room*, Greg thought, *in a good motel.*

He threw the covers aside and saw that he was wearing pajamas: unfamiliar, neither new nor old. He went to the window and adjusted the blinds, producing a scene from a picture postcard: lovely, tree-covered rolling hills against a background of blue mountains. The Ozarks? He shook his head and wondered why he wasn't screaming hysterically, he felt completely calm, but there was something provisional about the feeling; it was being borrowed from a hidden pocket within himself, like a twenty stashed behind a credit card for emergencies.

He continued his inspection of the room. Bathroom: immaculately clean, impersonal; a single toothbrush in the holder, a half-empty tube of toothpaste, not his brand, on a glass shelf. He gazed blankly at the contents of the closet: three suits, two sport coats, a windbreaker, three pairs of odd trousers—unfamiliar but, judging by the eye alone, roughly his size. He opened one of the jackets and stared for a long time at the Marshall Field label; he never shopped for clothes at the big downtown department stores in Chicago. He closed the closet door and tried the next one: by elimination, the exit. It was locked, with no latch on his side. Not a motel room.

A peach-colored telephone stood on a bedside table. It had no dial. He picked up the receiver and held it to his ear, half expecting to find it dead. It crackled briefly, then a woman's voice said, "May I help you?" He snatched the receiver from his ear and looked at it in disbelief. Then he put it back to his ear and said, still calm, "Yes. You can tell me where I am."

"Ah," she said. She drew the sound out for a long time, as if a blank space had appeared in the universe before her. "Wait just a moment. A nurse will be with you right away."

"A what?" he asked, but she'd already hung up. A nurse? A dressing gown lay across the foot of the bed—the sort of item he'd never felt the need to own. He put it on and turned to the door as the latch turned. A small brunette stuck her head in and said, "Do you need something, Mr. Iles?"

"Mr. Who?"

"Mr. Iles?" she repeated doubtfully.

"I'm not Mr. Iles," Greg stated.

She stared at him openmouthed. "Oh my," she said. "I'll be right back."

"Wait!" She turned back reluctantly. "What *is* all this?"

"All this?"

"Where am I?"

"I'll bring Dr. Jakes right away," she promised and headed down the hall.

"Why is the door locked?" he shouted after her.

"It's not," she said over her shoulder. "It's open."

Greg followed her as far as the doorway and saw her disappear down a long, carpeted hallway. Most of the hallway doors were open, and at one of them appeared a tall, gray-haired woman in tweeds. She glanced at the departing nurse, at Greg, then smiled and waved, and he pulled his head back hastily and shut the door.

"Jesus," he breathed. He sat down on the bed and looked around, wondering what to do. Obviously he had to get dressed. He could hardly walk out of the place in a dressing gown. Swallowing his reluctance to don a stranger's clothes, he pulled open a drawer and began to take out underwear.

He was dressed and looking through pockets for money in a mounting fury when he heard a knock at the door. "Come in," he snarled. It was recognizably a snarl, and Greg knew he'd just about run through his reserve of calmness. Holding the pants he'd been searching, he turned in time to witness the entrance of a short, blockish woman with close-cropped iron-gray hair. As if having trouble focusing, he blinked a couple of times and found himself looking into the eyes of Agnes Tillford.

"Agnes!" he gasped.

Her normally cheerful dumpling of a face was solemn as she studied him. She raised an eyebrow at him, and he took in her formal appearance: she was wearing the well-cut gray suit he remembered from her lecture at the library.

"What the hell are *you* doing here?" he asked.

She raised the other eyebrow and said, "Mr. Iles?"

"*What?*"

Her eyebrows drew down into a puzzled frown, and she nodded toward a pair of chairs in front of the window. "Let's sit down, shall we?"

"Agnes, what the *hell* is going on here?" His legs began to tremble, and he looked down stupidly at the pair of pants he was holding. Agnes eased them from his hands and tossed them into the closet. Then she took him by the arm, settled him in a chair, and sat down across from him.

"Now," she said gently, "tell me what's going on." He gawked at her and suddenly felt great bubbles of hysterical laughter quaking in his stomach. There was nothing he could do to hold them down, and Agnes watched gravely as he let them come welling out. At last he wiped his eyes and said, "That's really funny. You want *me* to tell *you* what's going on."

She cocked her head on one side but said nothing.

"Agnes, for God's sake, tell *me* what's going on!"

"Very well," she said agreeably. "Where should I begin?"

"Where the hell are we?"

"We're at the Glenhaven Oaks Sanatorium, a private institution some fifty miles south of Louisville, Kentucky."

"You're kidding. What the hell are we doing here?"

"Ah. Well, *you're* doing one thing and *I'm* doing another."

"Agnes, Christ's sake, just tell me what's going on."

She studied him with baffled concern. "Mr. Iles, believe me, I'll tell you anything you like."

Greg looked at her. "What is this *Mr. Iles* shit?"

"Perhaps I don't have it right. That's not your name?"

He sprang out of his chair. "Cut it out, Agnes. Don't do this to me anymore. It's not funny."

"I'm sorry. I'm really not trying to be funny. Please sit down, Mr. . . . Please sit down."

"I don't feel like sitting down. I'm getting out of here." He looked around wildly. "Where the hell's my money?"

"Your money?"

"I had at least fifty dollars on me last night. I want my money and my billfold and my credit cards. Right now."

Agnes put an elbow on the arm of her chair and rested her head on her hand. "Very well. But I'm afraid the cards and things in the billfold will have the name Richard Iles on them."

"Bullshit." Greg turned and started walking, but got only as far as the door before realizing he had nowhere to go. He stood facing the door for a moment, then turned back. "Agnes."

"Yes?"

"*Come on.*"

She gazed at him. "I think you're getting tired of this."

"I am, yes."

"Then sit down and let's see if we can straighten it out. Okay?" He eyed the chair with distaste, shrugged, and sat down. "Something seems to have happened here this morning," she said. "Will you tell me what it was?"

"Something happened during the goddamned *night.*"

"All right. Tell me what happened."

He shot her a look of disgust. "You don't know."

"That's right. I don't know."

"Someone brought me here from Chicago."

She stared at him. "From Chicago. I see. Then this is something else I don't know: What were you doing in Chicago?"

Greg interlaced his fingers, turned his hands palm out, and

106

pushed, cracking half a dozen joints at once. "That's it," he said. "Finished." He looked around grimly, then went to the phone and picked up the receiver.

"May I help you?"

"Yes," he said. "A while ago you sent a nurse to this room."

"Yes?"

"Is she available? I'd like to ask her something."

"She's right here. Do you want to talk to her?"

"Could you send her here?"

"Certainly. She'll be right along."

Greg opened the door and sat down on the bed to wait. When the small brunette arrived, he asked her if she remembered talking to him a while ago.

"Of course I do." The question seemed to startle her.

Greg smiled at her. "Will you tell me your name?"

Her eyes grew wide. "Why, my name is Wendy, Mr. Iles. You know that."

"I don't know that, Wendy. There's been some confusion here, you see. I'm not Mr. Iles."

She gave Agnes a bewildered glance and said, "Oh."

"Wendy, when you left here, you said you were going to get a doctor. I don't remember the name."

"Dr. Jakes. That's right."

"Good. Is Dr. Jakes the person in charge here?" Again she glanced at Agnes. "Well . . . yes. *One* of the persons in charge anyway."

"Good. I'd like to see him as soon as possible, Wendy. Him or her. Can you arrange that?"

Wendy's jaw dropped and she gaped at him. Agnes said, "It's all right, Wendy. Run along, everything's under control."

Greg turned on her, his face red with fury.

"Since you knew my first name, I naturally assumed you knew my last," Agnes said. "I am Dr. Jakes."

XV

THAT," GREG SAID, "IS ALL A FUCKING LIE."

Agnes gave him a thoughtful look. "Does that mean that you know me by another name?"

He shook his head stubbornly, and Agnes sighed.

"All right. You won't talk to me. You think I'm playing some kind of trick on you. You think I already have the answers to the questions I'm asking. Is that right?"

"You know it's right."

"Okay. Since you won't talk to me, I'll talk to you. How's that?"

"Go ahead."

"Sit down first, please. Thank you. Now." She paused to think for a moment. "Let's begin someplace easy. Last night around eleven a man named Richard Iles went to sleep in this room, in that bed over there. How does that sit with you?"

Greg shrugged.

"He went to sleep in this room and in that bed, and during the night the door didn't open once." She waited for a reaction to this and, getting none, went on. "This morning at nine, the man who slept in this room, in that bed, picked up the phone and asked the nurse at the desk to tell him where he was."

"That," Greg said, "is a lie."

"Okay. Am I right in assuming that you went to sleep last night in Chicago?"

"That's right."

She shook her head in wonderment. "Then would you kindly explain how the devil you got *here*?"

"I assume I was *brought* here."

"By whom? Why?"

"I don't know."

"How was such a thing managed, for heaven's sake?"

He glared at her, then at the lush blue hills outside. After two minutes of furious thought, he turned to her with a triumphant smile. "We can settle all this very easily. I should have thought of it sooner."

"That's wonderful. I'm delighted to hear it."

"Can I use that phone to make a long-distance call?"

"Certainly. Just give the operator the number."

A few moments later he was listening to the buzz of a phone ringing in Chicago. A woman's voice came on the line, and Greg said, "Ginny?"

"You must have the wrong number," the woman said.

"Is this 328-9494?"

"Yes. But there's no Ginny at this number."

"Wait," Greg said and stood blinking for a few moments. "Are you *sure* this is 328-9494?"

The woman hung up.

Greg got the operator back and asked her to dial Chicago information for him.

"Directory Assistance. What city?"

"Chicago. I'd like the number of Ginny or Virginia Winters on Dearborn."

After a momentary pause, "I have no listing for a Ginny or Virginia Winters anywhere in Chicago."

He swallowed. "Gregory Donner, Lake Shore Drive."

Another pause. "I have no listing for a Gregory Donner."

"D-O-N-N-E-R?"

"That's what I checked, sir. I have no such listing."

"You have to have one."

"Would this be a new phone, sir?"

"No."

"Then I'm sorry. There is no listing for a Gregory Donner."

"Wait. His number is 984-2754. Could you check that for me?"

"One moment . . . That number is not in service, sir."

"Not in service? What does that mean?"

"It means no one has that number, sir."

He stood staring blindly at the wall. The phone felt welded to his ear.

"Sir? Is there another listing I can check for you?"

He slowly lowered the receiver and replaced it. Then he turned to Agnes and said, "That's very good. How did you manage it?"

Agnes frowned at him. "I think you should have something to eat."

He heard himself laugh at this grotesque suggestion, felt it bucking in his chest, but it sounded like it was coming from a stranger. His knees began trembling and he sat down on the bed.

Someone said, "I don't like this," and Greg laughed again when he recognized it as his own voice.

"You're Gregory Donner, aren't you?" Agnes asked gently.

He nodded.

"Strangely enough, Mr. Donner, I believe you."

He looked at her in surprise. "You do?"

"Yes. I believe that you're Gregory Donner and that up till last night you lived on Lake Shore Drive in Chicago. That's the address you gave the operator, isn't it?"

"Yes."

"So we seem to be making some progress after all."

"But I thought . . ."

"Yes?"

He shook his head in bewilderment.

"I think I'm beginning to see what happened, Mr. Donner. We'll have it sorted out soon." She stood up. "But right now I'd like to see you get something to eat."

He frowned. "What is this obsession with eating? Are you a nutritionist or something?"

Agnes chuckled. "I'm not a nutritionist, Mr. Donner, I'm a psychiatrist. And, speaking as a psychiatrist, I have the distinct impression that you've just lost a hell of a lot of substance. Eating will help you put some of it back. Come along."

Greg followed her out of the room.

XVI

THE DINING WING WAS THERE on the ground floor of the Glenhaven Oaks Sanatorium, but Greg took it in only remotely, as if viewing it on a television monitor. A cocktail lounge, lush with velvet and chrome, glowed at his right; he noted that it looked inviting—and felt no invitation. A room at his left offered a cheerful, almost bohemian, coffeehouse atmosphere, with small tables oriented toward a spotlit stage; to Greg, it seemed as cozy as a corporate boardroom. Agnes led him past these to the main dining room, where an acre of glass pulled the viewer out into a vast green world apparently never visited by man. It was a large room, but one that seemed at once intimate and regal, formal and casual—a room as accommodating to evening wear and ball gowns as to jeans and tennis shorts. It was an impressive feat of interior design, and Greg noted that he was impressed.

They paused at the entrance and Agnes asked him where he'd like to sit.

"I don't care where we sit," he said. "Let's just sit." Agnes shrugged and told him to lead on. Greg headed for a booth in the far right-hand corner, beside the twenty-foot-high window and facing the entrance. When they'd settled themselves in it, Agnes smiled and said, "In change, however cataclysmic, there is always continuity."

"Meaning what?"

She nodded toward the approaching waitress.

"Good morning, Dr. Jakes," the waitress said. "Good morning, Mr. Iles. You must have slept in this morning."

"Yeah," Greg said, staring straight ahead.

"Just coffee for me, Ella, Mr., uh, Iles will have breakfast."

"I'll bring a menu."

111

Greg chewed his lower lip for a moment. "Dr. Jakes," he said experimentally.

"Please go on calling me Agnes," she said. "I take it you knew me . . . in Chicago?"

"Yes."

"And what was my last name there?"

He made a face. "Tillford."

"Tillford," she repeated thoughtfully. "And we were what? Friends?" He nodded stiffly, as if he had a sore neck. "It's no wonder you were disconcerted when I walked into your room this morning."

"Yeah."

"Order something," she told him. "The food's pretty good."

"I'm glad to hear that," he said dryly and glanced through the large, handsomely printed menu. When Ella appeared at his side, he ordered eggs Benedict.

"Tell me about you and Agnes Tillford," Agnes said.

"What do you mean?"

"Well, what was your relationship? Our relationship?" He shook his head. "You said we were friends."

"Yeah," he said wryly. "Drinking buddies."

"What did I call you? Gregory? Greg?"

"Greg."

"Is it all right if I call you Greg?"

"Don't humor me, Doctor."

"I'm not, honestly. How did we meet?"

Greg laughed. "We met at the Chicago Public Library. You were giving a lecture."

"A lecture."

"That's right."

"A lecture on what?"

He made a face. "On dreams."

"I see."

"You're supposed to say 'Very interesting.'"

Agnes chuckled. "Well, it *is* interesting. How long ago was this?"

He shrugged. "Three or four weeks."

"Very interesting."

"Agnes."

"Yes?"

He sighed and closed his eyes. "I keep *hoping* that you're going to stop fooling around and admit that this is all just a very bad, very cruel joke. I would *like* it to be a very bad, very cruel joke. Do you understand?"

"I understand. I think. You're telling me you'd forgive me if I said, 'Ha ha, April Fool!'"

"Yes, I guess so—provided you said it *right now*."

"I'm sorry, Greg. For your sake, I wish it was all just a very bad, very cruel joke."

"But it isn't."

"No. I'm sorry."

"I am too."

"It may not seem entirely bad when . . . you've had a look at it. Meanwhile tell me about Greg Donner. About yourself."

He carefully rotated his coffee cup in its saucer while thinking this over. "I already know about myself, Agnes. I'd rather hear your explanation of what happened here."

"That will come when I'm a little surer of my ground. And to anticipate your next question—I'll be surer of my ground when I've heard a little about Greg Donner."

"Christ. What do you want to know?"

"Just tell me about yourself, Greg. Who are you?"

He shrugged. "I'm a freelance writer. I live on . . ." He paused, blinking. "On Lake Shore Drive in Chicago. I grew up outside Des Moines, Iowa, went to college at Ames, started on a master's at the University of Chicago, then gave it up to go into publishing. . . . "After a couple years in publishing I quit and became a freelancer."

"Your family background? Wife? Children?" Greg shook his head. "No wife, no children. My father was a farmer. He died of a heart attack when I was fifteen. My mother still lives on what's left of the farm. It's a suburb now.

Agnes nodded. "Good. Tell me about the people close to you, the people who are important in your life."

"There aren't many of those, actually. I'm a loner, which is why I prefer freelancing."

"No women friends? Besides Agnes Tillford."

"One. Ginny."

"Ginny," Agnes repeated thoughtfully, as if tasting the name. "Tell me something about Ginny."

He sighed through his teeth. "She's a graphic designer. A stunning beauty. Flaming red hair, green eyes, beautiful complexion."

"Ah."

"Ah? Ah what?"

"She sounds attractive," Agnes answered ambiguously. "I'm not exactly sure what a graphic designer does."

"It's hard to describe. Does it matter?"

She looked at him curiously. "You find it hard to describe?"

"'To someone outside the business, yes."

"You mean the publishing business?"

"That's right."

"*You* understand what she does, but you'd find it difficult to explain to me. Why is that?"

He gave her an incredulous frown. "What *is* all this, Agnes? What difference does it make?"

"I'm trying to make sure of my ground, Greg. Trust me, just for a while."

"All right. She's involved in the production end of the business, and that's not my specialty."

Agnes raised her brows. "Now you seem to be saying you don't understand what she does after all."

"Jesus. Okay, I suppose you're right. What happens between the time I turn over a manuscript and the time the finished product comes out is pretty much a mystery to me—and the designer is the high priest of the mystery. I still don't see what difference it makes."

"You don't?" Agnes smiled. "You began by saying it was a

mystery an outsider couldn't understand and ended up saying it was a mystery to you as well. I have to consider that a notable difference."

He started to say something, then saw that Ella was bringing his breakfast. By the time she was finished serving him, he'd decided to skip it. "Can we get on with it?"

"I warn you that I'll have a lot more questions about Greg Donner's background, but those can wait," Agnes said. "Here's one that can't."

"Go on."

"How did you spend yesterday?"

"Oh." He sat blinking for a few moments. "Yesterday was a bit . . . complicated."

"Tell me about it."

"I had a deadline to meet. I was working like a madman up till seven. Then Ginny arrived." The doctor waited patiently as Greg thought about this. "After I put the manuscript in the mail, we went out. Then we came home and went to bed. Then . . . then I woke up here."

Agnes was examining him with interest. "Why do you say it was complicated?"

"Well . . . I guess the *actions* were simple enough."

"Something happened when you and Ginny went out?"

He shook his head. "Just the feelings were complicated, Doctor."

"'Doctor,' huh? I guess that means you don't want to talk about those feelings."

"That's right."

"Will you answer a question about them? Were they good feelings or bad?"

"Good."

"Important? Something to do with Ginny?"

"Yes. That's all, Doctor. It's your turn now." Agnes nodded but, having agreed, seemed reluctant to begin. "I expect the person you want to hear about right now is *you*—specifically, what the devil you're doing here."

"I'd say you were absolutely right," he replied dryly.

"The trouble is, there's not much I can tell you about *you*. The person I can tell you about is Richard Iles."

She seemed to be asking for Greg's permission, and he told her to go ahead.

"The story's not going to seem relevant at first, and once it *begins* to seem relevant, you're probably not going to like it much. But I'd appreciate it if you could contain yourself until you've heard it all."

Greg said he'd do his best.

"Two and a half years ago," Agnes began thoughtfully. She made it sound like a whole preamble: *I'm groping for the ends of all the threads; be patient, bear with me.*

"Two and a half years ago, some affair that was being supervised in the Soviet Union by the CIA came unglued. I don't know the details. There was some foul-up, and it was necessary to infiltrate an agent in a hurry. They looked around and—"

"Hold on, Agnes. You grabbed the wrong tape or something. This has got nothing whatever to do with me."

"I told you it would sound irrelevant at first, Greg."

"Well, it certainly does. I've already run through my entire supply of willing suspension of disbelief just listening to the first sentence. What the hell does something that happened in the Soviet Union two and a half years ago have to do with me?"

She gave him a look. "Do you want to hear this or not?"

With a groan, he told her to go on.

"All right. Where was I? The CIA was looking for a way to infiltrate an agent into the Soviet Union. Looking around, they discovered that a group of twenty U.S. school teachers was about to convene in Moscow to attend an international conference. One of them was approached. Let's call him Bill Smith. Bill Smith was approached and asked to give up his place to a CIA agent who would attend the conference in his name. He agreed.

"The conference in Moscow began, with the U.S. delegates in attendance, including the false Bill Smith. For the first week, all was well. By the beginning of the second week, however, it was clear that the Soviets had learned or guessed or perhaps come to suspect that one of the delegates was a ringer. They didn't as yet know which it was.

"Now at this point an unfortunate event occurred in the United States—at least it was unfortunate from the CIA's point of view. The FBI exposed a Soviet agent who had been buying low-grade military secrets from servicemen all over the country. What that meant to the CIA was this: The Soviets, lusting for vengeance and for vindication in the world press, would spare no effort to ferret out the ringer in Moscow before the end of the convention. If necessary, they figured, the Soviets would detain the entire delegation until they got him. To forestall this, it was decided that one of the delegates—not Bill Smith, of course—would be thrown to the wolves. Which delegate? There wasn't much time to decide and apparently not much basis for discrimination; a hasty check with the State Department indicated that none of the delegates were regarded as VIPs. Finally, somehow a choice was made. Incriminating evidence of great subtlety was planted in the innocent delegate's hotel room and duly discovered by Soviet agents, who took him into custody."

She paused, seeing that Greg was beginning to fidget.

"Agnes," he said, "give me a clue. Why am I listening to this third-rate John le Carré?"

"Because the delegate who was arrested was Richard Iles."

He smiled crookedly. "Amusing bullshit. Go on."

"Contrary to the CIA's expectations, the Soviets didn't publicize the arrest. They wanted more than the satisfaction of proclaiming their indignation to the world. They wanted to exchange Richard Iles for their own agent. Okay. When he was arrested, Iles disappeared from public view, and it was learned he was being kept in one of the Soviets' notorious 'psychiatric hospitals.' I guess they made no secret of this. They apparently wanted us to know—or to assume—that Iles was being systematically destroyed by drugs and perverted psychotherapy. The negotiations for the exchange began in the winter and continued through the spring. Early in the summer two years ago they were concluded. It was planned that, on July first, Iles and the Soviet agent would be exchanged.

"Meanwhile, apparently through powerful family connections, Richard Iles's wife learned the story behind the arrest, and, with this knowledge to use as a club, her lawyers managed to keep abreast of what was going on. As I've indicated, none of this was public knowledge—the State Department was desperate to keep it from *becoming* public knowledge.

"Finally July first arrived and the exchange was made, I suppose somewhere in Europe. Iles was whisked back to the U.S and installed in a government facility for examination. Mrs. Iles's lawyers demanded access to him but were put off for a week, then for a second week and a third. When their demands became threats, it had to be admitted that Richard Iles had been returned in a damaged—perhaps irreversibly damaged—condition. After three weeks of tests and observation, the physicians and psychiatrists could only shrug.

"Now another set of negotiations began, these between Mrs. Iles's lawyers and the U.S. government. They didn't take too long, because there was no question of the government going to court to defend what the CIA had done. The government would award Richard Iles four million dollars tax free and would pay all expenses for his treatment at an institution of Mrs. Iles's choosing for as long as it might take—for life if necessary.

"Within a few days of that settlement Richard Iles was delivered into the care of the Glenhaven Oaks Sanatorium. To be specific, he became my patient."

Agnes paused as Ella appeared to clear away the dishes. "How was everything?" the waitress asked.

"Fine," Greg replied dully. He barely remembered eating.

"More coffee?"

He nodded. When she was gone, he said, "So?"

"So. For a year and a half we looked after Richard Iles. He was what the nurses call an easy patient—pleasant, never any trouble, undemanding. But also completely withdrawn, completely unresponsive. Until one morning he woke up and gave everyone a hell of a shock by announcing that he wasn't a school teacher named Richard Iles, he was a freelance writer named Greg Donner."

Greg glared at her, his lips working angrily. "That," he said, "is absolute, unadulterated crap."

"I'm sorry, Greg. It's not *all* crap. I can't personally vouch for the story of Richard Iles's arrest and imprisonment in Russia; for all I know, it may well be crap—though why anyone would invent such a tale is beyond my understanding. But there is definitely no doubt that a person identified as Richard Iles was admitted to this institution a year and a half ago. And I'm afraid there's also no doubt that you were that person."

He shook his head stubbornly. "No, believe me, Agnes, *that* part is completely and utterly impossible. A year and a half ago I was right there in Chicago—and I've been there ever since, right up to last night."

"Right in your apartment on Lake Shore Drive?"

"That's right."

"The one with a telephone Ma Bell's never heard of."

He glared at her. "I've never ever been to Russia."

"That may be so. That's just what we were told."

"I'm not married."

"That also may be so. The woman who visits you here may be a fraud. I never asked her to produce a marriage certificate."

He closed his eyes and breathed through his nose for a minute. "I don't accept it."

"And I don't blame you for not accepting it. In your place, I wouldn't accept it either."

"But you do accept it."

"You have to understand, Greg. I've seen you sitting right here at this table day after day, for a year and a half. This is *your* table—Richard Iles's table. I've seen you and talked to you hundreds of times. You spent an hour in my office yesterday. It would be impossible for me *not* to accept what's happened. You went to bed Richard Iles and woke up Gregory Donner."

"What was I doing in your office yesterday?"

"Nothing you haven't done a hundred times before. Sitting. Answering questions when asked, but mostly just sitting."

"That's completely impossible."

"It *seems* impossible, because you have a different memory of how you spent yesterday."

"That's right. Where the hell did I get that memory if I was sitting in your office?"

Agnes nodded. "That's a point, all right. Would you like to hear my hypothesis?"

"I don't promise to accept it, but I'd like to hear it."

"Promises aren't required," she said with a smile, which slowly faded as she gathered her thoughts.

"You presented us with an unusual problem right from the beginning. You came to us without a case history. We had no idea what had happened to you in Russia and no way of finding out. This made it impossible to arrive at anything like a reliable diagnosis of your condition—and, without a reliable diagnosis, any course of treatment is just well-meant improvisation. In other words, we felt that all we dared do was keep an eye on you until we had some idea of what we were up against."

"You were by no means a zombie. You were unfailingly polite and would discuss any neutral subject. But you seemed to be a person without an interior life. You had no memories, no feelings, no worries, no thoughts, no desires, no anxieties, no expectations. It was our opinion that, left alone, you probably would have thoughtlessly starved to death."

"Okay. So what's your theory?"

"It's still pretty crude at this point, I'll admit, but I assume you want to hear it all the same."

"You know I do."

"Okay. Here goes . . . Most of us at one time or another have to deal with traumatic experiences—and most of us manage it pretty well, in very ordinary ways. We distract ourselves from the past, we find new things to focus on, we keep busy, we make plans for the future, and so on. These are all functions of the ego; that is, they're deliberate policies executed consciously. Usually this works fine; we put the trauma behind us and go on. But apparently the trauma you experienced as a prisoner in Russia was one that Richard Iles couldn't handle this way. It was too massive—it blotted out the horizon, blocked off all access to the future. He was theoretically free to resume his life but wasn't up to tackling it as a deliberate policy executed consciously. In other words, his ego was paralyzed. But, you see, even though his ego was paralyzed, his *unconscious* wasn't. His unconscious took on the problem and solved it in its own way and to its own satisfaction. In effect, it said, 'All right, you can't go on with your life as Richard Iles; that ego is finished, useless. So let's give you a new one. We'll start from the ground up: a new man, a new name, a new background, a new occupation—a whole new set of memories to live with that doesn't include any disastrous trips to Moscow. Okay? The ego that calls itself Richard Iles is going to go to sleep now—and is never going to wake up. Someone else is going to wake up in his place—a whole new person I've put together for you, by the name of Gregory Donner. Let's see how you do with *that*.'"

"Jesus," Greg whispered and shook his head. "Are you telling me my entire life has been a *dream*?"

"Not your *life*, Greg, your *past*."

"Is there a distinction?"

"Of course there is. In a very real sense, everyone's past is a dream; the past isn't a *thing* you can reach back and touch; it's just something in your head. Your *life*, which is what's going on here and now at this table, is as real as anyone's. And believe me, your *life* looks a hell of a lot more promising today than it did yesterday."

He laughed mirthlessly. "Thanks to my helpful unconscious." He closed his eyes and slumped back heavily into the booth. "I'm suddenly very tired. Exhausted."

"It's no wonder," Agnes said.

While walking back to his room, he said, "Agnes."

"Yes?"

He shook his head. "Does it really make any sense to *call* you Agnes? I just met you a couple hours ago."

"That's really not true, you know. I think you've got to trust your unconscious on this. It told you I was Greg Donner's friend—and I accept that. If I can accept it, why shouldn't you?"

"But are you the same *person*?"

"Greg, we've spent hundreds of hours together here. Your unconscious didn't make me up. The Agnes it gave you in Chicago was the Agnes it knew in Kentucky."

"Okay. I'm glad of that. Look, what I wanted to ask you . . . You said Richard Iles had a wife."

"That's right."

"Do you have to tell her about this . . . development?"

"Not if you'd rather I didn't. My first obligation is to you, of course."

"I would emphatically rather you didn't."

"Then I won't. Here you are."

Greg paused, staring at the door. "There was something else I meant to ask you . . . Oh, yeah. When I got up this morning, my door was locked. I mean from the outside. Why is that?"

Agnes smiled. "I don't really know. Richard Iles *asked* that it be locked. He didn't explain why."

"Oh."

"I'll tell the nurse to leave it unlocked from now on."

"Thanks." He opened the door.

"Is there anything you need? Anything you'd like?"

He looked around blankly for a moment. "Yeah. Would it be possible to have someone get my clothes from Chicago?"

Her smile faltered briefly and then was back in place. "We'll take care of everything. You have a good nap now."

Greg nodded, already half asleep. He got his clothes off somehow and tumbled into the bed. As he was dozing off, a stray thought crossed his mind: *I'll wake up back in my apartment in Chicago.*

But he didn't.

XVII

"WOULD IT BE POSSIBLE FOR ME to get a dial phone in my room?" Greg asked the voice on the phone.

"Certainly, Mr. Iles." She sounded a little hurt. "But I'm happy to dial any number you want."

"Yeah, well . . . I hate to keep bothering you. I've got a lotta calls to make."

"No bother, really, Mr. Iles. That's what I'm here for."

He suddenly appreciated rude phone operators: you can be rude back to them. Finally he said, "I really need the exercise."

"Oh," she said, as though that explained everything. "I see. I'll have one sent over right away. Just dial 9 for an outside line."

"Thanks a lot."

A few minutes later he was dialing a familiar number in New York. He got a recorded message: "The number you've reached is not in service at this time. Please check the directory. If you need assistance—"

Greg broke the connection. Well . . . numbers do change from time to time. For some reason. He dialed again.

"Directory Assistance. May I help you?"

"Yes. Do you have a listing for Ted Owens on the Avenue of the Americas?"

"One moment . . . I have a Ted Owens and Associates on Madison Avenue."

"You do?"

"Would you like that number?"

"I sure would." He dialed the number she gave him.

"Ted Owens and Associates."

"Wow," Greg said.

"Hello?"

"Can I speak to Ted?"

"May I say who's calling?"

"This is Greg Donner. In Chicago."

"Uh. May I tell him what it's about?"

"He'll know. I'm working on a project for him."

"One moment."

A moment later: "This is Ted Owens."

An unfamiliar voice. "Ted?"

"Do I know you?"

"This is Gregory Donner in Chicago."

"I'm sorry. You'll have to refresh my memory."

"Christ, Ted, I've worked on a dozen projects for you."

A pause. "You've got the wrong party." He hung up.

Greg made one more call to Directory Assistance, this time in Iowa. After that, he sat down beside the window and spent the rest of the afternoon staring out of the window.

"So you put it to a test," Agnes said.

They were once again seated at "Richard Iles's table" in the dining room. A friendly young waiter named Alan, tanned and muscled like a tennis pro, had served them drinks: a sherry for the doctor, a bourbon on the rocks for Greg. Watching him work among the tables, with a smile and a good word for everyone, Greg had been strongly reminded of someone, but he couldn't think who. He had, of course, seen him hundreds of times in this very room—presumably. But the memory he stirred wasn't Richard Iles's; it seemed to belong to Greg Donner.

"And your conclusion?"

Greg shrugged off his reverie. "You don't have to rub it in, Agnes. There's no one out there named Greg Donner and apparently there never was."

A familiar smile was playing on her lips as she asked, "Have you considered the significance of that name?"

"What do you mean?"

"I know of only one notable person named Donner: George Donner. In 1846 he led a party of settlers westward, was trapped in the Sierras by early snow, and ended by devouring his com-

124

panions." The psychiatrist smiled. "In a psychological rather than physical sense, that seems to be what you've done to your own companion, Richard Iles."

He rolled his eyes in disgust. "Yeah. Very cute. I suppose that's—" He broke off abruptly, blinked twice. "Something you once said. Except of course that it wasn't you who said it."

"I'd like to hear it anyway."

"You said, 'Such puns are very common in dreams.'"

She took a sip of sherry and smiled. "That's interesting. I'm sure I never said anything like that to Richard Iles, since he never talked about his dreams. But it's something I might well say."

"That's terrific," he observed and sent his eyes on a grim tour of the room. "Is there anything to stop me from getting out of this place tomorrow?"

"Whoa," Agnes said. "Hold on. You're not ready for anything like that."

"Why not?"

"Good heavens. I suppose I see what you're thinking, but you've got to be a little realistic. To you, Gregory Donner must seem like a completely stable entity who's trod the world for decades. In fact, Gregory Donner is a remarkable psychological phenomenon that's less than a day old. You must see that."

"So what do you think's going to happen, Agnes? Am I going to dissolve like sugar in the rain?"

"I hope not. But I certainly wouldn't want to put it to the test, shoving you out into a world you're not prepared to meet."

"I'm prepared. I *feel* as prepared as I ever did."

She shook her head wonderingly. "I suppose you can at least tell me your name."

He opened his mouth to speak, then snapped it shut.

"Who are you going to *be* out there, Greg? Gregory Donner has no money, no job, no home, no friends, no relatives."

"I'll manage somehow."

"I see. You're going to manage by turning your back on reality. And this is supposed to reassure me that you're in the pink of mental health."

"I don't want Richard Iles's life."

"Perhaps not. But this headlong flight hardly strikes me as a mature, reasoned decision."

"Do I have to be mature and reasonable to get out of here?"

Agnes sighed. "No, but I have to be mature and reasonable, because I'm responsible for your welfare. And to release you at this point would be an act of sheer medical recklessness. Shall I frighten you with possibilities? Is that what you want?"

Greg laughed sourly. "Yeah, do that."

"I hadn't intended to worry you with any of this, but I'd rather have you stay by choice than by compulsion. It's entirely possible that Gregory Donner is just a *trial* personality. Having tested the waters of reality, through you, the ego of Richard Iles may reassert itself, may say, in effect, 'Thanks, Mr. Donner, for reminding me of how it's done; I can take over for myself now—you're no longer needed.'"

"Jesus," Greg said. "That's frightening, all right. You think it's likely?"

"I think it's *possible*, and until I'm sure, I'm not about to sign you out of here."

He nodded sourly. "Yes, I can see that. How long do you think it'll take? For you to be sure, I mean."

"I'd say this depends on you. What we have here is a vacuum in the area of ego-identification. Your own identification is with a phantom by the name of Greg Donner, and Richard Iles himself has opted out entirely. The trouble is, this vacuum just *has* to be filled—*someone's* got to own up to being Richard Iles. If you refuse to do it, then I think one of two things is going to happen. Either Richard Iles is going to come forward to fill the vacuum—or you're going to be sent back for recycling." Greg winced. "You've just got to face this, Greg. The day you wake up and automatically think, 'I am Richard Iles, a school teacher, a married man, and a millionaire,' the vacuum will be filled—and I'll be ready to talk about your getting out of here."

He nodded, closed his eyes, and felt depression sink into his brain like a heavy oil.

XVIII

THE NEXT MORNING Greg found himself reluctant to leave his room. He showered, dressed, paced from corner to corner, stared at himself in the mirror and finally sat down and gazed out at the lush hills. He understood his reluctance well enough. To find his way to the dining room and order breakfast would be the beginning of the end of Gregory Donner. In the very act of opening his door, he would adopt the routine of Richard Iles, a school teacher recovering from a mind-breaking ordeal. Stepping into the hallway, he would be saying a first good-bye to a life and a woman he loved. Along with Gregory Donner, Ginny would also slip away into an imaginary past, her face and voice fading away little by little into nothingness like a photograph left in the sunlight.

At two o'clock there was a knock on the door, and, without stirring, he murmured, "Come in.

Agnes entered, hesitated, and said, "May I join you?"

He shrugged indifferently.

The doctor seated herself, crossed her legs neatly, and leaned back as if preparing for a long stay. Greg continued to stare out of the window.

"You didn't join us for breakfast or lunch," she observed.

She sat quietly for a few minutes as if considering the quality of Greg's silence. Finally she said, "What you're doing is fundamentally healthy, I think. Do you recognize what it is?"

He shook his head.

"You're mourning."

Without taking his eyes from the window, Greg sighed bitterly, as if in disagreement. But finally he nodded.

"It's a beginning, my friend. A necessary beginning that we all must make at one time or another. Do you understand?" She

127

stood up. "I'll leave you to it for now. But will you promise to be with us for dinner?"

Two minutes passed, but at last Greg nodded again.

He was grateful that no hush fell over the dining room as he entered, that no one called out his name or nodded as he made his way to the booth in the corner. He sank into it with a sigh, as if he'd reached a safe haven. In a moment Alan appeared at his side like an affable genie.

"Your usual, Mr. Iles?"

Once again Greg studied the young man's cheerful, healthy face, trying to place it, not succeeding. "That'll be fine," he said.

As he waited for his drink, he guardedly studied the people around him. With a few exceptions—a couple who stared vacantly into space, another who nodded brightly but without apparent relation to the conversation around her, another who sighed monumentally into every lull—they might have been patrons in any restaurant anywhere. Occasional ripples of hilarity swept the room, but the laughter was always refined and controlled. He considered that those who could afford treatment so manifestly expensive as this must make a better class of loony.

His drink arrived and soon thereafter so did Dr. Jakes. "May I join you? Don't say yes if you'd rather be alone."

He smiled ironically. "Please do, Doctor."

She slid into the booth and breathed, "Ah," as if she'd had a hard day.

He took a swallow of his drink and asked, "Don't you have any alcoholics here?"

"Yes. Why do you ask?"

He held up his drink. "Isn't it awkward to serve this stuff around them?"

She smiled indulgently. "I'm afraid your notions on the treatment of alcoholism are a bit dated, Mr. Donner."

"Probably," Greg said. "Look, what are we going to do about this 'Mr. Iles' - 'Mr. Donner' business?"

"What would you *like* to do about it?"

"I don't know. I suppose . . ." He shook his head emphatically.

"Yes?"

"I suppose I should start getting used to 'Mr. Iles.'"

"It would be a step. You needn't press it, but you're going to have to get used to it eventually. That is, if—"

"I know, I know," he nodded furiously. "Don't say it."

Agnes smiled gently and said nothing.

Without quite knowing why, Greg found himself acutely embarrassed. "So what do we do now? What's the program?"

"We talk. We pass the time. And, as ever, we try to live."

"What's that mean?"

"Owing to a set of circumstances beyond your control, this is for the time being your home." She sent her eyes around the room. "These are your neighbors. There are people to be met, friendships to be formed, things to be done."

He shrank back into his seat. "I don't feel any need for that."

"I understand. The longer you stay buried in yourself, the longer you can remain Greg Donner."

"Yeah." Greg bared his teeth in a grimace. "Okay. Christ."

The doctor chuckled softly. "Is the prospect really as gruesome as that?"

"Not gruesome . . . I just don't want to admit I'm *here*."

"I know. And having acknowledged that, you've taken a step forward." She thought for a bit. "Another aspect of trying to live is learning to recognize and do the things you want to do."

"Meaning what?"

"There *is* something you'd like to do, something you'd like to fix, to remedy."

"There is? How do you know?"

"You mentioned it yesterday. It's something that would make you feel more comfortable."

Greg looked up as Alan approached to ask him if he wanted another drink or if he was ready to order. "Both," he told him. He glanced at the menu and ordered a steak *au poivre*. The waiter nodded and turned away, and Greg said, "I don't remember saying anything yesterday."

"I should let you rediscover it for yourself, but it's no great matter. You'd like to shed the clothes of Richard Iles. You'd like to assert your own personality in the matter of dress."

"True. Is that unhealthy?"

Agnes smiled. "Not at all. Your task is to fit yourself into Richard Iles's life—not his clothes. If you like, you can go into town tomorrow and make a new beginning of a new wardrobe."

"I'd like that. You mean Louisville?"

"Well, that depends on you. If you're looking for something more formal, say a business suit, then it would have to be Louisville. If you're looking for casual clothes, there are several excellent shops in a resort town nearby."

"That'll do," Greg said. "And what do I use for money?"

"Don't worry about that. We have accounts in all the shops. Let's see if we can find you a guide." She turned in her seat and began to survey the faces around the room. Finally she nodded toward a table across the room where a morose-looking hulk sat with a jaw propped on a fist. Middle-aged, overweight, round-shouldered, and with a battered face, he looked to Greg like a retired longshoreman.

"Your friend Robert Orsini," Agnes said. "He'd do nicely."

"My friend?"

"He's spent a lot of time with Richard Iles. In addition to appointing himself your special protector, he seems to appreciate your boundless capacities as a listener."

Greg closed his eyes. "Christ. Do I really need a guide?"

"You need someone to vouch for you, someone to confirm your right to use our accounts. Besides," she added with a smile, "you'll like him."

Greg looked again at Orsini. Though their eyes didn't meet, they might have been exchanging scowls. "He's a patient?"

"He is." Agnes chuckled. "But I assure you he won't try to bite your neck. Shall I bring him over? Then the two of you can work out a plan for tomorrow."

He sighed. "Yeah, I guess so."

She got up, hesitated, and then turned back. "I assume you'd like me to brief him on this . . . latest development?"

"He'd be pretty confused if you didn't, wouldn't he?"

"Very true."

Agnes's departure coincided with the arrival of Greg's steak. As he ate, he was careful to keep his eyes on his plate or on the vacant seat opposite. His steak finished, he had ordered coffee and Drambuie by the time she returned with Orsini. She performed a quick introduction and asked to be excused.

Orsini shifted his mass awkwardly into the booth and stared at Greg as if he were an apparition.

"Robert, was it?" Greg asked, just to be saying something.

"Robbie. Dr. Jakes calls me Robert, nobody else." He raised his brows comically. "You honest to God don't know me?"

"Not from Adam."

"Wow, that's terrific, terrific." His bullfrog face was beaming.

In spite of himself, Greg laughed. "Is it? Why?"

"Well, sure. Wow, what a breakthrough. A whole new you. I wish I could do that."

"Why?"

Robbie laughed and shook his head delightedly. "Listen to this guy," he said to an invisible audience. "Everybody else in the goddamned place runs when they see me coming, 'cause I'm the world's biggest bore, and he says why would I want to be a whole new person."

"Well, why?"

Robbie laced his thick fingers together on the tablecloth in front of him. "I'm a depressive. Started five, six years ago." He looked up. "You ever been depressed?"

"Yeah, sure."

"Well, I'm depressed every minute, I wake up depressed, go to bed depressed, eat depressed, have sex depressed. Did you ever see the movie *Airplane*? I saw *Airplane* and laughed myself sick and was depressed every goddamned second."

131

"Sounds pretty awful."

"It is, pal. And the worst of it is that I can't figure out *why* I'm depressed. I got no reason at all to be depressed. I got money coming out the kazoo. I got a nice business, no problems. Good health, good family. And every morning I wake up wishing I was dead. Can you beat that?"

Greg shook his head.

"Hey, man, can I ask you a question?"

"Sure."

"Is it okay if I bite your neck?"

"*What?*"

The giant threw back his head and roared with laughter. Then he looked at Greg solemnly and said, "No kidding, I even make jokes depressed."

XIX

"HEY," ROBBIE SAID as he was driving them back from town the next afternoon, "I'm the one who's supposed to be depressed here." In just four hours, under Robbie's relentless urging, Greg had spent close to four thousand dollars on shirts, slacks, shoes, lightweight sweaters, and sports coats, any one of which he would have considered ridiculously extravagant in his remembered life. Where alterations had been needed, Robbie had cajoled, brow-beaten, and bullied to have them done right then, on the spot.

"I don't feel depressed, Robbie," Greg said. "I feel guilty. Monstrously guilty. I haven't spent four thousand dollars on clothes in my whole *lifetime*."

"Don't be dumb," Robbie said placidly. "You're a millionaire. You can't dress in jeans and sneakers anymore."

Greg looked at him curiously. "How do you know I'm a millionaire?"

"Huh," Robbie grunted. "You can have anything you want out at that dump—except a secret. It's like a small town—everybody knows everything about everybody. Besides, out there they wouldn't even hand you an aspirin if you weren't a millionaire."

"You're a millionaire?"

"Forty times over, kid," Robbie said indifferently, his eyes on the road.

Strange, Greg thought, how forty million could make four million sound like not much.

"And I'm *still* depressed," Robbie added heavily.

Dr. Jakes dropped in as Greg was putting away the last of his new wardrobe and asked if she could have a peek. Greg gestured to the open closet. She examined a collection of Italian shirts and delicately ran her hand down the sleeve of a cashmere jacket. *"Très élégant,"* she murmured in a lamentable accent.

"It was all they had," Greg said defensively. In his remembered life he would have sneered at such garments as "movie star clothes."

She turned back with an understanding smile. "You'll get used to it. Meanwhile I was wondering if you'd drop by my office when you're finished."

"What's up?" he asked, suddenly apprehensive.

"Nothing's up," she replied lightly. "My office is where I generally see my patients."

"Yes, but why do you want to see me?"

"To talk to you. To begin the program you were so anxious to hear about last night." Amused, she cocked her head and asked, "Is that satisfactory?"

"Yes. But I can come right now. I'm all finished here."

"That's fine," Agnes said and led the way to another wing and a large, airy, and elegantly furnished room that seemed neither office nor living room but a cross between the two, with a chrome and smoked-glass desk in one corner and several different seating arrangements scattered around the room: an el-shaped sofa, two Eames chairs face-to-face, and a traditional psychiatrist's couch and easy chair. Along the shelves of one long wall was arranged a collection of what looked to Greg like very valuable antique toys, all pristinely gaudy, as if they'd just been taken from under the Christmas tree. He paused, smiling, before a garish collection of tin figures mounted on a stage: Li'l Abner's Dogpatch Band, with Pappy Yokum at the snare drum, Daisy Mae at the piano, Li'l Abner ready to dance, and Mammy conducting from atop the piano.

"Are these yours?" he asked.

"Of course. This is my own personal madness. Please sit wherever you feel comfortable."

Greg looked around. "I usually sit in the Eames chair that faces the window, don't I?"

Agnes gave him an interested look. "Is that a memory?"

He grinned. "No, just a guess."

"Ah. Well, your guess is correct."

They sat down. "You probably don't realize it," the doctor began, "but you're something of a phenomenon."

"A phenomenon. You mean because . . ."

She nodded. "Of course, in itself, there's nothing new in the appearance of diverse personalities in one individual—even personalities that are unaware of each other. What makes the appearance of Greg Donner unique is that, instead of representing a psychological degeneration, it seems to represent a decisive step toward health."

"Yeah," Greg said. "For Richard Iles."

"For the person sitting in your chair."

"Okay. So?"

"You know I have an obligation to you as your psychotherapist. You should also know that I have an obligation to my fellow workers in the field to make a record of your case."

He gave her a crooked grin. "In other words, you're going to get a paper out of me."

"Naturally that's secondary to your treatment. You don't object, I hope."

"Not at all. Agnes Tillford's a writer too. Go for it."

Agnes laughed, shook her head, and picked up a large manila envelope from the table beside her.

"I have here some photographs. Some are of people you've never seen in your life. Some are of people known to Richard Iles. I'd like you to go through them and see if you recognize any of them."

Shrugging, Greg held out his hand for the envelope. Inside he found a bundle of twenty or so pictures, some five by eight, some eight by ten, held together by a large paper clip. He slipped off the clip and studied the face on top: a kindly looking elderly man. He slid it to the bottom and looked at the next: a chunky girl in her teens—a graduation picture. He slid that to the bottom and looked at the next, a grinning couple in forties clothes. He sighed and went on.

At the eighth his heart lurched and his mouth went dry. He looked up, stunned, and whispered, *"Ginny."*

Agnes nodded, obviously pleased. "Your wife."

"Jesus!" Greg shrieked, his face blazing. "Why didn't you show me this before?"

"Take it easy, Greg. I didn't show it to you before because I didn't *have* it before. It arrived in this morning's mail."

"Well, why didn't you at least *tell* me?"

"Tell you what, Greg? That the woman you described to me *might* be your wife? If you consider it a moment, you'll see that would have been most imprudent."

He looked at the photo again. "When can I see her?"

"We'll talk about that. Please go on."

Greg blinked. "You mean with the pictures?" At the doctor's nod, Greg took Ginny's and set it on the table at his elbow. The next three faces were unfamiliar. He frowned at the fourth. In a tone of disbelief he said, "This is Bruce."

"You know him?"

"Yes. Ginny and I met him in a bar the last night I was . . . the night before I woke up here."

The doctor raised her brows. "You liked him?"

"Yes, very much."

"He's your paternal uncle. Bruce Iles."

"Good lord."

"You say you met him that last night. That's interesting."

"Why is that interesting?"

"Because he evidently had no major role to play in your life as Greg Donner—yet he's there."

Greg frowned. "There? I don't get it."

"Richard Iles's unconscious evidently didn't want you to wake up to this life as an orphan, so it arranged for you to establish relationships with three key people you'd meet here. At least I have to assume that they're key people. Flatteringly, me. More obviously, your wife. And then, just at the last moment, your uncle. He seems almost an afterthought. What was his last name?"

"Let me think. Some famous name. He said, 'No relation.' Eddison. That's right—'Two D's, no relation.'"

"Hm. By association with the famous name, it suggests that Richard Iles's unconscious considers him a bringer of light. What else?"

He smiled. "He has a strange hobby. He collects and analyzes family snapshots."

Agnes nodded enthusiastically. "Yes, that's very good. Evidently Richard Iles's unconscious is recommending Bruce as someone to shed light on your family. You say he analyzes snapshots? How?"

"By expressions, gestures. By the way people arrange themselves in relation to each other." Greg laughed. "I told him he should meet you—Agnes Tillford."

"Ah. That's also suggestive. Why did you tell him that?"

"Because you analyzed dreams the way he analyzed snapshots."

"Goodness, I had no idea all this nifty stuff was to be found here. I analyzed your dreams? How did that come about?"

"I thought I told you. I was having a very weird series of dreams . . . and some very weird, impossible things were happening. I can understand it all now, since it was *all* a dream, but at the time it was baffling as hell—and you sort of . . . held me together."

Agnes allowed herself a self-satisfied smile. "Well, that does pretty well describe my role in this bizarre situation."

"Yes. It's starting to make some sense at last—even to me."

"I agree. I'm looking forward to hearing about all this in greater detail."

Greg said, "When can I see Ginny?"

She nodded thoughtfully, as if she'd been anticipating the question. "Let's give ourselves a month. That will give us time to . . . Oh my. I can see you don't care for that."

"I certainly don't. What'll you know in a month that you don't know now?"

"Well . . . for one thing, I'll know a great deal more about you than I do right now. And for another, if things keep on going the way they've been going, I'll be pretty well convinced that Greg Donner's here to stay."

"'Pretty well convinced,'" he repeated with a sneer. "What are you right now, Agnes? Doubtful?"

"No, I wouldn't say I was doubtful. I'd say I was . . . hopeful."

"Good. That's fine. You just get on the phone to Ginny and tell her there's been a hopeful development here. That's all I'm asking you to do. There's been a hopeful development, and it would be nice if she'd come down and have a look at it."

Agnes's bosom heaved with a weary sigh. "Greg, please don't ask me to do something that all my experience tells me would be reckless and risky. It just doesn't make any sense to plunge into something like this."

"Into something like what, Agnes? What is it you think we're plunging into?"

"I don't know, Greg. That's exactly the point."

He stood up. "Do you have a procedure for handling escaping inmates? If so, you'd better get it working."

"Don't be ridiculous."

He turned and headed for the door, pausing with his hand on the knob. "I'm not kidding, Agnes. I know my way around now. I think I can get back to Chicago, even without money."

"Ginny's not in Chicago."

He stared at her, frowning. "True. I forgot. Where is she?"

"Come sit down."

He swung the door open. "I'll find her."

"Sit down, Greg. I'll call her."

"Now?"

"Today. I promise."

"You'll ask her to come down here as soon as possible?"

"I will if you insist."

"I do insist—and I'm not in a mood to sit anymore."

"All right."

"Where is she?"

"She's been living with her father in New York State since all this began."

"Oh. And before that?"

"Before that, you were living in Libertyville, Illinois."

"Good lord." He stood blinking vaguely around the room for a few moments. "There was something else I wanted to ask. Oh. Right. All that preamble about studying me in the name of science. That's just guff, isn't it?"

Agnes shrugged. "Call it misdirection. It was designed to spare you a possible disappointment. If you'd recognized none of the faces in those photographs, you'd have dismissed it as a foolish experiment and thought no more about it."

"Yeah, probably."

"On the other hand, I *will* get a paper out of you."

He laughed. "You'll let me know what Ginny says?"

"Of course."

Back in his room, Greg found he was too restless to stay there, so he took himself on a tour of the facility, which proved to be what he expected: a country club on a lavish scale, with indoor and outdoor swimming pools, an elaborate gymnasium, an eighteen-hole golf course, tennis courts, a small theater, several game and common rooms, a chapel, and, to his disappointment, a meager library offering only the blandest of light reading. The grounds were so vast and the activities so varied that the twenty or thirty people he saw seemed like stragglers in an off-season resort. He avoided encounters and was careful not to see the few hands that were waved at him from the pool side and the game rooms.

At six o'clock he tried calling Dr. Jakes and was told she was with a patient. After fifteen minutes of fidgeting, he went back to the library, picked up an exhausted-looking English country house mystery, and took it to the dining room. With his nose buried in a book, he hoped Robbie would understand he didn't feel like company.

It wasn't until seven-thirty that Agnes sank into the seat opposite.

"So?" Greg asked, but the doctor was looking around for their waiter. When she'd caught his eye and ordered a sherry, she turned back to Greg, her eyebrows raised enquiringly.

"So?" he repeated.

Agnes sighed. "Your wife will arrive in Louisville on Wednesday morning at eleven."

"What day is today?"

"Monday. I'll be frank with you, Greg. I told her there'd be no harm in waiting a week or two, but apparently the suspense of not knowing is something she can't stand any better than you can."

"What did you say had happened?"

"I told her you were once again a fully functioning person and left it at that. She wanted to know if you'd shed any light on what happened to you in Russia, but I said we'd talk about that when she arrived. She'll be met at the airport and should be here by twelve-thirty, at which time you'll be having lunch." She gave Greg a frigid smile. "By that I mean I don't want you lurking in the corridors trying to get a furtive glimpse of her. Understood?"

"Understood."

"She and I will have lunch in my office, and I'll explain the current situation. An hour or so should be enough for that. Then I'll give you a call and you can join us." Seeing Greg's expression, she asked, "That's not satisfactory?"

"It's not how I was imagining it. I was thinking of something a little more . . . private."

She snorted in amused disgust. "Greg, I'd advise you to keep your romantic nature well throttled down. Candlelight and soft music are definitely not first on the agenda here. Just keep reminding yourself that the person Ginny married was Richard Iles, a school teacher of Libertyville, not Greg Donner, a freelance writer of Chicago."

Greg nodded contritely.

"Now," she went on, "for tomorrow. Thanks to you, events are rushing us. Before I talk to Ginny, I want to find out as much as I can about your life in Chicago, particularly about the 'weird events' you mentioned earlier. So I'd like to schedule a two-hour session in the morning, beginning at ten, another in the afternoon, and, if need be, another in the evening after dinner. Okay?"

"Of course. I'm at your disposal."

She nodded and drained her sherry glass. "I'm going to take myself off to bed. It's been a hectic day."

"Can I ask a quick question?"

"Certainly."

"It feels weird to ask such a question, but—how long have Ginny and I been married?"

The doctor smiled wearily. "I'd have to check my notes to be sure, but my memory is that it's six or seven years."

"And I assume you would have told me if we had any children."

"Your assumption is not well founded," she said with mock formality, "but no, you have no children."

XX

DURING THEIR MORNING SESSION, Greg recounted the first thirty years of his life: his childhood, his school years, his years in college, his years in publishing, the lean years spent establishing himself as a freelancer, the recent years when contacts had been cemented and work was steady. At the end of it, he asked, "When did I do all this? I mean, I've got thirty years' worth of memories. My feelings say I *lived* through all those years."

Agnes said, "I'm not sure what you're asking."

"Did I fabricate all this in a single night, the night before I woke up here as Gregory Donner?"

"We may never know, but it's not inconceivable. The subjective time of dreams has little relation to the objective time of waking life. In just a few seconds of dreaming we may have an experience that would last for hours or even days in waking life. The same is true in hypnotic trance." She paused, smiling. "Once, as a student, I reexperienced the entirety of the film *Gone With the Wind* under hypnosis—in just fifteen seconds."

"Really?"

"Really. I read all the opening credits, heard every word, saw every scene and every gesture, listened to all the music. It wasn't speeded up or distorted in any way."

"Interesting. So what's your theory about me?"

"At this point I've nothing but conjectures. You may have created Greg Donner in a single night—or it may have been the work of months. From a therapeutic point of view, the question's academic." She spent a few minutes scanning her notes. "An interesting pattern seems to be emerging, though it's more or less what I expected. 'Gregory Donner' isn't just any old alter ego: he's a wish fulfillment."

"Meaning what?"

"Richard Iles married relatively young, just a few years out of college. My guess is that in later years he regretted that, wished he'd spent a few years leading a carefree bachelor life—the way Greg Donner did."

"Yes, I see."

"Perhaps that early marriage thwarted some ambitions. He became a school teacher in Libertyville. Do you think that would have suited you?"

"I think I would have detested it."

"Perhaps you did detest it, as Richard Iles. Perhaps you yearned for a more glamorous life—the life of a single freelance writer living on Lake Shore Drive."

He smiled crookedly. "I'd hardly call it glamorous."

"Perhaps you would if you were Richard Iles, school teacher of Libertyville."

"True."

At the beginning of their afternoon session, she reviewed her notes for a few minutes, then said, "Up till now the story you've told has been pretty well confined to your professional growth. You've told me how a child of a farming couple in Iowa came to be a freelance writer of Chicago. Your involvement with others seems to have taken a back seat to this process. You had no close friends. Your romantic affairs were casual, not deeply involving. But I gather that recently—in terms of your remembered life—this changed dramatically."

"Yes."

"How long ago?"

"Well, three or four weeks ago."

"And strange things began happening at about the same time?"

"That's right."

She nodded. "Let's hear about that now."

Greg sat thinking for a moment. "Oddly enough," he said, "it seems to have begun with a dream."

* * *

143

When he was finished, Greg watched the psychiatrist tug on an earlobe for a few minutes. Then he asked how all this fit into her theory that "Greg Donner" represented a fulfillment of Richard Iles's wishes.

"It doesn't, of course. But it doesn't exactly contradict it either. The menacing dreams, the dunning phone call, the episode of the gun represent Richard Iles's anxieties on behalf of Greg Donner. He seemed to recognize that you were going to face some extreme confusion and disorientation when you woke up here—as you did, of course. Dreams and real life were suddenly going to become intermingled, just as they did throughout this period in Chicago." She paused, smiling thoughtfully. "Perhaps in his own way he was doing his best to get you used to it."

He frowned, dissatisfied. "That doesn't explain what was *happening* in the dreams. Who was the follower?"

"Well, who is it who lurks behind Gregory Donner?"

"Oh . . . Richard Iles."

Agnes nodded.

"But he was represented as a threat in the dreams."

"Don't you in fact *feel* he's a threat?"

He laughed shortly. "Yes, I guess I do. Who was the old man Ginny was making love to in the last dream?"

"That should be obvious. Who *is* the old man Ginny has been making love to?"

"I don't get it."

"Gregory Donner is the new man, isn't he? Then who's the old man?"

Greg winced. "Richard Iles. Again."

"That's how I read it. The dream expresses an anxiety that Ginny might prefer the old man to the new. But note that it doesn't end there. Richard Iles seems pretty sure that she'll ultimately come round to Greg Donner. This is, after all, what she did that last evening before you woke up here. She literally came round to Greg Donner."

"True." Feeling exhausted, Greg pulled himself out of his chair. "Is there any reason for us to meet tonight?"

"I don't think so," she said. "I've got plenty to digest, and you . . . Why don't you go to the movie tonight? It's a favorite of mine, even if it is a bit of a relic—the Trevor Howard *Pygmalion*."

"Good lord," Greg said heavily.

The doctor cocked an eyebrow at him. "Is that significant?"

He shook his head, suddenly weary of significance.

Back in his room, he fell across the bed fully clothed and was asleep within seconds.

It was nearly ten when he awoke hungry both for food and for company. He dialed Robbie's room, got no answer, threw on fresh clothes, and hurried to the dining room. Robbie waved at him from his usual spot, and Greg joined him gratefully.

Within seconds Alan was at his side, grinning cheerfully. "Get you a drink, Mr. Iles? Kitchen's closed, I'm afraid."

"Closed," Greg echoed bleakly.

Alan folded his arms and gazed into the distance as if considering the fate of nations. "I guess I could make you a sandwich."

"That would be a blessing, Alan."

"Roast beef okay?"

"Terrific."

With a sigh, Greg settled back to listen to Robbie's latest speculations about the source of his relentlessly mysterious miseries.

XXI

GREG SPENT THE MORNING becoming vaguely and unsatis-
factorily resentful. It wasn't until he was waiting for Alan to
bring him his second Bloody Mary that he identified the source
of his resentment. It was a door: the door to Agnes's office.

Checking his watch, he saw it was twelve-thirty. Behind
that door, Ginny would just be sitting down, would just be
answering polite questions about her journey and the weather in
New York. An hour or so, the doctor had said, beginning at
twelve-thirty. At the latest, he'd have to be back in his room at
one-thirty to be ready for her call.

And then he would face the problem of the door.

It would be closed when he arrived. Understandably, since
Agnes's talk with Ginny would be private. So. On arrival he was
going to confront a closed door—and what was he going to do
about it? Was he going to knock, like a schoolboy at the head-
master's office? Absolutely not. He was going to barge right in
and look like a lout.

Of course, there was a way to sidestep the problem. When
Agnes called, he could ask her to open the door before he
arrived. He tested a dozen different ways of making the request,
and all of them made him sound completely stupid.

Therefore he would barge right in, and to hell with it.

Who cared, anyway?

He had more important things to think about.

Such as the possibility that Ginny might not even recognize
him. Such as the possibility that Ginny might take one look at
him and shriek with horror.

Suddenly it occurred to Greg that there was another alternative: he could knock on the door and then enter immediately,

without waiting for an invitation. A neat compromise, it seemed to him — civil but not servile.

Yes, he decided, that was the way to handle it.

When he was summoned at last, an hour later, he found that the door to Agnes's office was standing wide open.

He walked in, his legs a bit wobbly, his smile a bit stiff, and saw that Agnes and Ginny were seated on opposite sides of the el-shaped sofa at the far side of the room. For a moment there was a certain blankness in their gaze as they looked up at him, as if he were an unexpected visitor. Then Agnes rose and gave him a welcoming smile. After a brief hesitation, Ginny did the same.

As he approached them, Greg said, "Great Moments in Psychiatry, folks," and held out a hand to Ginny. After a sidelong glance at Agnes, she took it and looked into his eyes. After a beat, she retrieved both her hand and her gaze.

Smile in place, he felt his heart sink; it had been unmistakably a greeting of strangers.

"Sit down over here," Agnes commanded brightly, indicating her former place. Then she put Ginny back where she'd been and sat down beside her.

Greg said, "Hello, Ginny."

She tried out a smile. "Hello, Di—" The smile faltered and her eyes flickered to Agnes and back again. "You really want me to call you . . . Greg?"

"To tell you the truth, it doesn't matter a whole hell of a lot, Ginny," he said, amazed at the serene (and wholly false) assurance in his tone.

"I'm sorry," she said. "Dr. Jakes explained. It's just that, after calling you Dick for all these years." She gave him a feeble smile and a helpless shrug.

"It really doesn't matter, Ginny. I'm going to have to get used to being Dick Iles sooner or later, so I might as well start now." He shot Agnes an accusing look that said, *Aren't you supposed to be running this show?*

She cleared her throat. "Greg, I've explained to Ginny

147

what's happened here, and I think she understands the situation well enough." She sent Ginny a glance and got back a confirming nod. "What she needs right now is just a little time to digest it all."

"Agnes, I have the feeling you're trying to tell me something. What is it?"

She gave him an indulgent smile. "What I'm trying to tell you is that I knew you'd want a chance to say hello to Ginny, but that's all it's going to be for today. We're going to give her a little time to adjust to all this. We'll meet here again tomorrow afternoon at three."

"I see," Greg said. Examining each face in turn, he had to struggle against blurting out: *Why do I begin to get the distinct impression that news of my extraordinary recovery has not been the cause of giddy rejoicing here?* Instead he politely asked Ginny where she was staying.

"At that . . . resort," she replied, not looking at him.

"Griffin's Lodge?"

"Yes."

"Do you have a car?"

"Yes."

"I'll walk you to it."

"Oh. Fine," Ginny said, standing up. She looked surprised and relieved to be getting away so easily.

Agnes was frowning as if she'd momentarily lost track of the conversation, and Greg said to her, "I'd like to see you for a few minutes when I get back."

"Of course. I've cleared the whole afternoon for you. I was expecting to . . ."

The words faltered and died away as she watched Greg take Ginny's arm and steer her toward the door.

"Ginny, what is it really?"

They were walking a graveled path that would take them the long way round the complex to the parking lot.

"*Really,*" she said, with a despairing laugh. "I like that."

"Why?"

"Because that's just the sort of question . . ."

"Yes?"

"It's your kind of question—Dick's."

"I'm not sure what that's supposed to mean."

She shook her head without looking up. "If you think I'm not *really* confused, you'd better think again."

They walked in silence for a hundred yards, then he stopped and said, "Ginny, look at me." Her glance touched his face like the wing of a moth and fluttered away.

"Please, Ginny, look at me." She looked at him. "Who do you see?"

"I see . . . Dick Iles."

"I don't know who Dick Iles *is*, Ginny. I don't have a single memory of his. I don't know where he grew up or went to school. I don't know what books he likes or what television programs he watches. I don't know how or where he met you."

Ginny blinked. "Then you don't know *me*."

"Christ, didn't Dr. Jakes *explain* this? Richard Iles couldn't cope with the memories of his own life, so he created a whole new set for a man who could take his place—a man called Greg Donner. He got rid of how and where he met you, but he didn't get rid of *you*. I met you my own way, but it was *you* I met, Ginny, you I fell in love with. Don't you see?"

She studied his face as if it were a puzzling photograph. "You seem to be telling me that you fell in love with a woman in your mind, an imaginary woman."

"No, Ginny. I fell in love with the woman Richard Iles remembered. He blocked out everything but you, and I fell in love with you. You are . . . my gift from Richard."

She gave her head a little shake and turned away. "You talk like Dick. You think like Dick."

"'What's that mean, Ginny?"

Her eyes closed. "I've heard you say that a thousand times, in just that hurt tone. 'What's that *mean*, Ginny?'

"God, Ginny. And what does *that* mean?"

She looked down into the palms of her hands, and his heart lurched as he remembered the gesture.

"Try to understand, Dick . . . Greg . . . I've had to get used to the idea that you might be here in this place for the rest of your life. I had to begin to think of our life together as . . . over."

"And now?"

"And now I'm in a state of shock." She took a step back as he reached for her arm. "Please don't ask anything of me right now, Dick. God, and please don't look so crushed—*please*. I just need some time to sort myself out."

"Okay."

"Please give me that time, Dick. I mean *really* give it to me. Don't make me feel like I'm stealing it from you."

He sighed. "I'm still living in a world in which, five days ago you spent the night in my arms. I'm sorry."

"Don't be sorry. Just tell me it's all right for me to take the time I need."

"It's all right," he said, managing a feeble smile. "If I weren't such a klutz, I'd have known you'd need it."

They continued along the path, and, groping for some neutral subject, he asked her what sort of place Griffin's Lodge was.

"Oh, plush. Pretentious."

"Maybe we could get together there if you wanted to talk," Greg suggested.

"Yes, that's a thought."

"In fact, we could have a drink here in the lounge before you leave. Just talk."

"I don't have any 'just talk' in me right now, Dick. Sorry—Greg."

"I don't care what you call me, Ginny." He grinned. "Just so long as you call me." She reminded him that they were scheduled to meet in Dr. Jakes's office at three the following afternoon. "I know, but that doesn't necessarily preclude all other contact."

"True," she said, giving him a smile that didn't commit her

to anything. Having arrived at her car, she let him open the door for her. A moment later she was gone.

"All right, Doctor Jakes," he began with deadly emphasis, "just what the hell happened here?"

"Happened?"

"Come on, Agnes, don't play games with me. I want the blow-by-blow account." They were sitting in their usual places in her office, facing each other in a pair of Eames chairs.

"Frankly," she said, "I don't think a blow-by-blow account is what you want at all."

"No? What do I *really* want?"

"I don't know. Why don't you see if you can figure that out for yourself?"

With a sigh, Greg pulled himself out of his chair and went over to the shelves arrayed with her collection of antique toys. He picked up a 1930s "G-Man Pursuit Car" in luscious red, purple, and blue and ran it along the shelf, producing an angry crackle of machine-gun fire.

His hand still poised on the car, he said, "Ginny didn't seem thrilled to have me back among the living."

"I agree. She wasn't exactly overcome with delight."

"Why?"

"I don't know."

"You didn't ask?"

"This isn't a branch of the Gestapo, Greg. She wasn't here for interrogation."

"I know, but . . . Didn't she say anything, give any kind of hint as to what she was thinking?"

"My feeling is that she was careful *not* to say anything, *not* to give any kind of hint."

"Why?"

"Again, I don't know. Conjecturally, because her thoughts were in a complete turmoil. As yours were the morning you woke up and found yourself here instead of in an apartment in Chicago."

"The two things aren't comparable."

"Not precisely, of course. But consider this. Ginny arrives here not knowing what to expect, is told that the personality she's known for many years as her husband has vanished—possibly for all time—to be replaced by that of an utter stranger. Would you necessarily and without hesitation identify that as a cause for rejoicing?"

"No, but . . . She knows her husband's personality hasn't been replaced by that of an utter stranger."

"How does she know that?"

"She said so. When we were walking to her car. She said, 'You *are* Dick. You think like Dick, talk like Dick.'"

"I see."

"Come on, Agnes. Haven't you talked to her about her life with Richard Iles? Don't you know where they stood with each other?"

She sighed. "Greg, the families of psychiatric patients come in two varieties. One variety understands that what we do here requires their active collaboration. The other variety drops off their children or spouses like appliances to be repaired, and when we try to question them they politely or impolitely tell us to mind our own business."

"You're saying that Ginny belongs to that variety?"

"Yes, but with considerable justification. After all, we *knew* what had traumatized Richard Iles—something intolerable happened to him in Russia. It had nothing to do with Ginny. That being the case, we had no more reason to probe into his relationship with her than if he'd been concussed in an auto accident."

"Yes, I can see that. But . . ."

"But didn't we talk about the things you want to know? We might have, but we didn't. She just didn't take me into her confidence about such things."

Greg picked up the "G-Man Pursuit Car" and peered in at the smiling, untroubled face behind the machine gun.

"Shit," he whispered.

XXII

THE DINING ROOM WAS EMPTY when Greg went in to lunch the next day. Checking his watch, he saw why: it was only eleven-thirty. Alan appeared after a moment, and Greg ordered a Bloody Mary.

When the waiter reappeared a few minutes later carrying a telephone, Greg thought he'd somehow misunderstood his order. Alan plugged the phone in and set it down before him, just as if it were a drink, and Greg gave him a baffled look.

"You have a phone call, Mr. Iles," Alan explained.

"Ah!" Greg cried, feeling like a complete fool.

When Alan was out of sight, Greg picked up the receiver and said hello.

"Greg?"

"Ginny?"

"Yes. I've been thinking about your suggestion."

"My suggestion."

"Yes, Uh. I think I'd better be honest with you about something. I'm not exactly looking forward to that meeting this afternoon."

"I see," Greg said. "May I ask why not?"

"I don't think Dr. Jakes has a very high opinion of me."

"Why do you think that?"

"I think she thinks that . . ."

"Go on."

"She thinks I neglected you."

"Neglected me. How?"

"She thinks I should have been a little more *on hand*."

"Ginny, you're being very oblique here. Where should you have been a little more on hand?"

153

"Here. She thinks I should have spent more time with you *here*."

"What good would that have done?"

"I don't know. I'm just telling you what she thinks."

"Okay." He closed his eyes, groping for the thread of the conversation. "So you're not looking forward to this meeting. Because you think Dr. Jakes is against you?"

"Yes."

"Well, she hasn't given me any indication of that, Ginny. None at all. Honestly."

A long silence.

"What are you trying to say, Ginny? That you don't want to meet with Dr. Jakes?"

"I'm not sure."

"You're not sure about what?" When that produced no reply, he said, "Is it that you want me to come there?"

"Well, yes, I thought maybe we could have lunch here. Then we could meet with Dr. Jakes if—"

"Yes? If . . . ?"

"If you really think we have to. I'd really rather not have to go through all this with her there."

"Go through all what, Ginny?"

"All our . . . personal business."

Greg thought for a moment. "All right, Ginny. I can be there by twelve-thirty or so. In the restaurant?"

"Yes. That's what I'd thought."

"Okay. See you then."

He hung up briefly, then asked the operator to connect him with Dr. Jakes.

"Agnes? This is Greg. Do you have a minute?"

"Sure."

"How do I go about getting a car?"

"What? Why do you want a car?"

"Ginny just called and wants me to have lunch with her over at the lodge."

"Oh . . . Well. I really don't think that's such a good idea at

154

this point, Greg. Tomorrow maybe, but not today. . . Frankly, this has caught me off balance. I'm a little boggled. What exactly was her thought?"

"To tell you the truth, Agnes, she's a little nervous about this afternoon's meeting. She has the feeling you're against her."

"Against her? Why?"

"She says you accused her of neglecting me."

"Ah. Well, it's true I thought it might conceivably help if she made herself a continuous presence in your life here. But you should know me well enough to know that I didn't *accuse* her of anything."

"She may not have used that word."

"I hope not. Accusation is just not my style."

"I know. But look. Let me talk to her."

Agnes's sigh transmitted itself clearly across the line. "Greg dear, when God was passing out his gifts and came to you, he must have said, 'Let's give this one lots and lots of brains but no survival instincts at all.'"

"Why do you say that?"

"Greg, you're absolutely fearless when it comes to making yourself vulnerable to psychological injury. If I haven't already told you that, I apologize. You may think this is a wonderfully charming quality in a man, but I definitely don't. In moderation, sure. But taken to the extremes you seem to enjoy, it's immature and neurotic and self-destructive. Believe me, I know what I'm talking about here. You just throttle down those kamikaze impulses for another three hours, and then we'll see where we stand. Okay?"

"Okay, Agnes."

He hung up, thought for a moment, and then asked the operator to ring Robert Orsini's room. When he had him on the line he said, "Robbie, I need a favor. Can you get me a car?"

"A car? Sure, no problem, buddy. What's up?"

The dining room at Griffin's was Hunting Lodge Plush, with acres of expensive-looking paneling, miles of smoky rafters angled up into a cathedral ceiling, and a stone fireplace big enough to roast a Rolls Silver Ghost in, but what Greg took in was Ginny at a table far away, looking tiny in a chair whose back would reach his chin. She didn't wave; she saw that she'd been seen, and she watched him without expression as he crossed the room and pulled out the matching chair opposite.

"Hi," he said.

She said, "Hi," and he sat down.

He sent her a smile that fell dead halfway across the table, and they both nervously scanned the room for a waiter. When one arrived, Greg nodded at Ginny's Bloody Mary and said, "I'll have one of those. Hot." He looked at her and added, "As punishment." She raised an eyebrow at him. "I'm AWOL. Dr. Jakes didn't think it was a good idea for me to meet you here."

She frowned. "I didn't realize you were going to tell her."

"Agnes is all right, Ginny. I'm sure you're wrong in thinking she's against you."

She shook her head and looked down at her drink.

"Isn't it strange?" he went on. "People who have a drink feel it's unfair to talk to someone who doesn't have one."

She looked at him coolly. "Are you going out of your way to make me feel awkward?"

Greg laughed and shook his head. "What's this in my mouth—a foot? God, Ginny, I have no desire in the world to make you feel awkward. I would love to see you relaxed and happy. I would love to see you smile. Believe me."

"I believe you, Dick." She gave her head a little shake. "I'm sorry—Greg."

"Call me Grick. Or Dreg."

She smiled faintly and glanced up at the waiter as he served Greg's Bloody Mary. Greg took a sip, winced as the Tabasco bit into his mouth, and gave her a long, serious look. "Who am I really, Ginny? I don't know. Dr. Jakes doesn't know."

She returned his look. "You're Dick."

"I see. Is that good? Or bad?"

"Don't be stupid, Dick. People are who they are."

Greg longed to say, *But you're Ginny and I wouldn't hesitate to tell you how good that is.* He said instead, "Who is Dick, then?"

"Dick is you, Greg. A sweet guy. An innocent. A man who wears his heart on his sleeve. A dreamer."

"Go on."

Ginny sighed. "You wanted to be a writer, Greg. I've never known anybody who wanted something so badly. You took writing courses. You read books on writing. You spent two hours every night in your room . . . working."

"Working," he repeated dully. "Working on what?"

"On short stories that wouldn't come together. On novels that never got beyond the first page."

"Shit," he said, closing his eyes. "You're telling me I was pathetic."

Ginny shrugged, embarrassed.

"I'm not pathetic now, Ginny." When she didn't meet his eyes, he said, "I'm not."

"Why? Because you're a writer in your dreams?"

"No. Because I know better now. I know I'm not a fiction writer. I wouldn't even waste a minute on it now."

"It's pointless to talk about it anyway, Greg. You can do anything you please. Thanks to my father, you're a rich man."

He blinked. "Your father? What's he got to do with it?"

"You mean they didn't tell you? It was my father who found out what really happened to you in Moscow, who bullied the State Department into bargaining for your release, who blackmailed them into that settlement after you got home."

"Oh," he said. "Tell him thanks for me, will you?"

"What's that? Sarcasm?"

"No." He sank back in his chair. "So, *I'm* a rich man."

"It's all yours, Greg. You suffered for it."

"And you want no part of it?"

Ginny looked away. "There's no nice way to say this, Greg. Before you left for Moscow, it was all settled. You knew I wouldn't be there when you got back."

Greg closed his eyes. "Why, Ginny?"

"Christ, Greg, you can't ask why a marriage breaks up. The years go by and . . . things don't work out."

"Was it me, Ginny? Did I want to end it?"

She shook her head. "It was me."

"But *why*?"

"Oh God, Greg. What difference does it make? The sort of life we had . . . the sort of life you wanted, it wasn't for me. I'm just not cut out for your middle-class, middle-brow, middle-western life." She made a face. "I'm a bitch. Can't you settle for that? I'm a bitch and a snob, and I bore easily. Don't you understand? Sweetness cloys. I need more than that. I need . . ."

The words were pouring out now, and Greg heard them clearly enough, at a distance. Somehow the sounds they made seemed to form a tunnel between them; there was a hollowness in their center, and into this space, he whispered, "Are you . . . happy?" He heard himself saying these words, and they echoed endlessly in the tunnel between him and Ginny, but she didn't seem to notice them. Looking through the tunnel was like looking through a telescope the wrong way: Ginny seemed far, far away, and he could no longer make out whether she was talking or not. Strangely, it no longer mattered; he felt very relaxed and peaceful.

Soon there seemed to be a lot of activity around their table. People darted in and out of his field of vision, but he paid no attention to them. At the end of the tunnel, Ginny had dwindled to a charm-sized figure, and he thought sadly that soon she would vanish altogether.

After a time, a voice at his side repeating his name again and again intruded itself into his consciousness. He looked up and said, "Oh, hello, Dr. Jakes. What're you doing here? Of course I'll come with you." Greg laughed, because he hadn't actually *heard* her asking him to come along. In some strange way, the question had appeared as an intelligible ripple in the tunnel in front of him.

"But I got it right anyway, didn't I?" he said, pleased with himself.

The ripple in the tunnel said, "You got it right, Greg."

"Dick," he said, laughing. "You can call me Dick."

"All right."

"And you don't have to hold me up, you know. I can walk by myself."

"I know," the doctor said gently, leading him out of the dining room.

Back in his room at the sanatorium, the tunnel was quaking in a way that filled Greg with dismay, and he whispered, "Don't cry, Ginny. Don't ever cry."

But the quaking went on, overlaid by the angry vibrations of the psychiatrist's voice, directed (Greg somehow knew) to Ginny. "There's nothing you can do, you silly, willful child. Do you imagine I would have asked you to come if I'd thought you intended to destroy him?"

There was a painful disruption in the quaking, and Greg knew Ginny was speaking in the midst of her sobs, but he couldn't make out the words.

"That can't be changed now," the doctor snapped. "Go away and strangle on your guilt while I strangle on mine for my own ineptitude. Please, Mrs. Iles . . . Nurse!"

The quaking in the tunnel began to subside, and he whispered, "Don't strangle." And then the surface of the tunnel became perfectly smooth for a long time.

Greg, sitting in front of the window, stared out at the beautiful blue hills.

After a while he realized that Agnes was sitting across from him and saying something. She was saying, "You're going to be all right, Greg. You're going to be fine. Soon you'll be living on Lake Shore Drive and having a wonderful time. Do you remember Lake Shore Drive?"

"I remember."

"You'd like to live there again, wouldn't you?"

"Yes."

"You will. You're going to be fine, Greg. Whether you

know it or not, you're a very strong person. Very resilient. Nothing can daunt you for very long. Did you know that?"

"Yes, Doctor. Don't worry."

"Will you have dinner with me this evening, Greg? I'd really enjoy that."

"Sure, Doctor."

"Shall I ask Robert too?"

"Whatever you say."

"Perhaps better just the two of us, eh?"

"Whatever you say, Doctor."

After the long afternoon and evening, Greg hung up his clothes, put on his pajamas, and slipped into bed. Staring up at the ceiling, he listened to the distant murmur of voices from the dining room and the endless racket of the crickets outside. Finally, not tired, not sleepy, not anything, he fell asleep.

And woke up the next morning, shaking uncontrollably, in his own bed, in his apartment on Lake Shore Drive.

PART
THREE

XXIII

GINNY!" GREG SCREAMED. "*GINNY!*"

She came running out of the bathroom, wearing one of Greg's shirts, and threw herself on top of him. "What's wrong?" she shouted, to make herself heard over her own name being shouted again and again. She wrapped her arms around him, as if trying to hold in his violent trembling. "Greg! Tell me what's wrong!"

"For Christ's sake, Ginny, what day is it?"

"It's Saturday, Greg. What else would it be?"

He covered his face with his hands and groaned. "God, Ginny, don't go away."

"I'm not going anywhere, Greg. I'm here."

He put his arms around her and pressed her against his chest. "Never again," he said. "I'm never going to sleep again. I'm not kidding."

"What happened?"

"I had a dream." He closed his eyes and shook his head. "The most horrendous nightmare of all time."

By the time he finished telling it, Ginny was sitting cross-legged beside him looking into a mug of coffee. Greg was puzzled by her silence and asked her what was wrong.

She glanced up and shook her head. "It's my fault. I'm sorry."

"Don't be ridiculous, Ginny. How could something that happened inside my head be your fault?"

"You'll see, I'm afraid." She slid off the bed. "Get dressed. There's something I have to show you."

"Where?"

Ginny headed into the bathroom. "At my place."

His other questions she ignored.

A few minutes later, when they were inside a cab and on their way, he asked her what it was all about.

"Let me do this my way, Greg. Believe me, all your questions will be answered in an hour."

So they rode downtown in silence, like strangers sharing a seat on a bus. Once inside her apartment, Ginny disappeared into her bedroom and returned clutching a videotape cassette.

"What's that?" he asked.

She shook her head and sat down on the sofa across from him. "I'm going to tell you the story of my childhood," she said.

He blinked at her, astonished.

"It's strange," she began, "the way children adapt to what's happening around them. No matter what it is, they assume this is the usual way life is lived. At least I did. I assumed that all men were like my father, that the role of men in the world was to make life hell for everyone around them."

She closed her eyes, then shook her head as if rejecting what she saw. "My father was a spectacular-looking man when he was young. He had a profile like John Barrymore's and he wore his hair long, so that he looked like a poet. I haven't told you his name, have I? Franklin. Franklin Everly Winters, and God help anyone who dared to call him Frank. He shouldn't have married my mother. He shouldn't have married at all, but in those days I guess one did." She looked up and said, "I'm sorry. I'm not telling this very well, am I?"

To Greg she seemed to have lost about ten years of her life, becoming an uncertain, fragile seventeen-year-old.

"Tell it any way you like, Ginny. I'll follow it."

She nodded and went on. "He was a womanizer—the only one I've ever known. I've known married men who've had affairs, and I've heard about them from a lot women they've had affairs with, but none were like him. He was like an alcoholic with women—he couldn't stop with one. He'd swallow one and go on to the next. And of course there was nothing subtle about it. He couldn't be bothered to hide it to spare my feelings or my mother's feelings. He was one of the wonders of the world, and it was unthinkable that he should be the exclusive property of any one woman. He thought it was very petty of us not to rejoice with him over his conquests.

"We lived out in the country about thirty miles north of Albany, in a house that had been in his family for three generations. Not that Franklin was around that much. He spent most of the week with the fashionable crowd in Manhattan. He knew everybody, or claimed to: Thurber, Tennessee Williams, Elia Kazan, Jackson Pollock. I've forgotten most of them, but they were names you saw in *Time* magazine every week. Mother and I lived out in the country and tried to pretend that Franklin was a distant relative who spent an occasional Sunday with us."

She looked up. "This begin to sound a little bizarre to you?"

"A little," Greg admitted.

"Anne—my mother—never talked to me about it, but I knew she wanted to divorce him. I heard them discuss it when they thought I wasn't around. Franklin wouldn't consider it, saw no sense to it, since he was perfectly content with the present arrangement. Anne had the grounds for a divorce, of course, but he made it clear that if she tried to use them, he would . . . He said, 'I'll see to it you spend the rest of your life repenting it.' And he would have. He was a man who never forgot a slight, never let go of a grudge—and was proud of it.

"I always felt I wasn't quite real to my father. He'd bring me out to show round like a beautifully made and expensive toy he'd acquired and then, having impressed everyone with his cleverness, he'd put me away again with complete indifference, as if I really were just a doll."

Ginny paused, staring at a space beyond her knees, and then went on with a sigh.

"One winter, when I was sixteen, he came down with the flu and spent a whole week with us. It was a miserable week. He hated being sick, hated missing out on all the fun—and took it out on Mother. Friday night rolled around, and I was all excited because I was having a real date. I don't even remember the boy's name, but we were going to a movie in Saratoga Springs. While I was getting ready, I crossed the hall in my slip to go into the bathroom, and Franklin saw me from his room at the end of the hall. He came charging out, grabbed my arm, and said, 'What the hell are you doing in *that* getup?' I told him I was getting ready for a date. He said, 'A *date*? You're not going on any dates at *your* age, young lady!' Then I told him Mother had let me start dating when I was sixteen. He looked thunderstruck, because I really don't think he knew how old I was. He told me to go back to my room and get out of those clothes, because, whatever my mother said, I was not going out.

"When my date arrived, Franklin sent him home. Mother told me he did it very nicely, but of course that didn't matter. I was completely humiliated, thought my life was over." Ginny gave Greg a rueful smile. "You can see that I was a completely normal adolescent."

"Yes."

"You understand that it didn't occur to me that my father's behavior was anything more than the usual fuss parents make over their kids' first dates."

Greg chewed on that for a moment. "Uh-huh."

"In any case, one week later Franklin arrived back at the house and told us he'd sublet his apartment in New York City. The car was packed to the roof with all the clothes he'd kept there, and he took us out to show it to us, as if he'd performed an amazing feat. 'Behold, the Prodigal returns!' he said and insisted we get dressed and go into Albany for a celebratory dinner. Of course Mother and I were simply dazed. Neither of us was sure we had anything to celebrate, but we had no choice in the matter.

"Oddly enough, Franklin seemed to be a truly changed man. There were no more affairs. To all appearances, he became a devoted husband and parent. He embraced the life of a country gentleman, dressed in tweeds, bought himself boots and a shotgun. These were all the things I'd prayed for when I was younger, and I tried hard to believe that we were now just an ordinary, happy little family, the way I imagined other families were. But there was something chilling and strange about what he was doing. It was too much, too perfect, too *theatrical*—but of course we couldn't complain about that. We couldn't even mention it. For my mother's sake, I pretended everything was wonderful—and I'm sure she did the same for my sake. At least in the beginning.

"My mother started to come apart after a few months. This seemed very unfair to me at the time. You know how kids are at that age—everything *looked* perfect, and that's what counts. So she should have been playing along with it, should have contributed to the communal image of bliss. Instead she started drinking heavily, started popping pills, turning herself into a zombie. Everything started falling apart—and suddenly it was Franklin who was keeping it all going."

Ginny shuddered.

"It was as if we were all under some horrible enchantment. Mommy, who'd always been the strong one in the family, was suddenly and unaccountably 'sick,' and Daddy, who'd never given a damn about his family, was suddenly taking care of poor Mommy and poor neglected little Ginny. You remember the gruesome snapshot Bruce Eddison showed us of that Russian family? We were like that—smiling into the camera through our derangement—and I didn't have any idea what was going on.

"Mother got worse. Have you ever known a paranoid? I don't just mean someone with paranoid leanings, someone who tends to think people are against him. I mean a real one."

Greg nodded. "A friend of mine once went that way. I spent an evening with him just before he was committed. It was an unforgettable evening."

"Yes. Well, my mother went that way too. At least that's the way it seemed at the time. She began taking me aside. Ugh. That's an understatement. We had to hide. She took me into the woods, till Franklin put a stop to it. After that, she took me into the cellar, into a closet. The things she told me Franklin was doing to her were breathtaking, unbelievable—but she believed in them absolutely."

"I know. So did my friend."

"You probably had the advantage of *knowing* they weren't true. I didn't. I didn't know what to believe. If what she was saying was true, then my father was a monster. I didn't want to believe he was a monster, but he already *seemed* like one. He had popped into the house like some horrible creature in a Grimm's tale, all charm and smiles, and the more he smiled the more nightmarish everything became. In the end it nearly tore me to pieces. If I listened to her, I became terrified of him—and if I listened to him, I became terrified of her."

"What exactly was she accusing him of?"

"Of trying to drive her crazy."

"Why was he doing that?"

"She told me, and I didn't understand. You see, he couldn't just get rid of her with a divorce, because she'd inevitably get custody. He *had* to drive her crazy."

"I don't get it."

Ginny closed her eyes as if in pain. "It was *me* he wanted, Greg—me without her. All for himself."

"Good lord." He stopped and frowned. "Wait a second. Was this for real or just your mother's fantasy?"

"I didn't *know*, Greg. He didn't rape me. He didn't even paw me. The things he did do *could* have been just affection. I simply didn't *know*."

"Did you ever see him do anything that seemed plainly *calculated* to drive your mother crazy?"

"No. Whenever I saw them together, he positively oozed benevolence and solicitude."

"But you believed what she was telling you?"

"Greg, how many times do I have to say it? I didn't know *what* to believe." He told her to go on.

"We had a housekeeper and a sort of general errand runner," she continued. "Franklin himself almost never left the house now, and when he did he'd call every few hours to make sure everything was all right. One day in the summer after I graduated from high school, he had to see his lawyer in New York. He drove to the station to take an early train and expected to be back by midafternoon. As soon as his car was out of sight, Mother told me she was getting me out of there, sending me to Chicago to stay with a friend. I was completely dumbfounded, of course. I didn't know what to do, but she took me by the arm, led me upstairs, and told me to start packing. I said, 'But when am I coming back?' and she said, 'You're never coming back.' Then I started crying and she shook me till my teeth rattled. 'This is your only chance of getting away from him,' she said, 'and you're going to take it.'

"I still didn't know what to do, whether I should go along with what she wanted or run away and hide till Father got back home. But she was standing right there waiting for me to pack, so I packed. When I was done, we took my suitcases to her car, then went back to wait by the phone for Franklin's call. It came at noon, and I said what she'd told me to say, that she was in her room zonked out on pills. Then she drove us into Albany and started withdrawing money from all her accounts. Finally I had a wad of traveler's checks worth almost fifteen thousand dollars.

"'That won't put you through school,' she said, 'but your father will send more.' I said, 'He will?' She told me he would. 'Don't you understand yet?' she said. 'Franklin's in love with you. He'll give you anything you want—as long as he believes he can get you back.'

"'Then why do I need all this money?' I asked her. "She shook her head as if I were being very stupid. 'This money forces his hand. Since he can't starve you into submission, he'll have to try to indulge you into submission. It's the only way he can hope to keep you. Play along with him until you can stand on your own feet, but don't ever come back—for anything.'

"'But what's going to happen to you?'

"'Don't think about me,' she said. 'None of this was your fault.'

"Then she took me to the airport and put me on a plane to Chicago. She'd told me a little about Nelson Herne, the man who'd be meeting me there. He was a friend from college days— a man she probably would have married if it hadn't been for Franklin. He was an attorney and turned out to be a very nice man indeed. He took off a whole day to go apartment hunting with me, and finally installed me in a Michigan Avenue high-rise.

"I didn't know what Mother had told him, and he didn't seem to want to say. I asked him if he knew my father. He made a face and said he did. Then he started asking me questions— very guarded questions. It wasn't till later that I realized that he was trying to find out how much I really knew about Franklin.

"There was one thing I hadn't thought to ask Mother— whether I should send her my address in Chicago. I asked Nelson Herne what he thought. He made another face and said, 'Don't bother. Franklin will know soon enough where you are.'

"I asked him how he'd know, but he just shook his head. Evidently he was right, because a few weeks later, after I'd started classes at the Art Institute, I got a call from my father to tell me that Mother had committed suicide. I wasn't really shocked; I guess subconsciously this is what I'd been expecting. Naturally he wanted me to come home for the funeral, but I told him I couldn't. You see, as soon as he told me that Mother had killed herself, I knew that this is what she'd been thinking of when she told me not to come back for *anything*.

"Of course it didn't stop with that. He tried every sort of moral blackmail on me, from saying that I'd shame him before the neighbors to pleading that he needed my support to survive this tragedy, but I held out. I still wasn't sure what the truth of all this was, but I felt I owed my mother this loyalty—at least until I *was* sure.

"A month later he sent me a letter full of saintly paternal understanding. It wasn't my fault that I'd let my mother turn me against him; I was too innocent to realize that she was demented. I'd see things in their true perspective eventually, and he'd be there to welcome me with a brave, sorrowing smile. To show me he wanted nothing but my happiness (however cruel I might be to him), he enclosed a check for fifteen hundred dollars and said he'd arrange with his bank to have one sent every month. So Mother's estimate of the situation proved to be exactly right.

"In the spring he wrote again, urging me to come to home for the summer break. He didn't want to rush me, but didn't I, in all fairness, owe him a chance to sponge away some of the mud my mother had thrown on him? I told him I still wasn't ready. This was the pattern for the next few years. Then he decided it was time for a new approach. On my twenty-first birthday he sent me an incredible diamond necklace from Tiffany's—and *this*." She patted the videocassette she'd brought from the bedroom.

Greg looked at her with raised eyebrows, and she gazed back as if willing him to do something he couldn't guess at. Then she wheeled over a television set and VCR, inserted the cassette, turned it on, and sat down.

For a few moments the set was silent, the screen blank, then a man's voice said, "Dearest Ginny . . . Just in case you've forgotten what your home looks like."

Abruptly a picture of a house appeared, obviously taken by a hand-held camera. It wobbled for a moment, grew steady . . . and Greg's jaw dropped. It was a stately old hip-roofed Georgian mansion—and, except for the fact that it had no dome on top, *it was the house of his observatory dream.*

The front door stood open, and the camera moved toward it unsteadily, mounted some stairs, entered, and panned across a broad hallway. A handsome staircase rose at the left, and Greg, too fascinated to speak, recognized it; he'd mounted that staircase in the dream that had ended with his gunshot suicide. Then the camera passed through a doorway and entered a large living room. After scanning the room's undistinguished furnishings, it approached a waiting tripod. The picture juddered wildly as the camera was set in place and made fast; then it was turned to focus on a leather wingback chair a few feet away.

A tall white-haired man in a dark green smoking jacket (presumably the camera operator) appeared at one side of the screen, went to the chair, and, with his back to the camera, attached a miniature microphone to his shirt-front. Then he sat down, turned his matinée idol's face to the lens, and smiled.

"Wait, wait, wait!" Greg shouted. "Turn it off!"

"My dearest Ginny," Franklin Winters managed to say before she hit the pause button.

"What's the matter?" she asked.

"I *know* this man," he said, staring at the face frozen on the screen. "I mean . . ."

"Yes?"

"I mean, I've *dreamed* about him."

Ginny sat down again. "Go on."

"You remember the night we met, I told you I'd been dreaming about you. You thought I was kidding, but I wasn't. It was a whole series of dreams, and in the last of them I found you there in that house . . . in bed with that man. Unmistakably *that man.*"

Ginny nodded. "I told you, Greg. That's what he wants."

He blinked at her. "What are you talking about? What *he* wants? What the hell does that have to do with what I *dream*? I don't understand."

"You will."

She turned the videotape back on.

XXIV

FRANKLIN WINTERS'S FACE CAME TO LIFE as if he'd been startled from a reverie. Although his long, fine features were blurred with age, they still composed a face that would draw attention in a crowd. It bespoke wit and charm, but it wasn't the face of a man you expected to like; his wit would be sardonic and his charm would be calculated to expose your own gaucherie. There was altogether too much calculation in Franklin Winters; he wanted you to see the self-confident set of his broad shoulders, the glittering awareness of superiority in his eyes, the gracefulness of his long, elegant hands.

He frowned with good humor and spoke with an actor's voice, in a pleasant mid-Atlantic accent.

"I hope this damned contraption is working, my dear. You know how little use I am around gadgets. Since you steadfastly decline to send yourself to me, it seemed the best way for me to send myself to you. If I'd come in person, you might have found my very presence a threat and refused to see me. This way, I am flattened, miniaturized, and reduced to a mere shadow of myself—and, best of all, you can banish me to nothingness with a flick of your finger. With all these reassurances, I trust you will not find my brief visit too onerous to bear."

He paused, and his lighthearted manner slipped away like breath on a mirror.

"It's time," he said, "that you knew who and what I am. If that sounds pompous, I make no apology for it. Thanks to a strange fate, I belong—thank God—to a class apart from the common herd of mankind, and there's nothing in that to be ashamed of."

The old man squirmed into a new position in his chair and for the first time seemed less than completely self-assured. He went on: "In the past three years I've spent many hours considering how I could tell you what must be told without arousing your scornful incredulity. In the end, I admit, my ingenuity failed me. I could contrive no explanation one-tenth as convincing as a simple demonstration. And so I decided to break a solemn vow I made to myself long ago.

"This vow," Franklin said, looking directly into Greg's eyes, "was designed to preserve your innermost privacy. I vowed never to trespass upon your dreams until such time as I might be invited to do so. Last night I broke that vow."

"Wait!" Greg cried, and Ginny paused the video. "What in hell is he talking about—'trespassing on your dreams'?"

"Just listen," she said through gritted teeth.

Franklin went on: "For you, this will not of course have been last night but rather several nights ago, depending on how long it takes for this cassette to reach you and how long you wait to view it. Nevertheless, you will remember the dream. I made sure of that.

"When I came to you in my own shape in the realm of dreams, you and a young companion were following a stream-bed, looking for something. You didn't recognize your companion, but it was yourself as a child. Nearby was a pool of luminous blue water, and I guessed she was leading you there to show you something in its depths. I intercepted you. You were startled. I could see that you wanted to come to me but were fearful. The little girl said, 'What have you done with my mother?'"

Franklin smiled. "Of course this brave child was simply verbalizing the question you've been afraid to ask me myself. I asked her if she wanted to visit her mother, and she said, 'Oh yes, please!' I looked up into the sky, summoned down a goose from a flock passing by, and sent the little girl flying away on its back."

Greg took his eyes off the screen and sent them to Ginny. She caught his glance and nodded.

"By now you know I'm speaking the truth, so I won't

bother recounting the rest of our adventure. It was all enchant-ing, and all the result of my own mastery. You see, my dear Ginny—and as you see from this demonstration—*I am a walker in the realm of dreams."*

Franklin Winters settled back in his chair with a sigh, as if the hard part were done.

"My dear, I can well imagine your bewilderment over this bizarre concept. *The realm of dreams?* It would be difficult to imagine anything more alien than this to your pedestrian education, which confidently teaches that our dreams take place strictly within the confines of our individual skulls. However, if you consult the knowledge and experience of ten thousand older cultures scattered all over the world, you will learn something different. In all these cultures, it's accepted without question that in dreams we inhabit a separate realm of reality that exists as surely as the one we inhabit in waking life.

"But I mustn't rush ahead to the conclusion of the story. I knew none of this when I began my sojourn into the unknown, half a century ago."

He paused, frowning over his next words.

"It seems to me important that you should understand something of the milieu in which it began—Princeton University in the middle of the Great Depression. It was a strange time for the children of the wealthy—and we were almost all children of the wealthy. We had, for some reason, been spared in the plague of poverty that was sweeping the world. We'd seen it carry off any number of friends, who could no longer afford to live in *quite* such large houses or attend *quite* such excellent schools as they used to. Though the plague spared our wealth, it carried off much of our enjoyment of it. Burdened by the survivor's vague sense of guilt and unworthiness, we couldn't give ourselves over to the pleasures of collegiate life with the sybaritic abandonment of our older brothers during the twenties. As a class, we were terribly nice, wholesome boys. I say 'as a class,' but I definitely was not one of them. I shared none of their feelings of guilt over my family's wealth—and I was very far from being a nice, wholesome boy. On the contrary, it was universally suspected that I had crawled out of one of the nastier stories of Arthur Machen or H. P. Lovecraft. "You see, my dear, in those innocent days I was accounted a dope fiend."

Franklin shrugged indifferently.

"I won't make more of it than it was. I was a boy and yearned to be deemed an original, and experimenting with drugs certainly made me that. If you've read Dashiell Hammett or Raymond Chandler—sophisticated men of the time—you'll know that in those days drug use was associated with depravity of the very blackest kind. In fact, it was such a rarity in middle-class circles that it was difficult even to locate drug dealers. These were not at all like the magnates of today, who handle nothing but what can be moved quickly at a tremendous profit. The dealers of my day—at least the good ones—were rather surprisingly like antiquarian booksellers. Their back room stock wasn't fifty kilos of cocaine, it was five hundred one-ounce phials of truly exotic materials collected from all over the world, each a treasure, each distinctive in its effect. Nowadays I'm sure you couldn't locate even a tenth of the great variety of drugs I sampled during my college career.

"I wasn't, you understand, looking for anything in particular in these substances, beyond novelty. Yet one night I found something, in the leaves of a plant from the interior of Brazil. I'd been told it was a hallucinogen used in the initiation of shamans of the Juruna, a tribe even then nearly extinct and now almost certainly so. Drugs of this sort were always a gamble. In their native habitat they were taken with foods that enhanced their effect, and these were unknown or unavailable to us. And the native users knew precisely what effect to look for, which we didn't, and success usually depends heavily on that. As a result, one's reward was often no more than a heavy sleep, perhaps with a vivid dream or two.

"That appeared to be the case with this drug, which was a smoke. I fell asleep and had an extraordinarily vivid dream. In fact, it was so vivid I didn't think it was a dream at all. I was quite certain I'd slipped out of my drugged body and was standing in the middle of my room, fully awake. I expected to see my body in the bed, sleeping away, and was surprised when it wasn't.

"I went out into the hall. A few yards away two black men in police uniforms were opening a door to another student's room. I didn't know what to make of this, and went over to see what was happening. The interior of the boy's room had been transformed into a prison cell, and the boy himself was handcuffed to a bunk, naked. The two black men were taunting him, pinching him, poking him with their nightsticks, and he was writhing, begging them to stop. Then they started taking off their clothes, and I hurried away. I didn't have any clear idea about what was about to happen there, but I wanted no part of it. The rest of the house was quiet, and I went outside.

"There was a meadow where the street should have been. I entered it and, soon came across a boy and his mother sitting beside an ornamental fish pond. Suddenly a small bird flew up out of the water, then another and another, and within a few moments the air was filled with birds rising out of the pond, and I realized that each bird was a drop of water. This phenomenon seemed to fill the child with an ecstatic delight, but it quickly ended when the last bird flew away and the pond was empty. A chauffeured limousine drew up, and a man I recognized as the actor Adolphe Menjou stepped out of the back and ushered the boy and his mother inside. They drove off, and the meadow dissolved and became a street once again.

"I won't bore you with a full account of that night's adventures. I went from one strange episode to another without even slightly understanding what I was seeing. When, in my dream, I was tired, I returned to my room, fell asleep, and on awakening was myself again. I didn't give much thought to the experience. Though they were uncommonly vivid, the things I'd witnessed seemed like perfectly ordinary dreams, and I attached no significance to the fact that they were peopled almost entirely by strangers. Then, returning from the library in the evening, I ran into the student who had figured in the first episode. I told him jokingly that he should watch who he admitted to his room. Giving me a rather belligerent look, he asked what the hell I was talking about, and I said, 'I'm talking about the two black men with clubs who visited you last night.'

"I didn't in the least expect him to understand what I was talking about—it wasn't even a shot in the dark. I was just maintaining my reputation as an exotic conversationalist. But understand it he plainly did. The blood drained from his face, and he cringed away from me as if I'd seared him with a blowtorch. Before I'd fully registered his appalling dismay, he'd scurried into his room and slammed the door.

"Even with this hint, I didn't begin to suspect the truth. I just assumed I had subconsciously noted a masochistic tendency in his behavior and had randomly worked this into my dream.

"I had enough material for another smoke, and I used it that night, hoping for more interesting results. I was a bit disappointed when, after drifting off to sleep, I awoke in my room, exactly as before. Once again I felt I'd left my sleeping body behind, was completely conscious and in control of myself and my environment. I left the room half expecting to find the two black policemen in the hall, but it was empty. I went to the student's room and without hesitation opened the door; it was just a normal room tonight and was untenanted. It was only later that I realized *why* it was untenanted; although he was sleeping, the boy was not as yet dreaming and so was absent from the realm of dreams.

"During that night's journey I decided, as a matter of experiment, to visit someone I knew, a young professor of English. I found him outside his apartment house—perched comically on the eraser end of a giant pencil standing in the middle of the street. He was stranded perhaps fifty feet up in the air—and he was truly stranded, because the only way he could keep the pencil balanced on its point was to sit right where he was. As soon as he tried to rescue himself by climbing down the side, the pencil began to topple, and he had to scramble back up to the top. I thought it was an amusing metaphor; it was well-known that he'd spent years working on a paper that was vital to his career—but, rather than risk submitting it to one of the scholarly journals, he kept revising it endlessly.

"The next day, I decided to test an improbable theory. I caught the professor after one of his classes and asked him if he'd ever managed to find a way down off the pencil. For a moment he just blinked at me without comprehension, then he got it and his jaw dropped down to around the middle of his chest. Naturally he wanted to know how the devil I'd learned about a dream he hadn't even mentioned to his wife, but I was too excited to bother with explanations. I rushed back to my room and called the dealer who'd supplied the drug. He told me he had no more of it and might never have it again.

"I was disappointed but not in despair, because I knew a little of how these things are used in shamanistic cultures. As they view it, there exists a special realm of power that the shaman can reach and master to his benefit. It is a vast realm comprised of many interconnecting principalities, and to each of these there is a path, which is hidden to ordinary vision. The function of any drug is simply to open the shaman's eyes to one of these paths. Once he's seen it for himself, he should, in theory, be able to find it on his own thereafter—without having to resort to the drug.

"I knew exactly where I'd been. The drug had taken me along the path and left me fully conscious in one principality of the shaman's realm of power—the principality of dreams. Now that I knew such a thing was possible, I felt sure I could do it on my own. After all, I visited that principality nightly in my own dreams—but only passively, rather like a clueless tourist limited to the movements prescribed by his guidebook. I felt that all I had to do was become *aware* of where I was. I had to be able to look around and say, 'This must be the realm of dreams. I can step out of the dream I'm having and order this reality to suit myself.' Then I could throw away the guidebook and enjoy the freedom I'd had under the influence of the drug.

179

"It was easy enough to imagine. Achieving it in fact was another matter. It isn't enough just to tell yourself very firmly that the next time you dream you're going to be aware that you're dreaming. It must become an obsession, so much so that the determination to achieve awareness-of-dreaming becomes *itself* the subject of dreams. Then one night—almost inevitably, I think—you find yourself in the midst of a dream and *wondering* if you are in the midst of a dream.

"That's all it takes: the slightest suspicion. Almost instantly—just on the basis of the suspicion—you sense a new sort of vitality and alertness in yourself. You're no longer just passively wallowing in sleep; suddenly you're filled with purpose. You have a hypothesis to test; if you are in fact in the realm of dreams, then certain things should be possible that are not possible in the waking world. You test the hypothesis . . . and then you *know*. And this knowledge sets you free—instantly, totally. Oh, at first you're a bit clumsy, like a lifelong cripple abruptly given the body of an Olympic athlete. It takes a while to discover how much or little exertion is required to perform the feats of a godling."

Franklin's eyes glowed with pride.

"Oh, yes. A godling. That's what I am in the realm of dreams. But what does that make me in the waking world? You might imagine it makes me nothing—but you'd be wrong. I am, in a way, the most powerful man in the civilized world.

"Does that statement strike you as grandiose? If it does, it's because you haven't had a chance to consider what I am capable of. In your own dreams, you travel across the world at the speed of thought, you visit the past and the future without hindrance, you converse with persons you could not possibly meet in waking life. All these things I can do as well; but I can do them *consciously* and *deliberately*, which you can't. If I wish to, I can meet with the President and ferret out the nation's most carefully guarded secrets; he will tell them to me happily. There is literally no secret I cannot learn, provided it's housed in a living mind. But, to tell the truth, I've never spent much time at this.

Secret knowledge is worth having only if you make use of it, and I have no taste for that; it's too much like work.

"The entire realm, alas, is never under my hand at once, and this is why I say I am a godling there and not a god. I can only be in one place at a time, can only focus my attention on one matter at a time. Nevertheless, within any given locale in the realm of dreams, I am truly like a god, ordering all to my pleasure: conjuring events, conjuring people, sending delight to one, terror to another. And through dreams I extend my power into the realm of waking reality. A *suggestion* offered by night becomes a *hunch* by day—a hunch in the subject's conscious life; repeated night after night, it becomes an obsession. Things I want done by day are associated in dreams with blissful rewards. Things I don't want done are associated with calamities and horrors. And if such tactics fail, there are others less subtle— but these you can readily imagine for yourself."

Franklin Winters sighed and sank back into his chair. He closed his eyes for a moment and then looked up with a smile.

"A few years ago, Ginny, you asked me quite ingenuously if I were a monster. Now you have your answer. Of course I'm a monster. The beast who stands at the center of the maze is always a monster.

"I've talked for quite a while now, my dear, and a pause is in order for both of us. When I return—"

Ginny cut him off. Then, without a word, she walked into the kitchen and began making a pot of coffee.

XXV

"I THINK I UNDERSTAND MOST OF IT," Greg said, breaking a silence that had lasted for more than half an hour while Ginny organized a sketchy breakfast and they ate it.

"There are parts of my own story you haven't heard," he added, and told her about the dunning phone call that had come after the dream at Armando's and about the gun that had been produced after the "suicide" dream at her father's house.

"Obviously," he said, "it was your father himself who called me posing as the bookkeeper from Armando's. And, posing as me, he set Phil Dobson to searching out the Reising Target Automatic." He shook his head in grudging admiration. "I must say, they were devastating tricks. I was ready to call in the men in the little white coats and have them take me away.

"But here's something I don't understand. Franklin didn't try to stop us from meeting—he practically *arranged* for us to meet. I mean, if he hadn't been putting you in my dreams for a week before the design show, I might not have talked to you at all. What sense does that make?"

"You've got it all wrong, Greg. He *wanted* us to meet, *wanted* us to fall in love."

"But why? That's crazy."

Ginny shuddered. "You haven't got the point of his little demonstration yet. It wasn't meant to warn *you*. It was meant to warn *me*. He's shown me exactly what it's going to cost to become involved with anyone but him."

"Good lord." He closed his eyes, thinking, and shook his head. When he looked up, Ginny was staring into her coffee cup, her jaw propped on a fist.

"So what do we do now?" he asked.

She gave him a twisted smile. "The demonstration's over, Greg. I guess we shake hands and say good-bye."

"Don't be silly. I won't do that."

"You won't, huh? You'll put up with another night like last night? And another one after that? And another one after that? How long do you think you'd last, Greg? A week?" He said nothing. "My mother lasted for two years—but Franklin wasn't giving her his full attention."

"You know this?"

She nodded. "It's on the second half of the tape."

"He actually admitted it?"

"He didn't admit it, Greg. He bragged about it. As one monster to another."

"He thinks *you're* a monster?"

"Of course. What else can the offspring of a monster be? He assures me I'll be reconciled to it once I've been initiated into the delights of monsterhood."

"What else does he say?"

"Oh," she said, jauntily waving a hand in the air, "he talks a lot about his plans for us. His—" She shook her head. "I don't want to discuss it, Greg. He's insane."

"Nothing that could help us?"

"Nothing."

"I know it sounds feeble, but haven't you explained to him that what he wants isn't going to happen?"

She twitched her shoulders in a weary shrug. "I told you— he's insane. He's perfectly sure that, once I get over my girlish scruples and accept the inevitable, I'll be happier than I ever could have imagined. No amount of reasoning, no amount of pleading can shake him from that."

Greg stared out into the brilliant sunshine of a perfect summer day for a few minutes. "You realize, of course," he said at last, "that he's depending on us to be less ruthless than he is. He's depending on us to throw up our hands in despair and meekly give up."

"Yes, I suppose he is. What else can we do?"

"Be as ruthless as he is."

"All right. And what would we do if we were as ruthless as he is?"

"I don't know. I haven't had a whole lot of practice being ruthless." Ginny's shrug said, *This is hopeless.*

"Is there anyone he cares about besides you? Anyone we could put pressure on?"

She thought for a moment and shook her head. "I'm sure there isn't. He's been almost a total recluse for years."

"Well . . . is there anyone he depends on?"

"In what way?"

"In any way. For example, does he have people who look after him—take care of the house, do the cooking, and so on?"

"There's a housekeeper and a handyman, yes. At least there used to be."

"Could you command any loyalty from them?"

"God," she said, blinking. "I don't see how. What do you have in mind?"

"Could you get in touch with them, convince them that Franklin is ruining your life, and then . . ."

"And then what?"

"I'm not sure. I'm just groping for some leverage somewhere."

"Not there, believe me. These people are nothing to him. The most they could do is quit, and if he couldn't replace them, he'd do without them."

He took in a long breath and pushed it out. "You never heard from your mother after coming to Chicago?"

"No, why?"

"I thought maybe she wrote a letter—something that could be used against him somehow."

"Sorry. She didn't."

"Jesus. Let's see. You mentioned a man who looked after you when you first arrived in Chicago. Something Herne. From the way you talked, it sounded like he knew what was going on with your father."

"He may have. Unfortunately, he died while I was still in school."

He grunted, then produced a hollow laugh. "Do you know what Agnes told me—at the 'sanatorium' down there in Kentucky? She said that when God was passing out gifts and came to me, he said, 'Let's give this one lots of brains but no survival instincts at all.'"

"So?"

"Ginny, that was *your father* putting those words in her mouth. That's the way he's come to perceive me."

She said nothing.

"What do *you* think, Ginny?"

"I don't know. Maybe you do tend to. . ."

"Yes?"

". . . leave yourself wide open."

"I don't remember to put on my bulletproof vest when I go out to play."

"'That's right."

"Shit. Well, hell. How would I handle this thing if I was Michael Corleone?"

"Who?"

"The son of the Godfather. The guy who had half the Mafia assassinated while he was attending a baptism."

"Oh."

"Shit. You know how I'd handle it. If I was Michael Corleone, I'd go to New York and kill the bastard."

Ginny laughed harshly. "Are you going to do that?"

"I don't know. I'm thinking about it."

She shook her head, her mouth twisted in a defeated grin.

"I'm serious, Ginny. People who do what your father's doing forfeit certain rights, it seems to me. He's put our backs to the wall, given us no way out—except to kill him. We didn't set that up, he did."

"I see. You're trying to justify it intellectually. And if you manage that, do we zip off and kill him?"

"I don't know."

185

"Forget it, love. Ruthless people don't bother to justify hurting people, they just go ahead and do it. You're not cut from that pattern—and I'm glad you're not."

"You mean . . . you wouldn't go along with it?"

Ginny laughed. "That's a little like asking a woman if she'll marry you *if* you decide to ask her. Definitely out of bounds. I didn't give you this decision to make, Greg, and I sure as hell won't react to it in advance."

"No, I see that. I'm sorry." He stood up and jammed his hands in his pockets as if they were useless objects.

Ginny stood up too.

"Greg, don't torture yourself about this. It isn't your responsibility to make everything come out right. I tried to warn you that you *couldn't* make it come out right, but my heart just wasn't in it. If anyone should be apologizing, it's me."

He shook his head miserably. "I've got to think."

"I know."

"I'll call you later."

Ginny, making it easy for him, nodded.

XXVI

"DIRECTORY ASSISTANCE. WHAT CITY?"

"I think it would be Saratoga Springs," Greg said.

"What name?"

"Franklin Winters."

"I have a Franklin E. Winters listed in Woodford."

"That's him."

She gave him the number, and his hand trembled as he made a note of it. Without giving himself time to think about it, he dialed it and listened to the buzz at the other end.

Ten hours of stewing over the problem had gotten him nowhere, because, of course, it *wasn't* a problem: problems have solutions. This was simply a choice he had to make—an unthinkable choice between renouncing Ginny and confronting Franklin Winters with the intention of doing murder. Neither was acceptable to Greg Donner—to Greg Donner as he was. Ultimately, since he wanted to think about *something*, he thought about what he was, and concluded that he wasn't enough of *anything* to handle this crisis. An easier-going man would kiss Ginny good-bye and think, *Better luck next time, ole buddy*—or blow Franklin's head off and think, *Well, the bastard had it coming*. A more righteous man would kiss Ginny good-bye and think, *Not even for you will I do murder*—or blow Franklin's head off and think, *I've done a service to the world.*

It was just like grappling with one of Laocöon's snakes: whatever end of the thing he grabbed left an end free to strangle him.

At two in the afternoon he opened a bottle of bourbon. Whatever he decided would be a disaster, so it didn't seem to

187

matter whether he decided it rationally or irrationally, drunk or sober. By five he'd degenerated to the point of wondering what his father would do (renounce Ginny, unquestionably) and what a *real* man would do (murder her father, unquestionably); he alone seemed afflicted with this moral paralysis. At seven he remembered that, after all, there was a third choice—but couldn't recall what it was; at last it came to him: he could simply decline to make a choice.

He made a pot of coffee, put a frozen dinner in the oven, and, while it cooked, took a long shower. Halfway back to sobriety, he realized it was true: he wasn't going to make a decision tonight; it simply wasn't possible. He had to buy himself a respite—and there was only one person to buy it from.

He made another pot of coffee and drank it watching the sky grow dim over the lake. When he was able to make out the glow of lights from the Michigan side, he decided he was ready to tell lies to Franklin Winters.

"I imagine you know who this is," he said when Franklin was on the other end of the line.

"Sorry. I've always disliked telephone guessing games."

"This is Gregory Donner."

"Ah. Ginny's *beau*."

Greg, struggling to control himself, let a long breath out through his nose. "You can stop now. You win. I give up."

"You're giving Ginny up?"

"Yes."

"One of life's little tragedies."

"Yes."

"All the same, a wise choice. You would have found her too much for you."

"Yes."

"I presume you've told Ginny your decision."

"I'll tell her in the morning."

"I see. Then you haven't *quite* made up your mind."

"I've made up my mind."

"Then why put it off? You'll sleep better knowing the nasty work is done."

"You think so?" Franklin hadn't given the words "sleep better" any special emphasis, but his meaning was clear.

"Very definitely. But it must be done. You mustn't leave any grounds for false hope. That would be cruel."

"All right."

"You must break it off finally and completely. For all time. Without reservation."

"All right."

"You understand that I'll *know* if you don't. From *her*."

"Yes."

"Then that's all right."

"Yeah. Look. I want to hear this from you. You'll leave me alone if I do this?"

There was a disdainful snort on the other end of the line. "Do you imagine you're personally of some importance to me, young man?"

"No."

"I think you do, because I've taken a certain amount of trouble over you. Let me disillusion you. You are nothing to me, not even a plaything. You were simply a handy tool, and I used you to make a point. Do you understand?"

"Yes. That's what Ginny said."

"Naturally she would not misunderstand. As a person, I bear you no ill will whatever. Go in peace. Marry a shop girl and be happy."

"All right."

The line went dead, and Greg replaced the receiver. He stood thinking for a moment, then picked it up again and dialed Ginny's number.

An hour's rehearsal, he knew, wouldn't make it any easier.

She answered, sounding exhausted, and he said, "Ginny. . . I'm sorry."

"I know. It's not your fault."

"Is there no way at all? No way to hide?"

"No, Greg. You know there isn't."

You must break it off finally and completely. For all time. Without reservation. I'll know if you don't. From her.

"Then I suppose it would be best if. . .

"Yes?"

"There's no point in torturing ourselves."

"No."

"What I mean is . . .

"Greg, you don't have to spell it out. I understand. Good-bye is good-bye. There's no other way to do it."

"I'm sorry."

"Don't say that any more, Greg. Don't even think it. There's nothing you could have done and there's nothing I could have done—except keep you out of it."

"I'm not sorry about that."

"Good-bye, Greg. Be well."

"You too, Ginny."

And that was that.

Feeling numb, he went into the kitchen and poured himself a drink.

I can always take it back in the morning, he told himself.

Or simply let it stand, another part of him answered.

He hurled his glass against the wall and it exploded in a glittering shower. He stood for a few moments watching the amber stain drool down the wall. Then he took out another glass and reached for the bottle.

XXVII

WHEN HE AWOKE THE NEXT MORNING, Greg found that his confusion had evaporated during the night, leaving behind a hard crystal of certainty: he'd rather live out his life knowing he was a murderer than wondering if he was a weakling. It wasn't something he was proud of or ashamed of. It was a simple fact about himself, and he wasn't going to chew on it to see how he liked it; he swallowed it whole and went on. He showered, skipped breakfast, dressed in a suit and tie, and went to his bank, where he withdrew a thousand dollars. Then he stopped at a phone booth and dialed Ginny's number.

"Don't talk," he told her, "just listen. Everything I said last night I had to say to get your father off my back. I called and convinced him I was backing out, but that wasn't good enough. I had to convince you as well. Do you understand? It was the only way I could get a night's rest."

"I *don't* understand. What are you going to do?"

"Plan B, Ginny. I'm putting Plan B into effect."

"No."

"Yes."

"Listen. Will you listen?" He said he was listening. "It's too much, Greg. I thought about it too—yesterday, when there wasn't anything else to think about. It's too much for one person to do for another. I can't accept that much."

"I'm not doing it for you, Ginny. I'm doing it for me, so I can go on living with myself."

"Look." She paused. "If I could get us out of this mess by cutting off my right hand, would you let me do that?"

"No. But that's not the same. If I thought I was mutilating myself, I wouldn't do it."

"Greg, please . . ."

"Look, Ginny, I've made my decision. Now let's have yours. If you tell me not to go, I won't go. Easy. Just tell me not to go, and that'll be it. Good-bye, and the best of luck to us both."

"Christ . . ."

"Well?"

"I won't tell you *not* to go."

"Fine. Then I'm on my way."

"Wait a second. If you're going, I'm going."

"No."

"Then don't go. I mean it. You're not the only one around here who has to live with himself. Do you understand?"

Greg laughed. "Yes, I guess so."

"Besides . . . I have a gun. My mother slipped it into my luggage before I left."

He thought for a moment. "Yes, that would simplify things. All right. I'll be there in ten minutes. See if we can get a direct flight to Albany."

Ginny made the journey to Albany in a furious silence because Greg, when they'd picked up their tickets, had reserved seats on a 6:15 return flight. It wasn't the reservation itself that infuriated her; that could easily be changed. It was his offhand approach to the thing, his bland assumption that it was all going to be a snap—and this she couldn't challenge until they were alone three hours later in a parking lot outside the Albany airport.

When they found their rented car, Greg handed her the keys and said, "You'd better drive."

"Thanks," she replied in a tone that made him ask if something was wrong.

When they were inside the car, she said, "Yes, there's something wrong. Are you thinking we're going to do this in broad daylight?"

Greg was startled that she'd thought anything else. "It's out in the country, isn't it?"

"It's out in the country, yes. But this isn't Wyoming, you know. The house isn't sitting in the middle of a section, it's sitting in the middle of forty acres. There are people around."

"Can we get in without being seen?"

"Yes, probably."

"Then what's the problem?"

"The problem is that a shot's going to be heard, Greg."

"Okay. But wouldn't it be heard at night as well?"

"Yes, but—"

"And wouldn't a shot at night be more suspicious than one in the daytime?"

"Yes, but—"

"I mean, there are lots of things to shoot in the country in the daytime, but the only thing you shoot at night is your fellow man."

Ginny collapsed with a bitter sigh.

He said, "Couldn't we talk about this while we drive?"

She started the car and headed away from the airport. "Why," she asked, "are we in such a fucking *hurry*?"

"Because I don't see any point in dawdling. I want to get it over with and go home."

"I see. We'll explain that to Mike and Mrs. Doherty."

"Who are they?"

"The handyman I told you about. And the housekeeper."

"Oh. Would they be there on a Sunday?"

"Maybe not. If they are, I guess we can just kill them too."

"Take it easy, Ginny. There must be some way of finding out."

"I suppose we could call Franklin and ask."

He gave her a long, baffled look, which she ignored.

"Ginny, what is it? What's the matter?"

She kept her eyes on the road ahead for a couple miles. Then she said, "Sorry. I guess this is just my reaction to a bad case of nerves. Go on with what you were saying."

"Well, what I was saying was: How do we find out where Mike and Mrs. Doherty are?"

Ginny sighed and thought for a moment. "I can call Mrs. Doherty's house and see if she's there. I don't know Mike's last name, so I can't call him."

"I just doesn't seem likely he'd be working today. Did he ever work on a Sunday when you were there?"

"I don't think so."

"Besides, we'd see a car or something, wouldn't we?"

"I suppose so."

"Then I'm not going to worry about it."

He reached into the back seat, opened the suitcase that had ridden in the baggage compartment of the jetliner, and took out the pistol Ginny's mother had given her. He'd looked it over at the apartment, but he did it again now. It was a solid piece of work in blued metal, a Smith & Wesson revolver. He didn't know the caliber but assumed it was a .32 or .38. He broke it open, took out the cartridges, and examined them one by one. He closed it, pulled the trigger; the hammer drew back, snapped forward with a satisfactory click, and the cartridge chamber advanced. It seemed to be in working order. He reloaded it and put it in the glove compartment.

"What exactly are we going to do?" Ginny inquired.

He'd already asked if she still had her keys to the house; she did. He now asked if there was a spot to park that was out of sight of both the road and the house; she said there were plenty. He settled a few more points and outlined a plan. Then he asked how long it would be before they arrived.

"About half an hour."

He glanced at his watch and nodded without betraying the fact that his stomach had lurched at the news.

There wasn't another car in sight when they pulled into a road that looked to Greg like a footpath in a forest. A small, weathered sign at the side read: WINTERS, PRIVATE.

They had stopped at a shopping mall outside Saratoga Springs to check on Mrs. Doherty. Since Ginny's voice might be recognized, Greg made the call; he learned that the housekeeper was at home cooking dinner and was no relation to a mythical aunt of his in Poughkeepsie. When he returned to the car, Ginny was nowhere to be seen, and he'd fumed for ten minutes until she returned with her purchase: two pairs of rubber gloves. He frowned over them but finally said, "Yes, I suppose so."

They bounced their way up the road for a hundred yards, and Ginny pulled into an opening in the trees.

"This is about halfway to the house," she said.

He nodded and checked the time. It was 3:27, local time. He got the revolver from the glove compartment and slid it into the side pocket of his suit jacket. Then, feeling ridiculous, he put on the rubber gloves and opened the car door.

Keeping well back in the undergrowth, they circled the house, with the expected result: there was no sign of Mike or any other visitor. Bypassing the front door, which opened more or less directly into the living room, Ginny led them to a side door, which opened into the kitchen. Greg stepped inside with gun at the ready. The room was empty.

After a few moments, the door at the right, leading to the dining room, opened a crack, and Franklin Winters stuck his head in.

He frowned at them with startling composure and said, "I *thought* I heard someone come in back here."

Neither Ginny nor Greg had arrived with an opening line.

Franklin threw open the door to the dining room.

"You may as well come in," he said, and turned to lead the way into the living room.

"Hold it," Greg said.

Franklin gave him and his gun a scornful glance and said, "Poop." Then he disappeared into the living room.

Greg gave Ginny a baffled look, and she said, "Don't let him take charge. He'll turn it into a social call."

He shrugged helplessly and followed the old man, who was heading toward an arrangement of three mismatched chairs. One of them was the leather wingback in which he'd taped his video letter to Ginny. He sat down in it and crossed his legs.

195

"Don't sit down," Greg said.

"Why ever not?" he snapped. "If you're going to shoot me, I may as well be comfortable."

"Get up."

Franklin gave him a disgusted look. "Poop," he said again, and smiled. "I don't recall ever having used that word before, but it seems wonderfully apt in these circumstances. I wonder if it's even in use today. In my boyhood it was a genteel four-letter word." he shook his head sympathetically. "You look damned silly standing there in those rubber gloves, with that gun in your hand."

Greg felt damned silly.

The old man leaned forward to peer around him. "Ginny, why don't you make us some coffee?"

Ginny, still standing rigidly in the doorway, said, "Greg, don't let him talk."

"And poop to you too, my girl," Franklin said, sinking back into his chair. He looked up at Greg and murmured, "You know, I dislike having people hover over me like this." He nodded to a chair opposite. "You could just as easily shoot me from there."

"Greg, for God's sake!"

"Cut it out, both of you," Greg said. "Ginny, go see if you can find a shovel and some work gloves." Glancing over his shoulder, he saw that she hadn't moved. "Did you hear me?"

She disappeared down the hallway. Greg slipped the gun into his jacket pocket and sat down.

"So," the old man remarked cheerfully, "you deceived me."

"I deceived you."

"And what exactly is your grand scheme at this point?"

When Greg merely stared at him, he said, "Gracious! Am I really to be terminated with extreme prejudice? How thrilling!" Then, suddenly serious, he leaned forward and said more quietly, "Be careful not to let it get out of hand."

"What the hell do you mean?"

"We both understand why you're here, young man. You're here to save face, to reestablish yourself as a hero in Ginny's eyes. I made a mistake, I grant you; I pressed my advantage too forcefully. I should have left you with some graceful way out."

"Some graceful way out of what?"

"Come now, don't be dense. Believe me, I'm not sorry you've come. Ginny will remember your affair less bitterly if it ends with this gallant little gesture of yours. But if you humiliate yourself by trying to carry the gesture too far, she will be humiliated as well, and that would be unfortunate."

"I see. And what is it you have in mind?"

"Take a month to bring it to an end any way you like."

He gave him an incredulous frown. "You really are something."

"When Ginny comes back, just tell her we've come to an understanding. She'll accept that with relief, believe me."

Greg shook his head.

A few moments later Ginny appeared to say that the shovel and work gloves were waiting at the backdoor.

He walked over to Franklin's chair and told him to get up.

Franklin gave him a disgusted look and stood up. "Remember what I told you," he muttered. "Don't let the gesture carry you away.

"Let's go," Greg said.

Franklin sighed.

Twenty minutes later they fought their way out of the tangled underbrush into a clearing under a massive oak tree, and Greg said, "This'll do."

"Idiot," the old man hissed. He sat down on the grass, leaned back against the trunk of the oak, and closed his eyes.

Greg shed his jacket and slipped the work gloves on over his rubber gloves. Then he picked up the shovel and looked around for some place to begin. Since it all looked equally unpromising, he set the point of the shovel in the ground in front of him, put a foot on the blade, and pushed. The point sank about an inch, and he pushed again. After a third try, he turned the first spadeful.

Behind him, Franklin sighed, bored. Ginny stood awkwardly nearby, shivering in the deep afternoon shadow.

Forty-five minutes later, he was bruised, stiff, dirty, and blistered, and the hole was three feet wide, three deep, and six long. He straightened up painfully and blotted the sweat on his face with a shirt sleeve.

"That's good enough," Ginny said.

He stepped out of the hole and looked at it critically. "Do you think so?"

"Yes."

He checked the time and winced: 4:50. He stripped off the work gloves and tossed them into the hole, thinking he'd be justified in taking a short break. Just a few minutes to catch his breath. He looked at Ginny and found her watching him doubtfully.

He worked the gun out of his jacket pocket.

"'I shall despair,'" Franklin cried out in mock agony. "'There is no creature loves me; and if I die, no soul will pity me.'" He leered up at them. "*Richard the Third*. Appropriate, no?"

Greg told him to stand up.

"Poop," he said, looking away disdainfully.

"Stand up," Greg repeated.

Franklin sneered at him. "Young man, you are tiresome. Dreary. Boring. Your role models come from comic books."

Greg hovered over him, the gun pointed down at his forehead. "Get up."

"'Get up!'" he screeched. "'Get up or I'll plug ya where ya sit, ya varmint!'"

Greg's hand began to shake.

The old man leaned to one side to look around him. "Ginny, you can't possibly be in love with this big booby."

The gun suddenly seemed to weigh twenty pounds, and Greg had to bring up his left hand to steady it.

Pull the trigger, he told himself. *Now*.

Franklin Winters looked up at him and shook his head in disgust. "Stop making a fool of yourself and go home."

Now. Greg's finger refused to move.

Now!

There was a shattering roar and the gun leaped in his hand. Franklin's head snapped back against the tree, and for a moment Greg thought he'd missed. Then he saw that the bullet had caught him in the crown of the head and had exited through the temple, spattering the tree trunk with blood and brains. He gulped back a wave of nausea, straightened up on wobbly legs, and looked down at the gun in his hand. A thin wisp of smoke curled from the barrel as if to answer his unspoken question: *Yes, it was this gun, in your hand, that did it. It wasn't a lightning bolt.* With a convulsive lurch he turned and hurled it into the underbrush. Listening for its crash, he saw Ginny out of the corner of his eye. He wanted her to say something, but he didn't know what.

He waited for a moment, then reached down, grabbed the old man's ankles, and started to drag him toward the hole.

They caught their return flight with twenty minutes to spare. They still hadn't exchanged a word, but the pressure of Ginny's arm, wrapped around his as they walked to the gate, seemed to convey what he needed to hear.

XXVIII

FILING INTO THE AIRPORT IN CHICAGO at seven thirty in the evening, they were momentarily bewildered. The corridors seemed a chaos of hurtling bodies and clamorous voices. Feeling like astronauts newly returned from a year on the dark side of the moon, they made their way out to the cab line and took their place alongside weary executives and laughing groups of salesmen. After a few minutes of placid waiting, Ginny began to giggle, and Greg put an arm around her shoulders. Their turn finally came and they headed eastward toward Ginny's apartment, headlights flaring around them like lasers in a *Star Wars* battle scene.

When they turned off the expressway into the relative calm of Ontario Street, Greg said, "I think there's something we have to do before we're finished."

"What's that?"

"We have to celebrate."

She gawked at him. "You're joking."

"No. What you celebrate you don't grieve over. I want to celebrate."

"Good lord. But I see what you mean. Okay."

"I'll pick you up at ten. Let me be old-fashioned this once."

"No. You want to celebrate. Okay, that's a good idea—let's celebrate at the Casbah. But let me meet you there. Let me make an entrance. Then it'll be . . . like the curtain going up on the next act, starting a new part of our lives. Okay?"

He put an arm around her and held her till they arrived at Dearborn Street.

* * *

"God, you're breathtaking," he said, meeting her just inside the lounge. "In less than two hours I'd forgotten."

Ginny laughed. "It's the dim lights — and a lot of expensive makeup carefully applied. Without them I'd look like the strung-out hag that I am."

After a moment a dark, mustachioed giant in evening wear appeared at their table, and Greg said, "Nuri, I'd like you to meet my fiancée, Miss Ginny Winters."

The waiter bowed gracefully. "I'm very pleased to meet you, Miss Winters."

"You *are* my fiancée, aren't you?" Greg asked. "I mean, you are my sunshine, my only sunshine, and the apple of my eye, and my everything, and all that other stuff, so I just took it for granted you were my fiancée."

Ginny smiled up at the waiter. "He has a knack, hasn't he? Have you ever heard a more romantic proposal of marriage?"

"Never," Nuri replied solemnly. "I believe it's a record for the Casbah."

Greg and Ginny laughed delightedly. "In celebration, may I bring you something from the bar? With my compliments, of course." They said he could.

An hour later Ginny said, "There's something you might be able to reassure me about if you wanted to."

"I definitely want to."

"I didn't let myself think about this beforehand, but I knew it'd have to be thought about sooner or later . . ."

She stared into her drink for a while. "Little Ginny Winters has made the man she loves into a murderer."

He grunted. "Yes, I can see that's something you'd have to think about, but you can stop thinking about it now. Because nobody can make me into anything. Not even you. I may not be much, but what I am I make myself. Entirely on my own."

"Go on."

"I'm stubborn as hell, Ginny, and you may as well know it. If you think you made me into a murderer, then you're just deluding yourself. What I am is my own doing, and you'll never be responsible for that. That's something you can count on."

"Okay," Ginny said. "That sounds like something worth counting on."

And that was the last time they ever talked about the killing of Franklin Winters.

Two weeks later, Ginny got a call from a deputy at the Saratoga sheriff's department asking if she had any information about her father's whereabouts. His whereabouts?, Ginny asked. Wasn't he at home? She was told that, according to his house-keeper, he'd disappeared. Ginny said that her father was an eccentric and not a very considerate one. If he was gone, she was sure he'd turn up again when it suited him.

When another month had passed, the deputy called back to say that her father was still missing. She asked him what he intended to do about it. "Not much I can do, actually," he said. "No sign of violence at the house. If someone wants to leave home and go someplace else, it's none of our business. No reason to think it didn't happen that way."

Ginny wondered if she was being a bit too offhand about it.

"I told you he's an eccentric, but, to be honest, he's never been *this* eccentric. He likes the comforts of home too much."

"Do you want to list him officially as a missing person then?" the deputy asked. She asked what that meant exactly. "It means we put out a description, a photo. These'll be checked against unknowns who show up at hospitals and morgues."

"That sounds harmless enough."

"Harmless?"

"I mean, if he prefers to stay missing, he wouldn't appreci-ate being the object of nationwide manhunt." He assured her there'd be nothing like that. He advised her to find someone to stay in the house, and she said she'd attend to it.

As months passed she received calls from her father's attor-ney, stockbroker, and accountant; she told them to do the best they could.

The body in the shallow grave remained undisturbed.

XVIII

BY THE TIME GINNY AND GREG WERE MARRIED the following spring, the harrowing events that had ended with the murder of Franklin Winters had become encysted within plainer and brighter memories. If recalled at all, they were like scenes from a horror movie: frighteningly realistic, but too fantastic to be real. Soon after their return to Chicago, Greg became involved in a new project, one of the silliest in his experience—a book linking the personal computer and fitness. The editors who had bought the idea were sure a book bringing these buzzwords together would be an irresistible piece of merchandise, and to Greg's surprise (and disgust) they were right. *Compute Your Way to Fitness* was destined to make slow, steady gains, and even bobbed up into the best-seller lists for a few weeks, and this did Greg's reputation no harm (even though the names on the cover were those of his consultants).

The *Bizarre* project went forward in the fall, and he managed to train three clipping services to recognize the sort of stories he wanted for it. The publisher wanted someone's name on the cover, and he reluctantly agreed to let them use his. It was a decision he regretted when, four months after publication, the book began appearing on the remainder tables. To everyone's annoyance, Ted Owens—who had denounced it as a turkey even as he sold it—did a lot of jocular gloating over its failure.

Bored with writing for hire, Greg took out a few weeks to work up a proposal for a mass-market series, Time-Life style, called *The Genius of America*, a celebration of American daring, defiance of tradition, ingenuity, and resourcefulness, and sent it to Ted. The next time Greg talked to him, he asked what he thought of it.

"Not bad," Ted said without enthusiasm. "I was wondering why you sent it to me."

"Well . . . can't you do something with it?"

"Like what?"

"Like sell it."

"No way."

Greg asked why.

"Because, if you were an editor at Time-Life, you might talk your boss into spending a hundred grand to test the idea. But from the outside, forget it. Hopeless."

"You couldn't sell just the idea itself?"

"Don't be such an innocent, Greg. If they buy an idea to test from an outsider, this is like admitting they don't have any ideas of their *own* to test. Which they're not about to do even if they don't, which they do. If you see what I mean."

Greg said he saw what he meant. Ted gave him a verbal pat on the head and told him to stick to writing.

Ginny's star, already well above the horizon when Greg met her, continued to rise, attracting bigger jobs and bigger budgets. Within a year of their marriage, she was working with two assistants in a Michigan Avenue office. The following year, when one of the city's best-known designers retired, she was invited to become one of the prestigious Chicago 27, which placed her near the top of her profession nationwide.

At the next annual design awards show, she collected an impressive number of prizes—and was noticeably pregnant. When the baby was born in July, they named her Anne, after Ginny's mother, and began to plan a "Coming Out" party for the Labor Day weekend—as much to celebrate their new Gold Coast apartment as the baby's arrival. Greg was ecstatic over all three—his wife, their sumptuous apartment, and the baby (though Anne seemed so minute and delicate that he was afraid to touch her).

August they declared a holiday from work, and so they nearly worked themselves into a shared nervous breakdown over preparations for the party. The invitation—their first collaboration—had to be a masterpiece not only of wit but of graphic brilliance, and they began by disagreeing fundamentally on its concept. An hour's conversation over it finally degenerated into a shouting match, which so startled them that they reversed themselves completely, each insisting it be done the way the other had originally wanted—so that they nearly had another shouting match advocating each other's idea. In the end Greg found a third approach they both liked better anyway.

The guest list, originally planned for a hundred, grew uncontrollably, on the grounds that if you invite A, you certainly have to invite B, and if you invite B, you really should invite C—and then won't D wonder at being left out? When it grew to three hundred, they eliminated the C's and D's. That left them with a hundred and eighty, and they decided to make it an open house starting at four in the afternoon.

One name hadn't appeared on any list: Agnes Tillford's. After dealing with her as Agnes Jakes, psychiatrist of Glenhaven Oaks Sanatorium, Greg had never felt like renewing contact with her—and still suffered an occasional twinge of guilt over it.

The party was so meticulously planned that, by three o'clock on the day, there was nothing for them to do but sit around wondering whether anyone would show up. At Greg's insistence, a nurse had been hired for the day to attend to the baby. At Ginny's insistence, drinks would be served in real glasses, food on real plates, and one of the caterer's assistants was unpacking them while another was installing a special dishwasher in the kitchen. The caterer himself was fussing over the food arrangements and table decorations. Ginny and Greg, feeling superfluous, were sipping Virgin Marys, having resolved to stay more sober than their guests. They figured the last stragglers would leave by ten-thirty or eleven and planned to slip off to the Drake for a nightcap while the caterer restored order to the place.

At 3:59 Greg suggested they run off to Kankakee for a romantic weekend. "When we get back, we can call someone and find out how the party went."

At 4:20 the first guests arrived, and for half an hour it was a small, intimate affair. Then the flood began, and Ginny and Greg became full-time hosts, greeting new arrivals, making introductions, starting conversations, pulling loners into groups, spending a little time with everyone and almost none with each other.

By eight o'clock the early arrivers had departed, and most of the people who were going to come at all were already there and settled in to make an evening of it. The party was under way and self-sustaining, and Greg and Ginny could have left without being missed. Feeling relieved and happily exhausted, they found an unoccupied corner of a sofa and allowed themselves the luxury of being guests at their own party for a few minutes.

"Not bad," Greg observed. "Everyone seems to be having a good time."

"You can hardly miss if you have enough good people, booze, and food together in one place," Ginny said.

"Did you meet the guy over there?" He nodded toward a tall, carelessly dressed man in animated conversation with one of Ginny's assistants.

"I don't remember. I don't think so."

"He's the head of Britannica's mail order division. I've done a few things for him. He just offered me a job on the editorial staff."

"Really? Doing what?"

"Directing projects. Sort of a managing editor."

"What sort of things do they do?"

"Same as Time-Life, basically."

"Are you interested in a staff job?"

"I'm not sure. Who's that, by the way?"

"Who?" she asked, looking around.

"The tall, distinguished-looking gent by the window. Gray suit. I know him from somewhere, but I can't place the face."

"I don't see him."

"He's talking to one of your clients, the lady in the forties dress."

"Oh." She paused, frowning. "Good heavens, it's Bruce.

Bruce Something . . . Eddison, two *D*'s, no relation to the inventor. He's a physician. You remember—we met him at Blinkers."

"Of course. Did you invite him?"

"No. He must have come with someone else."

"I'll go over and say hello."

As Greg approached, Bruce gave him a smiling glance, which the woman in the forties dress followed to its destination and took as an excuse to drift away. The two men shook hands.

"It's nice to see you again," Greg said.

"Nice to see you," Bruce replied. "I see things have worked out wonderfully for you and Ginny."

"Yes, they have indeed."

"Could I possibly have a peek at the cause for celebration?"

Greg shook his head apologetically. "We had to make a policy about that for the party. No visits to the nursery, without exception. Otherwise . . . You understand. Ginny'll bring her out later, if she's awake."

"Of course. By the way," he added a bit guiltily, "I hope you don't mind my crashing your party. I came with a designer friend."

"Not at all. In fact, I'm sure Ginny would love to get together with you some evening—just the three of us, I mean."

"That's very kind of you. You're a lovely pair."

After a moment of awkward silence, Greg remembered the doctor's curious collection of family portraits and asked if he'd made any interesting additions to it.

"You remember my strange passion? My friends know better than to ask me about it, lest I pull out my current favorite and start expounding its virtues."

"You have one with you? Let's see it."

"You're sure? I don't want to become a bore in the midst of your party."

Greg laughed and told him to drag it out.

Looking around guardedly, Bruce drew a black-and-white photo from his inside breast pocket and handed it to Greg. "This one's quite special, as you'll see," he said.

Puzzled, Greg studied the picture. Without the visual cues of color, he couldn't make it out. Its masses of light and shadow seemed to resist forming a recognizable image. With an embarrassed laugh, he held it at arm's length to see if it would come together, but it didn't.

Bruce smiled. "The shadows make it a bit of a puzzle. It's like an optical illusion. You have to sort of twiddle your eyes to get the right of it."

Greg brought the photo closer, gave it a slight turn, and suddenly a dappled shape at the left became a familiar figure: it was Ginny, leaning forward as if about to take a step. At the right, with his back to Ginny, was Greg himself, bending awkwardly, the gun in his hand inches away from the forehead of Franklin Winters, sitting on the ground, his back against a tree.

Gagging, Greg reeled back and tried to thrust the picture away from him. Conversation in the room died away and fifty pairs of eyes turned to him apprehensively. Still gagging, the photo still in his hand, he felt his back arch convulsively. His eyes rolling up into his head, he toppled backwards into an endless darkness.

And woke up screaming in his room at the Glenhaven Oaks Sanatorium.

PART
FOUR

XXIX

THE MAN IN RICHARD ILES'S ROOM was howling, was bellowing incoherently, and for a few moments the nursing staff was stunned into immobility, then routine and training took over. A nurse was dispatched to summon a couple of male attendants. Another was sent to lock Mr. Iles's door. Another called Dr. Jakes, who listened, gave instructions for the preparation of an injection, and said she'd be on hand momentarily.

By the time she arrived, the roaring had subsided to a low, rhythmic moan. At a nod from Dr. Jakes, one of the attendants unlocked the door and entered. Greg, shrouded in sheets and blankets, was rolling mechanically from side to side in his bed.

Agnes approached, sat down cautiously on the edge of the bed, and put her hand on his shoulder.

"Greg," she said gently.

He looked at her, recoiled, and began howling again.

She held out her hand for a syringe and the two attendants immobilized Greg while she administered the injection.

Later that morning, when Greg regained consciousness, a nurse was on hand to ask him if he'd like some breakfast. He stared at her without interest.

"You'll feel better if you eat something, Mr. Iles. I'm sure of it." His face registered absolutely nothing.

The nurse stepped to the phone and quietly asked that Dr. Jakes be called. When she turned back to Greg she said, "Oh my." Her nose told her he had just wet his bed. After a moment of uncertainty, she decided to wait for Dr. Jakes. She arrived a few minutes later, took in the situation, and asked the nurse if she'd called for assistance.

211

"No, Doctor. I didn't know how you'd want to handle it."

"We'll handle it in the usual way." She nodded and left, and Agnes spent a moment looking at the man in the bed. "Shall we get you into some dry pajamas, Greg?" she asked.

He looked vaguely out of the window.

"You have another pair, don't you? Where do you keep them? I'll get them out for you." He gave no sign that he'd heard. "Come on, Greg, hop out of bed. We'll get you a fresh mattress and put some dry clothes on you."

She threw back the covers, but apart from a brief dis-interested glance, he took no notice of her.

"You know, Ginny and I had a long talk yesterday, Greg," Agnes said half an hour later.

They were sitting in front of the window, Greg in a fresh set of pajamas and a bathrobe. He hadn't resisted being moved, cleaned up, and dressed, but neither had he helped in any way. He stared at the blue hills outside, his hands folded in his lap.

"She realizes now, of course, that the things she said to you yesterday were very hurtful. . . . You must be very angry with her," she added, hoping to provoke a denial. She provoked no reaction at all. "I'm sure she'd like to have another chance to talk to you, Greg. Would you like that?"

Nothing.

"Shall I see if I can arrange it?"

As if profoundly bored, he sighed and crossed his legs.

"I know you must be feeling very discouraged at this point, Greg. I certainly would be if I were you. To tell you the truth, I probably wouldn't be taking it as well as you are."

But neither self-pity nor flattery seemed to be tempting baits. Agnes sighed and rubbed her eyes. "You know," she said brightly, "I believe I could do with a bit of lunch. How about you, Greg? I left specific instructions for them to hold your booth for us. You look as if you could do with a drink. I know I could. How about it? Maybe we could ask Mr. Orsini to join us. Yes? No?"

Not a flicker of interest.

"Well, let's have a tray sent in then. Rumor has it the prime rib is especially luscious today. Very tender, very juicy. I know you like it rare." The doctor watched carefully for any sign of salivary reaction: swallowing, working of the tongue. There was none.

She sighed, went to the phone, and ordered lunch for two. "And," she added, "if possible, I'd like Alan to serve it. . . . Yes, I realize he doesn't come on till five. I said *if possible*. If he's on the grounds and is willing, tell him it would be a special favor to Mr. Iles."

She turned back to Greg and smiled. "Isn't that nice? Alan's going to bring us lunch." She sat down and put a hand on his knee. "I hope you'll cheer up a bit for Alan's sake. You know, he's had a lot of trouble of his own lately." Agnes sat back in her chair. "Oh yes, indeed. The girl he was engaged to—a perfectly lovely child—has contracted leukemia. Dreadful. In spite of this, Alan still wants desperately to marry her, but she refuses to put him through the agony to come. Tragic. But you'd certainly never guess it to look at him, would you? He's so unflaggingly cheerful and supportive of everyone. Still, I worry about him— truly. Behind that happy-go-lucky facade is a young man capable of being deeply hurt, and he's in a sensitive condition just now, as you can well imagine, I'm sure. He'd be very upset to see you in this state, Greg. Terribly upset. Especially now, you understand?"

She went on to describe the shattered wedding plans, the bridal gown returned, the weeping mothers, and the couple themselves, struck down by grief but doing their best to smile through it bravely, until she heard Alan's cheerful whistle approaching down the hall.

"Please don't let Alan down," she urged. "It would mean so much to him. Just a word, Greg. Even a nod, just to let him know you understand what he's going through."

Greg stared blankly out of the window.

Alan sailed through the door, a large tray of dishes poised

over his shoulder. "Good morning, folks," he said, gracefully wheeling the tray down onto the bureau. "Or afternoon, or whatever it is. You're looking a little down today, Mr. Iles," he observed as he began setting their places.

"Yes," she said. "He's had a bit of a shock. Very like yours."

Alan paused, blinking. "Very like my what?"

"Shock."

He stared at her without comprehension.

"How is your lovely fiancée, Elizabeth, Alan?"

His eyes widened.

"The doctors give her no hope, I understand. No hope at all." She nodded meaningfully in Greg's direction.

"Oh," Alan said enthusiastically. "Right. No hope at all!"

"Do you hear that, Greg?" She looked up at Alan. "Greg has just now learned that your fiancée has leukemia."

"Oh?"

Agnes groped for the next line. "I'm sure Greg's sorry about it, but . . . he's not feeling very well himself just now. Are you, Greg?" She reached across the table to put her hand on his. "But you'd like to say something to Alan, wouldn't you, Greg? I mean, if you weren't feeling so blue, you'd like to talk to Alan, wouldn't you? You don't have to say anything. Just nod, Greg. Please. It really upsets Alan to see you like this."

She shot the waiter a look.

"It sure does," Alan said earnestly. "Makes me feel, uh . . ."

"As if you didn't care about him, Greg. As if he were insignificant to you. As if nothing mattered to you but your own problems and your own feelings."

Without taking his eyes off the window, Greg yawned.

Agnes sighed and slumped back in her chair.

"Shall I serve now, Doctor?" Alan asked quietly. She nodded. "The prime rib is really super today, Mr. Iles. So they tell me." He set their plates down before them and looked critically at the low table. "These tables really aren't much good for dining."

"It's all right, Alan. Thanks."

214

"Shall I, uh . . .?" The waiter made knife-and-fork motions over Greg's shoulder.

She shook her head glumly. "Thanks, Alan. It was kind of you to serve us during your off-hours. I appreciate it as a personal matter."

"Any time, Dr. Jakes." He paused at the door. "And you get better in a hurry, Mr. Iles. You hear? I'll save your table for you. You come to dinner tonight and I'll buy you a bourbon on the rocks. Personally, from me to you."

The doctor smiled her thanks for the effort. Alan gave her a wink and disappeared into the hallway.

"Did you hear that, Greg?" Agnes asked, cutting into her prime rib. "You're a popular guy around here. You're needed. People depend on you." She stifled a sigh and went on eating in silence. When she was finished, she leaned back in her chair and studied Greg's impassive face for a few minutes.

"When you woke up this morning," she said at last, "you were screaming, Greg. Do you remember that?"

He blinked and went on staring into the hills.

"Why were you screaming, Greg?" Agnes waited for a reaction through a full minute. "Did you have a dream?"

Greg sighed.

"Did you have a dream like the other one? Were you back in Chicago?"

His lips parted fractionally, then closed again.

"That was it, wasn't it, Greg? You dreamed you were back in Chicago." But whatever reaction she'd provoked had subsided. Greg was once again gazing listlessly out of the window, and she paused to tug thoughtfully at an earlobe. "That was my fault, you know. Entirely my fault. I can see that now. Yesterday I told you you'd be living on Lake Shore Drive again in no time, and you acted on this as a *command*, Greg. You're intelligent enough to appreciate this. You were in a state not far different from hypnotic trance, and when I told you you'd soon be back in Chicago, you took this as a command to return to that dream. Do you understand?"

215

If Greg understood, it was a matter of complete indifference to him.

"What happened in your dream, Greg? Was Ginny in it?" It seemed to her that his eyes closed for a fraction of a second longer than a blink. "Did things . . . turn out well for you and Ginny?" His lips tightened slightly, and she paused to reflect on this. "Was Ginny *happy*, Greg?"

His jaw muscles tensed and almost imperceptibly his head quivered in a negative gesture.

"You shook your head then, Greg. Does that mean she wasn't happy or that you don't want to talk about it?"

Greg closed his eyes, and after a few moments his face relaxed. He opened his eyes and, once again calmly gazed out into the hills.

"You don't want to talk about it. That's it, isn't it? You and Ginny were happy together in Chicago, and you want to cling to your dream. As long as you say nothing here, do nothing here to admit that this is real, you can go on living forever in that dream. Isn't that it, Greg?"

But Greg had receded to a point beyond reach of words.

"I can understand that very well," she went on. "All of us are tempted at one time or another to retreat from reality into the security of our dreams. Everything's perfect there. Nothing can go wrong there, nothing can . . . You shook your head again then, Greg. Why? Did something go wrong in your dream?"

The doctor watched in alarm as Greg's stare became fixed and his muscles locked into rigidity.

"We won't talk about it right now, Greg," she said hastily. "It's all right. We won't talk about it anymore. Everything's all right. *Shit.*"

She grabbed the phone and ordered a muscle relaxant on the double.

Greg had stopped breathing.

At bedtime she visited him again. Greg was lying on his back staring up at the ceiling, his hands folded across his chest.

Earlier, the nurses had managed to pour a couple of glasses of orange juice into him. Agnes judged that a day's fast would do him no harm. If it came to that, they could begin feeding him intravenously the next day. At all costs, she wanted to avoid stabilizing him in his present condition.

She spent a few minutes chatting about this and that, from time to time asking an innocuous question. Finally she began the routine for putting him into a hypnotic trance, but, locked in his own private reality, he simply continued to stare up at the ceiling. She decided she'd have to rely on suggestion alone; using drugs, she could put him into a sleep too deep for dreaming, but, since she didn't know exactly what she was dealing with as yet, she hesitated to use them.

"You're going to have a good sleep tonight, Greg," she murmured soothingly. "A very long and restful sleep, and if you have any dreams, they'll be very happy, pleasant dreams. You will not dream about Ginny tonight or about your life in Chicago. If you dream at all, you'll dream about other things, and these will be pleasant and soothing. And when you wake up in the morning, you're going to feel cheerful and invigorated. You'll see. You're going to wake up and look around and see that you're young and strong and healthy and attractive, and that the world's a beautiful place to live in. Do you hear me, Greg? I'm sure you do. You're listening to everything I have to say, and you know I'm right and that I have your best interests at heart."

For some twenty minutes, she went on gently repeating her injunctions. Then she wished him a good night, adding that she expected to see him in the dining room the next morning, turned out the light, and left, closing the door quietly behind her.

Though there was nothing to see there, Greg continued to stare up at the ceiling until he fell asleep a few minutes later.

XXX

AT TEN THE NEXT MORNING, they were once again seated in their usual places before the window. A front had moved in during the night, and a steady, sluggish rain smeared the glass beside them. It seemed to make no difference to Greg.

"Now, Greg," she said gently, "we really must talk about the dream you had the night before last. You mustn't let our talking about it upset you. There's nothing to be upset about at all. But you mustn't keep it to yourself. That's the point, really. You must share it with me, so I can help you with it. You understand that, don't you?"

Greg, his hands folded in his lap, stared out at the rain.

"You told me yesterday that you were in Chicago again in that dream. You didn't mean to tell me and probably don't remember telling me, but you did anyway. In your dream, you were in Chicago. Do you remember?"

She paused, but he gave no sign of having heard her.

"You were in Chicago, Greg, and I'm sure Ginny must have been with you there."

Greg sighed, but then he sighed frequently; it seemed to have nothing to do with what he'd heard.

"She's very beautiful, isn't she, Greg? I'm afraid I don't know her well, but I can see why you're so much in love with her." She leaned forward and lowered her voice. "You want very much to be with her, don't you?"

A small crease of annoyance appeared on his forehead.

"You want very much to be with her, and you were with her the other night in Chicago, weren't you?"

His jaw muscles tensed.

"Everything's all right, Greg," she crooned. "Everything's

fine. I want you to be with Ginny too. Ginny is very good for you, and it's good you were together the other night in Chicago. That's right," she said as he relaxed again.

She paused uncertainly, like a surgeon about to cut into a body in a darkened room. "So you and Ginny were together. And you were happy, weren't you?" She studied his face and thought she saw a barely perceptible nod. "But then something happened. I don't know what it was, Greg, but you mustn't let it worry you. It's completely over and in the past."

With a slight flick of his head, he seemed to deny this.

"Yes, everything's all right now, believe me. Ginny is fine, and she'd like to talk to you again.

Another flick of the head.

"Greg, listen to me. Whatever happened in Chicago is all over now. You can tell me about it. Whatever it was, I'll understand it. I want very much to understand it. Between the two of us, we can handle it. There's nothing to be upset about." She paused doubtfully. "Now I'm going to see if I can find out what happened, but you needn't be upset. I'm going to ask some questions and you mustn't become excited if I ask the wrong ones. Do you understand, Greg?"

He stared at the rain-bleared window.

"Did something happen to Ginny in Chicago, Greg?" she asked quietly. "Was she hurt in some way?"

Greg sighed, bored.

"Good. I'm glad nothing happened to Ginny. She was well when you . . . left her? She was happy?"

His lips twisted disdainfully.

"Yes, that was a stupid question. Of course she was. But *something* happened. Something that upset you. But you needn't be upset by it now, of course. Whatever it was is over and done with. You know that." Agnes paused and rubbed the bridge of her nose thoughtfully. "Did something happen to *you*, Greg?"

He closed his eyes for a long moment.

"That's it, isn't it? Something . . . upsetting happened to you in your dream. I understand. Dreams can be frightful sometimes, but it's all over now . . . Did the person you call the follower appear in this dream, Greg? Did he do something to you?"

Greg's nostrils flared in disgust.

"No, not the follower." The doctor sighed and sat blinking for a few moments. "In your other dreams, Greg, some very strange things happened. You remember. Someone called to collect a debt you didn't owe. Someone tried to sell you a gun you'd dreamed about. These things upset you a lot. Was it something like that?"

His lips were compressed into a stubborn line.

"That's it, isn't it? Something bizarre happened."

The muscles in his cheeks were jumping.

"Something bizarre happened that made you think—"

"*Go away*," Greg whispered savagely.

Agnes expelled a long breath. "You want me to go away?"

"*Yes.*" Although he continued to stare out of the window, his eyes were blazing now.

"Are you sure? I don't want to leave you if you're upset."

"*Go away!*"

"All right, Greg, I'll go. But may I come back in an hour?"

"No."

"Well, then . . . may I come back this afternoon sometime?"

"Yes. Go away."

"Will you talk to me when I come back?"

"Yes."

"You promise, Greg?"

"Yes. *Get out!*"

When he heard the door close, Greg blinked and felt hot tears course down his cheeks.

Two hours later there was a soft knock at the door. When it wasn't acknowledged, Alan entered hesitantly with a tray. "Dr. Jakes said I should bring you some lunch."

Greg, staring into the rain, said nothing, and Alan began setting a place at the table. Greg glanced at what he was doing and said, "No."

The waiter straightened up. "No? You should eat something, Mr. Iles. Really."

"Take it away."

"I could leave it just in case."

Greg closed his eyes. "*Please.*"

After gathering up the silverware and dishes, Alan paused at the door. "Anyway I'm glad you're . . . feeling better."

"Thank you," Greg whispered.

When Agnes arrived at three, Greg acknowledged neither her knock nor her presence in the chair across from him. Although blowing rain continued to streak the window, the clouds were breaking up, and his eyes were fixed on the sky.

"You said you'd talk to me," she pointed out. He shrugged. "But you'd rather be left to your brooding."

"Yes."

"You've had four hours to brood in, Greg, and it wouldn't help to give you another four or another forty. At the end of it, you're going to have to face what has to be faced."

He said nothing.

"Among the things you have to face is that you're alive here and now in a rest home in Kentucky, and you've had a miserable shock. The woman you love has rejected you."

Greg shook his head.

"She hasn't rejected you?"

"No."

"Greg," she said gently, "you can't hold onto the dream. Or rather, you *can* hold on to it—but only at the expense of your sanity and your life. Is that what you really want? To sit here in this room staring out the window for the rest of your life, lost in a fantasy?"

He set his jaw stubbornly.

"I see. It *is* what you want. And just a couple of days ago you were all in a rush to be released so you could return to normal life. You demanded to know what program I was going to put you through before giving you your freedom. But now you want to sit here and feel sorry for yourself forever, while you gently rot away among your delusions. Poor, pathetic creature."

"Shut up."

"I'll surprise you, Greg." She stood up. "I will shut up. I've managed to drag you back from the edge of cataplexy and psychosis, but if you actually prefer to throw yourself into that chasm, go ahead. I have other patients to attend to, and most of them, unlike you, are frantic to return to health."

She turned to go, and Greg whispered, "Wait. Tomorrow."

"Tomorrow what?"

"Give me till tomorrow morning."

"No, Greg. That's what the addicts say. 'Give me till tomorrow. Give me till tomorrow, but let me be drunk today, let me be stoned today.' And so they stay drunk and stoned forever, because it's never any easier tomorrow. And it won't be any easier for you tomorrow either. It'll probably be harder, in fact, because self-pity is like any other habit—the longer you indulge it, the stronger its hold becomes."

Greg's face twisted. "I don't want to."

Agnes sat down. "You don't want to what?"

"I don't want to . . ."

"Yes?"

". . . be here."

"I know, Greg. I know. But you *are* here."

"I don't want to be."

"I know. This is why you won't eat, won't talk. To do these things is to admit that you're *here*." He nodded. "I understand, Greg, I really do. And, strangely enough, it's all right. You don't have to want to be here. You just have to acknowledge that you *are* here."

"I don't want to do that either."

"I know. But, you see, you've already done it. You can't rescind that acknowledgment now. You couldn't even if you tried." Agnes waved all this away. "That phase is finished, Greg. Now we can begin to do something constructive."

"Such as what?"

She sighed and settled back into her chair. "Do you remember the conversation you had with your wife two days ago?"

"Two days ago. Christ." He closed his eyes as if in pain. "Yes, I remember."

"Ginny was deceived by your appearance of health and stability, Greg. So was I, for that matter. And because she was deceived, she delivered a nearly mortal blow to your ego—and in this case I'm using that word in its technical sense, not as a synonym for *pride*. The ego that you identify as Gregory Donner was shattered and for a few hours was replaced by that of Richard Iles. During those hours you were once again the person you were when you arrived here—completely docile, completely malleable—as empty of emotional tone as a doll. Do you remember?"

"No, not really. I remember sitting in the restaurant talking to Ginny, and then at some point everything became . . . vague."

She nodded. "We brought you back here, and I gave you some emotional first aid. I tried to resuscitate Greg Donner. I was afraid that . . ." She waved this away. "At one point, I foolishly told you, by way of encouragement, that you would soon be back in Chicago, living on Lake Shore Drive, and everything would be fine again. And evidently when you fell asleep that night you made this prediction come true—in your dreams."

Greg sighed. "Yes."

"I'd like to hear what happened in that dream."

He shook his head wearily. "What difference does it make?"

"I won't know what difference it makes until I hear it, Greg. What I do know is that in the morning you woke up screaming hysterically."

"I woke up screaming hysterically because I didn't want to be here. I didn't want to believe this was happening to me *again*, that I'd . . . lost everything *again*."

"I understand. Nevertheless . . ." She leaned forward

earnestly. "Please trust me on this, Greg. This dream represents a gap in my knowledge—in our collective knowledge—of the development of the person known as Gregory Donner. I'm not just indulging my curiosity here. If I'm going to help you back to health, I must know what you know. This dream may well be a vital part of your personal history."

"Okay," Greg said wearily. "But not right now, okay? We could do this tomorrow, couldn't we?"

"Greg, I'd really rather not put it off. In all my experience, in all my reading, I've never known therapeutically significant developments to occur at this terrifying rate. This is why, in the last twenty-four hours, I've literally assaulted you. I've battered and browbeat and tricked you relentlessly. I've taken unforgivable risks to force you to talk to me—precisely because I don't know what the devil's going on here. Your condition is so obviously volatile that I felt the risks had to be taken—and I don't dare say to you now, 'Sure, Greg, take your time. Another day doesn't matter.' It *may* matter. I just don't know."

He let out a long, hopeless sigh. "Okay." he closed his eyes for a few minutes, then shook his head and muttered, "God."

Then he began.

When he was finished, the doctor closed her notebook and shook her head sympathetically. "I'm sorry, Greg. Truly. I can see now why you reacted so violently. You had everything you wanted—and thought it was all nailed down for good." She checked her watch. "Shall we take this conversation to the dining room? You must be famished."

Greg shrugged indifferently.

"Hey, Mr. Iles!" Alan said, greeting them at the door, "This is great!" He picked up a couple of menus and led them to Greg's table. "You remember I said I was going to buy you a drink?"

"I remember," Greg said. He managed a feeble smile as he slid into the booth.

"It'll be right along."

"Bring some bread first, Alan," Dr. Jakes said. "A bowl of

224

soup. On a stomach as empty as his, a drink is definitely not recommended."

"You got it, Doctor."

Alan disappeared, and Agnes took out her notes and began to read through them. After a few minutes she looked up and said, "Do you understand what the dream is about in a general way?"

"No. I haven't thought about it . . . as a dream. I don't *want* to think about it that way."

"I know, but you're going to have to make a decision now, Greg. You can hold on to it, try to pretend it *wasn't* a dream, or you can try to face it, understand it, and go on from there."

"Go on," he said wearily.

"If you feel like I'm rushing you, you're absolutely right. I want to get this thing out in the open, where you can't brood over it—and the sooner the better."

"I *told* you to go on."

"Okay . . . Waking up here a week ago was a devastation. You'd lost a career you loved, a woman you loved, a life you loved. Then, briefly, it seemed that at least one of these things would be given back to you—Ginny. But again reality rose up and slapped you in the face. Unlike the Ginny of your dreams, your wife rejected you. Utterly. Finally. Why? This was the question you were asking yourself when you fell asleep two nights ago after your shattering experience with her. Why? Why had the splendid life of Gregory Donner been so ruthlessly destroyed? You had to have an answer to this question, and you sought it in the realm in which you were born—your dreams."

Greg sighed.

"And why would the answer be there, Greg?"

"I don't know."

"I think you do, but you're not ready to look at it. Greg Donner has no memory of the life that Ginny and Richard Iles shared; there is nothing in *your* memory that could explain her rejection of you. For this, you needed to draw upon the memory of Richard Iles—and that you can only do in dreams."

"I don't see what you're saying, I'm afraid."

Agnes thought for a moment. "You remember the dream you had in which you found Ginny in bed with an old man."

"Yes."

"My interpretation of that dream—dead wrong, as it turned out—was that Richard Iles was worried that Ginny might prefer the old you to the new you. It's obvious now that the person he was worried about was not the old you but rather Ginny's father. In that dream Richard Iles was telling Greg Donner something *he* knew that you didn't—that your rival for Ginny's love was Franklin Winters."

Baffled, Greg shook his head.

"Greg, where is Ginny right now?"

"In New York, I suppose."

"That's right. Living with whom?"

"Her father."

"Why?"

"I don't know."

"Come now, Greg, time to be realistic. I gather that the Winters family is well-off. She can presumably afford to live where she *prefers* to live."

"I suppose so."

"And where does she *prefer* to live?"

He frowned. "Okay. She prefers to live with her father."

"Exactly. According to what she told me before she left here, Richard Iles knew when he went to Russia that Ginny would be gone when he returned. He knew that she would be in New York, living with her father."

"Yes."

"So you see. When you went looking for the truth in the realm of dreams two nights ago, Richard Iles gave it to you. Franklin Winters is the source of all your miseries. He has never stopped controlling Ginny's life—and because he controls Ginny's life he controls yours as well. He can make her do whatever he wants—and because he can make *her* do whatever he wants, he can make *you* do whatever he wants. Do you see?"

"I guess so."

"Franklin Winters, according to Richard Iles, exerts a kind of magical power over your lives and your destinies. And if you want to win Ginny and control your own destinies, you're going to have to do what?"

"Kill him."

"Not literally, I think. You're going to have to kill him *as far as Ginny is concerned*. In other words, if you want Ginny, you're going to have to get Franklin Winters out of her life once and for all. Once you've done that, you'll have everything you want. This is what you were told in your dream the night before last."

"Yes, I see."

"I hope you also see that the situation isn't as hopeless as you originally thought."

"What do you mean?"

"I just told you, Greg. You *can* have everything you want— if you're strong enough"

"Strong enough?"

"Strong enough to take Ginny away from her father."

He shook his head. "If she really prefers life with him to life with me . . . to hell with her. She can have it."

"You're not emotionally ready to make such a decision, Greg. Give yourself a little time to get your priorities in order. If you really want her—and I think you do—you may not feel like giving her up so easily. Believe me, you're not the first man who's had to vanquish a father to have a wife."

Greg shrugged. "Not my style."

Laughing, Agnes shook her head. "'Not my style.' That's the spirit. Keep it and I think you'll be fine. Now, are you in the mood for something to eat?"

He was surprised to find that he was.

XXXI

THIS EPISODE, TRAUMATIC IN THE SHORT RUN, had one beneficial effect for the long run: it brought home to Greg his vulnerability and made him appreciate the support he received within the Glenhaven Oaks Sanatorium. He stopped agitating for immediate release and no longer thought of his stay in terms of days or weeks. Within a few days, he told Dr. Jakes he was ready to accept the name Richard Iles, but warned that he would continue to *think* of himself as Greg Donner; Agnes saw no harm in that, at least as a transitional matter, comparing it to a security blanket that would be abandoned when it was no longer needed.

In the beginning they met as doctor and patient three times a week, and Greg talked. After a month of this, Agnes had to agree that (apart from a tendency to wear his heart on his sleeve) there was nothing much wrong with him, and they agreed to meet twice weekly for a while. By the fall they were meeting once a week and spent the hour more in gossip than in any form of psychotherapy. On Halloween he told her he thought it was time he took his leave of the Glenhaven Oaks Sanatorium.

She asked, "Whose life are you going to head?"

"My own."

"Don't play games. Are you going to lead Richard Iles's life or Greg Donner's?"

"I don't know anything *about* Richard Iles's life."

"Very true," Agnes said. "And?"

"And what?"

"You don't know anything about Richard Iles's life, and therefore . . . what?"

He shook his head. "I don't know what you're trying to make me say, Agnes."

"Where were you thinking of settling, if I may ask?"

"Well . . . Chicago."

"Okay. I'll ask it again. Whose life are you going to lead?"

"And I'll answer it again. My own."

"And out of all the cities on earth, living your own life, you want to be in Chicago."

"That's right. I *like* Chicago."

"You do."

"Yes, I do."

"You've lived there?"

He was opening his mouth to say, "You *know* I have," when he stopped and glared at her.

"You've *lived* there?" she repeated.

"All right, Agnes. What do you want me to say? That I want to live in Seattle? I've never lived in Seattle either."

"But you *have* lived in Chicago, haven't you? How else could you know that you like it?"

"Okay. I *think* I'll like it."

"Based on what? Your reading? What you've seen in movies?"

"Knock it off, Agnes."

"*You* knock it off. You think you'll like it based on your dream experiences as Greg Donner. That's whose life you're going to lead, isn't it?"

Unable to think of any reply, he got up and stalked out, his back rigid with indignation.

There was (he was sure) some profound injustice in Agnes's approach to this thing, but by the time his next appointment rolled around he hadn't found a way to articulate it. Being unable to fling it in her face (as he'd hoped to do), he settled for informing her, rather coldly, that he wanted to make arrangements to leave as soon as possible.

After a few minutes, during which she simply sat and stared at him, he said, "Well?"

"I'm thinking, Richard."

"What are you thinking about?"

"My obligations."

"Go on."

"We've never talked about it explicitly, but I assume you realize that you were legally *committed* to this institution. Your wife signed a piece of paper committing your welfare to us, making us answerable to her. Do you understand?"

"Yes."

"Since that time there's been a change. I didn't think it would matter to you and didn't want to bother you with it, but now I guess I'd better. After talking to you, Ginny evidently decided it wasn't appropriate for us to be answerable to her alone. She wanted to share the responsibility with someone in your immediate family, namely your uncle, Bruce Iles. In the circumstances, I have to agree that this makes sense."

Greg frowned. "Go on."

"What we now have is a piece of paper that makes the two of them *jointly* responsible for committing you to this institution and that makes us answerable to both of them."

"Shit," Greg said.

"Not at all—at least from your point of view."

"Why? What do you mean?"

"I told you I was considering my obligations. If you'll think about it, you'll see that they're a little different now. If I was answerable only to your wife, I'd have to discuss your request for release with her; I'd have to tell her that, since what you have in mind is to settle in Chicago—out of contact with either her or me—I'd strongly recommend against it at this point. I'm sure she'd take that recommendation. But the fact that I'm now answerable to your uncle as well changes all this. Since your uncle lives in Chicago, part of my argument against your release is diminished."

"I don't quite see what you're saying."

"In discussing the matter with your uncle, I'd have to point out that, though I'm opposed to releasing you now, I'd be *less* opposed if I had his assurance that he'd keep an eye on you. If he gave me that assurance, I'd then have to call your wife and tell her so. Under these circumstances, she might very well direct me to release you."

"In spite of your reservations."

"That's right."

"In other words, if I'm prepared to insist on it, I can probably get out of here."

Agnes nodded.

"But you really think it's a mistake."

"Yes, I do. I think you intend to go to Chicago and recreate the fantasy of your dreams."

"How can I persuade you that that's not my intention?"

"Let's say that nothing you've said so far persuades me to the contrary."

He sighed and spent a moment in thought. "Look, you once said that the Greg Donner dreams were a kind of wish fulfillment on Richard Iles's part. They represented what he wished he'd done with his life. Right?"

"Right."

"Well, they also represent what I want to do with *my* life. What am I supposed to do, Agnes? Stop wanting what I want? Will you let me go with your blessings if I tell you I want to go to Zurich and become an apprentice cuckoo clock maker?"

Agnes chuckled. "I'd be more inclined to do so, yes, because I'd feel reasonably sure you weren't following some deeply hidden agenda that was going to get you into trouble."

"You think I'm following some deeply hidden agenda?"

"I think you may be, yes."

"And what's on this deeply hidden agenda, Agnes?"

"That's precisely the point, Richard. I can't know what's on it, because—if it's there—it's hidden, even from you."

Grappling with this amorphous phantom, Greg found his face growing hot. "This is why psychiatrists never lose an argument, Agnes. There's no way on God's earth I can *ever* prove I'm *not* following a hidden agenda—even if I sit here for a century."

"I know that perfectly well, Richard," she said with an

unruffled smile. "This is why I'm prepared to suppress my misgivings and let you have a shot at doing what you want—provided your uncle agrees to keep an eye on you. Under those circumstances, I couldn't reasonably refuse."

"Well, great," he snapped, getting to his feet. "Are you going to call him or shall I?"

"I'll call him. Today."

"Thank you. Will I have a chance to talk to him?"

"Certainly. I'm not going to rush this, Richard. I'm going to ask him to pay us a visit so we can discuss the whole thing."

"Shit."

"Richard, your uncle is a physician himself. If he's going to take on a responsibility, I'm sure he'll want to know exactly what it entails. What's the sudden urgency?"

"There wasn't one before. You've made me feel like an errant schoolboy being released from the reformatory."

"I'm sorry. I don't think of it that way at all, believe me. It's just that I have an important obligation here and want to discharge it in a responsible fashion."

"Yeah, I know. But let's get it over with. Okay?"

"Richard, I'd better warn you. I'm going to argue against your release—but I promise you I won't delay it by a minute if I can help it."

"Fair enough."

Five days later Greg and Bruce Iles occupied adjoining seats on an afternoon flight to Chicago.

Their reunion hadn't been as awkward as Greg had expected. Bruce seemed to grasp the situation more firmly than Ginny had and treated it with casual good humor. As with Ginny, the Bruce of real life was subtly different from the Bruce of his dreams. The pale and rather wistful good looks were the same, but Bruce Iles carried with him an air of disappointment and bitterness that had never hovered around the gentle, courtly Bruce Eddison. If Bruce Iles was gay (as Greg assumed), he would never admit it to Greg—and Greg would never ask. Greg might have counted Bruce Eddison as a friend—Bruce Iles, never; he took his unclehood a little too seriously.

At their conference, as Agnes explained her misgivings, Bruce had listened with so much professional detachment and sympathy that Greg began to despair. When Greg's turn came, however, Bruce had readily (and smilingly) acknowledged the force of his simple counterargument: if you locked up everyone until they proved they weren't following a hidden agenda, the streets would be empty. In the end, he settled it all very easily, with a question directed to Greg: "If I ever become convinced that you're not handling your life in a sane, sensible way, will you accept that judgment? Will you agree to come back here for treatment without making a fuss?"

"Absolutely," Greg said.

Because, after all, he had no other intention than to handle his life in a completely sane and sensible way.

XXXII

IT WASN'T A CHATTY PLANE RIDE, but this was more Greg's choice than Bruce's. Bruce said he must have a lot of questions about the family lost somewhere in the recesses of Richard Iles's memory, but in fact he didn't. His biological parents were people he didn't know, would never know, and felt no need to know. He learned that, after their death in an auto accident in 1966, he and Bruce had been close for a time, and Bruce had served as a surrogate father during his high school years. Greg didn't want to hear about it and was too distracted by his plans for the immediate future to pretend otherwise.

They parted at the airport, since Greg's destination was downtown and Bruce's was Glenview, where he lived. Greg promised to call when he was settled and agreed that getting together soon for dinner was a fine idea; privately, he hoped his uncle wasn't going to start thinking of himself as a probation officer.

A few minutes later the city skyline rose up before him on the horizon and his heart rose up to greet it.

Greg's suite at the Drake was magnificent, and he felt a little underdressed in it. That was something he planned to remedy the following day. He was by now no longer embarrassed by Richard Iles's fortune; he felt he'd earned it in the ordeal of becoming Richard Iles, in shouldering this stranger's future. He couldn't conceive of ever needing to touch the principal; his ready assets, this quarter's earnings, represented an infant fortune in itself.

Over the next week he managed to unburden himself of a sizable part of it in half a dozen Michigan Avenue men's shops, where his visits came to be anticipated as an awesome phenomenon of nature; he was a walking gusher of money. With his hotel closets jammed with suits and shoes, his bureau drawers overflowing with shirts and silk underwear, and more of everything on order (all of this to be handmade), he abandoned the men's shops for the galleries. These he prowled more cautiously, merely doing a preliminary reconnaissance. He nodded mutely over old master drawings, an early Kandinsky, a breathtaking Hans Hofmann, a charming Degas bronze, a luscious small Monet—but left them all alone for now. He needed a place to live first.

In what he'd come to think of as his "second dream," he and Ginny had lived just around the corner from the Drake in one of the older, smaller lakefront buildings that had always put him in mind of the classic apartment houses of Paris. The building was there, much as he remembered it, but he didn't go in to inquire about vacancies; he was pleased to note that he wasn't tempted to.

He was no longer in the mood for Old World Elegance; he wanted something modern, sleek, and open, and so he went to the John Hancock Center and leased an enormous corner apartment with Olympian views of the lake and city. After that, he took himself and a floor plan to an interior designer, who agreed that, with a budget of sixty thousand dollars (not to include fine art acquisitions), they could put together a reasonably smashing living space in the Milanese style; after two weeks of shopping together, Greg was giddily exhausted and fifteen thousand over budget. It was all in place by the middle of December, and he moved in just a week before Christmas. The next day he visited an antiques dealer who specialized in toys, and in the midst of thousands of dolls, banks, fire engines, hansom cabs, nodders, roly-polies, cannons, and puzzles finally found something he liked, a classy gray Hubley trimotor airplane from the late twenties that he had sent to Agnes Tillford to add to her collection. With this, he considered his Christmas shopping done; he'd reconciled himself to the fact that Ginny was out of his life, and he didn't quite see himself exchanging gifts with his uncle.

He and Bruce had met twice for dinner, relentlessly polite affairs; Greg tried delicately to point out that, unencumbered by a family relationship in his dreams, the two of them had been something very like friends. His uncle chose to construe this as an interesting gloss on the nature of dreams, and Greg decided to let it go.

Three days before Christmas, when he felt finally settled, he called Bruce and invited him over for a drink. He was puzzled by his uncle's reaction to the apartment. Walking into the living room, he stopped, obviously stunned, and muttered, "Good lord."

Greg looked around quickly, hoping it all looked reasonably sane and sensible. It did, at least to him. It was extreme, perhaps even a bit weird, with its severe lines and masses in black and white, but—

"Did it *come* this way?" Bruce asked.

Greg laughed and confessed that he'd done it with his own little checkbook.

Once again Bruce said, "Good lord."

It was then that Greg recognized what he was seeing in his uncle's face. To his astonishment, it was *envy*—not over what Greg had assembled here (he obviously detested it) but over the sheer size of the expenditure needed to assemble it. The realization was dismaying, because it had never occurred to him that a physician (and an unmarried one at that) could be anything but wealthy himself. Embarrassed for both of them, Greg invited him to sit down and hurried off to the kitchen to make drinks.

They chatted halfheartedly through a dismal hour and Bruce at last departed with a feeble "Merry Christmas," which Greg returned with an equal feebleness, reflecting that Richard Iles detested Christmas as much as Greg Donner had.

XXXIII

CHRISTMAS WAS A LONG, LONG DAY. He slept late, dressed slowly, had brunch at the Drake, went to a matinée, and came out depressed that it was still bright day. Back in his apartment he settled down with a fat family saga he'd saved specially for that purpose.

Turning the last page at 8:30, he changed clothes and took a taxi to the Ambassador East, telling himself firmly that there was no reason in the world why a lone diner shouldn't have as much fun at the Pump Room on Christmas as on any other day. Whole platoons of captains, waiters, sous-waiters, and sommeliers took turns trying to cheer him up, and he had a thoroughly miserable time.

Falling into bed at midnight, he reminded himself that, if nothing else, it would at least be another ten months before Bing Crosby started moaning again for sleigh bells in the snow.

He woke up with a feeling of glad relief, knowing that the city had by now risen from its hushed trance and was once again open for business, he got dressed and, without pausing for breakfast, went to an Oak Street gallery and purchased a pre-Columbian terra-cotta figure he'd had his eye on. Returning, he installed it on the top shelf of a glass and chrome étagère in the living room and studied it with an interest he could never have felt over something inside a museum case; this one was *his*. It represented a dignitary of the Zapotec culture, from around the time of Christ. Wearing something rather like a diaper, a tall stovepipe hat, a heavy necklace, and a handsome pair of boots, he looked to Greg like a magistrate in a satiric mode. He stood with his legs well apart and his hands thrown up in dismay, his face a mask of horrified astonishment, as if he'd just come upon someone peeing on the altar. Whatever else he acquired, Greg had the feeling this would remain his favorite.

By the end of January, there was nothing heft to buy. He'd spent an agreeable week reassembling the library that had vanished with his dreams. He'd spent another week ordering films for his VCR. He'd spent three in the galleries, bringing home posters by Cassandre and Toulouse-Lautrec, a magnificent figurehead from an eighteenth-century ship, a small primitive portrait of a sea captain from the same period, and paintings by Adolph Gottlieb, Dado, Ernst Fuchs, Jules Ohitski, and, incongruously, Maxfield Parrish.

At the end of the entry hall was stationed an object of which Greg was especially fond: a death cart that had been used in the rather sinister Easter processions of the Penitentes of northern New Mexico. Perched in the cart was a stylized human skeleton, life-size, brandishing a hatchet in one hand and a huge knife in the other, leaning forward as if eager to strike, its emaciated face set in a perpetual shriek of rage. He'd been told that, in the Penitente tradition, this figure was a woman, and he'd dubbed her Matilda. It was plain from her eyes that she saw nothing of what was going on around her in *this* world; what lived in her eyes were visions of another world entirely: the world of nightmare. And so Greg thought her an appropriate talisman for Richard Iles.

When it was all in place, he took a solemn, silent tour of his own apartment, pausing for minutes before each piece. Then he made himself a drink and stood at the vast east windows, looking out over the lake and puzzling over his sudden depression. He realized now that he should have been prepared for it; finishing an exciting project always has to be paid for with a letdown. Worse, he'd foolishly jammed a year's enjoyable occupation into two months and now had nothing to look forward to. And with no one to share them with, his fabulous apartment and its fabulous contents might as well be a suite in an expensive hotel. Richard Iles, whose name was on the lease and on all the receipts, was too insubstantial a person to possess anything. He needed someone who could ratify his existence by saying, "This is *ours*."

By imperceptible degrees he found himself thinking of Ginny, and he sighed, remembering that just a few weeks ago he'd imagined he was reconciled to losing her. He plainly wasn't. In a sense, everything he'd done here from the very beginning had been with Ginny in mind, with the wordless expectation that this bold new statement about himself would force her to revise her estimate of him. He had—as Agnes had predicted—been following a hidden agenda, and it wasn't even a very bright one. Anyone can spend money; Ginny wouldn't be impressed by that.

He spent a few minutes with the yellow pages and, finding nothing much to choose among them, dialed a travel agent on Michigan Avenue to book a flight to Nassau for the following morning. Hotel accommodations? Yes, the best, whatever it was. A suite, of course. For one. Richard Iles, I-L-E-S.

Twenty hours later he presented himself at the Eastern Airlines check-in counter, where he exchanged a set of ostrich skin luggage for a ticket, a gate number, and an order to have a nice flight. With thirty minutes to kill, he wandered around the terminal, had a cup of coffee, bought a Jack Higgins novel to read on the plane, and stood studying the arrivals/departures board for omens.

Then, without knowing exactly why, he returned to the check-in counter and told the agent he'd changed his mind, he wasn't going to Nassau after all. There was a little fuss, but half an hour later he left the terminal with his ostrich skin luggage, got in a cab, and headed back to his apartment.

A light snow was falling, turning the air into a glittering veil over the city.

XXXIV

THERE WAS A LONG PAUSE on the other end of the line, and Bruce said, "I'm beginning to feel like you're avoiding me."

It was a difficult charge to deny, since for two months Greg had been dodging Bruce as if he were a process server.

Bruce said, "You understand that I have a certain responsibility toward you."

"You know, Bruce," Greg said, "I might look forward to seeing you if you could give your sense of responsibility a rest. I mean, I could use a friend, but I really don't need a keeper. I'm a grown man and I've been out here for five months, and the closest I've come to aberrant behavior was to tell a man at Maxim's that his cigar was bothering me. Believe it or not, he didn't even call the maitre d', much less the men in the little white coats. He just apologized and put it out. I don't start knife fights in bars, I don't expose myself in public, and I don't hang around playgrounds with my pockets full of candy. Hell, I don't even mumble on the bus. If you really want to get together, let's just go someplace and have a few drinks like ordinary people, and you can tell me what's happening in your life and I'll tell you what's happening in my life. How does that sound?"

Obviously stunned by this tirade, Bruce agreed that it sounded fine, though from his doubtful tone he might have been agreeing to spend a night freebasing cocaine. They made a date to meet at the Tip Top Tap at six that evening.

Greg went determined to Make a Real Effort with Bruce; he even came ten minutes late to give the older man the psychological advantage of choosing the table, having a drink in hand, and being kept waiting. It didn't help much, and after half an hour of the usual small talk, he decided on a frontal assault.

"Did Dr. Jakes ever tell you how you figured in the Greg Donner dreams?"

"She said something about family snapshots." He thought for a moment. "She said I'd been 'recommended' to you as a link to your family background."

"Did she tell you where we met? We met at Blinkers."

"Blinkers?"

"You know the place?"

"I've been there," his uncle admitted cautiously.

"Why do you suppose my subconscious chose that particular spot as our meeting place?"

"I have no idea."

"Come on, Bruce. It was because at some point in time I formed an opinion about you."

"I don't know what you're getting at," Bruce said, with dignity but not much conviction.

"In the dream, Bruce, you were completely up-front with me, and we got along fine. That's what I'm trying to tell you."

"You can't force someone to be up-front by putting a gun to his head," Bruce said coldly.

"What gun? Look, I'm just saying that in that dream we weren't saddled with being an uncle and a nephew, we were just two people who enjoyed each other's company, and I'd like it to be that way now. Is that putting a gun to your head?"

Bruce glared out over the glittering lights of the city. "What is it you want me to say?"

Greg sighed. "Look, you've interested yourself in my life. Isn't that so?"

"Yes."

"Well, are you *really* interested, or do you just want me to go on lying to you?"

He frowned. "You've been lying to me?"

"Of course. Why shouldn't I lie to you, Bruce? That's the way you've got it set up here. You lie to me and I lie to you. You pretend to be one thing and I pretend to be another."

"What am I pretending to be?"

"The Upright Uncle."

"And what are you pretending to be?"

"The Sane and Sensible Nephew. What else?"

"Are you telling me you're *not* sane and sensible?"

Greg shook his head. "I'm telling you nothing, Bruce. That's the agreement as it stands right now. You tell me nothing and I tell you nothing. I can live with it if you can, but don't expect me to look forward to getting together with you, because I won't."

"I see," Bruce said thoughtfully. "Yes, all right." He sank back in his chair. "So you've guessed the truth about me. What am I supposed to say now?"

"Forget it, Bruce. I'm not interested in wringing admissions from you. I'm just trying to open things up between us so we can talk like ordinary people. Am I the only straight person in the world who knows you're gay? Aren't there others?"

"Yes."

"Well, do you pretend with them that you're some solemn, prissy expert on what's sane and sensible and what isn't?"

"No. Hardly."

"Then why pretend that with me, for Christ's sake?"

"I'm sorry. Have I really been solemn and prissy?"

"Unremittingly, Bruce. From the word go."

Bruce laughed with undisguised embarrassment, and for the first time Greg saw in him something of the charming person he'd known in his dreams.

Later, after a few drinks, they got around to a few confidential admissions.

Much as he had in Greg's dream, Bruce admitted he wasn't a very good or very successful doctor; in fact, he said, he wasn't much good at anything, and secretly fantasied being an English squire tramping his grounds in shabby old tweeds. Greg in turn admitted he was far from being ready to break entirely with the remembered life of Greg Donner. Puzzled, Bruce asked why.

"I suppose because I'm far from being over Ginny. She was mine in that dream, and I just don't want to let her go."

Bruce nodded thoughtfully. "Yes. I didn't know the two of you well. But in the beginning you were . . . a golden couple."

Greg winced and changed the subject.

After telling the waiter to bring a check, he asked if Bruce would like to come with him to the annual design awards show the following month.

"Why?" Bruce asked.

"Well, you might like it." he laughed. "I suppose actually I was thinking there are a lot of attractive designers to meet."

"I'm not in need of meeting any attractive designers, thank you. But why are you going?"

"A sentimental journey, I guess. That's where I met Ginny. In my dream, I mean."

Bruce frowned. "Is that wise?"

"Mooning around in scenes of my fantasies? Probably not."

"I don't think it's something to joke about. It sounds like just the sort of thing Dr. Jakes was worried about."

Greg shrugged, laid a hundred dollar bill across the check, and stood up.

"Here, part of that's mine," Bruce protested.

"You can get the next one."

"But aren't you going to wait for your change?"

Greg said, "It's only forty dollars. Let's go."

A strange look swept across Bruce's face like a puff of wind on the surface of a pond. Then in an instant it was gone, and he silently followed Greg to the elevator. A hundred other sensations were competing for Greg's attention at the time, and he was scarcely aware of having seen it. A few minutes later, however, after they'd said good night and Greg was walking toward the Hancock Center, he remembered the look and thought about it. A trick of the light? An involuntary response to a twinge of pain?

He wasn't prepared to believe it was what it appeared to be: a look of pure, seething hatred.

The worry was swept away by a sudden smile. He'd just thought of something else he wanted to own.

XXXV

BY THE TIME THE DESIGN AWARDS SHOW rolled around, Greg wasn't sure he wanted to attend after all. He wasn't reluctant because of any scruple that he might be trying to re-create the fantasy of his dream; rather it was just the opposite. He was reluctant because he knew he would *fail* to re-create that fantasy. He would go, mope around the exhibits for an hour, and leave as much an outsider as he'd arrived. The experience could only underscore his irrelevance to the world, his isolation from all meaningful activity, his estrangement from the family of man. The past month had been bad enough. This would probably only make it worse.

After his evening with Bruce, he'd spent an enjoyable week shopping for a word processing system. It was no strain in the end to decide on a Sony, a dedicated word processor that would enable him to put a book-length manuscript on a single disk small enough to carry in a shirt pocket. All he needed after that was a book-length manuscript.

In his last, disastrous meeting with Ginny at Griffin's Lodge, she'd told him that Richard Iles had tried rather pathetically to make himself into a fiction writer. Greg had protested that he knew he wasn't a fiction writer, that he wouldn't waste a minute on it. Now, with an infinity of minutes to waste, he had decided to prove himself wrong. He felt sure he had an advantage over Richard Iles. Richard Iles had failed (Greg decided) because he was writing in desperation, was trying too hard, thinking of it as his only way to escape a life he hated. Greg, not working under any such pressure, could afford to relax and take his time. And so, relaxed and taking his time, Greg had begun casting around for an idea for a novel.

Relaxed and taking his time, his mind remained a blank for a week, two weeks, three weeks, four weeks. He told himself that getting the idea was the hard part, that even successful novelists went idealess for years; it didn't cheer him up.

And now, on the evening of the design show, he would have felt more like joining that throng of busy, productive people if he'd been able to say, "I'm busy and productive too. I'm working on a novel."

Just in case he found someone to say it to.

In a year, he'd forgotten just how assaultive such a gathering could be to the senses. He'd made the mistake of coming early, when the crowd was at its most clamorous, and amplified voices whacked down on him from every surface like the laughter broadcast in a carnival funhouse. Light dazzled from a thousand miniature floodlights, rippled across plastic showcases, flashed from glass-fronted exhibits. Here and there some of the more bizarre of the season's high fashion monstrosities blossomed with an air of curious menace, like carnivorous plants in a field of daisies.

Greg found a spot well out of the way and stood taking it all in, swirling a puddle of bourbon and two ice cubes around in a plastic glass and scanning the crowd for familiar faces he knew wouldn't be there. After a while he became aware that his face was fixed in a meaningless grin, and he made it go away. He finished his drink, went to the bar for another, returned to his place, and wondered what the hell he was doing there.

It wasn't an entirely rhetorical question. He'd kept his eye out for the date of the show and had noted it on his calendar. He'd looked forward to it. In his mind, he'd argued with Agnes about it and won. He'd had a haircut, bathed, shaved, and dressed for it. And here he was. What was supposed to happen next?

He thought about it for a bit and smiled; it wasn't very mysterious after all. He was like a man who goes out in a thunderstorm, climbs a hill, and stands under the tallest tree he can find: he was trying to attract the lightning bolt. That being the case, he thought wryly, it was a bit pointless to stand there sheltered from the storm.

Shaking his head, he moved out into the crush. What he was feeling was not a tingle of anticipation but rather a touch of weary self-disgust; never again was he going to let himself be hoodwinked by this tedious romanticism of his.

Half an hour later he was puzzling over a simulation game called Small World, with enough components to furnish a moderately Large World. He wondered how anyone ever figured out how it worked—and then wondered why he was wondering. He shrugged and turned to the next exhibit—and it was then that the lightning bolt fell, and the hair on the back of his neck rose. He closed his eyes and told himself not to be a fool.

It wasn't Ginny.

It couldn't be Ginny. Ginny was eight hundred miles away, in her father's house, where she wanted to be.

He opened his eyes, and she was still there, a few yards down the aisle, turned three-quarters away from him, her hair a flame around the shoulders of a lime-green dress of nubby wool. Moving of their own volition, his feet took him closer, disclosing by degrees the shape of a cheek, a russet eyebrow, a fine, clearly drawn nose. Then he was beside her looking down. Sensing his presence, she swivelled her head up to give him a look that said, "Yes?"

And of course it wasn't Ginny; it was only her twin.

"Uh," he said. "Have you seen my cat?"

Her eyes widened—emerald pools.

"The one that got my tongue," Greg explained. Her eyes got wider still, and he laughed. "I have to admit that for a moment I thought you were someone else, but now that I've met you, sort of . . ." He cleared his throat and tried to gather his wits. "Uh . . . do you come here often?"

She laughed and shook her head. "Are you crazy?"

"Yes, actually I am. But I'm harmless."

"I'm glad to hear that."

"Yes, well, my name is Greg Donner. Whoops. No. For a second there I thought *I* was someone else too. My name is Richard Iles. Perfectly harmless."

She gave him a thoughtful look. "Actually I did see a cat, but it didn't have your tongue. I think it had your whole head."

"Yes, yes," Greg agreed, nodding enthusiastically. "That must have been it. I could tell something was wrong. I mean *really* wrong, not just superficially wrong."

She lifted an arm to point. "I think it went that way."

He looked behind him and wondered if it was only by coincidence that she'd pointed back toward the entrance.

"You could help me look," he said.

"Where would we begin?"

"Well," he said, thinking furiously. "I know this cat. I mean, I know its habits."

"Yes?"

"I'm pretty sure it would head for Armando's."

"Armando's. I see. An Italian cat?"

"Well . . . a neutral, actually."

She laughed. "And suppose it's not at Armando's?"

"We could have a couple of drinks and think about it."

She gave him a perplexed smile. "Are you doing this on a bet or something? You know, 'Ten dollars says I can whisk that girl off in two minutes flat.'"

"No, no bet. I just never learned to meet girls in a civilized way."

She laughed again. "I can see that."

She hesitated for a moment longer and then said okay.

Her name was Carol Hartmann. Incredibly, she was a graphic designer, and she lived in the neighborhood, as Ginny had in his dream. If she'd been more like Ginny as a person, it would have been rather spooky. Even so, it was a bit disorienting to look into a face so like Ginny's and be denied Ginny's special presence.

He felt oddly divided during their conversation over drinks and dinner; he was there, keeping up his end, laughing, listening, but he was also standing gravely to one side to measure and compare, taking part with silent observations:

Ginny wouldn't have said that.

Ginny would have known what I meant.

Ginny wouldn't have let that pass.

Ginny wouldn't have bothered to evade that question.

Oddly, it didn't detract from his enjoyment of the evening. Carol was in some ways easier to be with than Ginny, lacking Ginny's sharp edges and shadowy depths. But he remained divided as he walked her to her apartment; it was as if a silent companion strolled with them, ignored and superfluous, a little bored with being the odd man out.

They parted at her door, sealing the evening with a kiss that was like an ambiguously worded promissory note.

XXXVI

THE NEXT MORNING GREG AWOKE feeling that he'd proved something—and that he'd turned a corner.

He'd walked out into the thunderstorm, called down the lightning bolt, and survived. Agnes Jakes, if she'd known what he was doing, would have been hysterical. She would have said that, by reenacting his first encounter with Ginny, he was trying to weave a spell that would ensnare him in his ghostly past. She would have been right—if he'd truly mistaken Carol Hartmann for Ginny Winters and fallen in love. But he hadn't.

Far from weaving a spell, he knew now that he'd broken free of one at last. Whatever else he might do, he would never again return to the places he'd shared with Ginny hoping to evoke some strange magic that would bring her back. He was finished with that foolishness for good, thanks (in large part) to Carol, who had reminded him that it was possible to have a good time with a woman without being madly in love with her. He felt no seismic stirrings of passion toward Carol—and didn't regret it. He was not in any great rush to find someone who would accept what Ginny had rejected. That could wait, perhaps for a very long time. He had scaled his ambitions down to a more realistic and manageable size. He was, after all, young, attractive, wealthy, and unattached; it was time to start acting like it.

And to hell with Ginny.

Even as the thought slipped past his guard, he sighed at it, disappointed to find it there at all.

Ginny is gone, gone, gone, he told himself. *Leave her out of it.*

He went to the jacket he'd been wearing the night before and dug a business card out of the breast pocket: Carol's card.

Looking at it, he reflected on the fact that designers' business cards were either very plain ("I'm too busy to design for myself") or very elaborate ("See what I can do?") and rarely anything in between. He'd never known it to be an infallible guide to superiority either way, but he felt vaguely pleased that Carol's was of the first type.

He settled by a phone, dialed her number, and waited through half a dozen rings before it was answered with a simple hello. He opened his mouth to speak, and the breath went out of him as if he'd been punched in the stomach.

"Hello?"

It was unmistakable. Just those two syllables, and it was unmistakable.

Whispering, because he still had no breath, he said, "Ginny?"

"You have the wrong number," she said, and hung up.

The dial tone was humming in his ear, but he didn't hear it. He was listening to that voice, wondering if he could be wrong. It didn't seem possible . . . but of course he *had* to be wrong.

He pushed the redial button; this time the phone was answered after the second ring.

"Hello."

Hello.

It wasn't Ginny's voice. It was nothing *like* Ginny's voice.

"Hi," he said. "Carol? This is Richard Iles."

"Oh. Hi, Richard. Did you just call here a second ago?"

"No. Why?"

She grunted. "Just a heavy breather, I guess. He caught me washing my hair."

"Sorry. Would you like me to call back?"

"It'll keep, it's all wrapped up in a towel now. What's up?"

"Well, if you're open to suggestions for the evening, I have a bunch in mind."

"I wouldn't mind flying to California for a bowl of chili at Chasen's."

"That was on the list. Suggestion eight, in fact."

"However, I can't. I'm expected at a cocktail party this evening. I'm not all that keen on it, but I've gotta go."

"Ah," he said with a pang of disappointment.

"Would you like to go with me?"

"Well..."

"Actually, I almost mentioned it last night, but I didn't want you to think I was pushy or anything."

Greg laughed. "I'd love to go with you. I haven't been to a party in a decade. But will I be welcome?"

"Are you kidding? They'll shackle you to a radiator. The place'll be packed with unattached females."

"Well, I can hardly pass up a chance like that, can I? What time shall I pick you up?"

Later, standing watch over the lake with a Bloody Mary in his hand, Greg wondered how much he was going to have to think about mistaking Carol's voice for Ginny's. Even as he posed the question, he recognized its deviousness. He hadn't "mistaken" Carol's voice for Ginny's; if he had, there would be nothing to think about. He had *heard* Ginny' s voice.

No mistake.

He could easily imagine what Agnes would say about it: he had dialed Carol's number, but the person he was really trying to reach was Ginny. Never mind that the voice he *expected* to hear was Carol's. The voice he *wanted* to hear—and had heard in fact—was Ginny's. It was no use pretending he'd simply made an error. He'd had an aural hallucination.

And what was he going to make of that?

After some thought, he decided to make as little of it as possible. Since he knew very well that he had no intention of doing anything about it, there was nothing to be gained by stewing over it. He went out to lunch at Don the Beachcomber's and afterwards bought himself a new tie, a festive paisley in rich blues, yellows, browns, and reds.

As far as Greg could see, there were only a handful of un-attached females among the thirty or forty guests at the party,

251

but he'd certainly been made to feel welcome. The hostess, a tall, angular woman with a wide, humorous mouth, had glommed on to him almost the moment he'd stepped in, gracefully separating him from Carol to lead him around the small, elegant Elm Street apartment, introducing him to everyone as if he were the guest of honor.

It was a younger crowd than he'd expected and apparently had no connection with graphic design or publishing in any form. After a little eavesdropping, he concluded that most, if not all, of them were involved in some way with the Goodman School of Drama. It accounted for the trained voices and the occasional larger-than-life gesture.

For Greg, the principal attraction of any party was more in observation than participation, but he wasn't allowed to follow his inclination for long. He'd shamelessly allowed himself to be introduced as a writer, and it was on this basis that he was drawn into a discussion of *Saint Joan*. A young man with very thick glasses was asserting that, judging from his introduction, Shaw had misunderstood his own play. The others in the group thought this an impossibility and wanted Greg's expert opinion. His attempt to evade the question on the grounds that he was unfamiliar with both the play and the introduction was waved away. Was it possible, they wanted to know, for an author to miss the point of his own work?

With a gleeful inner shrug, he obliged them with an opinion he only half believed himself: an author is very much like a parent; he may be too importantly involved with his brainchild to see it for what it is. They scoffed, and he sidetracked them with an irrelevant example. Herman Melville, he said, didn't really understand what *Moby Dick* was about when he started writing it; he began by insisting repeatedly that Captain Ahab was a "monomaniac" but stopped using this label entirely around the middle of the book, because he'd seen a greater potential for Ahab if he *wasn't* a monomaniac but rather a visionary obsessed with a great truth. Greg's listeners were outraged by what they took to be a slur on this great literary genius, and he proceeded to outrage them some more by telling them that if Melville had seen himself as anything more than a writer of adventure stories, he would have rewritten the first half of *Moby Dick* to bring it into line with the second half.

Greg's eccentric literary views won him the swooning attention of a smoky-eyed brunette, who spent the next hour being languidly fascinating while he told her absurd tales of growing up in Laos, the son of missionaries ultimately slain by Communist guerrillas.

"You ought to write a book about *that*," she told him earnestly.

"Maybe someday," he replied. "I'm too close to it now."

Face by face, the group around him changed, but it was always there, and, oddly, he always seemed to be the center of it. It was an unusual and flattering experience, and he wondered if his superior age intrigued them or whether a man who carries three thousand dollars in his pocket as spending money carries a special aura with him as well.

Around midnight he began to look around for Carol. Even with her back to him, she was impossible to miss, and he excused himself to walk across the room to join her. He picked up a fresh drink and stood at her side to catch the drift of the conversation. After a few moments he glanced down at her, and, as if sensing his attention, she looked up and smiled.

Greg's heart plummeted, and his glass slipped through his fingers unnoticed. His mouth suddenly dry, he stared at her and croaked, "Ginny?"

For there wasn't the slightest doubt of it: the woman looking up at him was Ginny, not Carol.

Her smile faltered, withered, and was replaced by blank bafflement.

"Ginny," he repeated, "what are you *doing here?*"

She glanced doubtfully at her friends, as if one of them might explain what was going on. A few of them shrugged; others kept amused eyes on Greg, tensely awaiting the punch line of the joke.

"Ginny, come on. *Stop it.*"

"'Ginny,'" she repeated with a thoughtful frown. "Someone called this morning and asked for Ginny. It was you."

"Ginny, please. For God's sake."

Shuddering as if his relentless gaze had touched her physically, she drew back a pace. "Are you crazy or something?"

Greg stared down at her, a feeble half-smile frozen on his lips. He felt helpless to move, to resolve the situation.

She sent a wild eye around her circle of friends. "Look, somebody tell this guy my name, okay?"

"Ginny . . ." he pleaded.

Suddenly her face blazed into life. "What the hell's the matter with you? Can't you remember it? It's Carol. Carol! C-A-R-O-L!"

He laughed uneasily. No matter how hard he looked, it was Ginny standing there, Ginny glaring at him, Ginny telling him that her name was Carol. He turned to the now silent group around them and met stares that were puzzled, worried, hostile.

"Come on," he said, appealing to them weakly, "you can *see* this isn't Carol. What's going on here?"

The woman who wasn't Carol turned abruptly and marched off toward the bedroom where coats had been left.

The entire room was silent now, as everyone turned toward the center of the drama. Greg picked out the face of the hostess and said, "Look, you saw who I was with when I arrived. *That* was Carol."

She shook her head and frowned down at her shoes.

He turned to the smoky-eyed brunette and asked her if she knew Carol. She nodded.

"Well, was that Carol I was just talking to just now, for God's sake?"

She studied him gravely and said, "Yes, as a matter of fact, it was."

He started to protest, but at that moment Ginny/Carol emerged from the bedroom and headed for the door.

"Wait," Greg said, catching her by the arm.

She stopped and peered down at his hand. Then she looked around and said, "Will somebody get this guy off me?"

Two men separated themselves from the crowd and moved toward Greg.

One of them said, "Gently now," as if soothing an alarmed horse.

Greg dropped her arm but started after her as she once again made for the door. The two men interposed themselves, and one of them said, very politely, "I have the impression she wants to be by herself. Okay?"

Sagging, Greg watched her leave.

There was a long silence, then someone muttered, "Where the hell did *he* come from?" He was answered with a few nervous laughs, and conversations were gradually resumed in a hushed murmur.

Greg, still confronting the two men, said, "Is it all right if I leave now?"

They exchanged a glance.

"Let's give her a few minutes, okay?"

Haying no choice, he nodded.

They let him go after ten minutes, and he walked out, his back stiff with a dignity he didn't feel.

XXXVII

GREG HAD ONCE TOLD GINNY he'd spent an unforgettable night with a friend who was going round the paranoid bend.

His name was Larry Fielding, and he and Greg had shared courses as graduate students at the University of Chicago. Greg had taken to him for his unflagging good humor, his refusal to take anything too seriously or to let anyone spoil his gracious style or his evident enjoyment of life. As they'd become closer, Greg envied him his almost uncanny ability to put people and events into perspective. Larry was younger than Greg, but he seemed infinitely more poised, more comfortable with himself— more finely balanced than Greg, with his doubts, awkwardness, wild swings of emotion, and ready sense of guilt.

They gradually lost touch when Greg left the university. Then one night Larry showed up at Greg's apartment and said he needed someone to talk to. This in itself was puzzling, because Greg had always had the impression that Larry was well endowed with friends; later he understood why their doors were no longer open to him.

Greg learned that, in the time since they'd been close, Larry had dropped out of graduate school, done a little undergraduate tutoring and term paper writing, and finally drifted away from education. For a while he'd sold encyclopedias, then worked in a men's shop. After that he'd managed an adult bookstore. Greg was astonished to hear that he was now a process server and general errand runner for a firm of court reporters, but it seemed that even this rather shabby job was in jeopardy. Someone in the office was arranging for him to be given instructions that were just far enough off to make him look like a blunderer, and because it was always done by phone there was no way to prove it, no way to defend himself against it.

Greg asked why anyone would want to do this, and Larry, with obvious reluctance, explained that while managing the adult bookstore he'd accidentally learned some things about a child pornography ring, things that were not healthy for an outsider to know. The result was that a handful of very unpleasant people wanted to drive him out of the city. They were persistent, well connected, and had all the time in the world to make Larry's life miserable. They would, for example, run in ringers for the people he was supposed to be serving papers on. They would bribe receptionists to send him on wild goose chases all around the city, while his target was sitting right there in the office.

But surely, Greg said, that must happen to process servers all the time. Larry agreed with a weary smile; this was different. After pulling stunts like that, they'd *call* to let him know they'd done it.

They didn't stop with petty annoyances. They visited his apartment when he was gone and rearranged things just enough to let him know they'd been there. Once, by intercepting a check he'd sent and subsequent warnings that payment was overdue, they'd contrived to have his electricity turned off. He managed to put up with these things pretty well, but lately they'd started increasing the pressure. He was being followed much of the time. He came home to find men lurking in the hallways of his apartment building.

Their threats were becoming more overt. Just recently, his boss had asked him to run a supposed client out to the airport. Out on the expressway, with Larry driving sixty miles an hour, the client had reached over the back seat and slipped some chloral hydrate into the coffee Larry was drinking.

Unbelievably, it wasn't until Greg had heard this absurd tale that the penny dropped. Larry had told it with such composure and conviction—even laughing ruefully at "their" cunning and his own helplessness—that he'd accepted it all without a qualm. Feeling stunned and immensely sorry for his friend, Greg said, "Larry, you've got to realize that that didn't happen. No one—no one at all—is going to risk knocking out the driver of the car he's riding it at sixty miles an hour."

Larry had given him a wounded, discouraged smile. "That's what makes it so goddamned infuriating. They do these completely grotesque things deliberately, *knowing* that no one will believe me."

"Larry, you're missing the point. No one's going to go *that* far—no one's going to risk his *life* just to discredit you. It doesn't make any sense."

In the end, Larry had talked cogently and calmly about committing himself for psychiatric treatment. "Everyone seems to think I ought to, including you. Right?"

"Yes, I really think so, Larry."

"It's harder than you think, Greg. I understand what you're saying. I know it all sounds completely fantastic, I really do. But I saw it happen, just the way I see you sitting there. How do you go about denying the reality of your own experience? What would you do if people started telling you that the things you were seeing and hearing weren't real?"

Greg had no very good answer for him at the time.

And he still didn't.

One thing Larry had made abundantly clear: he *felt* completely sane, as sane as he'd ever felt in his life.

Just as Greg did now.

He never found out what happened to Larry Fielding. Like Larry's other friends, he'd closed the door on him with a shudder of relief, telling himself he'd done all he could do. He'd given Larry his best advice, the only advice it was possible to give under the circumstances. Wise advice, offered in the kindliest spirit. *Seek help.*

The question now was: was he going to take that advice himself?

Larry had probably answered it the same way: no.

Not yet.

In the hours following the fiasco at the Elm Street apartment, he'd framed a bargain with himself. He even wrote it out to prove his sincerity.

He would go to Carol's apartment in the morning and knock on her door. If Carol answered, he would make an abject apology and that would be the end of it. That's what he hoped would happen. He would never see Carol again—would never want or dare to see her again. He might even leave Chicago, settle far away. Wyoming. Take up ranching. Anything. But if Ginny answered the door, he would turn around, come home, pack a bag, and go back to Kentucky for treatment. No more stalling, no more excuses, no more tests.

That was the bargain. When he went to bed at three in the morning, he was sure—reasonably sure—that he'd keep it.

But seven hours later, dragging himself step by step toward the actual moment of confrontation, he wavered, paused, and decided that a small revision in the bargain was permissible. There was no reason why he had to come face-to-face with whoever might answer the door of Carol's apartment; humiliating himself wasn't part of the bargain and would serve no purpose. He could just as well learn what had to be learned by keeping watch on the building from the coffee shop across the street. Eventually she'd make an appearance at a window or on the street, and he'd know the truth.

There was, after all, no great hurry. Whichever way it went, a few hours weren't going to matter.

He installed himself in a booth by a window that gave him an unobstructed view of Carol's apartment, laid a hundred dollar bill on the table, and told the waitress he was renting it for the day; anything left over from the hundred after lunch, dinner, and the occasional cup of coffee was hers. Her eyes popped as if she were having hallucinations of her own, but she gathered up the bill and folded it into a pocket quickly enough.

After an hour it occurred to him that Sunday was an unpromising day for such a vigil. It could very well be that the only thing she'd go out for would be a newspaper—and she might have done that before he'd arrived. On the other hand, she might have gone out to brunch, in which case she'd be returning in an hour or two.

Three hours passed with leaden slowness, and he crossed off brunch. She was probably right where he'd expected her to be: inside her apartment. But by six o'clock he'd begun to doubt even that. After last night's catastrophe, she might conceivably be anywhere—staying with a friend, gone home to mother. For all he knew, she might have taken a handful of sleeping pills and be lying there in a coma.

A phone call could settle all this, of course. But a phone call wasn't in the bargain. He wanted the evidence of his eyes, not his ears.

He breathed a sigh of relief when her lights went on at 6:30. At least he now knew where she was. At 7:15 she moved past a window. Perhaps she was getting ready to go out. At 7:30 a lone man entered the building: a date? He didn't pause to push a bell in the foyer, but that didn't mean anything. As Greg knew, the foyer door was unlocked. A minute later the lights went on in the apartment above Carol's: not a date, just another tenant.

At 8:30 he decided to give it another half an hour; the probability of her going out after nine seemed minute.

In the end, he left at 9:30. He stood on the sidewalk for a few moments looking up at her lights and thinking, *All I've got to do is walk over and knock on the goddamn door.*

But he couldn't bring himself to do it.

XXXVIII

AT 8:30 THE NEXT MORNING Greg slid into the same booth and laid another hundred on the table. The waitress—the same one from yesterday—said, "You a private eye or something?"

"Something," he said, and ordered scrambled eggs and sausage.

He was about to take a sip from his third cup of coffee after breakfast when a cab pulled up in front of Carol's building. A man in the back seat leaned forward to hand the driver some bills, then got out and closed the door behind him.

It was only for a tenth of a second that he was facing Greg, but it was enough. Groping for the saucer, Greg blindly replaced his cup and watched, fascinated, as Bruce Iles turned and entered Carol's building.

Bruce Iles.

Visiting Carol Hartmann.

Of course there were half a dozen other people he might be visiting in that building. But the coincidence was too big to swallow.

Bruce Iles and Carol Hartmann.

And Ginny.

The pieces of the puzzle shifted and came together to form a pattern—a pattern almost too bizarre to be believed.

He looked out into the street again, but the cab was gone and Bruce Iles had disappeared into the interior of the building.

Bruce Iles, Carol Hartmann, and Ginny.

He looked again at the pattern and thought about what his paranoid friend Larry had said: *I know it all sounds completely fantastic, I really do. But I saw it happen, just the way I see you sitting there.*

Bruce had known he was planning to attend the design show.

Is that wise?

Sane and sensible?

Greg had told him that he'd met Ginny at the design show.

Carol Hartmann, Ginny's double, had been at the design show. And was now entertaining Bruce Iles.

Ginny: stationed in Carol's apartment, answering the telephone whenever it rang . . . *until Greg called*.

The party: all staged for Greg's benefit, peopled with actors. The hostess nimbly separating him from Carol. Ginny waiting in a back room, ready to change into Carol's clothes. Carol shipping away while a smoky-eyed brunette flattered him. Ginny unobtrusively taking Carol's place while wave after wave of admirers kept him occupied.

Ginny looking up into his face, outraged.

Can't you remember my name? It's Carol.

All designed to get him ready for recommittal to the Glen-haven Oaks Sanatorium.

He could well imagine the next step in the plan. Bruce Iles would "hear a rumor." A rumor about another Iles who'd behaved strangely at a party: very strangely, raving, hallucinating about someone named Ginny.

It would be child's play to call in Greg's promise to go back to the sanatorium "without making a fuss." Back to the sanatorium, where there was a piece of paper in a file that would, Greg was sure, give Bruce and Ginny control over Richard Iles' fortune.

Except that Ginny had said she wanted no part of that fortune.

For a moment the pattern blurred.

Then he got it back in focus. Ginny wanted no part of that fortune *if it meant taking Richard Iles with it.*

She'd been happy enough to have the use of it while Richard Iles had been a vegetable. It was only when he'd shown signs of recovery that she'd disavowed it.

And it was only then that she'd made herself and Bruce *jointly* responsible for committing him.

She knew she was going to need Bruce. If they were to succeed in separating Richard Iles from his millions they were going to need each other. And a Ginny look-alike.

I know it all sounds completely fantastic, I really do.

Greg shook his head. This was no delusion.

Not unless seeing Bruce Iles in front of that building was a delusion—and he was certain it wasn't.

I saw it happen, just the way I see you sitting there.

Goddamn it, this was something he could *prove*. Right now. If Bruce was in Carol's apartment, chances were that Ginny was too. All he had to do was go over there and confront them.

Yet he went on sitting through another minute, the muscles in his arms and shoulders jumping and twitching as if chilled by an arctic wind.

"*Go,*" he whispered. Gripping the sides of the table, he pulled himself out of the booth.

"Get you some more coffee?" his waitress asked, hurrying over.

"No. No, I'm leaving now."

"Well, you have a good day then."

Greg lurched through the door, staggered across the street, and, carrying his body like an awkward burden, mounted the stairs to Carol's apartment.

Taking a deep breath, he knocked on the door. It opened after half a minute, and Carol peered up at him, shook her head, and started to close it. Greg blocked it open with a foot.

"I want to see Bruce," he mumbled.

Her eyes widened. "Look, will you just go away? There's no one called Bruce here."

He put his shoulder to the door and pushed his way in. Looking around, he saw an array of living room furniture and a pair of drafting tables side by side with the usual litter of proofs and layout sheets.

There was no one there but Carol, gaping at him. "Where's

the bedroom?" he asked, then answered his own question by turning down a hallway to the left, throwing open doors as he went.

There was no one in the closets, no one in the bedroom, no one in the bathroom.

When he returned to the living room, Carol was punching out a number on the telephone. He took it away from her and hung it up.

"Where are they?" he demanded.

"Listen," she said, her eyes blazing, "you are fucking crazy, you know? You need help!"

"*Where are they?*"

"Where are *who*, for Christ's sake? There's nobody here but me. You can see that."

Speaking very slowly, through his teeth, he said, "Where are Bruce and Ginny?"

Her eyes grew very wide and her face went white. "Look. I don't know who you're talking about. Honest to God. I don't know anybody named Bruce, anybody named Ginny."

Before she could move, he took her by the shoulders.

"The people who arranged all this with you, Carol. The man who hired you to go to the design show. The woman you changed places with at the party."

"Oh Jesus," she whimpered.

"Where are they?"

"Please, Richard. Please don't do this to me."

He dug his fingers into her arms and started shaking her.

"Just tell me where they are."

"They're . . . they're in the kitchen."

When Greg looked up and relaxed his grip, Carol twisted away and broke for the door. He caught up with her in two long strides and wrapped an arm around her waist, half pulling her off her feet. He felt her take a deep breath to scream and clapped a hand across her mouth.

She bit him, hard, catching the knuckle of his index finger, and he slung her away.

Falling backwards, she twisted in the air. The side of her head slammed into the corner of a drafting table, and she crumpled into an untidy heap, one arm caught beneath her, her cheek against the floor, a look of slack astonishment in her staring eyes. Greg knelt down beside her, brushed the hair back from her face, and winced over the bloody dent in her temple. He groped for a pulse at her throat and wrist but his fingers were frozen, numb, and he found nothing.

He stood up, made his way to the telephone on wobbly legs, and called 911 to report an accident and ask for an ambulance. Then he sat down and put his head in his hands.

After a few minutes he went back to the phone and dialed the number of his uncle's office. When he identified himself, the receptionist told him that Dr. Iles was with a patient.

"That's all right," Greg said. "Maybe you can help me. Do you know how long he's been there?"

"Been here?"

"What time did he arrive this morning?"

"Oh. Just a few minutes before nine. His first patient was due at nine."

"And he hasn't been out? He's been there ever since?"

A puzzled silence. "That's right. Why do you ask?"

"It doesn't matter," he said, and hung up.

He waited until he heard the lugubrious hee-haw of the approaching ambulance, then he slipped out of the apartment, leaving the door open.

XXXIX

WHEN HE CALLED THE SANATORIUM, he was told that Dr. Jakes wasn't in her office. He checked his watch and saw that it was just noon—one o'clock in that part of Kentucky.

"She's probably still in the dining room," he said. "Would you check, please? It's an emergency."

"One moment."

It was nearly ten minutes before Agnes's reassuring contralto came on the line.

"Agnes," he said, "this is Richard Iles."

"Ah, Richard. How are you?"

"Not well, Agnes. I need your help."

"I'm sorry to hear it, Richard. But you know I'm always available."

"I need you here, Agnes. In Chicago."

"In Chicago," she repeated thoughtfully. "Why in Chicago, Richard? I can't do anything for you there."

"You can, though. I'm in deep, deep trouble."

A half-minute's pause. "Richard, I think you're asking a bit much of me. You know where I work. You know that I have patients here. Much as I might want to, I can't go running off to answer distress calls all over the country."

"Agnes, please. I'm begging you."

She sighed. "What exactly is the problem?"

"I . . . I've been hallucinating."

"Richard dear, that isn't something we can tackle in an overnight house call. Come back to Kentucky. Or, if you like, I can send someone to Chicago to pick you up. Alan perhaps."

"You don't understand. Someone's been . . . hurt."

"Hurt. Hurt by you?"

"Yes."

"Do you mean *physically* hurt?"

"Yes. Badly, I'm afraid."

"I see. Are you telling me that you're in custody?"

"No, but I'm afraid that's just a matter of time. A lot of people knew we'd . . . been together recently."

"Oh, Richard, Richard . . . All right, I'll come. I don't know what flights there are, but I should be there by early evening. You're at the address you sent at Christmas time?"

"Yes. Do you want me to meet you at the airport?"

"No, you stay right where you are. And Richard . . ."

"Yes?"

"Try not to brood. I'll talk to our lawyer about this. I hope it'll be his opinion that you'd be within your rights to return with me to Kentucky. I really think that would be best for you all round if we can manage it."

"All right, Agnes. Thanks."

"You understand . . . you'll have to sign some papers."

"Yes. Okay."

"Try to take it easy till I get there. Get some rest."

After hanging up, he poured himself a drink, took it into his bedroom, kicked off his shoes, and lay down on the bed. If he could, he knew he'd be very happy to pass the next few hours in sleep. He felt not the slightest temptation to brood over what had happened. He would cheerfully turn it all over to Agnes and let *her* brood over it. Cheerfully and mindlessly, relieved to be rid of the responsibility for his own life, his own actions.

His eyes closed and, shielded by a forearm, he took a sip of bourbon and, in memory, saw Bruce step out of the cab in front of Carol's apartment. He'd glanced out over the roof of the cab for the briefest of moments, looking a bit haggard. Straining at the image, Greg imagined Bruce wasn't as carefully groomed as usual, his morning shave a bit sketchy.

And at that moment, while the Bruce Iles of reality was with his second or third patient of the day, Greg had never felt saner in his life.

267

He took another swallow of bourbon, reminding himself that he wasn't going to brood about it.

In a way, it was a pity. He'd had the whole conspiracy so neatly worked out. Even now it seemed like a masterpiece. A bit melodramatic, of course, but not as screwy as Larry Fielding's drugged coffee. Not quite. The notion of the very upright-seeming villain substituting one woman for another had come from some movie or other. Was it Hitchcock? Yes. James Stewart, Kim Novak. *Vertigo.*

So, not entirely original, but a pretty good idea all the same.

And he'd told Carol in the first minute that, though crazy, he was perfectly harmless.

Emotionally exhausted, he was teetering on the edge of sleep when he was jerked back to wakefulness by the imagined sound of an ambulance siren approaching Carol's apartment.

Eee-aww, eee-aww, eee-aww.

He lay there for a while listening to it, his drink resting on his stomach, his eyes open now, staring at the ceiling.

Smiling, he remembered the old saw: *Even paranoids have enemies.* Maybe the man Larry Fielding drove to the airport was a lunatic himself. Maybe he carried chloral hydrate to knock out his *own* delusional enemies . . . like Larry. Stranger things have happened. Greg hadn't thought of it at the time; maybe the joke was on him after all.

Eee-aww, eee-aww, eee-aww. The old horselaugh.

That raised a good question: do the police of Nassau ride horses? He somehow didn't think so, but he couldn't be sure, since he'd never been there to see for himself. But suppose he'd gone to Nassau after all. Would the police be on horses or not?

Big to-do at the police station as Greg's plane taxied to a halt at the airport.

White uniforms? *Absolutely, Sah!* Bahamian accent? *You bet, Sah!* Big grins? *Big islahnd grins, Sah!*

Horses? *Ah. Not quite sure about that.*

Your Bahamian accent slipped there.

Ah. Not quate shu-ah about that, Sah!

That is a *lousy* Bahamian accent. I can't *do* a Bahamian accent, but I can sure as hell recognize one when I hear it, for Christ's sake!

Sorry, Sah.

Maybe we'd better skip Nassau.

I really think it would be best, Sah.

Grinning, Greg sat up, swung his legs over the side of the bed, and looked around. Idly, he switched on the lamp beside him, switched it off, shrugged: of course. Something as obvious as his electricity wouldn't be neglected.

He looked around some more and went to a closet, switched on a light and stood contemplating its contents. He slid a jacket from its hanger and held it for a moment as if judging its weight; then he turned it around and, grabbing the fabric on either side of the vent, ripped it up the back. He examined the open seam carefully and frowned.

Well, whaddya know. *Real thread.*

He dropped the jacket on the floor and looked around again. Still frowning, he slipped a tie from a rack: the paisley he'd bought on Saturday. He ran it through his hands, looking for a break in the pattern; at the center he paused and examined it more carefully; there was no break in the pattern. He threw it aside, took another one from the rack, and went through the same procedure. Then he went on to the next and the next and the next. All the ties in his closet were flawless.

Very cunning. He allowed himself a grin of triumph, then self-consciously wiped it away.

God may be watching.

He stood staring down sightlessly at the tangled pile of ties for a while. Then he left the bedroom and walked to the kitchen. He took a hammer from a drawer, sent his eyes around the walls, and picked a spot beside the light switch. He went over and smashed the hammer into the Sheetrock and started pulling chunks away with the claw. After a couple of minutes, he stopped and thought, *This is going to take forever. What I need is a crowbar.*

He stood for a moment as if trying to remember where the crowbar was. Then he went to the pantry and found it leaning against the wall beside the broom and dustpan.

The work went much more quickly with the crowbar, and he'd soon opened a hole about a foot and a half in diameter. It was big enough to see that there was nothing hidden behind the Sheetrock. Nothing at all.

He looked around for another place to try. There was only one area within easy reach that wasn't tiled, around a plate of electrical switches, and he attacked that next.

Except for bare studs, there was nothing behind that wall either. Very cunning. But not cunning enough.

He shoved the crowbar down into the garbage disposal unit as far as it would go, then went into the living room. As he passed the skeletal figure of Matilda raging from the seat of her death cart, he paused to give her a conspiratorial wink.

His eye fell on a bookcase, and he wandered over to study the titles. At last he smiled and slipped out a copy of the first *People's Almanac*, which he considered one of the best reference works of all time—except for its index, which was so obviously and annoyingly inadequate; however, what he wanted was there under the *D*'s, and with an air of triumph he turned to page 1394, glanced down to the bottom of the page, and burst out laughing. He stood there for a while, reading and nodding, then reshelved the book and looked around again.

He walked across the room to the glass and chrome étagère and nodded a greeting to a familiar object a few years older than he was, but in better shape: Li'l Abner's Dogpatch Band. Out of a sense of diffidence, he'd always resisted the temptation to see exactly what it did. Now he took it down, wound it up, put it back on the top shelf, and switched it on. With a fixed smile, he watched the madcap dance and listened to the furious rattle of drums. When it started to run down, he switched it off.

"Now you know what it's like," a voice behind him said.

Chuckling, Greg turned to the sofa where Larry Fielding sprawled. Wearing a dark blue three-piece suit, he looked the

270

way Greg remembered him from graduate school, before he'd been reduced to delivering legal papers.

"You know," Greg said, "I've always felt guilty about that last night."

Larry shook his head, smiling gently at this slow learner. "You've always been big on guilt, Greg, from the time you started feeling guilty about your brother's suicide—guilty for being alive when he was dead. You've always measured yourself against him, always expected too much of yourself. People aren't perfect—even you."

"I know. All the same, I could have been a little more . . . compassionate that night."

"Forget it. I was a spooky person. I know that."

"I take it you . . . recovered."

"Don't try to push it too far, Greg. I'm just saying the things you want to hear, after all."

"I don't understand."

"All these years, you've wanted me to be well, wanted me to come and reassure you that you didn't hurt me too badly that night." He shrugged. "'So here I am, well and reassuring.'"

"I see. In other words, you're just a hallucination."

Larry chuckled ruefully. "Just a hallucination. I like *that*."

Greg checked his watch and was surprised to see that it was after seven. He made himself a drink, which he nursed through the next hour, while the southern windows became a blaze of city lights. Then he made another, promising himself it would be the last until Agnes arrived, and took it to the eastern windows, overlooking the lake.

Though clear, the sky was still the milky gray of twilight. Over the next half hour the gray deepened until a sprinkling of stars appeared like pinpricks in velvet. As he watched, one of them broke out of its place, arced briefly across the sky, and plunged into the pale glow above the lakeside towns on the eastern shore. Greg smiled and drained his glass.

Ten minutes later, a call from the lobby signaled Agnes's arrival.

271

XXXX

LIKE IT?" GREG ASKED. After giving hatchet-wielding Matilda a doubtful glance, Agnes had paused, stunned, at the entrance to the living room.

"It's a little extreme for my tastes, but it's very . . . chic, I suppose."

"I'm the Sheik of Araby," Greg stated in a matter-of-fact tone, and she turned and frowned up at him.

"Would you like a drink?" He held up his empty glass.

She shook her head.

"Come into the kitchen while I make one for myself."

"I really think it would be wise to go easy on the booze, Richard."

"I intend to. Come on."

She followed him into the kitchen, where she stared at the wrecked walls and the crowbar sticking up out of the sink.

"Aren't you going to ask what I've been up to here?" Greg asked, taking ice from the freezer.

"All right, Richard, what have you been up to?"

He finished pouring his drink, leaned against a counter, and used his glass to gesture to the walls.

"I wanted to see if there was any wiring behind the Sheet-rock."

"Wiring?"

"Electrical wiring. For the lights and things."

"I don't understand, Richard."

"There isn't any, Agnes. What do you make of that?"

Shaking her head doubtfully, she peered into one of the holes. "Aren't there wires inside this metal tubing?"

He came and looked over her shoulder. "By golly," he said,

unruffled. "You're right. You're absolutely right. I missed that completely."

"Richard . . ."

"I'll bet you noticed the crowbar."

"Yes, I noticed the crowbar."

"Do you know where I found it? Right in that pantry, beside the broom."

"So?"

"There was no crowbar there yesterday, Agnes. What in the world would I want with a crowbar?"

"What are you trying to tell me, Richard?"

"I'm telling you it's an *invented* crowbar. Watch. I'll make it go away."

He closed his eyes. After a moment he opened them, and his eyebrows arched in surprise.

The crowbar was still there.

"Interesting," he said.

"Richard, I think it would be best if—"

"Come on. There's something I want to show you in the bedroom." He turned and walked away, and Agnes followed, her face a study in baffled uncertainty.

He paused at the doorway to his bedroom and gestured to the tangled heap beside the closet.

"All my ties are made from a single length of material."

She gave him a puzzled look.

"That's an obvious mistake. Ties are always made from two pieces, with a seam that falls at the back of the neck."

As she started into the room, he said, "Don't bother, Agnes. I know you can fix them so they're right. The point is, they weren't right when I first looked at them."

Without waiting for a reply, he turned and walked back into the living room, where he took *The People's Almanac* from its shelf and handed it to her.

"Turn to page 1394, Agnes."

"Richard, let's sit down and talk."

"Page 1394. Please."

273

With a sigh she found the page, scanned it briefly, and said, "What am I supposed to see?"

"The story at the bottom, entitled 'Gregory Donner, the Man Who Dreamed.'"

Without even glancing at it, she handed it back.

The story at the bottom was entitled, "Ghosts and Hauntings."

He sighed and closed the book. After thinking for a moment, he looked over at the chrome and glass étagère. Li'l Abner's Dogpatch Band, which he'd appropriated from Agnes's collection in Kentucky, was gone. In its place stood the familiar terra-cotta figure of the outraged pre-Columbian magistrate. Greg shook his head, acknowledging defeat with a rueful smile.

"All the same," he said, gazing wistfully out at the lake, "I made a star fall out of the sky."

"Richard," she said gently, "let's sit down."

With abrupt cheerfulness, he said, "Sure, Dr. Jakes," and threw himself onto a nearby sofa.

Agnes sat down on the edge of a matching sofa opposite his and gave him a long, searching look.

"You know, Richard, I believe it was a mistake for you to try living alone so soon. I think you've had too much time on your hands and have spent too much of it just . . . thinking, wrapped up in your own imagination."

She paused at Greg's sudden grin.

"Do you know where you went wrong?" he asked.

"What?"

"Do you know what tipped me off?"

"Richard . . ."

"It was the siren."

He waggled his eyebrows at her comically.

"Richard, we'll have plenty of time to talk about these things when—

"*Eee-aww, eee-aww, eee-aww,*" he mimicked. "That's wrong, Agnes. Ambulances don't use that electronic howl—police cars do. Ambulance sirens sound like *sirens.*"

"I'm sure you're right, Richard, but—"

"That's what got me started. Then I thought about Nassau."

"Richard, please listen to me for a minute."

"I'm sure you know I tried to go to Nassau, Agnes. Just after Christmas. I really *wanted* to go. I had my ticket, I had a hotel reservation, everything. I went to the airport to catch my flight, and then, for no reason at all, I just couldn't bring myself to get on that plane. I felt compelled to turn around and come home. So I did.

"Now at that time I didn't think that much about it. I'd wanted to go to Nassau, but when it actually came down to doing it I found I really wanted to stay home. That's the way it seemed. But then, after the siren business, I thought about it some more. Why exactly hadn't I been able to go to Nassau? Let's do some supposing. Suppose I couldn't go to Nassau because neither one of us could *manage* Nassau, Agnes. Suppose neither one of us knew enough about it to make it convincing. *I've* never been there, so I had no memories to work with. And I'll bet *you've* never been there, so you had no memories to work with either. Even between the two of us, I'll bet we couldn't come up with a convincing Bahamian accent, for example. There would be all sorts of other mistakes, like the mistake with the siren. And the sum of those mistakes might have made me suspicious, might have made me wonder what the hell was going on. And once I started wondering, it was only a matter of time till I figured it all out. So a visit to Nassau was just too risky, Agnes. When I got ready to board the plane, you made me turn around and come home."

Agnes sighed. "Richard, please . . ."

"Then I went looking for other mistakes, like the seams missing in the ties, like the lack of wiring in the walls. Natural mistakes to make, Agnes. I mean, how many people ever notice that ties are made from two pieces of cloth? How many people ever tear down the walls to see if there really is wiring behind them?"

He held up a hand as Agnes tried to interrupt.

'Then I made some experiments. I conjured up that crowbar. That must have given you a shock, but there was nothing you could do about it. You'd obviously seen it, so you couldn't get rid of it. And of course you couldn't let *me* get rid of it once you'd admitted it was there. But that wasn't so bad; it was at least *possible* that I'd have a crowbar.

"Then I put my name in the index of *The People's Almanac*, I put in a story about me on page 1394. You couldn't let that stand, of course, because that was obviously impossible, so you put it back the way it had been. Then I swiped your Dogpatch Band from Kentucky and put it on a shelf over there. Again, that was something you didn't want to deal with, so you got rid of it as soon as you saw it."

He chuckled.

"I suppose you could even put the star back in the sky, if you knew which one it was."

He leaned forward and looked into her eyes.

"It's all very simple once you understand, isn't it, Agnes. *In a dream*, you can have things just the way you want them. *Anything's* possible in a dream."

She sighed with weary relief and sank back into the cushions of the sofa. "So *that's* what this is all about. You believe we're in the midst of a dream. Is that it?"

"You know it is, Agnes. There is no sanatorium in Kentucky. There is no Richard Iles. Greg Donner is asleep somewhere, and we're running around in his dream."

Agnes gave him a look that was half a smile, half a puzzled frown. "Richard, think. When you called me this afternoon, you said you were in deep, deep trouble. You said you'd hurt someone badly. Isn't that right?"

Greg shrugged.

"Exactly. Now you shrug. Now you're no longer worried about that. Why? Because you've come up with an explanation. This dreadful thing—whatever it is—didn't actually *happen*. It was all just a dream. Isn't that right?"

"That's right."

"So you're completely off the hook."

"Well, yes, that's true."

"Come now, Richard, summon up your intelligence for a moment. Doesn't this explanation strike you as being just a bit self-serving? Just a bit too convenient?"

He shifted uncomfortably in his seat. "Yes, I admit that. But it also happens to be the truth."

"Which you've demonstrated by conjuring up a crowbar that you say you've never owned. Which you've demonstrated by discovering that there's no wiring in the walls of your apartment, even though there is. Which you've demonstrated by discovering that your ties are made from a single length of cloth—though you don't care to have me confirm this. Which you've demonstrated by seeing things in a book that I can't see, by seeing things on a shelf that aren't there. Richard, do you remember what you told me this afternoon when I asked what was wrong? You said, 'I've been hallucinating.'"

"These things weren't hallucinations," he snapped.

"Ah. *These* things weren't . . . but evidently some *other* things were. And you can tell the difference."

Greg shook his head stubbornly.

"Very well. Let's explore this theory of yours for a bit. You say we're in a dream. Greg Donner's dream?"

"That's right."

"I see. So you've turned everything on its head again. Richard Iles is the dream and Greg Donner is the reality."

"That's right."

She paused, frowning. "Let me see if I can work it out, Richard. Greg Donner has a dream in which he wakes up as Richard Iles at the Glenhaven Oaks Sanatorium. At the end of this dream, he wakes up and learns that Franklin Winters, the diabolical dream-walker, is responsible for it. Am I right so far?"

"Yes."

"Greg Donner then goes to New York and kills Franklin Winters. With the dream-walker eliminated, Greg lives happily ever after with his beloved Ginny—except that he doesn't. In the midst of a party celebrating the birth of their daughter, he loses consciousness—and wakes up *a second time* at the Glenhaven Oaks Sanatorium. But this too is a dream?"

"Yes."

"I see. So at this moment, Greg Donner is lying unconscious in the midst of that party."

Greg frowned.

"Well?"

He shook his head.

"You're beginning to see the impossibility of it, aren't you, Richard? If Greg Donner *killed* Franklin Winters, then there is no dream-walker. And this is not a dream."

He leaned back, closed his eyes, and sullenly chewed on his lower lip.

"No," he said at last. "This dream didn't start when I collapsed at the party. It obviously had to start before that. It had to start *before I killed Franklin Winters.*"

"Because you need a dream-walker to blame it on?"

Greg laughed. "That's right."

"Come, Richard. If this is a dream, *when did it start?*"

"I don't know."

"And if this is a dream, whose is it? You say it's Greg Donner's. But where is Greg Donner as he's having this dream?"

"I don't know that either."

She shook her head regretfully. "I'm sorry, Richard. You've been grasping at straws to keep this theory afloat, but it's just not working. And you're intelligent enough to know it."

She checked her watch. "I took the precaution of booking us on a flight that leaves at eleven-thirty. If you haven't yet packed, you'd better start now."

But Greg, sprawled contentedly on the sofa and gazing up at the ceiling, didn't seem to be listening.

"Do you know what the trick is, Agnes?"

She gave him a weary smile. "What trick is that, Richard?"

"The trick of dream-walking. Franklin explained it on that videotape he sent Ginny."

"Richard, please. It's been a very long day, and it's far from over."

"He said it's just a matter of becoming *aware* that you're dreaming. Once you've done that, you're free. Just like that."

He snapped his fingers.

She stood up. "Alan's waiting out in the hall, Richard. If you like, he can help you pack."

He grinned at her. "Brought some muscle along just in case I get difficult, huh?" Greg too stood up.

"I don't mind leaving, Agnes, but let's not go to Kentucky. Let's see if Franklin's right. Let's go somewhere else."

Agnes sighed and folded her arms in resignation.

He looked around thoughtfully. "I would have tried this before you came, but I was afraid of attracting attention. This is a little more ambitious than conjuring up crowbars."

"Get on with it, Richard. I've had about all I can handle for one day."

"Now don't fuss at me, Agnes. This takes concentration."

He closed his eyes, held a deep breath for a count of five, and opened them again.

The walls of the room undulated briefly, as if under water, then steadied and became solid.

"Almost," he said, and closed his eyes again.

When he opened them, the lights were dimming, the walls flowing. Beginning at its center the ceiling dissolved like cellophane held over a flame, revealing a more remote, curved ceiling overhead.

They were standing just inside the entrance to a vast domed observatory. A few yards away, the black mass of a telescope reared upward toward a slot in the roof.

"Well, damn!" he crowed, looking around triumphantly. "What do you think of that, Agnes?"

Agnes, her arms still folded, gazed at him with concern.

"What is it you're seeing, Richard?"

"It's the Celestial Mirror, Agnes! Ginny and I were nearly trapped here in one of those early follower dreams."

279

"Oh, Richard," she said, shaking her head in obvious disappointment.

"Come on, there's an elevator over here." He strode across the room and Agnes reluctantly followed. Arriving at the far wall, he had to spend a few moments looking for the remembered red button set in the apparently seamless expanse of metal. When at last the elevator door slid open, he started to step inside and nearly walked into a second door that was blocking his way. He drew back, startled.

And saw that the door was his own front door. He turned around and saw Agnes frowning up at him solemnly, framed by the familiar setting of his apartment.

"Oh," he said. "We're back."

"Richard," Agnes said firmly, "we never *left*. You led me over here, poked at the doorjamb a couple times, then almost smashed your skull walking into your own front door."

"Oh no," he replied, shaking his head violently. "No, no. We were at the Celestial Mirror."

"Richard, for Christ's sake, wake up! You were *hallucinating!*"

But Greg went on shaking his head. "No, I see what it is. It's a matter of will. I wanted to be at the observatory and you wanted to be here. I wasn't prepared for that, so you won."

"Richard, *please* . . ."

"Let's try something else," he said, and closed his eyes.

And immediately felt himself falling backwards.

"Whoops!" he said, and started waving his arms in a frantic effort to catch his balance. As he continued to plunge, he tried to open his eyes, but his eyelids seemed to be as heavy as lead.

Suddenly his fall was broken and his head snapped forward.

Someone beside him said, "Had a little nap, huh?"

XXXXI

GREG BLINKED, LOOKED AROUND groggily, and realized that he was riding in the front seat of a car.

The driver of the car glanced at him, and Greg recognized the battered face of Robbie Orsini, his depressed friend at the Glenhaven Oaks Sanatorium.

"Everything okay?" Robbie asked.

Greg looked into the back seat and saw that it was piled with boxes and clothes bags. They were just returning from the expedition they'd made into town to replace Richard Iles's wardrobe with one of his own choosing.

"This isn't right," Greg said.

Robbie glanced at him, his eyebrows raised.

"This isn't where I wanted to be."

Frowning, Robbie drove in silence for a few moments. Then he grumbled, "Kid, nobody exactly *wants* to be here."

"That's not what I mean. This is just a dream."

Robbie shook his head. "Take it easy, Dick. We'll be back in a few minutes. You can talk to Dr. Jakes about it."

Greg hunched down in his seat, closed his eyes, and tried to concentrate on returning to his apartment at the Hancock Center, but he felt panicked and disoriented, and the car just went on jouncing under him.

In a few minutes they turned into a long driveway, wove their way through the sanatorium's park-like grounds, and came to a halt at a side entrance. Robbie got out, opened the back door, and started gathering up packages.

"Leave 'em," Greg said.

Robbie straightened up, gave him a disgusted look, and said, "What the hell's gotten into you, Dick?"

"Oh, fuck it," Greg said, and started grabbing things.

When they reached Greg's room, they dropped everything on the bed, and Robbie said, "Hey, you want me to see if Dr. Jakes is available?"

"Yeah, Robbie. That'd be fine."

Looking back from the doorway, he saw that Greg was standing at the window, staring gloomily out at the blue hills.

"You oughtta hang this stuff up so it doesn't get wrinkled, Dick."

Greg turned to him with a sour laugh and said he'd take care of it.

He was just hanging up the last of his new clothes when he became aware that Agnes was standing behind him, watching him gravely.

"Well?" he snarled.

"Tell me what you're doing, Richard."

"I'm putting away the goddamned clothes, Agnes."

"What about those?" She nodded toward a tangled pile of neckties at his feet.

He stared at them for a few moments, as if trying to place them. Then he turned around and saw that they were standing in the bedroom of his Hancock Center apartment.

"Oh," he said, "I'm . . ."

"Back? Richard, believe me, you never left. After you closed your eyes, you stumbled backwards into a sofa. You sat there for a while talking to . . . someone, then you got up, walked behind the sofa, and it looked like you were picking something up. Then you came in here. Where did you *think* you were?"

He shook his head, preoccupied.

"I've got to figure out what I'm doing wrong."

He turned and strode out of the room.

As he entered the living room, Agnes caught him by the arm. "This has to stop, Richard. I mean it. You're playing a sort of Russian roulette with your sanity, and one of these times . . . you're not going to make it back."

Greg gazed down at her.

And behind them one of the huge windows exploded outward. For ten seconds they stood transfixed, listening to broken glass cascade down the sloping sides of the building to the concrete below.

"You can't pretend *that* didn't happen, Agnes. Your eyes gave you away."

"Richard . . ."

"Watch." He nodded toward a heavy black leather chair, and it began to glide toward them.

"Sit down, Agnes."

When it was a few feet away, it suddenly dipped, pushed up a wrinkle of carpet, and pitched forward.

Before he could move, one of its floppy cushions sailed through the air and wrapped itself around his face. Staggering under the impact, he tried to pull it away, but it clung like a plastic film, blinding him, smothering him.

As he wrestled with it, the absurdity of what was happening struck him, and in spite of himself, he barked out a laugh—and was immediately sorry he had. Having expended the breath, he found he couldn't get it back: his stomach shriveled in panic, and he sank to his knees.

The cushion seemed to have no substance, seemed to have *disappeared*. He felt his hands stirring the air in front of his face—air that he couldn't get into his lungs. He clawed at his mouth. There was nothing there, nothing between him and the oxygen he needed; it was as if he'd simply forgotten how to breathe.

It's just a dream, he screamed without sound.

He felt his fingers actually fumbling in his mouth, touching his teeth, his mouth—yet no air followed. He simply couldn't make it come.

Wake up!

The blackness around him turned blood red and he fell to the floor, his arms leaden weights.

For a few moments the roar of blood filled his ears like a raging sea, then, as he lost his hold on consciousness, it began to subside into a murmur of jumbled voices.

What happened? Is he all right? Shouldn't you . . . ? Raise his head. Please move back! Here, let me . . . Loosen his collar.

Suddenly an icy column of air rushed down Greg's throat, and his lungs seized it greedily, surged up for more.

It's okay, it's okay. What happened? Take it easy. Shouldn't someone . . . ? It's okay. He's a doctor. Is he all right? . . . heart attack?"

His eyes fluttered open, and the room swirled around him, faces passing like figures on an airborne carousel. Gradually the carousel slowed and stopped unsteadily, and he recognized the closest face, peering down at him from a few inches away.

It was Bruce's face.

And behind that, over Bruce's shoulder, another face: Ginny's.

Rolling his head from side to side, he saw a dozen others that were dimly familiar.

"I'm awake," he whispered.

He tried to push himself up on an elbow, but Bruce pressed him back to the floor. "Just take it easy for a minute," he said.

"What happened?" Greg asked.

Bruce smiled apologetically. "Well . . . it looks like you fainted."

"Fainted?"

"We were talking, and I showed you a snapshot. And while you were looking at the snapshot, you . . . collapsed."

Greg looked around again, wonderingly.

"This is the party?"

"The party?" Bruce laughed gently. "Yes, this is the party."

"Let me see the snapshot."

"That's nothing. Just take it easy."

"Show me the snapshot. Please?"

Shaking his head, Bruce retrieved the snapshot from the floor beside Greg, smoothed it out, and handed it to him.

He held it up, blinked a couple of times to get his eyes in focus, and peered at it without comprehension. Suddenly he remembered what Bruce had said about it: *The shadows make it a*

284

bit of a puzzle. It's like an optical illusion. You have to sort of twiddle your eyes to get the right of it.

The last time he'd twiddled his eyes to get the right of it, he'd seen himself bending over Franklin Winters with a pistol in his hand. This time he saw a young man in thirties clothes offering a plate of sandwiches to a girl sitting on a blanket under a tree.

He handed the snapshot back and said, "I'm sorry I crumpled it."

"It's nothing, Greg. Forget about it."

Greg looked up at Ginny.

"So you're here."

"I'm here, love. How are you feeling?"

"A little shaky."

"When was the last time you had a checkup?" Bruce asked.

"I don't know. A decade or so."

"Time for another, I'd say."

Greg nodded.

The crowd around him was breaking up quickly now, as it occurred to everyone that, like the excitement, the party was over, and it was time to go home. Back on his feet, Greg said good night to the last of them, closed the door, and turned to Ginny.

"Still feel like going out?" he said with a smile.

They'd planned to go to the Drake for a nightcap while the caterer cleared up.

"Don't be an idiot," she said. "You're going nowhere but to bed."

"I suppose that would be prudent," he agreed with a sigh. "Bring me a drink?"

"Do you think you ought to?"

"I'm all right, Ginny. Just a little wobbly in the legs."

"All right. You get into bed and I'll bring it."

When she came to him a few minutes later, he asked her how long he'd been out on the floor.

"Couple of minutes. Maybe three."

"Huh. Would you like to know how I spent those two or three minutes?"

"What do you mean?"

"Sit down here beside me."

She sat down and Greg told her what he meant.

When he was finished, Ginny went on staring broodily into space.

"So?" he asked.

"So what?"

"You're obviously thinking *something*."

"I don't know what. Except . . ."

"Yes?"

"You told Agnes at one point that the dream had to start before . . ."

"Before I killed Franklin."

"Yes."

"But obviously it didn't."

"No."

Ginny frowned, dissatisfied.

"What's the matter?" he asked.

"I'm *worried* about you, goddamn it!"

"Why?"

"I don't know exactly. I guess I'm worried that you're going to *make* something out of this."

"Shouldn't I make something out of it?"

Ginny stood up abruptly and started pacing the floor.

"*That's* what's worrying me. You're making something out of it, and I don't know what it is."

"I'm just thinking about it, that's all. I don't see how I can *help* doing that. It was just exactly like the dreams I had when . . . when your father was alive."

"Goddamn it!" She sat down on the bed and put her hands on his shoulders. "You *know* he's dead."

"I know, Ginny. I'm not crazy."

"Then what are you *thinking?*"

286

"I don't know what to think. I really don't."

"Do you think he's pulling stunts from beyond the grave?"

"No."

"Then *what?*"

"I don't know, Ginny. I just know that it *happened*, and I'm trying to figure it out."

"Look, will you do me a favor? *Don't* try to figure it out. Just leave it alone. It was just a *dream*, for Christ's sake!"

Greg nodded, his face expressionless.

Ginny sighed. "All right. Do you want to know what I think?"

He nodded again.

"When you looked at that snapshot of Bruce's, you saw yourself bending over Franklin with a gun, when in fact it was a picture of someone else entirely, doing something else entirely. Right?"

"Right."

"Greg, you don't have to be a genius to figure out something like that. After all these years, your subconscious—your guilty conscience, whatever you want to call it—snuck up behind you and gave you a whack on the head."

"Yes, that's about what I thought myself."

"Time for a little self-punishment here, Greg."

"Yes. You mean the dream? You think the dream was a little self-punishment?"

"Yes. Yes, I do. Don't you see? You punished yourself *exactly the way Franklin would have punished you if he'd been alive.*"

Greg laughed mirthlessly. "Yes, that's it. That's very good. Let me up, I'm going to have another drink."

She stood up and followed him into the kitchen. As he got out the ice and the bottle, he said, "It's amazing how everyone keeps coming up with *explanations* for everything—all completely plausible, all completely contradictory. Agnes Tillford gave me wonderful explanations of all those dreams I had just before I met you. Then Agnes *Jakes* gave me a whole different set of explanations for the very same dreams. Then, in the dream I just had, she gave me an explanation of why I *wasn't* dreaming. And now you've given me an explanation of why I *was* dreaming. I love it."

"And what's *that* mean?"

"That's *my* line," he said with a laugh, and carried his drink into the living room.

"I just want to know, Greg. You say all that as though it's supposed to *mean* something."

"It's not important, Ginny. What's important is, what do I do now? What do I do about my guilty conscience? Do I just ignore it? Wait and see if it's going to make a habit of sneaking up and slugging me from time to time?"

"No . . ."

"What then?"

"You really want an opinion?"

"Absolutely."

'Then I think you should talk to someone about it."

"Someone like a psychotherapist."

"Maybe."

He chuckled. "I love it. I could be the only man alive with two psychotherapists—one in waking life and one in his dreams."

"It doesn't have to be a psychotherapist."

"A priest? It would have to be someone who could keep a small murder just between the two of us, after all."

Ginny frowned. "Why are you being this way, Greg?"

"I'm sorry. Am I being some way?"

"You're being . . . sort of manic."

"Sorry, I'll be serious. Who do you think I should talk to?"

"Well, you could talk to Bruce. I think he'd . . ."

"You think he'd what? Keep my dark secret? Yes, I suppose he would, since he has dark secrets of his own to keep. Do you think I should call him?"

"I don't think it could hurt."

Greg nodded and headed for the phone.

"I didn't mean this *second*, for God's sake!"

But Greg was already punching out a set of numbers.

"Greg, it's one o'clock in the morning!"

He gazed at her placidly, the receiver at his ear. After a few moments he said, "Hi! Bruce? This is Greg Donner. Listen, Ginny and I have been talking, and we think it would be a good idea for us to get together—I mean, you and me. What? Well, yes, it's connected to what happened tonight. In a way. There's some deep stuff going on here."

Greg paused, raised his eyebrows at Ginny, and turned the receiver toward her as if to demonstrate that Bruce was silently thinking it over.

"Yes?" he went on, putting the receiver back to his ear. "Are you sure? It could wait until Monday if you'd rather not break into your weekend. Great. Why don't you let me buy you brunch at the Drake? Say . . . eleven o'clock? Fine. See you then."

After cradling the receiver, he took his drink to a window overlooking the lake, threw back the drapes, and stood staring at his reflection in the black glass.

"Now that really is amazing," he said.

"What is? The fact that he'd see you on a Sunday?"

Without turning, he smiled.

"No, not that. The fact that I've never known Bruce's telephone number, never called him in my life. But all I had to do was pick up the phone, punch in some numbers, and there he was."

Ginny said nothing.

"Isn't that remarkable?"

"I don't know. What does it mean?"

"It means, my love, that I have an appointment elsewhere. For tonight, your charms have faded. The woman I want to be with is Agnes, and I imagine she's right where I left her."

He spun around and was once again surrounded by the stark blacks and whites of Richard Iles's living room.

Noticing that he was still in his pajamas, he laughed.

Agnes, standing just where Ginny had stood, glared at him reproachfully.

XXXXII

IT'S NO ONE THING, IS IT, AGNES. It's not just willpower, not just concentration, not just having a very specific thing in mind. It's like learning to ride a bicycle—one minute you're wobbling all over the street and the next you've got the hang of it, and it's impossible to say why."

"Enough, Richard," she said, her eyes ablaze with fury. "This has got to stop now. I mean it."

"It does indeed, Agnes. It's showdown time."

She shook her head, turned, and started walking across the living room.

"Showdown," he repeated, and Matilda, the skeleton that stood guard at the front door, rose up out of her cart and rushed toward Agnes with a screech, brandishing her hatchet and knife.

Agnes paused, startled, and Matilda's head flew off.

Headless, Matilda continued to race forward. She staggered back a step when her rib cage exploded, regained her balance, and came on. A foot twisted off and was left behind, and she went on stumping forward. Finally, as a thighbone parted from her hip, what was left of her crashed to the floor and disintegrated, her hatchet sailing off harmlessly to one side and her knife rolling to a stop at Agnes's feet.

Kicking aside the debris, Agnes took a step forward.

And sank into the floor up to her waist.

As she struggled, red faced, to extricate herself, Greg strolled over and hunkered down beside her. "Cement, Agnes. Fast drying. That'll hold you for a bit while we have a little talk."

She closed her eyes disdainfully, and Greg laughed.

"You know," he said, "I guessed the truth about you a long time ago, Agnes. You must have realized that."

Her eyes still closed, she gave no sign of hearing him.

"Are you ready for it, Agnes? Here it is. You're not Agnes at all. You're *Franklin*. Franklin *in drag*."

Her eyes popped open, and she glared at him.

"Tell me something, Agnes. Did you really bring Alan here?"

She went on glaring but said nothing.

"Why, Agnes? What was he supposed to do?"

Before he could go on, there was a discreet tapping at the window behind him, and he stood up to see what it was. On the other side of the glass, obscured by the reflected lights of his living room, he could just make out the figure of a man, beckoning to him. He switched off a lamp, walked over to the window, and experienced a moment of *déjà vu*.

On the other side of the glass was the balding old magician in shirt sleeves who had "entertained" Ginny and him in one of his dreams. In that dream, he had stood slightly above them, in a storefront window, while they watched from the sidewalk. Now their positions were reversed. The old man was looking up from the very same sidewalk, and Greg himself was standing inside, in the storefront window. Beyond the sidewalk lay the same dismal street, jammed with dusty, abandoned cars.

Just as he'd done before, the old man very carefully rolled up his sleeves, waggled his hands to show that they were empty, reached into a pocket, and pulled out what looked like a silver dollar. He held it up briefly for inspection, then pressed it against the glass.

When he took his hand away, the coin remained, clinging to the window. Having accomplished this feat, he just as carefully rolled his sleeves down, buttoned the cuffs, crossed his arms, and looked up expectantly.

Greg smiled and reached for the coin, which, as before, had passed neatly through the glass. On the front of it, he expected to see a mist-shrouded Charon ferrying the dead across the river to Hades, but it was nothing like that. It was so different, in fact, that it took him a few moments to make it out.

It was the living room of Ginny's apartment on Dearborn Street, detailed in such exquisite relief that he could see each piece of furniture as he remembered it, drawing table laden with proofs and layout sheets, racks of press type, tabourets littered with brushes, pens, rulers, pencils. Down a hallway at the back of the room, a door stood open: Ginny's bedroom. And inside, a shaft of moonlight fell upon the bed where she lay sleeping. He could see her face plainly; it was contorted with anguish, her mouth falling open in a voiceless moan.

Shaking his head, Greg turned the coin over and studied what was printed there:

ASLEEP, SHE
TOO DREAMS.

He looked up, puzzled.

And saw Ginny wandering in a daze down the sidewalk.

A chill skittered up his spine as he understood. This was not one of the Ginny-facsimiles that Franklin had conjured up to move through his dreams on demand. Those, like his own conjuration of Larry Fielding, had been akin to hallucinations.

This was the *real* Ginny, the Ginny who, in sleep, inhabited the realm of dreams: alone, defenseless, as easily manipulated as a puppet . . . by one who knew how it was done.

As she drew near, gazing round in confusion, the old man caught Greg's eye and nodded meaningly to the coin in Greg's hand. Greg glanced at it and saw that a second legend had appeared under the first:

IN DREAMS, THE
DEAD AWAKEN.

The old man stepped aside with a bow and a flourish, and in the car behind him at the curb a groping hand appeared at a window and slid down the glass, smearing it with gray. A moment later the hand was replaced by the face of what had once been a man, slack and empty-eyed, and Greg remembered: when he and Ginny had moved among them, all these cars had been tenanted by corpses.

The car door swung open, and the thing inside lurched out onto the sidewalk.

Ginny, her eyes cast upward to the darkened windows of the street, saw nothing of this.

Another car door opened behind her, and this she heard.

She turned as a body pitched forward onto the sidewalk and staggered to its feet. Terrified, she backed away from it, then turned again—and ran into the outstretched arms of the one in front of her. Her momentum knocked him down, but he held her, rolled over on her, and, nuzzling her, pressed her face to the cement with his own.

"No," she whimpered. "Please . . ."

All along the street now, car doors were opening and twisted bodies were shuffling forward.

Shaking off his paralysis, Greg stepped through the glass of the store window and made for the man pinning Ginny to the sidewalk. Finding nothing better, he grabbed a handful of hair and pulled.

The scalp came off in his hand.

Retching, he threw it away, got an arm around his throat and heaved him off. Lifting Ginny to her feet, he put his arms around her and said, "Don't be frightened. It's only a dream."

A heavy hand shammed onto Greg's shoulder and an arm coiled around his throat.

"Run, Ginny! Please!"

She stared at him, wide-eyed with terror.

"*Run!*"

She turned and ran.

Another pair of arms wrapped themselves around Greg's waist, and he was pulled down and engulfed in pulpy, rotting flesh. Even as he struggled for air and mobility, elbowing limbs out of his way, pushing his way upward, sinking his fists in torsos, a part of his mind remained aloof, analyzing the conditions of warfare in this realm. It seemed that, in any given battle, the upper hand automatically belonged to the one who chose the battleground. Greg had no power over this situation on the street, could only struggle with it, because Agnes had created it. If this was true of Agnes as well, then she was no better off than he was. She was struggling to work herself out of the cement trap he'd sunk her in.

Another body fell on top of the heap crushing him into the sidewalk, and Greg decided that, since struggling with Agnes's initiative seemed useless, a new initiative of his own was his only hope.

Taking a deep breath of the fetid air, he allowed himself to sink *into* the sidewalk. Once beneath its surface, he turned in the heavy liquid, and with slow, labored strokes began to swim back toward the apartment.

After a few moments he realized he was never going to make it on the single breath he'd taken. *My initiative*, he thought, *my rules*, and began breathing normally. He couldn't, however, make the swimming any less labored: this was the medium that had to hold Agnes in check.

After what seemed like half an hour but was only a handful of minutes, he angled upward toward the surface, which he expected to be the floor of his own apartment.

It was. He bobbed up midway between the windows and Agnes, who was just then pulling herself free. By contrast, he dragged himself out quite easily.

My initiative, he thought again, *my rules*.

By the time he got to his feet, Agnes was at the front door.

He said, "I don't know what help you expected from him, Agnes, but you're too late. *Alan's dead.*"

XXXXIII

AGNES THREW OPEN THE DOOR, started across the threshold, and found herself teetering on the edge of a dark abyss. Fanning her arms to keep from toppling into it, she stepped back and saw that she was standing on a subway platform. It was the abandoned station in which Greg and Ginny had become separated after escaping from the observatory.

In the train well, on a table straddling the tracks, lay a body covered by a white sheet. She knew without wondering whose it was.

"Alan!" she commanded harshly, "Get up!"

The body stirred, and the sheet slid away from Alan's head and shoulders as he struggled to sit up.

"Need me, Dr. Jakes?" he asked weakly.

A public address system crackled into life, and Greg's voice echoed off the walls: "*Dead!*"

Alan slumped back onto the table, his staring eyes lifeless.

Greg's voice pounded out of the speakers, "It's *power*, isn't it, Agnes? That's what this is all about! *Power!*"

The power rail in the train well sizzled and sparked, and an edge of the sheet dangling from the table began to smolder. Suddenly the table itself burst into flames, and Alan's body was engulfed in the inferno.

Agnes glanced around and, satisfied that she was alone, hurried toward the back wall of the station and promptly disappeared. Anyone watching might have thought she'd walked through a solid cement block wall; in fact, she'd slipped into an opening masked by a cunningly placed mirror.

On the other side of the wall she threaded her way through a maze of corridors, passing a score of identical rooms, windowless boxes, all empty. At last, without hesitation, she turned into one no different from the rest and entered a dim closet at the rear.

She paused there for a moment until her eyes, adjusting to the darkness, picked out a flight of stairs that rose up at the back of the closet. She kicked aside a box of old toys and squeezed herself into the stairwell, which was little more than a foot wide. After a few steps, it turned at a crazy angle, and she had to suck in her stomach to get around it.

Shaking her head in disgust, she looked up, where, a few feet farther, the stairwell turned again.

It had once, she somehow knew, been the central feature of a playhouse that Ginny had visited many times in her childhood dreams.

She sighed and went on.

When she was midway to the next turning, the wall at her right, with the shriek of a hundred nails being drawn, lurched in on her by an inch.

Startled, she let out a squawk, then thundered, "*Back!*"

But instead of moving back, the wall slowly began to bow away from her, the wood beneath whining ominously as the pressure mounted. Suddenly it buckled and collapsed, boards exploding into dust, nails and splinters flying like shrapnel. In a final explosion, a massive beam crashed through the shattered wall like a battering ram and came to rest against her stomach.

Breathless, she began to edge herself around it. And the wall behind her lurched forward an inch, pinning her to it.

"Stop!" she gasped.

Greg stuck his head around the corner above and grinned down at her.

"Fun, isn't it?"

The wall behind Agnes shuddered another inch closer.

She twisted in an effort to free herself, and when that proved futile, the features of her face began to writhe and flow like wax heated by the fury within. Her pudgy nose thinned as it elongated and drooped. The flesh of her plump cheeks flowed away from the bone until it hung in flaps from her jaw. But by then the fury-filled eyes, the long, drooping nose, and the wattled jaw no longer belonged to Agnes's face. They belonged to the face of Franklin Winters.

"More comfortable in your true form, hmm? You're a little leaner than Agnes, aren't you."

Wallowing foolishly in Agnes's dark suit, the old man threw him a look of hatred as sharp as a dart.

And the wall behind him rumbled forward another inch.

Franklin screeched.

"That's all right, Frank. I've got you now. Tell me, have you ever done battle with anyone else in the realm of dreams?"

The old man shook his head.

"That explains it then. I picked up a trick even you don't know. I learned it out there on the sidewalk, playing with your pet corpses. Needless to say, I'm not going to share it with you."

Franklin shrugged.

"I want some answers now, Frank. I want to know *when* this dream is taking place. Is this the same night I called to tell you I was giving Ginny up?"

Smirking, Franklin nodded.

"And 'the next morning,' when I got up and decided to go to New York to blow your head off, that was actually the beginning of the dream — *this* dream."

He nodded again.

"You checked up on me while I was asleep and found out I hadn't really decided to give Ginny up, so you decided to give me another dose of your medicine — a really big dose. That's right, isn't it. No, don't nod. I want to hear your voice, Frank."

The old man set his mouth in a stubborn line.

And the wall behind him trembled.

"Yes, that's right!"

"Thank you. Now, just out of curiosity, what was Alan supposed to do, Frank? What was he along for?"

His mouth curled in a smug smile. "That's the wrong question, young man."

297

"What's the right question?"

"The right question is, *who was Alan?*"

"All right, who was Alan?"

"He was, after Ginny and perhaps your parents, the most important person in your life."

"Don't play games with me, Franklin. Who was he?"

"Your brother."

Stunned, Greg stared at him, slack jawed.

"What the hell are you talking about?"

"Alan was your brother, assembled from your own repressed memories of him—your own *discarded* memories."

"You're crazy. My brother was ten years older than I was."

Franklin shrugged. "In your memory of him he's just a youngster. In the realm of dreams, he will *forever* be a youngster."

"Okay. And what was he supposed to *do* to me, Frank?"

"Ah. At the appropriate moment I would have seen to it that you recognized him at last. Perhaps you yourself don't realize how deep your feelings of guilt toward him are. Properly orchestrated . . ." He sighed wistfully. "I assure you, it would have been a devastating reunion."

Greg shook his head in rueful admiration of the old man's unabashed wickedness. "And, now that I've caught you properly, what do you think I'm going to do with you, Franklin?"

"You're going to let me go," he answered promptly.

Greg sighed. "Yes, I suppose I am. You'll stay out of our dreams now, because you know I wouldn't be so kind if I caught you a second time."

"I know," he said, a bit sulkily.

Greg paused, frowning. "Do you really care for Ginny at all?"

Franklin looked away, his expression thunderous, and Greg knew he would get no answer to this question.

"Perhaps, if you asked nicely, like a normal person, Ginny might come and visit you some day. I can't promise it, but it's possible. She might."

The old man nodded stiffly, once.

Suppressing a smile, Greg asked him if he needed any help getting out of there.

"You know I do," he snapped.

"Think small," Greg advised—and shrank him to the size of a cockroach.

Franklin got to his feet with enraged dignity and shook his fist at Greg, screaming an imprecation that sounded like the chittering of an infuriated gnat.

Greg bent over and with a puff of air blew the little man head over heels down the stairs.

The same puff of air carried Greg up and away from there, into the black sky over Chicago. He hovered there, admiring the long sweeping curve of lights along the shore of Lake Michigan, a view far outstripping the one he'd had in his apartment in the Hancock Center. He smiled, wondering if he would ever have such a dwelling in waking life.

Here and there below him he saw figures moving on the street and behind the windows of apartments: countless figures of people wandering through their dreams. For all his disapproval of Franklin Winters, he could sympathize with the temptation to take a hand in those dreams: perhaps to help—to save one from drowning, another from falling off a roof; perhaps just to play a few tricks . . . have a little fun . . . play God for an evening. He shook his head. The temptation was resistible.

He looked vaguely to the north and wondered what Agnes was doing, the *real* one—Agnes Tillford. As if propelled by some unconscious homing instinct, he found himself in motion, and was soon hovering over a building he didn't recognize from above. Gliding down to street level, he saw it was their old meeting place, Freddie's.

After taking a moment to refurbish his appearance, he entered that establishment's perpetual midnight and was greeted by a maitre d' in stunning evening wear (an innovation for Freddie's). Greg told him he was meeting someone in the bar and from the man's hurt expression realized that, for this evening at least, the bar was *the lounge.*

It was easy to see why. Its vinyl booths had been replaced by velvet banquettes, its candles flickered in the midst of crystal glassware, set on gleaming white tablecloths, and its patrons were dressed to the maitre d's standards.

Agnes waved to him from a distant table, and he was glad she had. He wouldn't have recognized her as she was in the dream—ten years younger and twenty pounds slimmer, dressed in a gown that looked like a Chanel. The dazzlingly handsome gentleman beside her rose as he approached, measuring Greg's potential as a rival.

"Greg dear, what are you doing *here*?" Agnes asked.

"Just passing by. Thought I'd drop in and say hello."

"How nice," she burbled. "Of course you scarcely need an introduction to my friend."

"Scarcely," Greg said, and gravely shook hands with Cary Grant.

Agnes leaned forward to whisper, "We come here so he won't be pestered by autograph seekers."

"I understand," Greg said.

They exchanged a few pleasantries and, after declining an invitation to join them, Greg took his leave.

Rising again into the air, he drifted southward along the lake until he reached the Near North Side. At Armando's, he descended to within a few yards of the street and followed a familiar path down Dearborn to Ginny's apartment.

Her living room lights were on, and, hovering outside, he watched her laboriously sifting papers at one of her drafting tables. It soon became apparent that Ginny was in the middle of one of those frustrating work-dreams in which nothing ever gets done or stays done. She would pick up a galley and be unable to lay her hands on the type ruler she needed to measure it with; finding that, the galley would be misplaced. Getting both together at last, no pencil would be at hand to mark the galley. Having at last marked the galley, the scissors would be missing.

The scissors found and the galley cut, the layout sheet she was working on would have gone astray.

Finally Greg glided through the window. Still absorbed in her hopeless task, she didn't notice him until he went to her and laid a hand on her arm.

She looked up, startled.

"Oh, Greg," she said, her face a picture of desolation, "I just can't make any of it come out right!"

He took her in his arms and brushed away her tears. "It's all right, love," he said. "It's all going to come out right now."

Although it was dark night in the realm of dreams, the sun was peeping over the eastern shore of the lake, and in his apartment on Lake Shore Drive the sleeping Greg Donner rolled over and smiled.

Made in the USA
Lexington, KY
25 August 2019